Sweetie

Jenny Tomlin is happily married and lives in France. With continuing support from her two children Martine and LJ, she still loves to write and enjoys family life to the full. She champions the causes of those charities that fight to wipe out abuse in all its forms, including Barnardo's, Refuge, Red Cross and domestic violence units. Her other works have been in non-fiction: *Behind Closed Doors*, *Silent Sisters* and *Not Alone*.

Also available by Jenny Tomlin

Non-fiction

Behind Closed Doors
Silent Sisters
Not Alone

JENNY TOMLIN
Sweetie

arrow books

Published in the United Kingdom by Arrow Books in 2008

3 5 7 9 10 8 6 4 2

Copyright © Jenny Tomlin, 2008

First published in the United Kingdom in 2008 by Arrow Books
First published in paperback in 2008 by Arrow Books

Arrow Books
The Random House Group Limited
20 Vauxhall Bridge Road, London, SW1V 2SA

Addresses for companies within The Random House Group Limited
can be found at: www.randomhouse.co.uk/offices.htm

The Random House Group Limited Reg. No. 954009

www.rbooks.co.uk

A CIP catalogue record for this book
is available from the British Library

ISBN 9780099509837

The Random House Group Limited supports The Forest
Stewardship Council (FSC), the leading international forest
certification organisation. All our titles that are printed on
Greenpeace approved FSC certified paper carry the FSC logo. Our
paper procurement policy can be found at
www.rbooks.co.uk/environment

Typeset by SX Composing DTP, Rayleigh, Essex
Printed and bound in Great Britain by
CPI Cox & Wyman, Reading, RG1 8EX

This book is dedicated to the little souls lost, gone from us but never forgotten

Acknowledgements

I love doing this bit! To Alan, always there with endless cups of coffee, kisses and encouragement, thank you. To Martine, my angel and friend. To Jack, a timeless musician. To LJ, my big man and special boy. To Kim, my sister and nutcase always! To my wonderful agent Jaine for all her never-ending support, and for the introduction she gave me to my lovely publisher Mark Booth and all the gang at Random House. Mark, you're a lovely man with real insight and great creativity. To the lovely Deb, my mate, guardian, angel and helper – here's to a lasting friendship. To Dawn for all her help in giving me time to work and for watching over my ironing and stopping it from spreading. To Matt Pullen and his family for always coming out late at night and fixing my computer and teaching me to cut and paste! To all my friends, up North, down South, and in France, the UK and Spain, for being there for me. I love you all.

Introduction

Throughout my life, I have been told many stories – some true, some not so true – and when I was given the opportunity to extend my writing into the fields of fiction, I decided to write what I knew about. I'm not a world renowned expert, but over the years I feel I have got to know real people, with real stories. Most of these stories have touched my heart, moved my spirit and shown me the true meaning of life, love and survival. I feel humble and grateful to have the opportunity to write about some of the memories I have and to transpose them into fictional stories.

I've never been slow in coming forward, and I've always believed that there is a right and a wrong. I can be quite self opinionated and stubborn at times, but I do have my own faiths and beliefs. I try never to sway or compromise anyone though and all of this is personal to me, but when asked what I think on certain subjects, I do say it how I see it and I suppose there may be times when I offend. I don't mean to do this however; I find it hard to keep my mouth shut. I believe in fairness and justice and I believe it should be every person's fundamental right to have it, providing you don't abuse it! Unfortunately, children are not always lucky enough to be treated in this way.

As a child I was abused, sexually, mentally and physically, and no one seemed interested in the scruffy little girl with a dirty face, no shoes, and a pervert for a father. My rights were stripped from me because of my age, and the choices made for me by adults were often wrong and damaging. With the love of siblings and a great aunt on my mother's side, who truly loved me, I made it through, but I long to see the day when you don't just survive, you strive, achieve and fulfil.

My father lived on into his late seventies. After abusing all of us throughout our childhood, he continued to beat my mother senseless until the day he died. I ask myself sometimes why he was never punished. Instead he led a full life and gained pleasure from other peoples misery. Never once did he regret his actions or offer any pity or remorse. I can still remember the voices of the authorities, "It's a domestic. She's lying, making it all up! Don't speak until I say you can." I grew up disbelieving most adults, too scared to talk, too afraid to act.

It would be true to say that as a parent, I haven't always got it right. When that baby pops out, it doesn't come with a set of rules on how it all works, but you don't need rules when you have an over-powering instinct to love and protect, and generally in most cases, its enough to get you started! Like an empowered large wild cat, I protected, fed and cared for my cubs, hoping that their lives would reach the potential we all hope for in our offspring, and more than anything, I wanted them to be safe.

What kind of world do we all live in when a child is taken, snatched away, generally by someone trusted and respected, then harmed, murdered even, while we are left powerless, wondering what we did wrong, and why we were not there when they needed us? What gives someone the right to take away what was not theirs? And what greater power gives them their lives back without the justified punishment?

As parents what can we do to protect the young and innocent? Protection and punishment comes in many forms, and I know that retribution is not always the answer, but ask me what I would do if someone took my child, abused them and then murdered them, I would, quite honestly reply that I'd kill them myself. Why? you might ask. The answer is simple. I am not brave enough to carry on with life if my children were not in it. I would have to try and stop anyone that hurt them ever hurting another child again and I would do it myself for the law does not dish out the punishment that fits the crime committed in my view: a life for a life. I am pro-capital punishment and always will be, but can never see it being re-introduced into our society until a referendum vote, on this law, is given back to the people. I believe we need something to stop the tidal wave of murder that's ever present in our lives today. What deterrent is there to stop these terrible crimes today? Life does not mean life and the only thing that keeps someone behind bars is the outcry and publicity surrounding the crime. While they are taking educational exams, or painting or making pottery, the parents, pay for their rehabilitation and sit at home looking at the pictures of children lost and dreaming of the day when justice will be served.

I can not, and will not, try and justify the way I think and feel it's just me and the way I am, but of one thing, I am sure. Whatever goes through a parents mind once they know the horror that their child suffered in their final moments, I don't know. I don't know how they cope, and to me, they are amazing! A life sentence is handed out to the victim and their families, not the criminal.

The argument will rage on for a long time and I don't expect a lot of people to agree with me, or the way I think. A lot of the time the terrible things that happen can only instigate change when it affects you personally, then you may feel differently and want things to change. I'm not a politician, and I'm not looking to change the whole judicial system, but something needs to be done. A premeditated crime of sexual assault and murder ranks as one of the worst possible offences, its total devastation can not be measured in time, but for the families who need justice; this is all that is offered. One child's loss of life has unbearable consequences, and a loss that no time can measure, give back or make right and the suffering goes on through generations.

Surely all parents have the right to know if there is a known, registered sex offender living in the flats down the road, or even worse, working with children in the community. They gave up their right to anonymity when they first took away a child's innocence, so why close ranks and protect them? A register is the only way to raise awareness, and it comes with the territory that if you have an unhealthy view of children, you should be named and shamed. The majority of parents are not out to break the law or take the law into their own hands, but surely they should be aware of possible danger. Its prevention, not cure that parents need and I personally believe that it's the least we can offer as a way of protecting our children.

Children are our immortality and the future society in years to come. If we let them down, what kind of society are we? I champion all children's charities in the tireless work they do, and their never ending fight for the rights of all children everywhere, but most of all, I champion those wonderful, courageous parents, who fight on for the justice and memory of their lost little ones. My heart aches for them all, but I have to believe that one day, they will win and real justice will be served. Let's hope for a change in attitude and in the law: as parents, we may live to see a time when the talking stops and the action starts and all children can see a future where they are protected, loved and most of all – safe!

Chapter One

Grace Ballantyne stood at the sink and wiped her forehead with the back of her hand for the third time in as many minutes. She stretched her long, graceful neck and closed her eyes for a few moments, twisting her head from side to side in a bid to release the tension she felt throughout her whole aching body. Nobody had managed to get a good night's sleep in weeks and everyone was feeling tired and irritable as a result, but Grace had never been a good sleeper. Her nights were always filled with nightmares from her childhood; she was always running and running, and when in her dreams her parents asked her where she had been, a strip of masking tape across her mouth prevented the words from coming out.

The heat in the small kitchen was stifling; even though the windows and doors were open no current of air swayed the net curtains. Grace had woken that morning and looked at the leaden skies with a sense of foreboding. There had been no rain for weeks, it had been the same all over the country, and now Bethnal Green, her small corner of the East End, was dusty and grimy, littered with fag ends and rotting rubbish in the gutters, which filled the stagnant air with the stench of decay. Flies and maggots made their homes in the rubbish and everyone was being bitten and driven insane by buzzing black swarms. The day before, Sunday, she had taken her four-year-old son Adam and his baby brother Luke for a walk down Columbia Road, hoping that the smells from the flower market would lift her spirits. Even before she had had money, Grace had been in the habit of spending what little she had on filling her home with fresh blooms, believing it lent an air of elegance to their modest surroundings; Grace by name, Grace by nature.

She and her husband John had recently moved into their own home from a flat on the Baroness Estate, where they had both grown up – the first in their close-knit circle of family and friends to buy their own home – and now Grace liked to choose great armfuls of flowers every Sunday to fill its freshly painted rooms. John liked to tease her about it, calling her the Duchess, but Grace took pride in everything she did, from her own stylish sense of dress to the way her children were always kept immaculately turned out on each and every occasion, and her new home gleaming and dust-free.

But in recent weeks her energy had begun to seep away, the unshakable confidence that was her trademark fraying at the edges and her sense of her own invincibility quickly eroding. It wasn't just Grace who felt this way. The Devil had come to the part of the East End where she lived, had claimed a defenceless victim and set everybody on edge. People who had known each other for years were beginning to eye their friends and neighbours suspiciously, and mothers were snapping at their children if they went out of sight for more than a moment. The worst of it was that the rape and murder of Chantal Robinson was to be only the first in a series of sexual assaults and murders during the long hot summer of 1976, when the sun beat down relentlessly, the rain just would not come, and the brash untouchable confidence of this tight-knit community gave way to a siege mentality.

No one had been prepared for the wave of misery and fear that the events of the last week had brought in their wake. Chantal Robinson had been a striking child. Of mixed-race origin, the twelve-year-old girl was tall and dark-skinned with long black curly hair. As she had developed into a voluptuous baby-woman, she'd become aware that boys were attracted to her and would quickly remove her glasses whenever they were around. But glasses on or off, Chantal was a beauty. She liked to walk down Hackney Road with her head in the air and her pleated grey kilt skirt turned over at the waist to show off her long, slim, legs. She loved the whistles of the boys as she strutted her way to school. Chantal was very popular and always in the middle of a crowd, so no one could understand how she had become separated from her usual group who went everywhere together, how she had become the victim of a sex killer. The first victim.

Her body had been found in the narrow alley at the back of the Bingo hall, near the rear gates of Haggerston School. She was naked from the waist down, laid on her stomach with her legs spread-eagled and bent at the knees out to the side of her body. Her throat was wrapped in wire which had been pulled back tight and looped under the strap of her very first bra. Her eyes, shorn of their lashes, were starting almost out of her sockets and her tongue swollen and blue. Semen was found in the back of her throat.

A pool of blood had soaked into the pavement around her, caused by the internal injuries she had endured when a piece of arrow-pointed railing had been inserted into her vagina. It had penetrated her anus, causing internal rupture and bleeding. Considerable force had been exerted, and the autopsy revealed that the object had been used in a ghastly travesty of sexual intercourse.

The stench of urine and faeces from the body had swiftly attracted all manner of insects and vermin. The once-beautiful child was reduced to a stinking corpse. Even more baffling, though, was the lollipop. Stuck to her cheek was a fruit lolly known as a drumstick, a popular piece of confectionery that was notoriously hard to chew.

Chantal was discovered by a road sweeper. Before

the police even had the chance to inform her waiting parents that their worst nightmare had become reality, the gossip spread like wildfire. Darren Robinson, known as Robbo, Chantal's father, raced to the scene. He was totally unprepared for the sight that greeted him. As he leaned heavily against the wall, Robbo felt his head jerk forward involuntarily. Vomit oozed from his mouth and nose. He struggled to see through eyes clouded over with a thick bile of snot and tears. His first-born, his beautiful girl, was dead in the vilest way. Some fucking lunatic had raped and violated her.

A police constable came slowly towards him, his own face white with shock at what he had found. Dry thunder rolled in the skies and the sunlight was blocked by rainless clouds. In his hand the policeman carried a pair of glasses. He held them out to Robbo.

'Sir, I . . . her glasses, sir.'

Robbo cradled them in his hand and stared at the policeman. 'What am I gonna tell her mum? What can I . . .' And then the sickness overcame him again.

The local toddlers' group, or the One o'Clock Club as they called themselves, met every Monday in the main room of the Baroness Working Men's Club. Here, mothers who had known each other all their lives – had gone to school together and then to each other's weddings – were now bringing up their own children together. They'd had their differences and squabbles, but the shared history and sense of community was stronger than any minor fallings out. There were petty jealousies and rivalries within the group, but when trouble hit they pulled together and worked for the common good.

Feeling out of sorts and unable to concentrate on the talk and speculation this morning, Grace had left the other mums in a conspiratorial huddle as they endlessly picked over the details of Chantal's rape and murder, searching for clues to the attacker's identity. She was sick of hearing about it, sick of thinking about it, and on the pretext of getting Adam a drink had escaped to the kitchen. Grace didn't want this in her life again.

Memories of her own childhood flooded back unbidden, and the thought of what she had endured as a young girl made her feel physically sick. Her Uncle Gary had been the suave, smart dresser, the man with money, the person everyone looked up to. A real East End guy done good who liked to put on a show whenever he turned up to visit. Uncle Gary who bought all the kids cream soda and crisps. Uncle Gary, the ladies' man, who was loved by one and all. Uncle Gary, the man who robbed Grace of her innocence and made her do things she didn't understand, terrorising her into silence and fear. Uncle Gary who had finally died at the wheel of his new sports car, and Grace hadn't cared, she'd been glad!

She steeled herself not to keep checking on Adam

as he played in his little red and yellow bubble car in the small enclosed garden, telling herself not to be paranoid. While all the other mums and children were seeking the shade indoors, little Adam seemed unperturbed by the blazing sun and continued on his circuits of the garden.

'Adam, come in and get a drink, love,' called Grace from the doorway.

'Brmm, brmm, Mummy!'

'Yeah, I know, brmm, brmm, but come and get a drink.'

'In a minute, Mummy.'

Grace stood in the doorway and watched him; looked at the wire-mesh fence which enclosed the garden, and the shut gate, and told herself to get a grip.

'For crying out loud, Grace! Come and sit down and stop hovering over that kid, he's all right,' Sue Williams, self-appointed leader of the One o'Clock Club and ringleader of the women in the neighbourhood, shouted over to her. 'None of us would let him play outside if we thought there was any problem. Besides, it's the girls who need to watch out . . .'

Grace gave Adam one last glance over her shoulder and went back to the other women, still huddled in their group. She was well aware that she wasn't universally popular with all the mums in the group – something to do with the Ballantynes' success. Her John worked all the hours God sent in his small building firm and they'd been able to buy their own house. John drove a Jag when he didn't use the van for work, and Grace had that effortless sort of beauty that stood out in any crowd. But she didn't care if they didn't all like her; she smiled widely, revealing her beautiful white teeth, and held her head up. This was where she was born, where she belonged and where she would stay. Not even Uncle Gary had changed that.

Although Sue was the most verbal in her criticism, Grace knew that she could trust the other woman with her life. Sue was the solid core of this neighbourhood, she knew everything and everyone, and although she could be domineering and opinionated, she had the best interests of the community at heart and respected Grace for not moving away to some nice leafy suburb, even though she could have afforded to. Now Sue was busy regaling the group with an account of what had happened to her the night before.

'So my Terry comes in last night, knows he's in the shit from the night before because he got drunk, and I'm just about to give him a proper tongue-lashing when he gives me this little box – he's only gone and got me another belcher chain! Well, I'm stumped then, I don't know whether to slap him or kiss him.'

Sue laughed and they all laughed with her, and then she proudly showed off the newest addition to the mass of chunky gold chains which adorned her neck. Grace smiled weakly and gazed towards the doorway; not a gold chain girl herself, she wore only a pair of pearl drops in her ears and the diamond-encrusted eternity ring on her wedding finger. She didn't need anything else. Grace turned away from the group and walked towards the doorway.

'Where are you going now?' bellowed Sue.

'I'm hot,' said Grace.

'Well, you won't cool down out there. It's like a bloody oven in that garden.'

'I know, I want Adam to have his drink.' Her son meanwhile was still busily brmm-brmming around the garden when a second little boy went to join him, banging on the door of the bubble car for Adam to come out, 'Me go, me go!' Adam shook his cousin Benny Jr off roughly, slammed the door of the bubble car and moved away, leaving the other child to dissolve in a pool of tears.

Grace checked over her shoulder to make sure that neither Sue nor his mum Gill had seen. There had been problems with this sort of thing before. Adam did not like to share and Sue had had words with Grace, telling her she needed to sort it out. Grace, in her usual laidback way, hoped it would sort itself out come September when he started school. He'd soon learn then, he'd have to. The teachers would make him. Anyway, Grace didn't see it as the big problem Sue liked to make out. His baby brother Luke had only just arrived on the scene after Adam had had four years of his mum all to himself, never having to share before. No wonder he was asserting himself now.

But Sue had very pronounced views on every aspect of motherhood and childcare, and would vehemently scold any child who refused to share its toys or let others join in their play. A mother of four, she was brisk and tough but a loving parent. Everybody knew where they were with Sue, including her husband Terry. His job was to bring in a wage. She liked to deal with the rest. Grace was more passive at home, preferring to let John take the lead, make all the decisions.

The beaker of squash she had poured for Adam and left by the doorway had turned warm and so she went to fetch another.

'For crying out loud, Grace, will you just settle? You got St Vitus' Dance or something?' Sue joined her in the kitchen, putting the kettle on to make another round of teas.

'I dunno, Sue, I just don't feel right. I woke up this morning feeling sick, like something really bad was going to happen, do you know what I mean?'

'Yeah, I do, love. You ain't up the spout again, mate, are ya?' Sue started to laugh; Grace had to giggle too.

'No, course not. You're such a tease, Sue.'

'Anyway we're all feeling a bit dodgy with what's

been going on, and this bloody weather doesn't help, but the men are gonna sort it.'

'What do you mean, Sue?'

'They're gonna go and pay a little visit to that Steven Archer.' Sue had a triumphant gleam in her eyes.

'What, that backward boy?' asked Grace, alarmed.

'Well, it's obvious, isn't it? None of this happened before he came back from that boarding school for nutty kids,' Sue said decisively.

Grace laughed nervously then muttered, 'Christ, even the cold water is bloody warm,' as she ran the tap. 'But how can you say that, Sue, when your TJ has cerebral palsy? And anyway, how do you know it's Steven?' she continued. 'He's only fourteen and seems a gentle enough soul. I've seen him waiting to be asked to play with the other kids, and helping some of the old dears with their bags and stuff.'

'Because he's always hanging around, just staring. He gives me the creeps.'

'But what proof have you got?'

'I don't need proof, I *know*.' Sue tapped the side of her nose.

Grace knew better than to argue with her when she got an idea into her head. Then they were interrupted by the familiar sound of baby Luke waking up from his nap and crying for his bottle. The thought of a brutish attack on a simple young lad left Grace's thoughts for a little while.

11

She put the beaker down on the draining board and walked out of the kitchen and over to the push-chair where she pulled her hot clammy baby out of his resting place. His nappy was wet through and the damp had travelled up his babygro. Grace removed the towelling suit and nappy expertly with him balanced on her lap, the large pin held in her mouth while she fixed a dry terry nappy on to her four-month-old. She pulled a lukewarm bottle of milk out of her bag and placed it in the baby's wailing mouth, immediately silencing him.

As she fed Luke she walked back over to the open door and called for Adam to come inside. 'Come on, love, you'll get sunstroke out there. Come in and have a drink.'

Adam ignored her. Grace tutted to herself and decided to finish feeding the baby before physically dragging her other son back inside to pour the juice down his throat. He was a tough one, her Adam, and seemed able to withstand incredible physical hard-ship. She still remembered the time she and John took him over to the park when he was tiny, only about eighteen months old. He had been walking since he was about eleven months and already they had to run to keep up with him. It was a freezing cold day in January and all the muddy puddles had frozen over, but that didn't stop their Adam from lying down in each and every one of them and giving himself an ice-mud bath. They had both laughed with a mixture of horror and pride as he delightedly got himself soaked to the skin, his thick nappy soaking up the dirty water and becoming so heavy that his trousers sank halfway down his legs, revealing his frozen bum.

In the heat, too, he never showed any sign of wilting, his stocky little figure just kept on going. He had a bullish head of dark curls and a perpetual look of sheer determination on his face. Adam just pushed on regardless of any obstacle in his path. Grace and John adored their little first-born and felt sure that he had some special destiny in store for him.

Life with John and her boys was more than Grace had ever hoped for. When she first met John, she was timid, tense, unsure what she felt, but he showed her love and tenderness, and that its physical expression could be a pleasurable thing. It had been a while since Uncle Gary had left her bedroom, but having sex with a man brought back the memories of his brute strength and rough penetration of her.

She had been only twelve when she was first raped by Gary, and could still remember every little detail. His roughness, his overwhelming smell of Brut aftershave, and the way he'd torn her knickers, yanking them off. Also that dreadful song had been playing over and over again on her small portable record player. Gary would leave the seven-inch single on repeat to cover the noises he made. It had played four times before he had finished with her. How she hated that song! Tommy James and the Shondells,

13

singing 'Mony Mony' over and over again, and each time the chorus came to the 'yeah, yeah' sequence, Uncle Gary would sing with them as he thrust ever harder into her frail body, cupping his hard hand over her mouth to stifle her screams.

Bruised, battered and tear-stained, Grace was held by the throat until she thought she would die from suffocation. On Uncle Gary's handsome face above her was a grimace of gratification and triumph. As he held her slender neck in one hand he snarled at her, 'You're mine now, little Gracie girl, and we're gonna 'ave lots of fun, you and me. I'm gonna teach you things you never even imagined, and you will never say nuffink to no one about it 'cause it's all your fault. They'll lock yer mum away because of you, if ya tell.'

Grace had been rigid with fear throughout the ordeal. When he finally released her, she slumped back on the bed and buried her face in the covers until she heard the door shut and realised he had gone. She put one hand to her vulva in an attempt to ease the soreness and bleeding. Blood mixed with a creamy, sticky fluid that seeped through her fingers. Quietly she left her room and made her way to the bathroom. She could hear Uncle Gary talking to Mum downstairs as normal as she slipped into the bathroom and washed herself, over and over again.

Still reluctantly reliving the events of the past, something suddenly compelled Grace to hand the baby over to Sue. 'Hold on to him for a minute, will you?' The other mums were putting away the puzzles and building bricks and emptying the water trays. Grace wiped her damp hands on the back of her shorts and strode out into the garden where she saw that the little bubble car was parked perfectly parallel to the wire-mesh fence. Adam was not inside it and Benny Jr who had also been playing in the garden was not visible either.

Telling herself they were around the corner of the building playing together, Grace stifled her rising sense of panic and called her son's name: 'Adam, time to go, love. Come on.' Silence. 'Adam? Come on, love, where are you?' She checked under the little climbing frame, wondering if he was playing silly buggers and hiding from her. Not there either. 'Oh, please God,' she said quietly then ran back into the hall and called, 'Has anyone seen Adam?'

The other mums looked at each other, waiting for someone to reveal his whereabouts, but nobody spoke up except for Sue who finally said, 'He must be around somewhere. There's no way he could have got out. Go and check the toilets.'

Grace ran into the loos, opening each stall and calling louder each time, 'Adam, come on! Stop mucking about, we have to go now.' And finally, in anger, 'I mean it, Adam, I'm going without you if you don't come out – *right now*.' But she already knew he wouldn't answer. She went back outside to check the garden one last time. The other mums had gathered there. A horrible silence hung in the still air as they realised that it had happened again.

Then Grace's nephew, little Benny Hoare Jr, crawled out from under a large shrub at the back of the garden. 'Benny, have you seen Adam?' cried Sue, gripping him by the collar in frustration. 'Benny, where's Adam?'

'Man, Sue, man!' he cried, pointing to the wire-mesh fence behind him. They could all see that it had been pulled or sheared away for several feet next to one of the metal uprights and bent back. The space was large enough for an adult to crouch down and get into the garden. Or for a small boy to scramble through and out on to the road.

Grace's sister Gillian, Benny's mother, ran over to him then and held him so tight he couldn't breathe. 'It could have been my Benny!' she screamed.

The other women just stared at her. Shamefaced after her outburst, she released him and joined the others who had huddled around Grace and were attempting to place steadying arms around her waist and shoulders. But despite their efforts to hold her up she sank to her knees and cried heavenward like a wounded animal, 'Oh, God, help me, please! Please . . . my baby, my baby.'

Chapter Two

Adam was found alive but unconscious at 6.30 p.m. that same day, in the alley behind the bookmaker's on Hackney Road. The bookie, Harold Kowitz, or Harry the Horse as he was known locally, only discovered the boy by chance when he went out to the bins looking for a betting slip carbon he thought he might have inadvertently chucked out. He would normally have shut up shop and left by 5.30 but that night could not get his books to balance. Beset by his perpetual fear that his staff were robbing him blind, he had determined not to leave until he had located the missing carbon. As he rifled through the bins the smell of rotting rubbish made him gag and he cursed the heat, not for the first time that summer.

A small sound, part-whimper, part-gurgle, stopped him in his tracks and he listened for it again. He thought at first it must be a cat, but as he rolled a dustbin away from the wall, he saw a little boy, pale and still as a marble cherub, looking for all the world like he was just taking a nap rather than lying unconscious from shock and pain.

At first Harry assumed this was just a kid who had wandered off from home, plenty of local children roamed in feral packs in the neighbourhood, but this child was too young to be out alone and he was beautifully dressed. He gently nudged the boy and said softly, 'Come on, little 'un, what you doing down there? Get up.'

But the little boy did not respond and a cold, sick, sinking sensation in his gut told Harry that something was badly wrong. He saw the grass and blood stains on his expensive clothing, the leaves and twigs stuck in the child's hair, and most peculiarly of all, a drumstick lolly stuck to his head in a sticky, soggy mess above his right ear. There was a cut just beneath the inside corner of his right eye, with a patch of dry blood on it. That was when he noticed that this child had no eyelashes, just a stumpy line where his long, silky, small child's lashes should have been.

Harry carried him into the shop where he cradled him in his arms until the police and ambulance arrived and they were able to match the boy's description to that of a child reported missing that morning.

The grass stains led the police to believe that after the boy had been snatched from the toddlers' group, he must have been taken to Haggerston Park a quarter of a mile away and wandered away after the assault, looking for his mummy. How nobody spotted a small child walking alone on a busy East End street was a question no one could answer.

*

After the relief of their child being found, Grace and John were distressed that they weren't able to take Adam home. Although he had been roused from his unconscious state by the nurses at the Queen Elizabeth Children's Hospital before Grace and John arrived, he still would not speak except to whimper, tugging at the lolly still stuck to his hair and skin above his ear, 'It hurts, Mummy.'

They sat in a hospital side ward with a young police officer, PC Ian Watson, and a nurse in attendance. John was leaning against the windowsill, staring out at the grey skyline, his hands clenched and knuckles white. He was breathing heavily to stop the shaking inside him. The room was close and muggy, and sweat rolled down his back. Grace rocked Adam back and forth on her lap, her eyes gazing into the middle distance but seeing nothing. He cried as his mother held his hand down to stop him pulling at the sweet, sticky mass above his ear.

Suddenly she burst out, 'Can't we just cut this bloody lolly out of his hair?'

PC Watson had his orders that nothing should be done until the medical officers arrived, but after a few meaningful glances from the nurse who silently backed up Grace's request, he said softly, 'I don't see why not, we can keep it in a sterile bag.'

The nurse left the room briefly and returned with a stainless steel kidney bowl, scissors, swabs and antiseptic. She pulled up a chair next to Grace and in a

19

whisper said, 'If you just hold him still for me for a minute, we'll get that out of his hair and then he'll be more comfortable, won't you, sweetheart?'

Adam eyed the nurse with glowering suspicion and fear but her soothing tone and deft handiwork had the sweet removed in less than a minute. He cried out only once when she had to dislodge the sticky mess at the point it had become stuck to the skin above his ear, but she was quick and soon he was being rocked and soothed again by Grace, who mouthed her thanks. The nurse, feeling utterly at a loss for the right thing to say or do, stood up and declared briskly, 'Right, I'll get us all a cup of tea then.'

The police insisted that they should stay at the hospital until a medical officer was able to give the child a thorough examination and take tests and swabs. They were very kind to Grace and John, but things became tense between PC Watson and a casualty registrar when hospital staff insisted Adam be taken to surgery. Having just got him back, Grace did not want to let him go, and the police wanted to get what information they could from Adam as to who might have done this to him, but the hospital doctor was adamant that the wounds to his genital area and anus needed immediate attention. They could not risk delaying any longer.

PC Watson, on uncertain ground, tried to reason with the doctor: 'I have strict orders, sir.' To which the doctor immediately replied, 'No doubt, Constable, but I have a child in urgent need of medical attention.' There was a slight pause and the doctor continued in a no-nonsense manner, 'Prepare him for surgery . . . immediately, Nurse.'

PC Watson stayed with Grace and John in the small ward, drinking tea and wondering aloud what kind of animal could do this to a child, but couldn't get a word out of either of them. Shock, he supposed. This was only his third year with the force, and though he had seen a couple of murder victims and some pretty horrific battery cases, this was his first experience of a sexual assault on a child, and such a young one at that.

He spoke of his own small children and his determination to catch the attacker: 'We'll get him, don't you worry. There'll be clues everywhere; it's just a matter of time. DCI Woodhouse is a top-drawer bastard – there's no way he'll let a pervert like this one roam loose for too long.'

John's resolve was beginning to weaken, the odd strangulated sob breaking from him, but Grace just sat there in silent agony, memories of her own shattered childhood running through her mind, numb with disbelief that this could be happening again.

Meanwhile Detective Chief Inspector Albert Woodhouse was waiting for feedback from his officers in

Dalston. They were searching the Haggerston Park area, looking for anything that could confirm that the child had been taken there to be assaulted and for any suspicious sightings in the area. Five officers were conducting door-to-door enquiries and he expected news to filter back soon. This was a neighbourhood where not much went unnoticed. Most of the residents knew each other by sight if not by name. Cases in these two square miles of densely populated East London terraced housing and tower blocks were notoriously difficult to close down unless you could get the right people to talk. A lot of covering up went on, but in a case like this, Woodhouse thought he could rely on local help.

He had worked at Bethnal Green for the last fifteen of his twenty-five years in the force and was a known figure in the area, respected if not liked. The gangs of organised criminals locally preferred their coppers bent, but nobody could ever accuse Woodhouse of that. A humourless man, he was a tall, lugubrious-looking individual whose suits and shoes were worn but well-kept.

Twenty-five years on the force exposed a man to the worst in human nature but there was something especially sickening about this case. A second sexual assault, the first resulting in murder, in a small area in the same week was suspicious despite the differences. Chantal Robinson was a young woman, hers could be a straightforward rape case that had turned

22

nasty if the girl had put up a fight, and Adam Ballantyne was so much younger. Woodhouse had yet to hear back from the medical officer, but it seemed clear from initial reports that the child had been anally penetrated. What kind of man got his kicks from buggering a four-year-old boy? However, although Woodhouse was uncertain, at this stage he suspected that the attacks had to be linked.

Woodhouse knew that a PC was holding the parents for him at the hospital while he scoured the area for any positive evidence he could present them with. Families of victims always bayed for immediate blood and Woodhouse knew from long experience that you had to be able to give them some proof that the case was progressing. Besides, he lacked the sympathetic touch necessary in these cases. Although he thought PC Watson was a bit too much of a soft touch to make a really good copper, he was just the ticket for work like this and could be relied on to make all the right noises. It wasn't that the DCI didn't care or have feelings; he just preferred to keep them to himself. In his job it was better not to give way to emotion.

Down at one of the local pubs, the Birdcage, the unofficial investigation was proceeding less dis-passionately. 'It's gotta be that spastic kid Steven Archer, my Sue's convinced.' Terry Williams, father of four and husband to Sue, was standing at the bar with his close friend and workmate Paul Foster, step-father to the recently murdered Chantal.

Privately, Paul had been rocked to his foundations by her murder, but for the sake of his wife Michelle, and for his own sanity, he was maintaining a calm approach. Beneath seethed anger and a fierce determination to find the bloke who'd done this before the police did. A life sentence would be too good for him. All the same, Paul wasn't going to batter somebody on the say-so of a busybody housewife and know-it-all. He thought the world of Terry but kept his feelings about Sue to himself.

It was talent night and the pub was packed, the stage with its mirrored backdrop reflecting the crowded bar and beyond to the pool table and darts board. Paul checked his watch to see if there was time for another drink before the first act came on. He usually liked to duck out before the show got going, not being a particular fan of middle-aged men crooning Frank Sinatra and Elvis favourites. The women tended to favour Shirley Bassey and Peggy Lee numbers, and liked to dress up for it.

'Who's she then, bloody Columbo? Same again.' Paul tilted his pint glass at the barmaid.

'No, but it's funny how none of this happened before *he* came home for the summer holidays. Sue says he gives her and the other women the creeps, the way he's always just standing around staring at the kids.'

'Might be because no bugger wants to play with him, poor little sod.' Paul handed a pound note over the bar and waited for his change.

'Yeah, but he's fourteen and wants to join in with little kids? Cheers, love.' Terry winked at the barmaid.

'That's because he's got a mental age of about five.'

'What are you sticking up for him for?' Terry grew instantly confrontational. 'I thought you'd be the last person, what with . . .' he paused here, unable to speak about Chantal '. . . well, you know.' Paul didn't reply, just stared into the mirror behind the bar reflecting back the sea of bodies in the pub behind him. It could be any one of these blokes in here, he thought to himself. Or none of them. The police had told him that in the vast majority of rapes and murders, the assailant was known to the victim. But who could it be?

Terry shifted uncomfortably from foot to foot, sensing he had gone too far and at a loss for what to say next. Finally he managed a feeble, 'Fancy a quick game of pool?' Paul knew that in his way Terry was trying to apologise. He turned and touched his friend's shoulder. 'Nah, you're all right, mate. I'm just gonna finish this then shoot off. Don't like to leave Michelle on her own too much, 'specially not with the funeral tomorrow.'

'Yeah, yeah. Course, mate. I'd better be getting home myself or Sue'll have my bollocks on the chopping block again like she did last night. But, listen, we'll see you there, mate. Christ Church, isn't it?'

'Yeah, eleven o'clock, then we've got the wake in here after. Maggie and John are closing the pub 'specially for us. Michelle wanted to do it at home but our place isn't big enough and I don't want a load of people in the house anyway. The other kids are upset enough as it is.'

'Are you bringing them?' Terry was fishing on instructions from Sue who wanted to bring all four of hers including the baby in a show of family solidarity. Terry didn't think it was right but wasn't going to go up against her.

'I dunno, mate. Aisha's definitely coming, but I think Trinity's too young. Still, it's Michelle's call.' Aisha was Chantal's younger sister, Paul's second step-daughter, a beauty like her. At nine she was old enough to understand what had happened to Chantal. Instead of forever riding around the estate with her mates on the Chopper she'd got last Christmas as she used to do, Aisha had refused to leave her room since Chantal's murder. Michelle wanted her to see a friend, do anything, just be normal for a while. But it was early days, they supposed.

Trinity, Paul's daughter by Michelle, was four and too young to understand what was really going on.

Her mum had tried to explain but Trinity just kept asking, 'When's Chantal coming back from heaven?'

Thinking of the kids suddenly caught Paul by the throat. He felt he might choke on the lump in it. He finished his pint with one long swallow, banged the glass on the bar harder than he'd meant to and, without saying a word, touched Terry's arm by way of goodbye. His friend started to say something but his mouth just opened and closed again. What could he say? Paul opened the door, ignoring the sympathetic glances of well-wishers, and walked quickly out on to Gosset Road where he cried all the way home.

Grace was having the opposite problem. She couldn't cry. She couldn't feel. John was doing enough of that for both of them. She had never seen her husband sob like this before and could only gaze at him in curious detachment as he crumbled before her eyes. She didn't even try to comfort him but spent her time instead just staring at her little boy as he lay sleeping in a hospital bed with metal bars at the sides. It reminded her of seeing him in his cot as a baby.

When John left, Grace spent the long watches of the night alone in the side ward with her boy, listening to the faint hum of the hospital incinerator somewhere in the distance. The night nurse popped in from time to time to check his temperature and make sure no infection was taking hold. Adam had needed eight internal stitches and three around the opening to his anus to repair the damage there. The doctors had warned Grace that they'd need to be very careful about what he ate in the next few weeks while the stitches healed, as going to the toilet was going to be exceptionally painful although he would be given medication for that. His penis had been badly bruised and was painfully swollen. There was no tearing to the skin, but puncture holes had been made in it deliberately, though hopefully surgery had corrected these.

John had finally gone home around 2 a.m. to relieve Lizzie Foster who had been looking after baby Luke. Lizzie was Paul Foster's mother, a tough old bird with a tight perm and flinty eyes. In their panic to find a sitter for Luke when the call came that Adam had been found, Grace and John had forgotten that Lizzie, as Chantal's step-grand-mother, would be at the funeral the following day and would probably want to rest up beforehand. It was only after Adam came out of surgery and was left sedated and in a sound sleep that the thought occurred to them.

John didn't want to leave Grace and Adam, but she was insistent. 'No, you go, see to the baby. I'm all right.' She was too, or so it seemed to John who had to suppress a flicker of anger at his wife for staying so composed – not thinking for a moment that what she was displaying was not composure at all but the numbness that comes by way of grace when feelings would be too hard to bear.

Chapter Three

The Fosters lived in a spacious Guinness Trust Housing Association flat at the eastern, residential end of Columbia Road. Its red-brick foundations and façades were dotted with the white freshly painted windowframes of the sixty or so flats it contained. Michelle and Paul had slowly moved up the housing list during their first five years together with Michelle's two daughters by her first marriage to Darren Robinson. When their own daughter Trinity was born it tipped the scales that had moved them from a damp, cramped, noisy flat above a green-grocer's on Brick Lane to the relative luxury of this newly refurbished Guinness Trust block.

Tower Hamlets Council had referred them to the housing trust and they were rewarded with three bedrooms, a kitchen/dinette, and a twelve-foot lounge – unimaginable luxury after years of living on top of each other. The flats housed mainly young families like themselves and Paul and Michelle quickly established firm friendships with their neighbours, doing favours, lending and borrowing tools, food and clothing, and of course minding each other's kids. Everyone was part of the community here, from the small post office to the reproduction furniture factory outlets. Everybody knew everybody, and until a week ago none of them had any reason to think that their children were anything but safe. They might come in late for their tea; they might come back with rips or stains in their clothing, or even cuts and bruises from boisterous play, but they came back in one piece. Children here used to be seen pushing open a letter box and pulling the door key through from inside where it dangled on a piece of string. They'd let themselves in and wait alone for their mothers to get back from work. Now, though, hardly anyone went unsupervised, the younger children only rode their bikes in twos, and there was a general sense of foreboding and anxiety.

That old sense of security, taken totally for granted before, had quickly evaporated and fear and anger had taken its place. Now neighbours stood round in conspiratorial huddles, speculating on who could have done such things to Chantal and then Adam. Since Chantal's brutal rape and murder, the Fosters' neighbours had roughly fallen into two camps – the first too stricken, shocked and embarrassed by the news to do more than mutter their condolences, the second supportive to the point of being intrusive: knocking on the door at all hours of the day and night, offering to do shopping, washing, cooking, take the girls to school, or just come in and sit with them.

For the most part Paul wished they would go away but Michelle wanted to talk about it all the time, it was her way of coping. He envied his wife her ability to let it all out. When she wasn't sobbing loudly, she was angrily slamming pots and pans. Only at night, after she had taken the sedative prescribed by their doctor, did she grow still; but only temporarily, for even then, she would toss and turn and call out in the dark, her dreams shot through with horrific visions.

On the day of the funeral the sun came up hot and heavy as it had every day that summer. Michelle Foster sat on the edge of her bed, head slumped, staring at her feet. Her toenail polish was chipped and that wouldn't do. She had to look her best for her baby. Preoccupied with this silly detail, she didn't notice her husband Paul set down a cup of tea on the bedside table and gently touch her long black curls before going back downstairs to get the girls their breakfast. Reality came back to her then like a hammer blow to her head, the impossible truth bludgeoning her brain. My baby is going to heaven today, she kept telling herself, and yet still she didn't want to believe it.

Michelle didn't know how she was going to get through the day ahead; a part of her deep inside couldn't quite take in the fact that Chantal wasn't coming back, and occasionally when she heard Paul's key in the lock after work she half expected her eldest to shout up the stairs, 'Mum, I'm home,' before slamming the door behind her. Chantal was a real door-banger, it used to drive Michelle mad that she could never do anything quietly – now she'd give anything to hear the glass in the front door rattle in its frame, just as she'd like to hear her daughter playing her records too loud, especially 'Save All Your Kisses for Me' by the Brotherhood of Man. Michelle must have heard it a thousand times, usually with Chantal singing along tunelessly, shuffling about and mimicking the famous dance routine, but now all was silence behind her bedroom door.

Michelle had not been able to face going into that room since her daughter's mutilated body had been found in the alley behind the Bingo hall. There were still empty mugs and crisp packets on the floor from where Chantal had invited her mates round the day before her murder. Her baby had been so popular. She was such a good-looking kid. All the boys had loved her and all the girls wanted to be her mate. Their newly acquired phone would ring constantly and Michelle had loved to see that Chantal was so well liked.

Her possessions were littered around the flat as if she were still there to use them; her slippers kicked off in the bathroom, combs and brushes and beads on the kitchen table where she had been braiding her sisters' hair. In the kitchen, on top of the counter stood a pile of overdue library books that Chantal had been due to take back the day she was killed, and hanging over the back of a chair was a skirt of hers which needed hemming. Michelle wasn't ready to clear any of these reminders away, but ready or not the time had come to say goodbye formally to her first-born. In less than two hours she would be sitting in the front pew of Christ Church, Spitalfields, looking at her daughter's coffin – that white glossy coffin with the big bold brass handles, lined inside with white silk to cushion her girl while she slept.

After Chantal's father Darren had formally identified her body, he'd spoken to Paul and made it clear that under no circumstances was Michelle to see her daughter. Chantal's face had been horribly disfigured by the attack, and the husbands – past and present – agreed that this was a sight that could push Michelle beyond the limits of her endurance. That she was holding up at all, despite all the tears and outbreaks of rage, was something of a miracle. This was a pain like no other she had known, a grief so deep and fathomless that it weighed down her body like lead. Her breathing felt laboured and she kept sighing heavily, but somehow she managed to carry on living.

Michelle forced herself to stand up and stretch, then sat back down again from the effort of it all. She wondered briefly if she could get away with not going to the funeral, but the sound of feet thundering up the stairs and the little girls bursting through her bedroom door made her sit up straight and paint on a smile. By the time the carriage arrived at 10.30 she was dressed in black, toenails freshly painted, grim-faced but determined.

The funeral cortège moved slowly through the streets of the small community. Behind the horse-drawn hearse, two little girls, two young boys, two women and two men walked slowly with their heads bowed. This was Chantal's family. Michelle, her second husband Paul, their daughter Trinity, and Aisha from her previous relationship with Darren Robinson. Robbo, too, had remarried. By his side walked Chantal's step-mother, Charmain, and her two sons, Darren Jr and little Max.

The sun beat down remorselessly and the black horse struggled to pull the hearse down Columbia Road, its body etched with sweat and black plumage weighing heavy on its head. Patches of white foam appeared around its muzzle as it drew the dignified black carriage that carried the body of Chantal Robinson.

Following on were four large cars full of family and friends, all with their faces covered with hands or handkerchiefs to hide red swollen eyes. Grief had ripped through the Foster and Robinson families and the whole close-knit community. The police were present to show that they supported the families and were determined to find the perpetrator. Neighbours and friends lined the street in respect and sorrow, and groups of schoolgirls broke the silence with their wails and sobbing.

Traffic came to a standstill as the funeral cortège crossed Bethnal Green Road into Brick Lane near where Christ Church, one of Hawksmoor's finest churches, stood.

Michelle stepped into its cool interior and was amazed to find that every pew was filled to bursting; there must have been over four hundred people in that church, even the galleried area upstairs was full. She didn't know most of the people's names but recognised many faces. Local people had turned out en masse to express their shock and sorrow at such a young life being snuffed out so brutally. She hesitated before walking up the aisle to the front pew, taking in the sight of all those people in front of her; in that moment she knew that she would survive, that the human spirit could not be killed by the evil action of one man. She felt the love in that church and let it carry her towards her place near the altar as she held the hands of her two surviving daughters.

The service passed in a blur, afterwards Michelle could hardly recall it, she'd been staring so intently at the coffin bearing her beloved girl, and praying so hard that God would keep Chantal safe in heaven until she could join her. Michelle was only fully present for the hymn 'Lord of the Dance', when she'd had to smile at the memory of Chantal singing it as a young child, the first hymn she'd ever learned in infants' school. She would belt it out, loud and tuneless as always.

Chantal's father Darren sobbed throughout the service, as did Aisha. Trinity, at four, was too young to really take in what was happening. Paul clutched her firmly on his lap in the second pew and, by breathing deep and hard, was able to contain his own tears.

The Vicar intoned, deep and low, '"*I am the resurrection and the life, saith the Lord; he that believeth in me, though he were dead, yet shall he live; and whosoever liveth and believeth in me shall never die . . . We brought nothing into this world, and it is certain we can carry nothing out. The Lord gave and the Lord hath taken away; blessed be the name of the Lord.*"'

His words washed over Michelle unheard. Only at the burial after the service, as Chantal's coffin was being lowered into the ground, could she focus on what he was saying.

'"*Man that is born of woman hath but a short time to live, and is full of misery. He cometh up and is cut down like a flower; he fleeth as it were a shadow and never continueth in one stay. In the midst of life we are in death . . . For as much as it hath pleased Almighty God of his great mercy to take unto himself the soul of our dear sister here departed we therefore commit her body to the ground; earth to earth, ashes to ashes, dust to dust; in sure and certain hope of the Resurrection to eternal life . . ."'*

The Vicar nodded at Darren and Michelle, indicating that this was their moment to throw earth into the grave. They leaned into each other for support as they stepped forward to bid this final farewell to their little girl.

Paul stood to one side and fought back a flash of jealousy. He knew he shouldn't begrudge Darren this moment, Chantal was his daughter after all, but the way he and Michelle had their arms around each other made his stomach turn. What if this was the thing that brought them back together? He had always feared that his wife had never really got over Darren, and it was only when their little girl Trinity was born that he'd felt Michelle was really his now. Paul stared at his beautiful wife. For a moment he thought she might lose her composure, might hurl herself to the ground and beg God to give her back her daughter, but she stood firm.

'*"Almighty God, with whom do live the spirits of them that depart hence in the Lord, and with whom the souls of the faithful, after they are delivered from the burden of the flesh, are in joy and felicity; we give thee hearty thanks, that it hath pleased thee to deliver our sister out of the miseries of this sinful world . . ."'*

At these words Michelle straightened up and

consoled herself with the thought that Chantal was out of it now, away from all the pain and the crap of this life on earth, away from the monster who did this to her.

' ". . . *may have our perfect consummation and bliss, both in body and soul in thy eternal and everlasting glory; through Jesus Christ our Lord. Amen.* " '

And it was over. The mourners drifted away from the grave in small groups with their heads bowed, men loosening ties and women fanning themselves in the heat with their Order of Service. Only Michelle and Darren stayed by the graveside, silently, side by side, unable to walk away from their little girl for the last time. Paul gently touched her shoulder and whispered, 'I'll take the girls and go on, I'll see you there.' He didn't want to leave her with Darren but he had to allow them this. And besides, someone had to greet the mourners back at the pub.

The wake afterwards in the Birdcage was a muted affair. It was not uncommon for funerals in the neighbourhood to turn into parties as the beer flowed – a good send-off was considered standard practice locally. But there were no songs around the piano for Chantal today, no funny stories being told about things she had done. Instead groups of men and women sat in huddled groups, speculating angrily. Sue Williams was leading the lynch mob, arguing forcefully that Steven Archer needed to be dealt with.

'What's it gonna take, eh? Another kiddie being raped and murdered before we do anything?' Sue's husband Terry nodded his agreement, though after his conversation with Paul in the pub the night before he was beginning to doubt his wife's certainty. 'Fucking police are useless! I told them it was him but they haven't picked him up yet. I saw him this morning outside the greengrocer's, bold as brass, watching the hearse go by. It was all I could do not to get out of the car and throttle the sick bastard myself.'

Next to Sue was Nanny Parks, mother to Gillian and Grace. A widow, she was close to her girls and idolised her four grandsons, Adam and Luke by Grace, and Jamie and Benny Jr by Gillian. She had left Grace and John at the hospital this morning after visiting Adam. No stranger to hardship, she had little time for tears. After seeing her frightened little grandson cowering in his hospital bed, she had determined that all her anger and outrage would be directed at the person who had done this to him. Her mouth was set in a grim line and the sun shone through the windows of the pub, casting a halo around her purple rinse. 'I've always said he was weird, that kid. Someone needs to sort him out.'

'Exactly!' agreed Sue.

'The police will soon pick him up if he's guilty, won't they?' Terry offered gently.

'Humph.' Nanny Parks made an indignant noise and raised her eyebrows at Sue.

'No, Terry, we can't wait that long. Our kids aren't safe all the time he's walking around. Anyway, no one's asking you to *kill* him, just put the frighteners on him. Enough to make sure he goes away and never comes back.'

'Here, here,' said Nanny Parks.

'Another milk stout, Mum?' Grace's sister Gillian asked their mother, arriving at the table.

'What do you think then, Gill?' Sue asked.

'Think about what?' she replied.

'Steven Archer – me and your mum reckon it's him.'

'That's what I said to Grace the other day but she wouldn't have it. Maybe now this has happened, though . . . I can't believe what he did to Adam, it's fucking sick . . .' Gillian's voice rose dangerously. 'That sick fucker mutilated his little willy, it ain't ever gonna function like it should. John's beside himself.'

'Enough, Gill,' said Nanny Parks firmly. 'There's enough gossip going round without spreading any more. We all need to pull together and remain tight-lipped. Let's talk about who done this and leave ya sister to get Adam better.'

A muted atmosphere fell over the group. Chairs were pulled up and moved around. Sandra Potts, or Potty as she was known, made her way over to Sue's table. The women sipped their drinks and entered into whispered conversations.

Memories of that day stayed with the community over the weeks that followed. Bit by bit, more was revealed about the terrible way that Chantal had died. A shocked and distrustful neighbourhood waited for further developments. The police had launched a house-to-house enquiry, but nothing had been found to move their investigation along. Even a front-page splash in the local rag had jogged no one's memory about the day or time in question. All the police had were the lollipops found on Adam's and Chantal's bodies, the fact that both had had their eyelashes cut off and a matching blood group. They were also fairly certain that the attacker knew the area well enough to realise he would remain undisturbed during the attacks. No one had seen anything, no one had heard anything, and the murder of Chantal Robinson remained unsolved. But news had travelled fast about Adam's abduction and assault, and even if the police weren't confirming anything, locals believed that they had been committed by the same man.

Chapter Four

The mums loitered for longer than usual outside the gates of Columbia Row Primary School a few days later. The children had been ushered into the playground, made to line up and wait for the bell, all the while watched closely by mums and teachers alike. The tension in the air was sharp, Adam and Chantal still the only topics of discussion. With a lot of head-shaking, grimaces and tutting, the mums discussed Chantal's funeral and the attack on Adam, news of which had now spread not just across the East End but throughout London as the newspapers got on to the story. Even a couple of the nationals were covering it in small pieces, and everyone seemed to know what was going on. Comments ranged from 'Did you see the flowers, weren't they beautiful?' to 'Apparently he'll have to wear a catheter for the rest of his life.'

The highly volatile mixture of fact and rumour had Adam close to death and on life support, when in fact he was at home with Grace, albeit subdued by a powerful combination of sedatives and painkillers to dull the constant discomfort. Those mothers who hadn't heard the details of the attack from neighbours and friends had been alerted by the police as they conducted their door-to-door enquiries, asking if they had seen anything suspicious in the Haggerston Park area on Monday. Despite all their efforts, though, PC Watson had little to report back. It wasn't that people were being unhelpful; it was simply that no one had seen anything. DCI Woodhouse would definitely expect more, but as the weary constable peeled off his hot boots that night, he felt he had put in a lot of hard work to no avail.

This combination of police and press interest had naturally alerted the local bush telegraph, and stories and rumours were already rife. Women leaned against the railings outside the school, reading fresh significance into every movement in the neighbourhood over the last weeks, rocking pushchairs to soothe impatient younger siblings fed up with hanging around, hot and bothered in the stifling heat. Even a bag of cheesy Wotsits and a Ribena wouldn't quieten them down. The women, all in tight bell-bottomed trousers and small halterneck tops, puffed on their No. 6, jittery from their morning slimming pill which just made them talk and talk and talk.

By 9.15 it was already blazing hot and tempers too became inflamed. The stimulants of too much coffee, a Tenuate Dospan and one too many fags rapidly converted gossip to gospel truth. One person's prejudice had a way of becoming another's indisputable fact, and what had started out as faint suspicions about Steven Archer were rapidly transformed into confirmed sightings and definite proof of guilt. A kangaroo court of sorts, this finger-pointing was nonetheless harmless compared to the council of war currently being held in Lizzie's Foster's flat on the tenth floor of a tatty council block half a mile away.

Like Nanny Parks, Paul's mother was a survivor of the school of hard knocks, and nobody's fool. She lived in a two-bedroomed flat in Dunbar House, built in the early 1950s, already crumbling and given to swaying in high winds. It was one of three high-rise blocks built at the southern end of Ravenscroft Road to house locals made homeless during the Blitz. Although the lifts were frequently out of order, stank of piss, and were littered with used johnnies and scrawled over with a thick layer of graffiti, there was little choice but to use them if you lived above the fourth floor. The stairwells were even more disgusting, and at times dangerous. Washing hung from the littered balconies, but the careworn exterior of the flats was in stark contrast to the pristine cleanliness behind Lizzie's front door.

The lounge contained an old but immaculate Draylon-covered three-piece suite in faded gold arranged around a 26-inch Ferguson TV, a present from Paul the previous Christmas. Framed photographs of three mixed-race girls sat on the polished sideboard, along with a Spanish doll in a rich red and

45

gold flamenco dress together with another ornament depicting a shepherd and his lamb. On the wall, and just slightly off centre, hung a spiky brass sunray clock that ticked away the seconds loudly. Next to it was a bamboo-framed picture of a bronzed South Pacific beauty, smiling back demurely at all who gazed on her. The swirly-patterned carpet was threadbare in places but swept by hand every morning with a dustpan and brush.

Now a widow, Lizzie kept herself busy with relentless cleaning and regular sessions at the Bingo hall on Hackney Road. Since her husband's death two years earlier, she had enjoyed a welcome renaissance in her relationship with her son. Her husband Ted – a man of fierce prejudices and an insatiable appetite for drink – had made family life impossible. The days since his death had been bliss. No more empty bottles to take back to the off-licence or green Rizla fag papers scattered around her clean front room. No more loud racist abuse, booming out when he came home pissed and feeling aggressive. No, Lizzie lived life on her own terms now.

When Ted was alive, he'd kicked up something alarming after Paul and Michelle had got together. How could *his son* love a black woman? It was just disgusting; Ted didn't know how he was supposed to hold his head up amongst the blokes he worked with at the paint factory. None of them lot liked the niggers. They had all had family killed in the war, and saw immigrant labour as another threatened invasion. Spades, they called them. Just fucking apes, weren't they, swarming all over his country and taking all the jobs? They had bad habits, they smelled, and were thick and lazy to boot – but they always seemed to have the latest gear, fast cars, and a white woman on their arms! Many a young girl who crossed the line and went with a black man was bashed up by her dad or brother! If Paul was stupid enough to take up with one of them that was his lookout, but as far as the outraged Ted was concerned he no longer had a son. He had to keep face with his mates. How could he be expected to support his son's taste for a bit of dark meat?

Of course, Lizzie had had to stand by her husband. It was what you did, wasn't it? She would try from time to time to talk about Paul and persuade Ted to keep up with the times, but her husband was an old-fashioned, ignorant man, and his word was and always had been law in their little world. In the two years since his passing from a massive stroke, things had changed very much for the better. For the first time in her life, death had brought rebirth to Lizzie who redoubled her efforts to be a good mother and grandmother, and was now leading the charge to find out who had done this to Chantal.

The girl might not have been her grand-daughter by blood, but Paul had loved her as if she'd been his own and that was good enough for Lizzie. Just seeing them together had made her happy. She'd loved to see them giggle and laugh, and her heart had finally been stolen when Chantal had made her a special card, reading 'Nanny, I Love You', on her birthday. No matter what, she'd loved that kid and was going to miss her, and now she had the job of trying to help her boy come to terms with that baby's death. Some sick evil bastard had taken that kid's future, and Lizzie was determined to get to the truth and find the person responsible. Years of living with an abusive drunk had made her bullet-proof. She had no fear whatsoever, of anyone or anything, nor time for hand-wringing over moral dilemmas: in her opinion the guilty deserved to be punished.

Lizzie was holding a coffee morning to talk about the recent events. Nanny Parks was there, looking tense and angry and ready for anyone who dared to contradict her. She needed to offload, and a morning with the girls was just what the doctor had ordered.

Sue Williams, perhaps the most enthusiastic vengeance-seeker of all, was in fact a faithful lieutenant of Lizzie's, and always had been. The two of them went back a long way. Although Sue appeared to be the leader, it was Lizzie who often pulled the strings.

Gillian was round at Grace's that morning, doing the shopping and cleaning, but said she would pop in later. She had felt the need to do something.

Chantal's funeral was still on her mind, as it was on everybody's, but her first duty was to her sister and her family now.

The three women sat grim-faced and businesslike around the Formica-covered table, drinking strong tea from bone china cups and saucers. 'Kiss and Say Goodbye' by The Manhattans was playing appropriately on the kitchen radio. The washing-up bowl was upturned in the sink and the draining board had been rigorously Ajax-ed. The grey standard council-issue linoleum was similarly well-scrubbed and a strong smell of bleach permeated the room.

Everything had its place in Lizzie's kitchen. The paper-towel holder held a new roll, the tea, coffee and sugar canisters were neatly lined up, and the two-slice toaster gleamed in yellow and stainless steel. A gentle breeze lifted the pristine white net curtains above the kitchen sink and dispersed the clouds of smoke which hovered above the heavy glass ashtray in the middle of the table.

Sue Williams broke the silence.

'My Wayne was in the park after school and he says Steven was definitely there, hanging around the swings all afternoon.' Sue referred to her eleven-year-old son while she jiggled her youngest, three-year-old TJ, on her lap.

Born with cerebral palsy, TJ was the apple of her eye and was adored by friends and family alike. Always smiling, he was the easiest of her four children and, despite his problems, always happy just to sit and play contentedly with bricks or anything else he found lying around. Sue never had any problems finding people to watch or hold TJ. The child seemed to have a rare quality about him that made up for his disability.

'And it's no coincidence that this all started when *he* came back from that spastic school he goes to.' Any irony in Sue's observation was lost on her; having a child of her own with special needs in no way made her sympathetic to Steven Archer. TJ was still the baby everybody loved. She never once considered the problems he could face when he reached Steven's age. She was so sure that she'd identified the guilty party that she prompted the other women and exaggerated all the things Wayne had told her. 'My Wayne said he was sure he saw Steven fumbling with his willy. Bloody pervert! Probably getting off on seeing the young kids playing.'

Her words enraged the other women round the table.

Nanny Parks stubbed out her cigarette angrily. 'I've always said he was a weirdo.' She picked up her spoon and stirred two sugars into her tea. 'Don't you remember how he used to lose his temper and chuck stuff about? He always threw wobblies in the classroom. No wonder they wanted to send him away from other kids! I don't know how Eileen has coped with him all these years.'

Eileen Archer, Steven's mother, had already seen the second of her children leave home pregnant and bound for a shotgun wedding when she herself became pregnant with Steven at forty-four. She knew she was old and the baby could be at risk, but for her as a religious woman there was no alternative but to continue with the pregnancy. At the time there'd been lots of jokes and cruel remarks about the egg from the speckled hen. All sorts of old wives' tales flew about, and for nine months, Eileen was the talk of the neighbourhood. Everyone said 'I told you so' when Steven was born a spastic. Eileen struggled on as best she could. Even after her husband, unable to cope, had left them and moved down to the south coast, she stuck by her boy. He was hers, and he was called 'special' because he was. He wasn't the only child in the area to have cerebral palsy, as it was rightly diagnosed, and so Eileen stayed strong for her boy and trusted that Steven would one day grow into a fine lad.

Lizzie was fidgeting nervously. 'It's funny, you know, I haven't seen her around since this all started up. I reckon she knows he did it and is too frightened to come out and face us. She's protecting that sick bugger!' Lizzie peeled the cellophane off a fresh pack of Player's, screwed it up and placed it in the bin. 'But maybe we should go round and see her . . .'

They'd been friends a long time, and Lizzie still felt she owed Eileen that much, no matter what her son had done.

Sue pulled a face at her. Taking the red toy brick out of TJ's mouth, she weighed her words before she spoke. 'No, leave it, Lizzie. There's no point in talking to her, it's him that needs sorting. Do you want a drink, sweetheart?' she asked her son in the next breath.

'In there, Sue, bottle of lemon barley.' Lizzie pointed to a cupboard next to the sink. She felt sure Sue had sussed her, could read the doubts lurking in her mind, so couldn't afford to appear hesitant. 'Yeah, you're right, Eileen's weak as piss water.'

'Cheers, Lizzie,' said Sue. 'Poor Michelle, though, did you see the state of her at the funeral? I don't know how she stayed upright. I think she was trance-like, sort of not really with us.'

Lizzie twirled her fag up and down her fingers, a neat little trick she had. 'She'll never get over it. Losing a child is bad enough, but to lose one like that . . . well, it doesn't bear thinking about. She'll be after his guts when she gets her strength back.' Her thin lips drew hard on her cigarette. 'I don't think it's women's work, though, do you?'

Sue butted in again. 'Well, look, my Terry said to give him the nod and he'll go round with a couple of the blokes.'

'Sooner the better, I reckon,' said Nanny Parks, taking a Player's from Lizzie's proffered packet. 'Ta, Liz.'

'I expect Grace and John will be pleased,' observed Sue.

'Don't bank on it,' countered Nanny Parks, 'you know what a soft sod my Grace is. She's always felt sorry for that boy, given him sweets and what have you, so I haven't told her anything about this and I'm not going to. Her John's so wound up he's fit to be tied, but she just sits there on the settee holding on to little Adam. She's been in a world of her own.

'My brother Gary always brought the best out in her, ya know. Those two were inseparable when Grace was in her teens. He was never like that with Gillian. I remember, it put her nose right out of joint! Don't think Grace ever got over his death until she met John and moved on. Shame her uncle isn't around now to get her out of herself. It breaks my heart to see her and John so quiet and subdued.'

'Give them time,' said Sue, 'I expect they're still in shock.' A loud knock at the door made them sit up straight. 'That'll be Potty,' said Lizzie.

Sandra Potts was a formerly attractive woman, now in her early thirties, who had gone to seed from the effort of bringing up three children without any help from her husband Michael, who preferred to spend all his spare time down the pub with his mates. She had thought he was the answer to her prayers when they first met eight years before. She already had one daughter, Lucy, a mistake by a very good-looking young lad who had swept her off her feet and then unceremoniously dumped her as soon as she announced her pregnancy.

When she and Michael met and he had taken to step-fatherhood like a duck to water, Potty had thought she had it made. Back then, Michael was quite a catch. Lucy was calling him Daddy from the off. It was only once his own two had come along that he started staying away from home for increasingly long periods. There were rumours about his affairs with other women, and his drunken behaviour was obvious for all to see, but rather than confront him, Potty just let things slide. She took refuge in her TV and her radio. Her house was a mess. She never bothered using a scrap of make-up or tidying her unruly hair. Frayed flared jeans, flip-flops and cotton vests were her uniform.

After Lizzie had opened the door to her knock Potty barged into the kitchen laden with bags of shopping, which she let drop by the sink. Lizzie looked sharply from the shopping to Potty but said nothing.

'It stinks out there,' was Potty's opening line.

'Out where?' asked Sue.

'On the streets. It's this bloody heat . . . everything is going off and the bin men didn't turn up yesterday. We're all gonna get diseases if we're not careful.' The other women murmured their agreement. Even on the tenth floor, a faint sweet sickly smell filtered in on the breeze. The odour of rotting rubbish and decay hung over the East End like a pestilent fog. Flies and wasps buzzed angrily around melted ice lollies and piles of dog shit. Old chip papers stayed where they were, dropped in the gutter, and rats were feasting on stale doner kebabs, thrown away by drunks on their way home too late for their supper.

'Cup of tea, love?' asked Lizzie.

'Yes, please, three sugars.' Potty plonked herself down on the fourth chair around the table. Her face was red from the effort it had taken to carry her shopping, and her freckles stood out even more when her face was flushed. 'Kids break up next week and I'm bloody terrified! Least you know they're safe when they're in school. Not too worried about my Lucy, though. Do you know, she bloody nearly threw me across the settee with one of her judo moves, the little cow!'

'Or if you don't let them out of your sight.' Sue gave the new arrival a meaningful glance. She had known Potty since their schooldays and harboured a deep affection for her – who couldn't love Potty? She had a heart of gold – but she considered her a slouch, lying on the sofa all afternoon watching television while her kids ran wild around the estate. Most of Potty's conversation was about TV. She loved *The Generation Game* and dreamed of being Anthea Redfern.

'How's your Grace bearing up, Nanny?' asked Potty. Most people called Iris Parks 'Nanny', because she seemed to have been old for ever.

'Bloody awful. She's aged ten years overnight. Little Adam's in agony . . . can't sit, can't walk, just lies there with Grace on the settee. Every time the poor little fucker pisses, he has an audience. John's doing his nut and is ready to murder.' They shook their heads in disgust, saying 'Terrible'. The four women eyed each other knowingly then, none wanting to be the first to say it. Finally, Sue spoke.

'Terry said that him, John and Paul could pay young Steven a little visit tonight.'

'Not round his house they're not, I'm not upsetting Eileen,' put in Lizzie.

Sue eyed her again. 'What is it with you and Eileen? She gave birth to the sick twat and is protecting him, can't you see her game?'

The room fell silent. Everyone knew Lizzie would have to retaliate. She slowly brought her gaze up to meet Sue's stare.

'You listen to me, Sue Williams,' said Lizzie in a very authoritative tone. 'I was friends with Eileen while you were still in nappies, so I'm going to call her up and take her down the Bingo tonight. She's a decent, loving woman, left on her own to deal with a nutty kid, and it's not her fault. Who are you to judge her? Look at TJ, he's a lovely kid but we all know he's a slice short of a loaf. Now back off and leave Eileen to me. We go back a long way, she deserves some respect.'

Nanny Parks saw the sense in this and broke in to keep the situation calm.

'I agree. And it'll keep her out of the house for a few hours,' she pointed out. 'Lizzie can just say she hasn't seen her around for a while and wondered if she fancied a game.'

'But what if she doesn't?' asked Potty. 'And what if the police find out?'

'They won't,' said Lizzie emphatically.

'Yeah, but how can we be sure?' Potty was feeling scared now.

'Because none of us are going to breathe a word, are we?' Nanny Parks fired a warning look at Potty and pulled her polyester cardigan tighter around her chest despite the heat, moving closer to Lizzie as if to emphasise their bond.

'Do you seriously want to wait for Old Bill to sort this out?' asked Sue, staring at Potty. 'Aren't you worried about your own fucking kids? Mind you, you hardly worry about yourself nowadays, girl. You're always a mess, that TV of yours is always blaring, and you're lost in bloody *Crossroads* half the time. Michael's a drunk and a liability, good for only one thing . . . to be put down. You are a stupid woman, you really are!'

'Enough, Sue, that's a bit rough. Potty meant no harm, she was just giving her opinion, that's all,' said Nanny, seeing that Potty's eyes had filled with tears. She knew the truth about her own life, but it hurt her

57

that Sue had reacted so aggressively. They had been friends for a long time and now Potty felt betrayed.

'I'm sorry, Potts. I'm just a bit fraught and, if I'm honest, scared.' Sue placed a reassuring arm round Potty's shoulders. 'The point I'm trying to make is, don't we have the right to feel safe in our own neighbourhood?' She was working up a good head of steam now. 'Let's get the job done and sorted. Are we all in agreement? Steven gets his comeuppance . . . tonight!'

Potty just stared down at the cup and saucer on her lap. It had always been that way, ever since school – you didn't argue with Sue. Lizzie felt a stab of sympathy for Potty. She was a good girl who wanted to help really, it was just that she'd lost her bottle, being married to that useless sod Michael. He'd worn her down and now the old spark was gone.

She stood up and went to the lounge where she opened the sideboard drawer and removed what looked like a magazine. To break the tension, she raised her voice and asked, 'Anybody seen the new Green Shield stamps catalogue yet? I picked one up the other day. Reckon I've nearly got enough stamps for an electric kettle.'

The mood in the Birdcage had reverted to its usual buoyancy after Chantal's wake. Hot Chocolate's 'You Sexy Thing' blared out from the jukebox. It was crib night again – there were two a week – and male pensioners made their weekly trip out to the pub to nurse halves of mild and bitter while the Birdcage darts team were warming up for their match against the Royal Oak. It was a league fixture and men aimed for double twenties with grim determination, pausing only to take long draughts from their pint pots and an extra drag on their fags.

Life carried on, Paul Foster reflected ruefully as he sat at a corner table by the door which had been left open to let in some air. The funeral had been a difficult test, but he had got through it. Everyone was now settling back into normality and he too had to face up to life and what had happened to Chantal, if he could only get her tortured image out of his head. He was part of a subdued group which included Terry Williams and John Ballantyne.

John could stand being at home no longer. Grace was so silent; sad tunes rang out from the radio, and the whole atmosphere was dense and unpleasant. He felt as if she wanted him to do something, to put things right in some way, but he didn't know how and felt absolutely useless. The pub was a welcome release. They were waiting for the fourth member of their band, Michael Potts, to arrive.

It was another close night, the kind where you'd have to sleep on top of your sheets and blankets, dressed only in your underwear with the windows open, and still you wouldn't be able to get comfortable.

Paul was still twitchy after the funeral, not helped by the fact that Michelle had spent all of today with Darren in their flat, going through old photographs, looking for snaps of Chantal and reminiscing about their time together when the girls were young. He kept telling himself he was being paranoid but was still tormented by his old fear that she would go back to Darren. Michelle assured Paul that she loved him, but grief could do funny things to people. Maybe by sorting out Steven Archer he would be able to prove that he was her hero, the one she should look to for comfort and protection. Maybe this was all about him and the fact that he hadn't been there to protect Chantal.

'What's the time?' Terry Williams broke their uneasy silence.

'Half-seven.' John Ballantyne clicked his knuckles. Grace was always telling him he'd get arthritis if he didn't pack it in.

'What time are we going over there?' asked Terry.

''Bout half-eight, I reckon. Give Eileen time to clear off to Bingo. It's all been arranged.' Paul sounded a lot more certain than he felt. He had his doubts about what they were planning to do tonight, but John looked quietly determined and Terry was straining at the leash. The time was fast approaching for them to act.

He stood up and offered to get another round. As he moved over to the bar, Michael Potts made his unsteady entrance. He was half-cut and Paul decided then and there that he would not be joining them later. Potts was a liability; not only would he be unpredictable, he probably wouldn't be able to resist mouthing off later.

Michael Potts's shirt was rolled up to the elbows and large patches of sweat were visible beneath the arms. His flared jeans were stained all down the front and his shoulder-length hair hung in greasy clumps. He gazed around unsteadily until his eyes fixed on Paul at the bar and he weaved his way through the crowd, listing and lurching, banging into people and making them spill their drinks. 'Pauley! All right, my son, you getting them in then?' he said loudly as he reached the bar.

Michael had arrived home earlier to a tearful wife. As she sat with the kids, watching *Vision On*, an argument broke out. Potty was complaining about Sue and what had happened at the coffee morning. As usual Michael offered no support. He was intimidated by Sue and Terry Williams, and besides, they were right. Steven had to be dealt with. Lucy, Potty's twelve-year-old daughter, unable to listen to their squabbles any longer, made herself scarce and went to get ready for her judo lesson, leaving Mum and Dad to thrash it all out yet again. After half an hour, Michael couldn't stand the whingeing and left early to have a drink at the Royal Oak before meeting the other lads later at the Birdcage. One drink had

61

turned into another, and now he was well and truly liquidised.

'Yeah, sure, let me get you a large one.' Paul had decided that the easiest way to leave Potts behind would be to keep piling the drinks in. 'We're over there, mate, you go and sit down and I'll bring this lot over.' He exchanged knowing glances with the barmaid. It wasn't unusual for Michael Potts to be in this state. When Paul got back to their corner table with the drinks, John and Terry looked at him and raised their eyebrows. Michael Potts swigged down his drink in one and slurred, 'I gotta have a slash, back in two secs.'

'I don't think he's gonna be much help in that state,' said Terry.

'No shit, Sherlock.' Paul took a sip from his pint and wished he'd ordered a whisky chaser.

'I don't think he's gonna make it somehow, Tel.'

John took a cigarette from his pack and fished in his pocket for the silver Ronson lighter that Grace had got him last Christmas, engraved with his initials. He thought back to that holiday as he turned the lighter over and over in his hand. It had been such a happy time. All the family had come to them as they had the biggest house, and Grace had cooked a fantastic Christmas dinner. Her taste for the traditional was indulged to the full. Cards dangled everywhere; the real tree had a fantastic smell and was decked with expensive little glass ornaments. Candles were lit in the centre of the table, and everything co-ordinated in red and green, from serviettes to crackers. Grace had meticulously wrapped all the presents that she loved to give.

Everyone had been in a party spirit. The real coal fire gave off a glow, and they were all peacefully pissed and content after a giant Christmas dinner and the Queen's Speech. John remembered how he had sat there, brandy glass in one hand and cigar in the other, watching his family force one more Quality Street down themselves, and the way a few cashew nuts had spilled over on the coffee table. He thought of all the silly things he'd noticed. Adam's first fire engine toy; the look on his face as he played happily on Nanny's lap. Everyone so content. John wondered briefly if those days had gone for ever, if they could ever get that feeling back. He suspected Grace would never be the same again.

Sighing heavily, he snapped himself back to the present, putting his lighter back in his pocket. Conversation moved awkwardly around the topics of work and cars for ten minutes until Terry wondered aloud where Potts had got to – his empty glass still stood on the table. He didn't have to wonder for much longer.

A man came out of the gents' and made his way over to their table: 'Is he with you, that long-haired, dirty sod?' It could only be Potts he meant and they nodded yes. 'Well, you'd better sort him out. He's passed out in a pile of sick in there. Bloody disgusting! Shouldn't drink if he can't handle it.'

The man, a regular called George, a big bloke in his early fifties who worked as the school caretaker, was well known for moaning. He shuffled off, tutting to himself, and Paul decided this would be the moment to get out of the pub.

'Come on. Let's shoot off before he comes round.'

They drained their pints quickly and headed out of the pub. Once on the pavement they looked at each other, waiting for someone to make the next move. Finally Paul said, 'Come on, we'll wait near the garages until we see Eileen come out.'

They didn't have to wait long. The first fat raindrops of summer were beginning to fall when Lizzie Foster, accompanied by another woman, unwrapping a rain hat and placing it over her carefully shampooed and set hair, emerged from the staircase at the bottom of the block of flats. The two women paused to light cigarettes and then, placing their large handbags over their forearms, turned left on to Ravenscroft Street, chatting animatedly as they headed for Hackney Road.

'This is going to be a bit rough on old Eileen,' said Paul, thinking aloud.

'And it isn't rough on my Grace or your Michelle?' John's voice held a hint of steel. He was ready now, all the suppressed emotion rising rapidly to the surface.

'Yeah, come on, Paul, don't bottle out now.'

Emboldened by John, Terry had to put in his tuppence worth.

'Who said anything about bottling out?' Paul suppressed an urge to deck Terry Williams, the stupid twat, who was always ruled by his wife. 'Come on then, let's go.'

The three men found the lifts at Dunbar House out of order and walked the six flights up to Eileen's flat. They knocked and waited, then knocked again.

'He's not in,' said Terry. It seemed as if he was almost relieved Steven was out.

'Yes, he is,' John insisted.

'How do you know?' asked Terry, now starting to feel cramps in his stomach.

'Because I can hear the telly, and anyway, I don't expect Eileen lets him out in the evening, especially now everyone knows he's a fucking pervert.' John pointed through the glass panel in the front door. 'He's coming.' Steven's face appeared in the frosted glass as he tried to work out who was knocking.

'Open the door, mate.' Paul's voice sounded friendly, light. Steven hesitated for a few moments then slipped back the chain and opened the door. His expression was a study in confusion. These were faces that were familiar to him, but not so familiar that they would usually call at his house. He shuffled uncomfortably from one foot to the other then gingerly opened the door.

Terry asked, 'Mind if we come in and have a little

chat, son?'

Steven looked confused. 'My mum says not to let strange people in when she's out. I'm watching *The Two Ronnies*. I love the singing. I can make tea. We can be friends and watch the television and drink tea.'

'*And it's goodbye from me and goodbye from him,*' a voice announced from the television as Steven was pinned down on the floor.

Slow at first, the rain fell steadily thicker and faster, till huge drops pelted down on top of Lucy Potts's head as she made her way into Audrey Street from the school where she did judo class on a Friday evening. It had been a great night, and the music session afterwards had given her the chance to listen to some of her favourite pop songs. She had been dancing little steps with the other girls and loved 'December '63'. '*Oh, what a night*' kept ringing in her head.

Lucy had the same unruly head of wavy hair as her mum, but that was where the similarities ended. Lucy was determined to get on in life. A miserable marriage to a waster and no money to call her own weren't for her. She worked hard at school, and afterwards went to any and every club going – ballet, tap, judo, swimming – anything that got her out of that squalid flat so she didn't have to look at her mother, stretched out on the sofa like a zombie, watching the television. How she hated that Ken Dodd and his Diddymen! Mum would count every long hour until Michael came home, and for what? Another blazing row.

As the rain fell harder Lucy began to quicken her pace but soon her clothes and bag with all her kit were soaked and felt heavy next to her skin. She was still quite sweaty from class and now felt damp down to her bones. She wished she had showered, but conscious of her developing body had decided against it. Abruptly she did an about-turn, deciding to take the short-cut through the park behind City Farm. Her mum always told her she was never to go through the park at night, but it was still light and it would shorten her journey considerably. As she sang the catchy song out loud, she made her decision.

Sod it! she thought. She just had to get through the wooded area and on to Edith Street which bisected Haggerston Park and City Farm. Usually there would be gangs of boys on bikes hanging around, but the rain had driven them into the corridors and landings of the local flats and Lucy was grateful for that as she was busting for a pee.

The rain was now falling in sheets as thunder rumbled somewhere in the distance. Lucy ducked under a beech tree, hoping for some shelter and somewhere to go to the loo. She looked about her and, unable to see anyone, pulled down her tracksuit bottoms and pants and squatted, leaning against the trunk of the tree. The relief made her forget momentarily how uncomfortably wet she was. With rain dripping on her head from the tree branches above, she lost her footing and pee splattered on her plimsolls.

Fuck! she thought as she straightened up. Then the sound of a branch snapping behind her made her start, and with her trackie bottoms just at knee-height she couldn't turn in time to see what had caused the noise. Before she knew what had happened, she had been pushed over and pinned to the ground on her stomach. Momentarily winded, she struggled for breath. The next moment she felt a hot, stale mouth and prickly beard against the side of her head and started struggling to get away. His breath was so disgusting she felt nausea welling up in her stomach.

A hand roughly probed around her anus, squeezing and pinching, and eventually trying to force its fingers into her, but her tracksuit bottoms were too tight at the knees and prevented him from parting her legs. He took one hand away momentarily to unzip his trousers and try to force her legs apart. With its grip on her arm released, Lucy was able to jerk back her elbow with all her might. It landed a blow which hit home in just the right place. There was a loud groan and he rolled off her. Lucy seized her chance to clamber to her feet, pull up her trackie bottoms and run away as fast as she could, not looking back or even bothering to stoop and pick up her kit bag.

The earth beneath her feet was becoming slippery with the burst of unexpected rain. Despite the short downfall, the air remained sticky and hot, but she ran and she ran through the rain, crying, 'Oh, God, please help me! I want my mum,' until the traffic on Hackney Road came into view.

When she finally turned to look back there was nobody behind her but she kept running anyway, squeezing the cheeks of her bottom together, until she hit the main road and flagged down the first car she saw. Wet, bedraggled and red-faced, a sobbing Lucy slumped against the driver's door, begging for help.

The old couple who had stopped for her were from Bangladesh and spoke little English, but they understood the word 'police' and recognised the state that Lucy was in. They let her into the car and took her straight to the police station on Bethnal Green Road.

Unseen by anyone at that time was the drumstick lolly, tangled into Lucy's dishevelled hair at the back of her head.

Chapter Five

A throng of people exited the Bingo hall from all four sides. The usual moaning and groaning of 'God, that was close' or 'If only number twenty-three had come out' could be heard above the drone of voices as everyone spilled out on to Hackney Road before dispersing down the smaller side streets and alleyways.

'Do you fancy a quick cuppa, Lizzie?' Eileen Archer was in a buoyant mood after winning two lines. Not the full house she was hoping for, nor the pyramid game, but she was still a fiver better off than when she'd started, which would come in handy now that Steven was home for the holidays. She had forgotten how much teenage boys ate and it was costing her a small fortune. How Steven loved his food, and what a sweet tooth he had! Ali at the local news-agent's always made sure he kept aside a tenpence mixed bag for the boy every day. It was so kind of him. Steven loved the variety bag of flying saucers, blackjacks, white mice and a drumstick lolly. Ali had a bit of a soft spot for Steven, and no matter what the other locals might say, Ali wasn't just another Paki on the take, he was a genuinely nice fella.

The streets were still wet from the downpour earlier that evening but the rain had stopped, the air felt fresher, and the first strong breeze for weeks wrapped Eileen's raincoat closer round her as she walked. The rain had also dampened the rotting rubbish, washing away some of its stale smell. She felt her spirits lift in the fresh clean air.

'I don't think I will, Eileen. This damp has got into my bones, and you know what a martyr I am to bloody rheumatism. My ankles are swelling already.' Lizzie hoped her friend couldn't hear the nervous tremor in her voice. She had been unable to concentrate at Bingo, kept looking at her watch all evening and feeling sick to her stomach. She had lied to and deceived Eileen, and knew that the guilt she felt for that would stay with her a long time.

'All right then, love, I'll get back and see what that boy of mine is up to. Probably emptied the biscuit tin and drunk all the Cokes, if I know my Steven.' Eileen squeezed Lizzie's hand and smiled at her. 'Thanks for dragging me out tonight, Lizzie. I always feel guilty, going out when Steven's back for the holidays, but it has done me the world of good. You're a good friend. You've always been there for me and my boy, even when others turned their backs. Thanks, mate.'

'No trouble, Eileen. Any time you fancy another trip out, just give me a shout. I'm only stuck in that flat by myself, staring at the four walls and cleaning most of the time, so it's good for me to get out too.'

Lizzie turned away before Eileen could see the tears begin to well in her eyes. A huge lump had formed in her throat and her head began to throb. Christ, what had they done? Poor Eileen didn't deserve this.

It's for the best, she told herself firmly then. Someone had to put an end to it. But her heart was thumping in her chest nonetheless as she took leave of her friend and headed back to her flat. Eileen's parting words still rang in her head and by now Lizzie was seriously questioning what she and the others had done. God, she hoped they were right!

Eileen pressed the button for the lift, but of course it was out of order again so she started the long climb up six flights of stairs to her flat. She stopped every now and then to catch her breath, and in doing so took in great lungfuls of the stench of rotting rubbish from the large cylinder bins at the bottom of the rubbish chutes situated on each balcony. She inwardly cursed the council for never doing anything to tidy this place up. The stairwells were daubed with graffiti and smelled of stale piss and puke. Not for the first time she promised herself that she would definitely put in for a transfer. She was tired of cleaning her part of the staircase, tired of pouring tin after tin of Jeyes Fluid down the landing, and tired of trying in vain to get others to do their bit.

She reached her flat breathless but relieved to have

made it, and found all the lights blazing and the sound of the telly and a newsreader's familiar voice audible through the front door. She'd told Steven about staying up late and he'd promised her he'd be in bed by ten. She fished around in her large handbag, rummaging amongst her purse, peppermints, rain hat, fags and lighter, before finally coming up with the key, but as she went to push it in the lock the door swung open, thudding against the hall wall. Intuition or mother's instinct, call it what you like, lifted the hair on the back of her neck and she knew immediately that something wasn't right.

'My boy, my baby,' she murmured to herself, and then raised her voice: 'Steven?' When there was no reply, she called his name again and opened his bedroom door but he wasn't in there. His jigsaw puzzle lay untouched on the thin piece of cardboard he used as a makeshift table, a bottle of Coke stood half-empty on his bedside cabinet; his bed had not been slept in.

Eileen walked into the front room and staggered slightly at the sight that met her eyes. She had to fight down a wave of nausea. She'd never seen so much blood in her life, it was everywhere: all over the three-piece suite, the carpet, even up the walls. And lying in a crumpled heap on the floor was her little boy, her last-born, her baby. His face was unrecognisable, like a bloodied cabbage, his nose halfway across his face and swollen mouth gaping open to reveal his missing front teeth. Puke oozed out of his mouth and nose, congealed with blood and making a foul smell.

For several seconds Eileen stood rooted to the spot, too shocked to do anything. Then she knelt down next to her boy. She saw that the blood had already dried on his *Muppet Show* T-shirt and felt too afraid to touch him. She wanted to scoop him into her arms, to rock him, to beg God to help him, but found that she couldn't.

'Steven,' she whispered, 'say something, love. Talk to me.' A low groan came from somewhere inside him and she thanked God that her prayer had been answered and her baby was still alive. She put her arms around him gently and said, 'Can you sit up, love?' but he just groaned again. An ambulance! She had to get an ambulance, but had no phone to call one. 'Don't go anywhere, love. Mummy's gonna call for an ambulance,' she told him. 'Stay still, don't move, sweetie. I'm here now and I'm gonna help you.'

As if he *could* move! You've let him down, Eileen, was all she could hear in her head. Her own voice was torturing her now, blaming her for leaving her innocent child alone and vulnerable. Outside her flat, she ran along the landing, banging on doors and screaming for help. Neighbours came out in their dressing gowns and lights went on in flats all over the sixth floor as people woke up to her anguished cries.

'Please help me! Please help me! My baby . . . my baby.'

Eventually her voice trailed away into a whimper as she fell exhausted against the balcony. Big Geoff from two doors down took charge and called an ambulance, then he accompanied the stricken Lizzie back to her flat where the sight of Steven made him splutter, 'Jesus fucking Christ!'

Meanwhile, down at Bethnal Green Police Station, DCI Woodhouse had been summoned in from his night off to interview the latest victim. He had been putting in fifteen-hour days since Chantal's murder and so far had come up with very little. He was still finding it hard to believe that nobody had made a sighting and for a while toyed with the idea that there was some kind of cover-up going on. But he was grasping at straws, he knew. Who would cover up crimes like these? Robberies, handling stolen goods, sure; that was how many people round here made their living. But *this*? For the first time in ten long frustrating days he had an evening off at home and had planned to spend it watching a programme about Agatha Christie, his favourite author, who had recently died. He'd also wanted a hot meal and a good night's sleep, but it wasn't to be. As he wearily entered the station the sergeant on desk duty looked up and gave him a sympathetic nod. 'She's in the interview room with a WPC and the mother. The kid's all right, considering, but the mother's in a right old state. Good luck.'

'Has the doctor been in yet?'

'No, he's delayed over at Dalston. Usual Friday night carnage.'

Woodhouse drummed his fingers thoughtfully on the desk for a few seconds before drawing himself up and sighing, 'Right then, here we go.' He lit another cigarette, dragged on it long and hard, then walked slowly down the corridor to the interview room.

They knew from forensic analysis that the same person was responsible for the murder of Chantal Robinson and the attack on Adam Ballantyne. Semen analysis had proved that. Although no rape had actually taken place on Lucy Potts, that drumstick lolly was surely no coincidence. It had to be connected.

Several of Woodhouse's men were already at the park but didn't expect to come up with anything useful until morning. It was pitch black now. Apart from preserving the crime scene there was not much they could do. Woodhouse was tired and found himself wishing that he had Watson with him now, to say the right things. Give him a hardened criminal any day, he hated the softly, softly approach.

He paused outside the interview room then doubled back to the coffee machine, which dispensed something wet and warm that would hopefully liven him up a bit. The coffee was both bitter and weak and he wished he were at the station in Dalston where there was always somebody human around to make a proper cup of tea or coffee, not this machine rubbish.

Through the glass in the door of the interview room he could see the WPC comforting not the child but the mother, who seemed to be completely hysterical. She kept raking back her unruly hair then burying her face in her hands and rocking backward and forward. God, she was gonna be hard work! The girl was slightly out of his line of vision but as he entered the room he saw a plump redhead, in her early teens perhaps, wearing a red and white towelling tracksuit. She looked surprisingly composed.

Woodhouse introduced himself and the mother managed to calm down for a moment by holding on to the desk as firmly as if she were on a white-knuckle rollercoaster ride, until he said, 'Don't worry, Mrs Potts, we will get the man responsible for this,' whereupon she started up a fresh round of howling and crying.

At Woodhouse's nod, the WPC took Potty out of the room, ostensibly to get her a cup of tea. The DCI was well aware that he would get very little out of the girl while her mother was in the room hearing every word she said.

He couldn't begin his official questioning until there was a female police officer present, but there was nothing to prevent him from establishing a rapport with the girl.

'How are you feeling, Lucy?' DCI Woodhouse tried to keep his voice soft and low.

'All right, I s'pose.' She looked at her hands, clutched together in her lap, then mumbled, 'A bit, you know, sore . . . but all right. Your police lady's been really nice.'

Woodhouse nodded and managed an encouraging smile. This girl was strong, a real trouper, quite possibly the sort to give them some vital clues. He had an instinct for a good witness, and got a strong vibe from this kid straight away.

'I know this is difficult, Lucy, but I want you to tell me everything – from beginning to end. We'll just have to wait a moment until our WPC is back in the room. She's gone to get your mum a cup of tea. Your mum's taken all this pretty badly. Highly strung, is she?'

'Mum's pissed,' said Lucy, then reddened slightly.

'Well, she's bound to be upset, considering.'

'No, she's always like this lately. She's not getting on with me dad so well and they 'ad a row so she was pissed before I went off to judo tonight. Got herself in a right pickle about something to do with Dad and his mates.'

Lucy was still matter-of-fact and the DCI felt himself warming to this gutsy kid. 'I see. And how old are you, Lucy?'

'Twelve and three-quarters. I'm the youngest blue belt in East London,' she answered rather smugly.

Woodhouse smiled. 'Sounds like it came in handy tonight.' Lucy nodded and frowned at this reminder of her ordeal, and the way she'd got him with that judo move. She used to hope that someday she would be able to use her skills, but tonight's events had shown her how foolish that had been.

At the same moment the WPC came back into the room. She explained that she'd got Lucy's mum a cup of tea. She was now in the waiting room drinking it and would stay there until her husband showed up. Woodhouse winked lightly at her to indicate good work.

'OK then, love, are you ready for this?' the policewoman asked. Lucy nodded and the WPC took her hand.

'You're a very brave girl, Lucy,' said Woodhouse, and meant it.

The WPC squeezed her hand and nodded to her to tell the full story. Lucy gave an excellent account of her movements between leaving her judo club and reaching the Hackney Road where she'd flagged down a passing car. Her answers were clear and descriptive. She faltered only when Woodhouse asked her to describe exactly where her assailant had touched her. Her face went bright red and she looked like she wanted the ground to swallow her up. The

WPC told her gently then that she was doing really well, there wasn't much longer to go.

Lucy stared blankly at the wall in front of her. With eyes bulging and nose running, she started to speak with tears in her eyes.

'He had his hands all over me, pinning me down. I can't remember how he got me to the ground. I don't know if he knocked me down or pulled me down. I couldn't breathe, his arm was round my neck, and I tried to scream but just a silly sound came out. I didn't have time to pull my trackie bottoms up, really I never. My knickers were tangled up and I couldn't move.

'His fingers were hard and rough and he slapped me across my bum. Then he stopped groping me for a moment and started breathing heavily against the side of my face. He said, "You pretty little red-haired cunt," and then he tried to push his fingers up my bum hole but I squeezed my cheeks together. My bottom felt all cold and drops of rain were falling down on it from the trees.

'My eyes were closed the whole time and I had my teeth gritted. I felt all wet down below, he must have had spit or something on his fingers because they felt slimy and cold, and of course I hadn't had time to wipe the piss away. I kept hoping he would stop, but I knew he wouldn't. His fingers were pushing harder and harder. He sort of had a grip with one finger pushing into my bum hole and the other trying to push up my fanny hole. I didn't know I was gonna hit him back, it just sort of happened.'

A gasping sob interrupted her then and she started to shake. Tears rolled down her face. 'I want to go home now! Please . . . let me go home.'

The WPC wrapped both arms around Lucy. 'It's OK, sweetheart. You've been really wonderful and you are a very brave girl.' She and Woodhouse both knew just how lucky Lucy had been too, despite what that pervert had done to her.

The DCI knew he ought to call a halt to this. The kid was gutsy, but now the shock had hit her. He decided to press her just a little bit more. She hadn't seen his face, but she had heard the man's voice. Was there anything else? Lucy shook her head, started to say something and then stopped.

'Go on. You were going to say something, Lucy,' urged Woodhouse.

'Well, it sounds silly, but two things keep coming into my head. I could hear scissors snipping . . . and then there was the smell. He had this funny smell about him. Not just the bad breath and fags smell, but this weird smell . . . like cleaning fluid.'

Cleaning fluid? Scissors? Of course, the other kids were missing their eyelashes. The fucking pervert hadn't got the chance to cut off Lucy's.

Woodhouse didn't voice his thoughts but sat with his pen raised above his notepad and waited for the girl to finish.

'Yeah, like that stuff they use on the floors of offices and in the school gym. It stinks for hours.'

The next morning PC Watson was very busy indeed. Not only was he sent out to make door-to-door enquiries about the attempted rape of Lucy Potts, but there was the additional matter of the attack on Steven Archer. Could the two be linked? He doubted it, there was no sexual assault on Steven, but the attacks had happened within half an hour of each other and less than half a mile apart. Watson privately felt sure that Steven was not victim number four. No sexual assault, no nakedness, no lolly. His assault was different. Somebody at the flats must have seen or heard something, it had been a violent and sustained attack, but nobody was saying. Whoever had battered Steven Archer was probably known to the victim as there had been no sign of a forced entry at the flat. He was currently unable to give the police any description as he was still lying unconscious in Homerton Hospital, his desperate mother by his side. It was just a matter of time, though. Steven would wake up soon and then Watson would take his statement.

The boy had no fewer than thirty-five stitches to his face, four broken ribs, a shattered kneecap and three missing teeth.

All local police leave was cancelled. They had their hands full. A few officers had been sent to the hospital in case of any further attack on Steven. The rest were conducting a thorough search of the park, which, along with the nearby City Farm, had been cordoned off with yellow-and-black tape.

By the time Watson started his enquiries the bush telegraph had already been buzzing and there were few people locally who didn't already know about one or other of the attacks, if not both. Shopkeepers passed on every titbit that came their way and groups of women hung around street corners, gossiping, pointing fingers, then holding their children's hands tightly as the sickening realisation dawned that they had held the wrong man accountable when they had pointed the finger at Steven Archer.

At the bookmaker's the men were concentrating on the Saturday races as news filtered through about the attacks on Steven and Lucy. Smoke shrouded the ceiling of the bookie's cramped premises. Commentaries and forecasts blared out from the TVs clamped high on the walls. Harry the Horse perched on his stool behind the newly fitted shatter-proof glass counter, looking out over his punters. All the usual suspects were there, bright and early and ready to blow their week's wages on some useless nag. Bloody fools! Big Geoff, who had helped Steven the previous night and had seen the damage inflicted on him at first hand, wasn't afraid to voice his criticism.

'The kid's a retard. It's obvious he couldn't have done it.'

There was a mumble of general agreement. Some of those who had been all too willing to point the finger in Steven's direction were now starting to backtrack along the lines of, 'I never thought it was him in the first place.' Others more honest in their shame just stared at the floor, puffed hard at their roll-up fags, and then turned their attention to the racing papers, looking for a horse that might win, licking their stunted pencils and marking off the nags that deserved a place or win bet.

Most of the guys present were reluctant to come right out and say who they thought had beaten Steven Archer, even though the front runners were fairly obvious. In a neighbourhood as tight as this everybody was staying schtum.

George, the local misery, broke the silence. 'They were only doing what they thought was right. You can't really blame them, can you?' The majority muttered agreement then continued with their Saturday morning ritual. Only Harry looked heavenwards and asked forgiveness for those who had committed such a horrible crime.

As far as Grace Ballantyne was concerned, the world had suddenly gone mad. She had been half-asleep when her husband had come home the night before, and had woken to the sound of the bath running.

John never took baths, only showers in the morning. She threw back the covers and went to the bathroom to find a pile of red-streaked clothing on the floor and her husband sitting in the bath, trying to scrub dried blood off his hands using her nail brush. Her stomach churned. She didn't have to ask. She knew.

The only words she said to him were: 'How could you?' All sorts of thoughts filled Grace's head then. She had been a victim herself once, had wanted to maim or even kill her attacker but fear and help-lessness had stopped her. Now she felt only rage. John and his ignorant mates had brutally beaten an innocent, harmless soul. Her husband had tried to justify himself but Grace slammed the bathroom door behind her, and when he came to bed pretended she was asleep.

It was a long tense night. She lay awake, rigid with anger at him. John should have known better. Should have known that she hated brutality in any form after what she had suffered at the hands of her Uncle Gary for all those years. She had drawn strength from her marriage to a kind man and the birth of her children, which had helped her through the long dark nights of reliving those assaults, suffering the recurring night-mares. And for what? So that now she could learn that John was no different after all? How would she ever be able to trust him again?

She didn't want to know who'd been with him, she already had a good idea anyway. She didn't want to hear the ins and outs, she could guess. What had happened to Adam and Chantal was awful, but attacking a boy, especially one as soft as Steven Archer, didn't make things right. She drifted off to sleep somewhere around six o'clock and was woken at seven-thirty by the ringing of the phone; it was her mother with news of the attack on Lucy.

Grace listened in silence, feeling horribly sick. The room began to whirl and sweat broke out over her top lip as she experienced a vivid flashback. *'Rub-a-dub-dub,'* said Uncle Gary as he pushed her clitoris from side to side. *'Groan, Gracie baby, groan!'* 'Let Your Love Flow' by the Bellamy Brothers, was playing on the radio in the kitchen. Grace dismissed the leering, laughing face of Uncle Gary from her mind, and said goodbye to her mother. She switched the radio off angrily. Within twenty minutes she was dressed, had fed and changed the baby and put Adam in front of the telly with a bowl of Weetabix.

John came down the stairs to find her heading for the door. 'Where are you going?' he asked, scratching his head and yawning.

Grace took a moment to stare at his right hand, the knuckles swollen and grazed, before saying simply, 'Out! Adam needs a nappy, they're in the baby bag by the sofa.'

'Where are you off to this early?' he asked between more yawns.

'Never you mind,' she said, kissing the children.

She grabbed her house keys as well as the keys to John's Jag and headed out the door.

She had her thoughts and plans in place. She needed to feel angry; needed to let out some emotion. She had held it in for too long! First stop was Potty's. Grace had to knock twice before Potty answered it, wearing a tatty cotton dressing gown and followed by her six-year-old twins, Sara and Jessica, both crying and pulling at the back of her robe to reveal a pair of pale podgy legs that were mottled like corned beef. Her face was tear-stained and blotchy. In fact, Potty looked like death.

Grace hugged her nevertheless, and as she did so Potty began to cry. Grace ushered her inside the flat, picked the milk up off the doorstep and sat her down at the kitchen table while she rooted around in a sinkful of dirty dishes, looking for a couple of mugs to make them some nice hot sugary tea. The girls were still crying. It took Grace a moment to work out that they were hungry and wanted some breakfast. She rinsed a couple of bowls, filled them with Sugar Puffs, and while the twins argued over the little plastic toy that fell out of the box, Grace poured milk into both bowls and steered them into the front room. Lucy was there, sitting on the settee watching television.

'How are you, love?' said Grace after settling the younger ones, and ruffled the top of Lucy's red head. Grace liked Lucy. She was a determined youngster and, although far from a beauty yet, Lucy would have her time.

'I'm all right, thanks, Auntie Grace.' Grace wasn't Lucy's real auntie, of course, but all close female friends were called 'Auntie' – and besides, if Lucy had had her way, Grace would be her mum. She was so elegant and lovely, and kept her home so clean and tidy. She was kind and beautiful, too, altogether the type of woman Lucy longed to have in her life. Grace was Lucy's role model. One day, she would be exactly the kind of person Grace was. It inspired her to do well.

Now Grace sat down next to her and put an arm around her shoulders. 'Where's your dad?' she asked.

'Bed,' Lucy answered, disappointment in her voice. Michael just wasn't the same with her any more. These days he paid her little or no attention and Lucy was devastated by this turn in his affections. Once she'd been the apple of his eye. Now, that seemed a very long time ago. All Michael wanted these days was his next drink.

Grace wasn't surprised to hear it but the way Lucy's parents were behaving still made her angry. Lucy had been attacked and her wretched mother was in the kitchen wailing like it was she who had been knocked to the ground, pinned down and assaulted, while the girl's bloody step-father couldn't even be bothered to crawl out of his pit! Grace looked around her. This room was a disgrace. Dirty cups and overflowing ashtrays and beer cans were strewn across the coffee table; piles of children's clothing littered the room, waiting to be ironed. The curtains were still closed and the whole place smelled stale.

'Let's get some daylight and air in here.' Grace went briskly about the task, drew back the curtains and opened the windows as far as they could go.

'How's Adam?' asked Lucy.

Grace smiled and said, 'He's getting there, love. Still very quiet and in a lot of pain, but he's young and the doctors seem to think he'll make a full recovery. It's just going to take time.'

She felt humbled by Lucy's bravery and the fact that she should be concerned for Adam, having just escaped rape herself. Lucy turned her attention back to the TV; she'd had enough conversation. Grace had the tact not to push it and instead excused herself, saying that she was going to make a cup of tea.

'Watch the twins, Lucy.'

Back in the kitchen Potty was wiping her nose on a tatty tissue.

'I know it's hard but you've got to try and be strong, for Lucy. If she sees you falling apart . . . look, I know what that kid's going through.' Grace stopped herself then realising, she was saying too much. She only hoped Sandra wouldn't ask what she'd meant by that. Thank God, Potty was too distressed to pick up on the remark.

'It's not that, Grace, it's Steven. You might as well know the truth. You see . . . I knew they were going to do it. I could have stopped it but I didn't.'

Potty gave a tearful account of the meeting round at Lizzie Foster's and Grace nodded, unsurprised by what she heard. She'd known that her mother and Lizzie Foster were baying for blood, and in a way it was understandable given that their grandchildren had suffered, but what the hell did it have to do with Sue Williams? That fat cow! Meddling bloody busybody. Grace had realised Sue was jealous of her close-knit family and her money. Now she knew that Sue could be dangerous too.

'Fucking Sue Williams,' she spat.

'Please don't tell her I told you.' Potty was shaking with fear as she thought about the recriminations that would follow once the others heard she had betrayed them. Grace was sickened to see the hold that Sue had over her friend but said only, 'Course not. I won't say a word – providing you get yourself cleaned up and presentable. The police might come round and you don't want them to see the place looking like a shit hole. I'll help you.'

She stayed for another hour, washed the dishes, sorted out a bag of washing for the launderette, and got the twins dressed. She was feeling a little better herself by then. Somehow helping others was a great distraction from her own troubles. She worried momentarily that she should get back to Adam, but while she still had energy she wanted to complete her rounds and make another call.

With the arrival of their fourth child, TJ, the Williamses had been moved into a proper house with a garden on the estate, one of the few roads that hadn't been entirely given over to flats. When Grace pulled up in the navy blue Jag she received admiring glances from a gang of boys which included Wayne, the Williamses' eldest son. They were standing around outside Sue's small front garden, an immaculate patch of green bordered with busy Lizzies and nasturtiums. By the front door were two hanging baskets, dripping with bright pink fuchsias. TJ and Gillian's two boys played happily on the grass. So her sister was inside. How much did *she* have to do with Steven's beating? Grace wondered.

Sue clearly had a thing about gnomes. They were scattered about the garden, some with their heads knocked off after Terry had come home drunk.

Grace hesitated by the gate. 'Is your mum in, Wayne?' she asked.

'Yeah. Your mum's there too, and Lizzie.'

Makes sense, thought Grace. She scooped TJ up for a cuddle and then kissed her two nephews. 'Hope you're all being good,' she said.

'Course we are,' answered Jamie, Gillian's eldest.

'I'm playing with my bike today, Auntie Grace, but Benny's being stupid.'

Wayne interrupted him then.

'Can we sit in your car, please, Grace?' Wayne and his little gang of mates looked at her expectantly. She eyed them for a moment. 'Go on then, but don't touch anything or I'll 'ave yer guts for garters. Watch the others, Wayne.'

She knocked on the open door to the house. Terry Williams answered and seemed surprised to see her. Not looking her in the eye, he ushered her inside. 'Grace love, surprised to see you. How are you doing?'

She didn't answer but glared at him. Terry bowed sarcastically for her to pass him and she headed straight for the kitchen at the back of the house. She didn't know what she was going to say but she was bloody furious. The four women she found there looked up in surprise, as if they had been caught doing something they shouldn't. Grace just stared at them with a face like thunder.

'Cup of tea?' asked Sue, looking worried.

'Shut up you, ya meddling fat cow!' Grace spat at her, then turned to address her sister next. 'So you were in on this as well, were you? You always were a sheep, Gill. Can't think for yourself, that's your problem.'

Gillian reddened and the other two women, Nanny Parks and Lizzie Foster, glanced at each other uncertainly before Nanny Parks said, 'Don't speak to your sister like that, Grace, she was only trying to help. We all were.'

Gillian braced herself to interrupt. 'Shut up, Mum, I don't need you to fight my battles.' Then, emboldened, she turned back to her sister. 'What's up with you, Grace? I thought we were a team, all of us!'

'Team? Help? You pathetic bunch! That poor little sod is in hospital, battered to within an inch of his life. What's wrong with you fucking people? Call that *help*? And you of all people, Lizzie . . . Eileen's your friend. You know Steven. How could you do this?'

'That's enough, Grace. Sit down and get a grip on yourself.' Lizzie Foster fixed her with an icy glare, but Grace stood up to her.

'Whose stupid idea was this anyway? What made you think you had the right to play God?'

She stared at each of them in turn.

'Mum, what were you thinking of? I told you I didn't think Steven had it in him to hurt anybody, but you had to go and listen to the likes of her!' Grace pointed at Sue, whose mouth fell open.

'You've got it all wrong, Grace. We only did it to put a stop to his game . . . stop him hurting any more babies. Can't you see that? We were just trying to help.'

'And did it help Potty or Lucy? No, of course it didn't! Because you got it wrong. So now everyone is hurting, and meanwhile that fucking maniac is *still out there.* You're a gossip and a rabble-rouser, Sue, and it's caused untold misery and trouble to all of us. Don't you realise that when Steven wakes up, all our men will be charged with serious assault? And while the police are busy with them, that fucking sicko will be hanging round with time on his hands . . . time to strike again!'

At that point, Grace fell into a chair. 'It's all such a mess, and there's no way out. This whole fucking thing is falling in around us, don't you see?'

She began to sob then. All her pent-up emotion poured out. Sue was lost for words for once. Gillian and Lizzie looked at her in concern.

It was Nanny Parks who spoke up.

'Pull yourselves together, the lot of ya! We've made a mistake, OK, we admit it. But we are family. We just gotta get ourselves organised and get our stories straight. Nothing's gonna happen to the men, and nothing's gonna happen to us. Steven won't talk. Neither will Eileen. We'll see them straight, we owe them that. But let's not forget one thing. The Devil's at work round here, and our job is to find him. Things carry on as usual. We meet at Gillian's, tomorrow, eleven as usual.'

After that they sat in silence, pouring tea and lighting cigarettes. Grace's anger was spent. Her mother was right about one thing, they must stick together in the face of this threat. Despite the mistake they'd made, these people were her family and John was her husband and she must fight to keep them all safe. Though how she was to do that Grace had no idea. Adam was uppermost in her mind now and she wanted to go home to him. She scraped back her chair to get up.

Just then her nephew Benny came running into the kitchen.

'Juice please, Mummy. Can I have some juice?'

'Course you can, love,' said Gillian, glad of the distraction.

Sue nodded and started putting out beakers, taking a jug out of the fridge.

'Yeah, Jamie and the rest will be thirsty by now. Call them in, Ben. Call them all in.'

'No, not Jamie,' said Benny, shaking his head. 'Jamie not want any. Jamie gone.'

Chapter Six

The ground-floor maisonette could be reached in two ways. The first was through the front door facing the tower blocks on Barnet Street though he hardly ever used this, mainly because the road was always busy – in the warmer months, kids and groups of nosy-parker women hung around watching all the comings and goings – and it was nobody's business what time he came in or went out. He didn't like to draw attention to himself or his home.

The second entrance was the one he preferred. It was easy to cut down the alleyway housing the bins that ran down the side of his block of maisonettes. Rarely if ever used by anyone except the dustmen, it was dark, squalid and quiet. Just the way he liked it. It didn't bother him that rats infested the large bins, that rubbish spilled out over the ground, that the whole stinking place was rife with dirt and disease from the heap of crap that grew bigger every day. From the alleyway he could pop the latch on his gate unobserved and let himself in through the back door, using the key he kept under a nearby brick.

No matter what hours he kept, whether it was winter or summer, he always left his lights on and the front-room window slightly ajar, so that the sound of the radio playing could be heard should anyone come to call. You couldn't be too careful in an area like this. But he didn't get many visitors. He was recognised by many but known by few, and that was the way he liked it.

He had lived alone ever since his short-lived childless marriage had broken down over thirty years ago. What a fool he had been then! That stupid, skinny, frigid woman and her busybody old mother . . . what a pair! She wasn't the woman to give him what he needed; no woman could. This way he could have things just the way he liked, with nobody to argue or contradict or to tell him he wasn't right, like she had. Before he'd made her eat her words. Her and her old bag of a mother too.

But he wasn't a complete loner, he had Twinkle for company. He loved that cat; would feed her scraps from the fishmonger's instead of that tinned rubbish. He took less care over his own diet, happy mostly with Fray Bentos pies and tinned peas. On Friday nights he treated himself to fish and chips, always saving some of the choice white flakes for Twinkle. Costas, the big fat Greek at the local chippy, sometimes saved scraps and bits of old tail for the moggy, too. Besides, the chippie was a great place to mingle unnoticed; while putting salt and vinegar on his Friday night supper he could eye up the local kids, see who was a sort and who wasn't.

Standing in the shadows outside, watching the kids with their mums or dads, he could easily rub himself off. He never bothered about the wetness in his pants, that could be sorted later.

Every night when he returned from work he would place the cat on his lap and groom her. It was a kind of meditation for him, an escape which brought him a feeling of total satisfaction. All the time he soothed her with the words, 'You're a good girl, a good girl, Daddy's good girl.'

Twinkle was a house cat, he made sure of that. He didn't want her going outdoors where she could be stolen or run over. She was his baby, his purpose, and he took no risks with her. Instead he kept her litter tray in the kitchen, though he wasn't always scrupulous about cleaning it out regularly, but Twinkle didn't mind.

The entire maisonette smelled of cat shit, leftover food and stale piss, but it was always warm and even in summer he would have the heating on for a couple of hours, in the morning and evening, because he knew that cats hated the cold. Living alone meant that he could wash up when he felt like it, usually no more than once or twice a week when he ran out of plates and cups. This summer had been a terrible one for flies, especially in the kitchen. Twinkle's litter tray had hordes of flies' eggs on the stale cat shit, but he couldn't open the back door in case she got out. He was petrified of losing her so instead of opening doors or flinging the windows wide he hung fly papers in the kitchen and toilet. He liked to watch as they became stuck and struggled to get free. He would never have described himself as a cruel man, though. On the contrary: everything he did was for love.

He'd been lucky to get a two-bedroomed maisonette with a small garden. At least the silly cow he'd been married to had come in handy for something. He wouldn't have qualified for the place without her and his sick, ageing mother-in-law, so when he'd got shot of both of them, he had said nothing and no one ever questioned their disappearance. It had all worked out quite nicely really. This was his little castle now. As long as he paid his rent down the local housing office, no one ever said a word.

It made him giggle, the way no one had ever cottoned on, but with the wife and mother-in-law having no other living relatives it had been too easy. No one had ever seen much of them. Silly bitch always stayed with her mum indoors, never went anywhere. Getting shot of them had been a piece of cake. A bit messy at the time, mind you, but nothing that a good scrub hadn't cleaned away.

There were no distinguishing features to his home; no bright baskets of flowers or imaginative placing of garden ornaments. He wasn't much of a gardener, rarely even troubled himself to cut the small patch of grass outside the back door which had reverted to a kind of inner-city meadow with dandelions and cornflowers sprouting up between the tall blades of grass. Buddleia from next-door had seeded itself incongruously and butterflies hovered around it. In the corner of his back yard stood a shed filled with rusting tools and a bicycle that hadn't been used for years, but he still kept a lock on it at all times though no one seemed interested in his way of life or the little property that time had forgot.

The front of his home was similarly nondescript and offered no clues as to the tenant's personality. No one called, and no one bothered him. Even the electric and gas meter readers put cards through the door and he did the readings himself. The front door was painted standard issue council blue and the plastic numbers had long since fallen off. The front door was now jammed shut in its frame from years of neglect and only the letterbox, through which a meagre trickle of mail passed, was still in working order. The letters made a slapping sound when they hit the lino in the passageway.

He hadn't bothered to carpet the hall, stairs, kitchen or front room, and the grey lino was scuffed and in places buckled. It served its purpose, though. Only the two upstairs rooms had been crudely covered in off-cuts and remnants, which he'd laid over the stained floorboards after those two bloody women had gone. He had picked up oddments at local house clearance shops for next to nothing. He hadn't bothered with carpet tape or nails, so they shifted about, held down only by the barest of furnishings placed upon them. He didn't own a vacuum cleaner, just a manual Bex Bissell, yet the upstairs rooms held a semblance of order that was lacking downstairs.

He slept in the small, sparsely furnished bedroom on the double bed with its light green candlewick bedspread and two thin pillows. His clothes, such as they were, hung on wire hangers in a small heavy wardrobe above his two pairs of shoes. His underwear and socks lay in a pile on the floor. His ready-made curtains were a mustard yellow polyester mix from Woolworth's, kept permanently drawn.

On a sunny day, the room was bathed in a golden light and he liked to lie naked upon his bed and dream of all the love he had to give, the power he had in his body as he pinned a child down and they cried out, the masculinity of his rock-hard penis. He would judder in delight as he thought of small children's beautiful, untouched genitals. He liked to round off his perfect afternoons by rolling himself a fag and puffing hard on it as he basked in the satisfaction of a good fantasy session.

Only the second, larger bedroom, which he used as his living room, gave any real clue to this man's inner life. With the plastic blinds always kept rolled down, he was able to cover one whole wall with pictures of children of all ages and colours, cut from magazines

– ordinary magazines that he picked up from work or the doctor's waiting room, not his special magazines that he kept hidden under his mattress, and the even more special ones he had hidden beneath the loose floorboard, that only came out on special occasions. Those beautiful little kids, all naked and being made to do unspeakable things . . . He loved them. They were the best turn-on, his special treat, but lately he'd been finding they were not enough to satisfy him. He'd gazed long and hard at pictures of innocent children suffering at the hands of gangs of paedophiles, but still he couldn't ejaculate. He'd needed something more.

Two spotlights had been wired from the ceiling and shone on to the wall, giving the impression of cheeriness, light and colour. He never felt alone in this room. A long, low sofa of red leatherette was placed beneath the window and its matching pouffe next to the coffee table, which bore the rings of many mugs of tea. Twinkle liked the room too. He had placed a large cushion under the storage heater for her to sleep on while he was in there doing his cutting and pasting.

Occasionally, he would just drop his trousers and masturbate here, but longing was all he seemed able to feel and frustration was building inside him. Feeling cheated, he would throw down the magazines and put his head in his hands. After a cup of tea, he would calm down, smoke another roll-up, then continue with his cutting and pasting. He always whistled while he worked and sometimes put on the radio for company. When he had finished adding new pictures, he would lie on his sofa and gaze at the wall, smoke a roll-up and admire his handiwork.

Until recently he had been happy with just the pictures. He knew a shop near King's Cross where you could get the kind of magazines he liked. It cost a bit, kiddie porn, but he loved to look at the soft skin of the children and the strained expressions on their faces. They enjoyed it really, enjoyed all of it, even the pain. And if they cried sometimes, that was just their way of playing hard to get.

He hadn't meant to kill the black girl but she would keep screaming when he was only trying to make her happy. She had strutted about, showing off those lovely long legs, wearing that tight T-shirt that revealed the hard nipples on her developing breasts. She'd deliberately bounced that pert little black arse in his face, so she'd deserved a good seeing to. It was selfish of her really, to try and stop him, but he had loved the fight she had put up. When she'd screamed for him to stop, he made sure she got what was coming to her. The railing had been there, just ready for him to use. Her face had been a picture. He had managed to come that time and it had felt great. It was just a shame he'd had to squeeze the life out of her. He'd especially liked her curly black eyelashes. They'd still had tears on them when he cut them off.

103

He kept the eyelashes in blue Basildon Bond envelopes with smart watermarks on them. He'd asked the newsagent for the best envelopes he had, saying it was for something special. He liked the silky feel of them, and the way they held their shape in his little box files. He didn't write names on the envelopes, simply dates and times. This way, he could take them out and look at them and relive the moment anytime he wanted.

Chapter Seven

'You must have seen something, for fuck's sake!'
Gillian was screaming at Wayne. She had yanked
him from the car and pinned him firmly over the car
bonnet. His mates were dragging themselves out of
the Jag, looking bewildered and scared. Gillian was
going at him hell for leather, her face red and angry,
but really it was the face of a terrified mother. In hot
pursuit of her sister, Grace cast urgent glances up
and down the street as if looking harder would
make Jamie suddenly appear; he must be here
somewhere.

Jamie was a rascal and a flash little sod. Tall for
nine, he was handsome with a mop of blond hair and
an expression on his face like butter wouldn't melt in
his mouth. He would be sitting on a wall a couple of
houses down, scuffing his new baseball pumps on the
wall, oblivious to the worry he was causing. He must
be. Or maybe he was hiding, playing a trick on them,
enjoying the hoo-ha, waiting to jump up from behind
a parked car and point and laugh at their over-
reaction. He couldn't have just disappeared. Kids
were playing and roaming round all over the area,
someone would have seen him.

'Honest, Auntie Gill, he was here a minute ago. Let go, you're 'urting me.' Wayne looked flushed and stricken and guilty. He was the eldest of this group of boys, the tough one, the leader, and Jamie had pissed off without him noticing. Wayne felt embarrassed. He really hadn't seen anything, but then, he hadn't been looking. There were too many of them there for them all to get inside the car at once and they'd been jostling to take turns. Wayne had been in the driver's seat, busy looking at all the lovely controls and admiring the walnut dash and cream leather upholstery. He was dreaming that he was in control of a speedy race car and was winning the Grand Prix! They'd only been there five minutes, and he was aware the others were moaning for a go in the driving seat, but he had to pass the chequered flag first and then the others could have their turn. Jamie couldn't have gone far. Wayne didn't know why they were all getting so hysterical.

'Look, his bike's still here.' Wayne pointed to the bright blue Chopper leaning against the lamp-post where Jamie had carefully parked it. The other boys' bikes lay propped up or on the ground. Everything seemed untouched and unmoved, just as it had five minutes earlier. Gillian made sure her boys looked after their toys and bikes. It made them appreciate the value of money, but now all that seemed meaningless – Jamie was missing and his new Chopper bike could go to hell for all she cared.

'God, where is he?' she screamed into the air as if hoping for an answer.

She began to cry in deep anguished sobs. Her distress was infectious and the group of boys looked tearful and afraid as they lined up against the car. Each hung his head, and shifted uncomfortably from one foot to another. One of them – a good-looking boy with dark curly hair – wouldn't get out of the driver's seat, saying he'd only just got his turn, until Wayne said, 'Gavin, get out now, you prick! Auntie Gill needs our 'elp.'

The boys honestly hadn't seen anything. They were as baffled as anybody; Jamie had been with them, right there in the car only minutes ago, fighting over who got to sit in the driver's seat. He couldn't just be gone. But feeling chastened by this sudden volley of hysteria from his mum, they stood stricken and embarrassed, just like when they'd been caught nicking sweets from the Paki shop last summer. They'd all been frogmarched back and made to apologise, all over a few blackjacks and flying saucers.

Grace stepped in. 'Gill, keep calm, shouting ain't getting us nowhere.'

'Calm? Fucking calm! You stupid fucking waste of space!' Gillian continued to vent her frustration on the boy. It was as if Grace hadn't spoken. Gillian could only focus on Wayne.

Sue stepped past the other two women inside the house and came up to Gillian.

'There's no need to take it out on my Wayne, it's not his fault.' Sue was pale and confused-looking, still struggling to get a handle on what was happening.

'Oh, shut up, you stupid fat cow! He was with Jamie, he's the eldest, he knows he has to watch out for the younger ones.' But anger was deserting her now. Gillian's hands covered her face and she muttered, 'Oh, God, oh, God, please let him be OK.'

Grace's thoughts were only for her sister. Suddenly, Gillian looked alone and vulnerable. Grace really could understand everything that was going through her head in those split seconds. She had been there and was seeing it all flash before her eyes again. What if Jamie was being hurt right now? Her thoughts suddenly shifted to Adam, her baby, her boy. Could the same person be assaulting Jamie? Grace placed an arm around her sister and pulled her close.

They had been very different as kids. Gillian was always the tough, chain-smoking teenage rebel, unlike her dreamy withdrawn sister. Grace had been so alone in her own teenage years, struggling with the sickening sexual advances of Uncle Gary. She had never told Gillian, never once confided in her sister, and realised in that moment that she'd been tough too, and now she needed to be tougher than ever to help Gillian. Something inside her took control. In a flash, Grace had the boys organised.

'Right then, I want you to go off in pairs and find Jamie. Don't split up whatever you do, make sure you always stay together. He can't have gone far, it's not been long, he must be close by,' she said hopefully even as a cold, sick feeling settled in her stomach.

Wayne was relieved at this opportunity to get away, and the other boys were happy to get themselves out of trouble too. They quickly jumped on their Choppers, Grifters and racing bikes, and headed off in different directions around the estate. As they vanished down the numerous alleyways and side streets nearby it suddenly hit Grace how easy it was to hide round here. The person doing all this knew their way around so well, it had to be someone who lived close by. A shiver ran through her body, as if someone was walking over her grave. She shook herself and gathered her thoughts.

'Come on, Gill, let's go back inside. Jamie'll probably turn up in a minute, let's not panic yet.'

But Gillian stood rooted to the spot. 'I can't stay, Gracie, I gotta go and look for him. I can't do nothing!' Grace's heart felt like lead. All she could do was look despairingly at her little sister as Gillian stared up and down the road, desperate to see her son.

Lizzie was the first to speak and break the eerie silence that had descended over them.

'Listen, we're all getting too jumpy. I'm sure he's

fine. You know what these boys are like – they're a law unto themselves. Jamie's probably just gone round the shops to get some sweets.'

'What with, hot air? He hasn't had his pocket money yet,' spat Gillian, still peering up and down the street for a sign of Jamie.

Opposite Sue's house, by the entrance to a worn-out-looking tower block, a group of girls were playing hopscotch, using a grid crudely drawn on the paving slabs with a chunk of chalk dug from the earth by the swings. They were oblivious to the unfolding drama until an unearthly cry filled the air. They froze mid-game as Gillian's patience finally snapped. A terrible wail left her, and the name 'Jamie' could be heard ringing through the streets of the whole estate. Suddenly everyone was outside their front door, looking on, and gathering in small groups. Loud whispers filled the air. Jamie Hoare was missing!

Grace calmed Gillian down with difficulty, gripping her flailing arms and keeping them tight by her sides until Gillian's hysteria was spent and she leaned against her sister for comfort.

'Sue, come and get Gill. I'm just gonna ask those girls if they've seen Jamie.' It was a command, not a request. Sue obediently made her way over to gather up a by now limp Gill and take her back inside as Grace made her way over to the gang of girls playing opposite.

110

There were four of them, all around eleven or twelve years old. She knew them by sight but not by name. She was sure they knew Potty's Lucy, though. Typical little cows, all full of themselves and far too old for their years. She was surprised they were even playing a child's game. Normally they were hanging around with bold mascara-clogged eyelashes and white shiny lipstick, looking at all the boys and trying to be grown-up.

'Have you seen Jamie Hoare?' Grace demanded. The girls knew something was up and were slightly guarded in their response.

'What, blond Jamie with the long hair?' asked a cocky-looking girl in a pair of purple suede hot pants with long black criss-cross laces which tied at the sides. She shielded her eyes from the sun with the back of her hand to get a better look at Grace. Just like Lucy Potts, all these girls wanted to grow up to be like Grace one day. That sleek black hair, that tight-fitting denim mini-skirt, the large gold hoops in her ears . . . everything Grace was, they wanted to be.

She held the girl's gaze and tried to soften her own face into a smile.

'Yeah, Benny's big brother. He was here with Wayne and the others just now, but he seems to have wandered off somewhere. You didn't see him go, did you?' Beads of sweat were forming on Grace's brow, her cotton shirt was feeling clammy, but she remained outwardly calm.

111

'They were all playing in that flash motor. Is it yours?' The girl looked her up and down enviously, drinking in every little detail.

'Yeah. But did you see him go off on his own?' Grace tried to keep her voice calm but she could feel the panic rising.

'Nah. We ain't seen nothing.' The girl gave Grace another funny look, trying to work out what this was all about, then added in a quieter voice, 'Sorry, but is it that paedo again? We've all 'eard things, you know, about the sex maniac. Rumour has it he's hurt three kids. I knew Chantal, she was me mate. We ain't all silly, ya know. You grown-ups think we know nothing, but we know what's been 'appening round 'ere, don't we, Sha?'

The cocky girl gave her friend a knowing look. Sha just nodded back and the two others stared at Grace, waiting to see what would happen next. Unperturbed, she asked again.

'Listen, it's important, have you seen anyone or anything unusual? Look, what's yer name?' Grace wanted to get on better terms with this girl, who seemed sharp and worldly. Right now Grace needed all the help she could get.

'Kelly,' she said. 'Me name's Kelly. That Steven knew nothing. He was too stupid, just a poor twat.' Grace looked at them all, pleading in her eyes. 'I mean, what's to see round this shit hole?' Kelly went on. The girls all looked at each other then, sensing somehow that trouble was brewing. 'We've done nothing, lady. Just hung around, that's all.'

'I'm not accusing you of anything,' Grace replied. 'But we can't find my nephew, and just want some help. Have you seen any strangers round here, people you don't normally see?' Her voice was rising now, becoming shrill. She could feel herself losing it. Breathe deeply, she told herself, breathe deeply.

'No, no strangers,' answered one of the quieter girls, shyer and smaller than the others and wearing a pair of pink National Health specs fixed with a plaster at the side. 'Only Slimy George and Harry the Horse.'

'Who's Slimy George?'

'The caretaker from the school. He walked past a while ago, and so did Harry. Oh, and a couple of the old biddies from the flats, going to afternoon Bingo, I s'pose. But no one really.'

Grace knew Harry, of course. How odd that he had found her Adam and been around when Jamie had gone missing. But Harry was a right old softie, he wouldn't hurt a fly. Christ, she was getting paranoid!

'OK, girls, thanks. Keep an eye out for Jamie, will you? Tell him to go straight to Sue's when you see him, his mum is worried sick.' Grace turned away and headed back. She could hear the girls talk in quiet whispers to each other and then giggle. She resisted the urge to tell them that it wasn't funny, they could be next.

She braced herself as she reached Sue's front door. Time to get control of herself and this situation. Some bloody fool had the radio blaring out a few doors down. The irritating strains of 'In the Summertime' by Mungo Jerry seemed to haunt her. Terry Williams was loitering uselessly in the doorway, seemingly unsure of the best course of action; he usually relied on his wife for instructions but Sue was feeling uncharacteristically subdued by Gillian's outburst and busying herself instead by making a fresh pot of tea. Gillian sat stony-faced and lost for words at the kitchen table. Nobody spoke, each of the women tortured by her own thoughts, all of them shit-scared.

Grace pushed past Terry after a frosty sideways glance at his unshaven face. He really was a bloody hopeless character, totally pussy-whipped by that fat wife of his, never moving without her consent, always waiting for her nod of approval. Not her idea of a man at all. Suddenly she felt a stab of longing for her John. He always knew what to do, was always reliable, never hesitated . . . even if what he did was wrong. She felt bad for the way she had spoken to him last night. He had only been doing what he thought was right, and Grace had the wisdom to know that you had to let a man be a man. She couldn't expect them to think just like women did. Men were different: that was the whole point, that was why you needed them. And right now she needed

John badly. She could feel that terrible fear returning and wanted to get back to him and their boys and be safe in their lovely home, but she had to keep it together, for Gillian.

Come on, Jamie, you little sod, she thought to herself, show your face.

Doing nothing wasn't an option, Gillian was too agitated and Grace knew that, so she made her sister and Benny Jr go with her and together they combed the tunnels and balconies and alleys and side streets of the estate, finally heading up towards the main road where they reached the shops. They stopped in the post office, the City Farm and various factory outlets on the way, asking if anyone had seen Jamie. Keep busy, keep moving, don't think, just walk! They called into Ali's the newsagent's and then spoke to Costas in the fish and chip shop, but neither man had seen Jamie.

The women left behind in Sue's kitchen barely spoke. Only the sound of the boiling kettle and TJ banging his bricks together penetrated the uneasy silence. They occasionally cast worried looks in each other's direction, waiting for someone else to break the ice. Even with the front and back door open it was stiflingly hot and there was no breeze to relieve the oppressive heat. Nanny Parks removed her pink cardigan to expose the dimpled, wrinkled flesh of a woman twenty years older.

Still not quite fifty, Nanny Parks looked way older

than her years. She was a petite, fragile woman who'd been prematurely aged by hardship and a bitterly unhappy marriage to a vicious drunk. Her life had never really been her own. After all the beatings and bouts of rough sex with an uncaring husband, and the weight of the three jobs she'd held down to keep the house going and the kids in shoes, all she wanted now was a bit of time on her own, to enjoy herself while she still could.

Iris Parks had been a beauty in her day, and she'd had her pick of men, but like most women who'd survived a bad marriage, she had suffered lasting physical and mental damage. Her skin hung off her bones, paper-thin and powdery, and only the determined set of her narrow mouth betrayed her inner strength. First Adam, now Jamie. Why *her* grandchildren? Weren't theirs the generation who were finally going to have it good? And hadn't her family been through enough already? That nasty old bastard she'd married had drunk himself into an early grave, her beloved brother Gary was killed in his prime, and now her girls' babies, her pride and joy, were threatened. Her vision of a contented future seemed to be rapidly fading away.

Lizzie Foster studied her friend's face and saw the pain etched deep in its folds. She reached across the table and grabbed Iris's bony hand, gripping it hard. This simple gesture was too much for Nanny Parks. The tears began to roll down her cheeks. 'My babies, my babies, my little men . . . oh, God, Lizzie, what's happening to us all?'

Lizzie silently handed her a clean handkerchief which she had fished from her handbag with her free hand. The two women, both survivors of tough lives, needed no further words to be spoken. Sue felt like an intruder in her own kitchen. God, she wished Potty was here with her, to support and stand by her without question. Sue could feel the other women's silent hostility towards her, and turned away as tears filled her eyes. Everything had gone horribly wrong! Humiliated first by Grace, and then by Gillian, she was starting to feel the uncomfortable slide from ringleader to outsider. She knew how bitterly they blamed her, first for the mistake last night and now for this. The atmosphere was so dense and thick that she felt she wanted the ground to open up and swallow her whole.

Terry hovered in the doorway to the kitchen. 'Any chance of a cuppa?'

Turning on him, Sue spat, 'Why don't you do something useful, you twat? Can't you see what's happening here? Can't you think for yourself? Must I do all the thinking and fixing, all the time?'

Terry stood there looking gob-smacked. 'Like what? What can I do?' He sounded wounded and confused.

Sue's face twisted with anger. 'Go and bloody look for him, you pillock! Don't keep hanging around here like a spare part. Little Jamie's missing, for Christ's sake.'

Terry shifted uncomfortably from foot to foot, a reply on the edge of his lips, but stopped himself.

'Well, what are you waiting for?' Sue challenged him.

'Don't you think you might be overreacting a bit, love? I mean, he's only been gone half an hour, he'll probably walk his arse back through that door any-time now. Besides, Jamie's a tough kid, he can handle himself. Blimey, remember when he got a black eye from that big lump from Goldsmith Row? How Jamie thumped him back and wouldn't give in? You remember . . . he hid from Gill for hours afterwards, too scared to go home. Come on, love, loosen up. He'll be OK.'

Terry held his breath as Sue turned sharply towards him again. 'This ain't no after-school punch-up at the gates, Tel. We're all scared silly here. Don't you understand?'

It looked like he was going to answer her back then, and Sue was ready for him, but Lizzie got in first.

'Terry, there is a sex maniac out there somewhere and he's getting through our kids like a dose of salts. A nasty, evil thing, raping, murdering and torturing our kids. He gets off on it. He messes with their little parts and leaves them for dead. Jamie could be number four, for fuck's sake!'

118

'What, and I haven't tried to do something about it?' Terry's face was colouring under the strain of actually standing up for himself for once.

'You got the wrong bloody bloke, you fuckin' idiot!' Sue chipped in.

'Whose fault was that then? *You* swore blind it was him, swore on TJ's life it was, now you're trying to blame *me*! You told me what our Wayne saw and heard in the playground. You told me that Steven Archer wanked himself off over our kids. It was you that got us all going, you and these two old cows as well, so don't pick on me!'

Terry waited for a reaction from Iris and Lizzie but both of them stared into their teacups. He stepped towards his now subdued wife in the small kitchen, bearing down on her. TJ looked up to see his parents screaming at each other. His happy little face crumpled and he began to howl. As the whole place descended into bedlam, Lizzie stood up and tried to restore some order.

'Pack it in, the pair of you! You're upsetting the baby.' With that she scooped little TJ into her arms and hugged him. 'It's OK, precious, let's get you some juice.' She picked up his blue plastic beaker and headed for the bottle of Kia-Ora on the draining board.

'We're in a mess, but screaming at each other won't help,' she told the rest of them. 'We got it wrong, we know that. We all have to take some responsibility for what happened to Steven and his mum. It was a mistake, but it's done with and we can't change it. We have to forget Steven for now. Jamie's all that matters. We'll give it half an hour more, wait for Grace and Gill to come back, then if we get no joy we'll call the police.'

As if on cue, the front door swung open then and three boys stood on the step, laughing and jostling each other. The front door was banging against the wall and lots of shoving was going on. The other two pushed the one with the collar-length blond hair down the passageway in front of them, and there in the kitchen stood Jamie, cool as you like.

'All right, Nan? Where's Mum then? Gavin said she was looking for me.' And Jamie, as cocky as always, made his way to the fridge to help himself to a drink.

Lizzie, Sue and Terry just stood there open-mouthed with relief while Nanny Parks made her way over to her grandson. At five foot one she was an inch or two shorter than him, but that didn't stop her giving him a good clout round the ear.

'Ya big fucker! Where ya been, we've all been worried sick.'

'Ow! What d'ya do that for, Nan? I'm 'ere, ain't I?'

Jamie looked wounded, confused, and completely humiliated to be getting a crack like that from his nan in front of his friends.

'*That's* for going off without telling us where

you'd gone.' Then Iris stood up on tiptoe and kissed his cheek. 'And that's for coming back safe and sound.'

'What's everyone getting so worked up about? I only went to get Kevin Ferguson so he could see Auntie Grace's car.'

DCI Woodhouse had dispatched PC Watson on a special mission to visit Lucy Potts the morning after the attack on her. He had the gentle touch and Woodhouse hoped he'd get her to remember something else. She'd been a brilliant witness last night, but there was nothing better to jog the mind than a trip back to the crime scene. He was hoping Watson would be able to take her down to the park to retrace her exact route from the night before, taking her through it step by step so that every detail was covered. It wasn't going to be easy for her, but it was vital to their investigation.

Woodhouse was beginning to get some hunches about this attacker. He knew from long experience that this was evil on a different scale from anything he had encountered before. This animal had sprung out of nowhere and was targeting kids. Woodhouse knew in his gut that he wouldn't stop until he was caught. The three cases all had striking parallels. Those lollipops and his liking for trophies: the eyelashes missing from Adam and Chantal. Woodhouse felt certain it was someone local, someone who could hang around without arousing unnecessary suspicion. Someone who blended in with the community. Someone no one would ever suspect. An outsider would have been fingered by this lot ages ago. It was a close-knit neighbourhood. Too close-knit sometimes. The attack on Steven Archer had sickened Woodhouse, to the point where he'd lost sleep. The kid had been completely pulped and that experience would stay with the already confused lad for ever. God only knew what kind of flashbacks he would suffer in the future. It was exactly the kind of vigilante have-a-go heroism that muddied the waters of police work, but Woodhouse had no time to worry about that now. He had his suspicions about who had attacked Steven, but more pressing matters needed his attention first.

The attack on Lucy Potts was the third in two weeks and Woodhouse was getting jumpy. The attacker, having escaped the police so far, would be getting more confident – more likely to slip up, granted, but also more likely to have another go. The DCI had men permanently patrolling Haggerston Park but the first attack on Chantal Robinson had happened on the street; it was likely he would strike wherever and whenever the opportunity presented itself, so drawing up a list of suspects was essential. That way he could keep an eye on them, track their movements. He was convinced that this man was an opportunist, a monster who kept his eye out for a pretty child, left for a minute – or even a few seconds – by chance. All he needed was that one chance.

The little boy, Adam, hadn't been able to provide any information beyond 'nasty man, horrible man, smelly man'. This could have been child's talk but the details Lucy Potts had given about that familiar smell intrigued Woodhouse. A chemical smell – someone from the paint factory perhaps?

PC Watson arrived at the Pottses' flat somewhere after two to find Sandra sobbing on the sofa while Lucy warmed some beans in a pan for her twin sisters. What a pathetic figure the mother was. Her clothes were crumpled and stained down the front, her hair an unruly mess. She sat with her legs folded underneath her large backside, on a threadbare sofa, feeling sorry for herself. He hoped his face didn't betray the disgust he felt. He came across this all the time, kids who looked after their own parents, but Sandra Potts took the biscuit. What sort of parent was she? Her daughter had been the victim of an attempted rape less than twenty-four hours ago, and here she was looking after the family while her mother fell apart. Watson glanced at Lucy with new respect.

While he waited for her to finish washing up the lunch plates, Michael Potts staggered into the kitchen, having just got out of bed. He wore a filthy

T-shirt and underpants, and his face had the reddened bloated appearance of a man who enjoyed too many drinks. The smell of stale alcohol seeping out of his pores, combined with the heat of the tiny kitchen, made Watson feel quite nauseous. Not wanting to stay in the flat any longer than necessary, he moved towards the front door. 'When you're ready, love,' he said to Lucy, wanting to get the hell out.

'What about my girl then? Fighting him off. I wish I'd have been there, fucking mad bastard! What I wouldn't do to a man like that.' Michael Potts swaggered right up to Watson as he spoke.

Leaning back while trying to hide his distaste, he replied, 'She's a remarkable girl, you must be very proud,' then looked Potts up and down with barely concealed contempt.

'I've always taught my girls to stick up for themselves, I 'ave. See my little Jessica there, she can throw a punch, can't ya, babe?' Potts barely looked at the child as he fished a dirty glass out of the sink, filled it with water and downed it in one. Watson could hardly believe that this excuse for a man was trying to take the credit for his step-daughter escaping what could have been a brutal rape or even murder.

'I'll just put some clean clothes on.' Lucy smiled shyly at Watson who was touched to see that at least one member of this family observed the decencies. How she had turned out so well he really did not know. Michael Potts flipped up the bread bin lid and pulled out a crust of Mother's Pride. 'Is this all we've got?' he shouted to Sandra, mumbling obscenities under his breath.

'Well, I haven't exactly had time . . .' Sandra came into the kitchen snivelling. 'My girl's been attacked and I just can't get my head round it.'

'Fuck this! Ya nothing but a useless lump of lard. Get off yer arse and clean this dump up – and get some proper grub in. I'm going out!' Michael Potts stomped off to the bedroom where he slammed the door shut behind him.

'Off down the pub no doubt,' Sandra said to nobody in particular, and began to wail again. Watson took in her puffy face, caught between wanting her to snap out of it and feeling sorry that she was tied to such a useless man. As he looked at Sandra Potts he saw what she might have been. She wasn't totally unattractive but seemed to take no pride in herself or her home, a situation that was all too common among families on the estate. Watson cleared his throat.

'Is there . . . erm . . . somebody you can talk to? Have you any friends or family close by?'

The gentleness of his voice made Potty look gratefully into his kind, capable face. She smiled faintly. 'Well, my friend Grace was here this morning, she was good. She's had a bad experience too with this nutter. Her boy Adam was attacked.' Sandra twisted a soggy tissue around her finger.

So the Ballantynes and the Pottses knew each other? It was a small world. 'It's just that they reckon the best way to get something out of your system is to talk about it, if you can,' he said.

Sandra smiled weakly at him again. She'd probably been a good-looking woman once. What a waste.

'Who says that then?' she asked.

'Well, my lady indoors mainly.' Watson smiled bashfully, thinking of his pretty little wife.

'You're all right, you are,' said Potty. 'Most people hate the police around here, but you're really all right. Thanks.'

Watson gave one of his all-part-of-the-job shrugs, and was rescued by the appearance of Lucy, standing in the doorway of the kitchen in jeans and a thick jumper.

Her mother looked at her and said, 'It's boiling hot out there, what do you want a big jumper like that for? You'll roast, ya silly cow.'

'That's normal,' commented Watson, 'probably still in a state of shock and feeling cold.' He glanced from mother to daughter and caught the fleeting expression of disappointment on Lucy's face. The poor kid still needed her mum's attention and understanding, no matter how good or bad a parent she was. Lucy just wanted her mum to be a mum, to take charge and look after her. 'You can come with us if you like, Mrs Potts?' Watson asked hopefully.

'No, I'll stay here. I'll be OK, you just go.'

Watson concealed his distaste at the selfishness of her reaction.

'Right then, shall we?' He led Lucy out of the door, pretending he hadn't seen the tear roll down her cheek. How did this kid cope? By the time they'd reached the lifts Lucy had regained her composure. He spoke to her gently as they waited for the lift to drag itself up to their floor.

'You understand why we're doing this, don't you, Lucy? It's just so we can go over everything again, see if there's anything else you can remember, no matter how small or unimportant it might seem.'

'I know, and I remember everything,' said the girl with a determined set to her jaw.

'Yes, I'm sure you do.'

Grace finally arrived home with bags of shopping around half-past four to find John and the boys watching the women's final at Wimbledon on the telly. She glanced briefly at the TV and wondered how on earth the players managed to look so composed and fresh. John looked pissed off; he was probably still moody with her, smarting from the way she'd gone off that morning.

'Christ, we've had some right fun and games! It's all been going on today, I'm exhausted,' said Grace, scooping baby Luke off the floor and giving him a big cuddle. 'Oh, John, he stinks. When did you last change his nappy?' She flopped down on the sofa between him and Adam, Luke on her lap, happy and relieved to be home; she put her arm around Adam and pulled him in close to her.

She looked lovingly at her first son – her pride and joy – and wanted to scream at the injustice of what he'd been through, but she was grateful too. For the first time since the attack he was smiling and she gazed at him with a wave of love and optimism before going on with her story.

'I went round to Sue's and I'd only been there ten minutes when little Benny came in saying Jamie had gone – so of course we all thought the worst. Bloody hell broke loose, we were all running round like headless chickens – it was a nightmare. Gill was doing her nut and we were all out looking for him. Anyway, we got back to Sue's and there he was, sitting at the table eating egg and chips and having a Coke, like nothing had happened. I thought Gill was going to crown him!'

John sat grim-faced on the sofa, staring straight ahead at the telly and not speaking. Grace sighed and told herself to stop chatting. Her husband was obviously still upset with her; she wanted to make amends, tell him she was sorry and that she loved him. She took the baby off to change his nappy then came back to the kitchen where she flipped the kettle on and whistled to herself as she washed up the breakfast dishes still in the sink.

That business with Steven Archer was awful, really awful, but she had to put it behind her, forgive John and get back to normal. He was her husband, he idolised her and their boys, and she knew she was lucky to have him. The world was full of weak men like Michael Potts and Terry Williams, but her John wasn't one of them. Yes, he'd gone along with them and he had hurt Steven, but she had to forgive him one slip-up. Her life, her marriage, her whole future, depended on her getting things back to normal as quickly as possible. John worked hard, provided them with a beautiful home and a good life. He'd done what he had because he'd wanted to protect them. She understood that now. She came back into the front room with two mugs of tea in her hands and a bag of doughnuts from the baker's held between her teeth. She set the mugs of tea down on coasters and sighed with contentment. But still John didn't look at her.

'Look, love, I'm really sorry about last night and this morning, I just felt it was all getting out of control and I was frightened. You know I like young Steven – that I've always had a soft spot for him? I felt terrible about what happened to him, and even worse when I knew you were involved. We were talking today, me and the girls, and realise we all made a dreadful mistake, but let's not dwell on it.' Grace waited for a reply and when none came continued, 'John, I've said I'm sorry, don't be pissed off with me.'

'It's not that.' His bottom lip was trembling and she could see him physically shaking.

'Well, what is it then? We're all right, aren't we? Little man here is getting better, and Jamie came back.'

'Yeah, but Wayne didn't.' John still couldn't look at her. He dropped his head into his hands and began to weep.

'What do you mean?' That cold feeling ran through her again.

'Sue rang about ten minutes ago, Grace.' He raised his head with an effort and looked into his wife's ashen face. 'Wayne hasn't come back. He went off on his own to find Jamie and hasn't been seen since. Sue's just called the police.'

Chapter Eight

Kelly Gobber watched events unfold throughout the whole morning and early afternoon. She was bored with everything and now that Sha and the others had gone home for lunch she sat on the low stone wall, swinging her legs restlessly. Lunch for her would be half a loaf filled with chips and lots of salt and vinegar – all from the local chippy. As a latch-key kid, there was nothing for her to go home to. Her mum would be down the local with one of her many men friends, getting sloshed, and Kelly had become streetwise enough to look after herself. She needed nothing and no one. Money was handed over on a regular basis, to shut her up and keep her out of the way while her mum staggered home with a client and occupied the bedroom in a noisy fashion.

Kelly had known from a young age that sex sells. Her father had left before she was born, and since then it had just been her and her mum. Everyone knew that Cath Gobber was the local bike, but Kelly, with her money and trendy clothes, was a popular girl. Whatever her mum did, it never stopped Kelly being liked.

There was nothing left to see now that all her

mates had gone home and the street was quiet once more, save for that idiot who just wouldn't turn the radio down. Bored, hot and hungry, Kelly made her way over to the chip shop to get her lunch.

It wasn't Sue who worried first. For someone who spoke so vehemently about the need to deal with the sex attacker, she had a surprising amount of faith in her eldest boy's ability to look after himself. She was certain that Wayne had simply got sidetracked by some of his mates and would come back as soon as he was hungry or needed money. She didn't fret unnecessarily about her Wayne – he was a big boy, a tough little bugger, a bit of a ringleader like her, and more than capable of taking care of himself and his mates.

Wayne Williams was a known face in the neighbourhood and even boys several years his senior had learned to their cost not to pick fights with him. He wasn't a bully, though, and despite his rough and ready exterior, Wayne always had a soft spot for the underdog. Perhaps it had something to do with having TJ for a little brother – he adored him, could be sweet and protective with other young children, and took his position of eldest child in the family very seriously.

It wasn't unusual for Wayne to go missing; he often stayed out way past the time he was meant to come home. He'd been like it since junior school, and now he was in his first year of secondary modern he had met an older crowd and the nights just got longer. He'd often come strolling home at half-past ten, even on a school night, and Sue and Terry had given up trying to rein him in.

It wasn't that he was a bad boy; far from it. It was just that he was a bit of a lad. His frequent detentions at school were almost a badge of honour. Terry often bragged about Wayne's antics in the pub, and Sue loved to regale the other women at coffee mornings with his comings and goings and outrageous behaviour. The other mums all loved him too; he was always there to watch their little ones. Wayne Williams, a real character.

Terry began to have his doubts after lunch. Wayne was a fucker, but he didn't like to miss out on anything that was going on. Granted Jamie was back now, but it did seem strange that Wayne hadn't been home to check. Gillian had been so relieved when she got back to Sue's and found her son sitting at the kitchen table, eating egg and chips, and was full of apologies for turning on him earlier. The kettle had been switched on to celebrate and cigarettes had been lit and everyone felt their spirits lift.

'You nearly gave your mum a heart attack, going off like that,' scolded Nanny Parks. 'You must always tell her where you're going.' Jamie was in disgrace for a while, but things soon went back to normal. The boy was safe and that was all that mattered.

Grace had said she'd better get cracking as she'd been out all morning and would probably get home to find Adam and Luke still in their pyjamas. Slowly the other women drifted away; Gillian scooped up Benny Jr and warned Jamie he wasn't to step out of her sight, he was coming home with her. Nanny Parks and Lizzie Foster decided to jump on the bus together and go up to the hospital to visit Steven: 'Take him some of those *Spiderman* comics he likes, eh, Liz? Get the keys from Eileen and maybe go and tidy up the flat.' As if their collective guilt could be erased with a bit of bleach and a squirt of Mr Sheen – the East End mentality at its simplest. Having overcome their panic about Jamie they were full of goodwill towards their fellow men. Even the ones who, until just hours ago, they had thought needed to be taught a lesson.

Sue was quietly relieved to be back on good terms with Gillian and Grace, who she'd sensed pulling away from her. The Parkses had always been the local family to look up to. In spite of her old man, Iris had looked after her kids properly and gained the respect of the whole neighbourhood. Sue didn't want to be cast out of that inner circle. Grace, with her lovely clothes, beautiful hair and striking face, was starting to look down her nose at Sue and she couldn't stand that.

She knew she'd never be a match for Grace in the looks department, nor have the same beautiful home, flash car and a handsome, hard-working husband like John, but like her son Sue was a natural leader, a force to be reckoned with, and she wanted it to stay that way. She had to have some way of competing with the Parkses: her own natural authority. She wanted other women to look at her and think, There's Sue Williams, best not get on the wrong side of her. Safer to stay in with her. Even ruling by fear was better than not ruling at all.

She was cheerfully clearing the plates and mugs and wiping the kitchen table with a J-cloth, thinking how well the whole situation had turned out, when Terry appeared from the front room and stood leaning against the doorframe. His armpits were circled with sweat; he looked thoroughly hot and bothered.

'Tel, get TJ an ice pop from the freezer, will ya?' Sue never missed an opportunity to give orders to her husband.

'Don't you think it's strange that Wayne still hasn't come back?' said Terry as he fished around in the top drawer of the freezer.

'Nah, he'll be all right, you know what he's like.' Sue rinsed the crumbs from the cloth into the bowl of soapy water, squeezed it and wiped down the draining board. Her mind drifting, she thought about Gillian and the hard words she'd said. Sue had been called a fat cow twice today and she thought she'd better join that local slimmers' club – that would show 'em! She was in a world of her own, wearing a size ten dress, when her husband spoke again.

'Oi, dozy, pay attention. It's three o'clock and he hasn't come in for his dinner yet. You know what Wayne's like for his grub.' Terry tore off the paper top of the ice pop with his teeth and handed it down to little TJ who was standing with arms outstretched, waiting. Her daydream brought to an end, Sue came back to reality.

'Don't worry about it, Terry. Go and watch the tennis. I'm going to take TJ and the girls down the park for some fresh air, it's bloody cooking in here. Maybe a go on the swings will cool 'em down.'

But Terry was insistent. 'Look, go past the betting shop on your way and see if he's hanging around outside there.'

'Why would he be hanging around outside the betting shop?' Sue enquired, turning to look at her husband.

'Because that's where he goes to scrounge fags and get a tip on a dog.' Terry looked down at his feet, fearing the reaction to his admission.

'Our Wayne doesn't smoke, Terry, don't be daft. And pass me that broom behind you, those bloody crumbs have gone everywhere.' He retrieved the broom from its place behind the kitchen door and handed it to his wife.

'Yes, he does, Sue. Harry the Horse told me he's always hanging about scrounging off the blokes who go in there. He's even got some of the older lads putting a bet on for 'im. Got a good eye for a winner, ya know, our Wayne!'

'But he's only eleven!'

'So? I was nine when I started.'

'Yeah, but you were in a children's home, Wayne's got a proper family,' Sue said cruelly as she rattled the broom about beneath the kitchen table. TJ began to moan as he struggled with his ice pop. She let the broom clatter to the floor and went to sort him out. 'Open the bloody thing properly, Tel. You know he can't do it on his own.'

Terry's face flushed angrily as he considered a reply but thought better of it. He made to turn away then came back into the room and said, 'No, listen, you stay here. I'm going out to look for him.'

'But I'm going to the park with the other kids. You'll have to stay here in case he comes back, he hasn't got a key.' Sue wasn't used to her husband changing her plans.

'Tough.'

Terry went out of the front door and slammed it behind him. Sue lowered herself into a chair at the surprise of it all. What had got into him? She didn't like Terry calling the tune, the silly bugger, that was her job. But finally she shrugged to herself and turned to TJ. 'Oh, well, love, we'll just have to fill up the paddling pool, won't we?'

Kelly wandered around after having her fill of chips and Coke, feeling hot and bothered. A small crowd had gathered around the City Farm and, with nothing better to do, she made her way towards the small group to have a nosy, see what was going on.

'Well, what a surprise,' she said aloud. 'It's Lucy Potts, the big fat lump!' So it was true, Lucy had been attacked. Glancing round quickly, Kelly observed the tall dark handsome policeman directing events around Lucy. Lucky bitch, she thought, he's a bit of all right.

Out of the corner of her eye Lucy spotted Kelly, the most popular girl in the neighbourhood. Now was Lucy's chance to impress her. She made her way through the crowd. 'All right, Kel?' Kelly looked her up and down, unimpressed. 'I'm 'elping the police with their enquiries. I was attacked, you know, but I got away. Gave 'im a right thump I did. Police say how good and brave I was. I might even get in the paper.'

'Really? How fantastic,' Kelly replied sarcastically. 'So, is this what all the fuss is about? I mean, all these people. Did ya know Jamie Hoare went missing earlier, but he's back and he's all right? I spoke to his Auntie Grace, you know, the money bird. She was all right actually. Anyway, gotta go. See ya.' Without a second glance, Kelly turned on her heel and walked back up Hackney Road, leaving Lucy standing there, all the wind taken out of her sails.

Terry headed straight for the betting office, which was full of men feeling bold after a good lunchtime session at the Birdcage. He asked Harry if he'd seen Wayne, but the bookie just shook his head and said, 'He might have been outside but I ain't been able to get from behind this counter all day. One of my girls has called in sick. Sorry, mate.'

Terry thought he remembered Grace saying some young girls had seen Harry walking past his house earlier, but dismissed the thought. Standing in the corner, gazing at one of the TVs with a short betting office pen behind his ear, stood George, the caretaker from the local school. He knew all the kids round here, and had to be worth a try.

'George, you haven't seen my Wayne, have you?' Terry forced a smile though he'd never really liked this man. George was a scruffy, grimy sort of bloke, but seemed harmless enough.

'Not today. I've been in the betting shop all day.' George gave him a concerned look. 'You look worried, Tel.'

'Yeah, I know. To be honest, George, with all the goings-on lately, I'm just a little bit uptight. All these bloody attacks on our kids, it makes you paranoid, don't it?' He looked at the TV screen as a huge cheer went up in the betting shop. Someone's luck had just turned. A solitary fan stirred the stale, smoky air, heavy with the aroma of sweat and lunchtime drinking. Sober himself, Terry found the dense atmosphere choking.

'You're not joking, mate. I don't know what's happened round here, no kid's safe.' George hiked up his elastic belt, which was beginning to ride low. He had on old grey work trousers, shiny with wear, a piss stain near the fly and stale dry food deposits near his crotch. He wore a yellow nylon shirt and jacket. Terry thought he must be roasting in all that.

'Yeah, but that little Lucy saw him off, didn't she? Did you hear about that? Fucking amazing, she can't be more than five one.' Terry shook his head with wonder.

'Yeah, Old Bill were swarming all over the park this morning and that PC Watson has been talking to everybody. Useless, the police, haven't got a clue. Silly load of plods, they won't catch him. I reckon he's too clever for them!' George picked up a half-smoked roll-up from the ashtray and lit it. 'Anyways, the retarded kid was involved, I reckon, but he got a good 'iding, I 'eard. Still in hospital now, ya know.'

Terry looked down at the floor at this mention of Steven Archer. 'Well, Old Bill might know more than they're letting on. You never know with them, the shifty bastards. I hope they get a bloody move on, though, and catch him.'

140

Dragging hard on his fag, George went on, 'So it wasn't Steven Archer after all then?'

Terry looked at him, trying to read what he knew. 'No, I guess not,' he said.

'Don't blame whoever did it for trying, though.' George pushed back the lock of greasy, grey hair which fell over his eyes. His brow was shiny with sweat and Terry noticed white flecks of spittle in the corners of his mouth. Time to change the subject. 'You working today, George?' he asked.

'No, course not, it's Saturday. Why d'ya ask?'

'I dunno. You look like you're dressed for work, that's all.'

'No, just haven't been down the launderette yet, been here all morning,' said George, scrawling through a horse's name on his betting slip.

Grubby old sod, thought Terry. Still, must be hard to stay on top of things like the washing when you were on your own and working, with no woman around. Terry thought of Sue and her twin-tub, at it every day.

'Well, look, if you see him, tell him I'm looking for him, eh?'

'Tell who?' said George, looking confused.

'Wayne.'

'Oh, yeah, course, mate. Sorry, will do. Good luck, hope you find him.'

George winked and patted Terry on the arm as he made his way over to the counter where men were

141

pushing and shoving, trying to place their bets. 'One at a bloody time!' Harry was shouting. Terry had been a betting man once but couldn't afford it any more, not with four kids, and was pleased to push his way out through the multi-coloured plastic strip fly curtain and get back on the street.

The park! Of course, Wayne was probably down there having a nose at Old Bill. I'll kill him, thought Terry, I'll bloody kill him.

He walked up Columbia Road, looking in doorways, then crossed the main road and went up past the City Farm where families with pushchairs and hot impatient children were queuing to get in. As he neared the park behind the farm, where Lucy had narrowly escaped, he saw two patrol cars and a gang of kids hanging around, trying to see what was going on. Police tape cordoned off an area about thirty yards square, and officers were walking in a line across it, slowly combing the grass with sticks.

Beneath a tree in the far corner of the park he could see Lucy Potts with PC Watson and a few others. She was pointing and he was writing down notes in a little book. A crowd hung about, chatting excitedly to each other. Wayne will be in there somewhere, Terry thought to himself, nosy little sod, just like his mother.

But as he drew nearer and eagerly scanned the faces in the crowd, looking for Wayne's dark, shaggy mane of hair, he drew a blank. He saw a couple of the kids from school and asked them if they'd seen his son but they just shook their heads and turned back to the drama unfolding behind the police tape, uninterested in what Terry had to say. He moved further along towards the far corner until Lucy turned and he caught her eye. She smiled and waved with the carefree look of a girl at a birthday party, not one reconstructing a serious crime. A tall hippy-looking bloke was taking down notes and another feller in stripy jeans was snapping pictures with a camera.

Watson turned to see who she was waving at and raised a hand in greeting to Terry. The Williamses were not unknown to PC Watson who suspected Terry of regularly handling stolen goods which were distributed for ready cash around the local pubs. He had a bit of form but seemed to have been keeping his nose relatively clean for the last few years. Marriage often did that to a man. That eldest boy of theirs was a handful, too. Watson suspected it was just a matter of time before he was up on a few charges of his own.

'Lucy,' Terry shouted, 'you seen Wayne any-where?'

'No, been here all morning with the police. Did you hear what happened last night?' She was bragging like she'd just won a swimming gala or something.

'Yeah, I did, love. You all right?' Terry had to

143

smile. Lucy was a right little character. He nodded his acknowledgement of Watson.

'Yeah, I'm all right. What's up? Only I'm gonna 'ave my picture taken soon. I'm gonna be in the paper.'

'Oh, nothing really. Just haven't seen Wayne for a few hours, that's all. He went off looking for Jamie and he's not back yet. We want him home. If you see him, tell him to get himself back sharpish.'

Something in Terry's tone made Watson study him more closely and say sympathetically, 'Don't worry, he'll be back. We'll tell him to get off home if we see him, Mr Williams.'

Kelly wandered round aimlessly and eventually found herself at the bottom end of Hackney Road, a short way from the swing park. She never usually went down there unless she wanted to do a bit of acting on their big concrete stage or there was a small gang of them, ready to play 'drop the lolly stick' on the roundabout, but with no one much visible except for Lucy Potts being the big I am, she thought she'd go and have a look down there, to see if anyone else was about.

There were two entrances to the play park, one in a small back street off Hackney Road, which was the main entrance, and one round the side. It was a bit like a secret garden door, tucked away in a corner almost covered with shrubs. A set of stone steps led down to a muddy patch of earth, and a latched door opened off this into an alleyway behind. Only caretakers and park officials were supposed to use it, but most of the kids knew it was there.

Kelly entered via the main entrance. The whole park was deserted, apart from two old women with their grandchildren, who were playing in the sandpit. Usually, kids would be on the big umbrella, or swinging high on the swings, but today everyone seemed to be watching the police and Lucy Potts.

Kelly sat on a swing. As she looked around, and gently pushed herself to and fro, she took in the old red bus, the unused maypole, and the small coloured animals rocking on huge metal springs. God, she was bored.

Normally, she wouldn't think of actually going into the museum, but there was nothing else to do. Maybe later this evening she could get together a few of her mates and head down to Ye Olde Axe, watch the young lads filing in to get under-age drinks. Afterwards, she could head for the kebab house and get a doner with Sha and the others, but for now she didn't want to go back to her flat and listen to her mum and some bloke snoring so she decided to do a bit of sketching in the museum. It would at least kill a few hours.

Sod walking all the way round, she thought. I'll cut through the quick way. As she walked towards the side door, she wrinkled her nose. It was so smelly and there seemed to be thousands of flies here. The shrubs were all overgrown. As she pushed open the door, she felt it jam on something and tried to push against it. 'Fuck, fuck, fuck!' she repeated out loud. To make matters worse, the ground at her feet was soggy with mud. With no sunlight reaching it, the hollow in the bare earth had filled with water, and she was slipping and sliding all over the place. She put her shoulder to the door and pushed harder. Something was blocking it from the other side.

She shoved again and slowly the door started to ease open. There was a horrible squelching noise, and a dreadful smell filled the air once more. Shit . . . it was shit. 'Fucking animals have been crapping down here. God, my new espadrilles,' Kelly said to nobody. She finally got the door to open about a quarter of the way and slid sideways through the gap. She couldn't look down, but felt the sensation of something soft and slippery giving way under her.

As she emerged at the other side, she finally looked down. There was a puddle by her feet and in it was somebody's head.

Kelly felt the puke rise in her throat. It must be a joke, she tried to tell herself, it must be a doll or something. But she knew deep down inside that it wasn't. Thick mud, slime and blood oozed through the material of her sandals and started to turn her foot a funny colour. The smell here was overwhelming and she clapped her hand over her mouth

146

to stop the sick gushing out. No matter which way she moved, more of that terrible liquid splashed on to her feet and legs. She tried to keep her balance, but in the slimy blood-coloured swamp she lost her balance and sat down hard. She vomited stinking squashed-up chips and bread into her lap, instantly turning her hot pants a nasty orange colour with the acidic vinegar and gassy Coke. Panic-stricken, she clenched all her muscles in an effort to lever herself up, but gaining a foothold was virtually impossible. She shifted on to her knees by clinging to some of the overhanging shrubbery and slowly turning over into a kneeling position. Then, as she gazed down between her knees, a black head became visible. She couldn't see its face, which was pressed down in the mud, but that T-shirt was familiar.

The police were called by museum workers who heard a gurgling scream that seemed to go on for ever, like a World War II siren. By the time DCI Woodhouse arrived, a young girl was sitting wrapped in a blanket by the back door of an ambulance, ashen-faced, smelling of shit and puke. As he made his way down the small stone steps from the park he placed his hand firmly over his own mouth, shocked by the sight that greeted him in the alleyway beyond. Lying face down in a muddy pool was the body of a young lad. Woodhouse guessed his age to be around eleven or twelve. His hair was covered in human shit. His jeans had been pulled down to his knees and his bottom was slightly arched to show his anus, which was covered in shit and blood. Red welts were visible on the cheeks of his bottom, and beside the body was the wooden handle from a large shovel, the type used for furnace fires. The boy's fists were clenched as if he had fought like a heavyweight boxer. It was obvious there had been a considerable struggle. This lad had fought for his life but he had lost.

Woodhouse was sickened by the spectacle of a young life snuffed out in such a diabolical way. It didn't take a rocket scientist to see what had happened. The victim had been buggered with the handle and had literally shit himself. The killer must then have smeared it all over the boy's head.

As the detective edged closer to the pathetic body, he already knew what he would find. Stuck to the side of the boy's cheek was a lolly, and as he gently lifted the lad by his shoulder he noticed that his eyelashes had been cut away.

Dread and fear gripped Woodhouse. For the first time he felt completely beaten. It had happened again. He went back into the park and, concealed in the bushes, quietly wept.

The police siren and the ambulance bell alerted everyone to what had happened. The whole area was on full alert as the locals realised the killer had struck again.

*

148

Terry Williams held on to the kitchen table, his knuckles white with the strain. His fruitless search of the area had come to an end. There was the sound of a car pulling up outside, a door slamming, a knock at his own front door. Then . . . screams, the eternal screams of a mother receiving the worst news she can ever imagine.

Chapter Nine

An abnormal silence had fallen over the Columbia Row Estate. As the Sunday morning bells rang out from the few churches scattered amongst the community, people moved silently through the alleyways and side streets. No one wanted to speak. The unthinkable had happened again, and the whole area seemed to be shocked into silence.

Flower market traders set up their stalls quietly and efficiently. The vibrant colours of the flowers and shrubs shone in the morning sunshine. The smell of freshly made coffee and apple fritters filtered through the air and everything on the outside appeared normal. No respecter of grief, the sun beat down. By seven o'clock there was steam in the air and an oppressive heat hung over the streets.

Everyone's thoughts were with the Williams family, but no one even wanted to imagine what they were going through, it was too dreadful even to contemplate. Women and children were walking towards the churches, heads covered with scarves or hats, their faces turned to the ground. Their need to say a prayer for the dead child was paramount today.

*

Woodhouse was conscious of the smell of death. His suit jacket was still smeared with shit and vomit from where he'd wiped away the muck from his hands at the murder scene yesterday afternoon. The clothes would be cleaned but he would never be able to wash away the sight he had witnessed, which was without doubt the worst of his police career. Deep down Woodhouse knew it would never go away, never leave his mind. It would constantly be there as he rested his head on the pillow each night. That vision of Wayne Williams would haunt him for ever, would remain the last thing he saw before sleep released him from this mental torture every night. He had to catch this bastard, and catch him quick!

Right now, though, he needed to get to the family and give them a full update on the discovery of the body. In the immediate aftermath he'd been kept too busy. Young Kelly Gobber had stayed in hospital overnight, and he'd had to deal with her mother, Cath, whom he already knew quite well. The crime scene had been secured, and in the small hours the boy's body had finally been moved to a more decent resting place. Woodhouse then had to go and relieve Watson and other junior officers at the Williamses' home, to lend some kind of support and give such facts as he had to the family. Plus there was the dreadful fact that someone must formally identify the boy's body.

Now he sat in the driver's seat of his Ford Cortina.

151

His arse was stuck to the cover with sweat, and despite all the windows being wound down there was still no breeze or relief from the heat.

He had rehearsed what he was going to say over and over in his head, but felt shaky and nervous. He knew he had to do this, though. His years on the force had toughened him up to most things, but he doubted he'd ever been in a situation as bad as this before. He stared at the closed door to the house and shuddered as he visualised the bereaved parents' reaction to what he had to tell them.

If there was one thing Grace and Gillian knew how to do it was feed people. Iris 'Nanny' Parks had scrupulously taught her girls how to prepare simple, plain, wholesome food, and followed a strict routine when it came to planning her menus. She hated the big supermarkets and loved to go round the markets and small shops, supporting local tradesmen and getting that friendly personal touch that you only got from people who knew and liked you. Besides, the local shops were great for a chinwag and a gossip. They were the hub of the community.

Sunday morning always meant a cooked breakfast with egg, bacon, sausage, fried bread and tinned tomatoes. The lunchtime roast was the best cut of whatever the butcher had on special offer, together with roast potatoes and lots of boiled veg which you made sure always came from the market where it was fresher, cheaper and better. For tea there would be tinned salmon sandwiches, salad and a bit of cake.

Monday was cold cuts left over from Sunday's joint, served with boiled potatoes and pickle. Tuesday was shepherd's pie made from the leftovers. Wednesday was egg and chips, possibly with tinned fruit and custard for pudding. It was toad in the hole with mash and greens on Thursdays. The ends of the bread from the week would be used to make a bread pudding served with a bit of cream.

Iris's Roman Catholic upbringing meant fish on Fridays, always, sometimes from the chip shop if her old man when he was alive hadn't cleaned out all the money from her purse to go down the pub. She had often managed to hoodwink him over the years, though. She always stashed a few shillings in the tea caddy for emergencies, and if she ever got stuck there was always the local tallyman to lend you a few pounds which you could pay back monthly.

Saturday meant steak, which she beat with a meat hammer until you could nearly see through it, served with her own deep-fried chips and mushrooms. She disapproved of frozen food in any form but tins were fine as long as you knew which ones to pick. Never buy a tin with a dent in it was her motto. Woolworth's always had a great selection of broken biscuits you could serve up on a Saturday morning with a cup of tea, to keep everyone going until lunchtime.

She might not have been able to do anything about the fact that their dad was an unpleasant alcoholic, but she always made bloody sure that her children ate properly and would be able to look after themselves the same way when they grew up. Iris was a tough little cookie, with no time for fools. Strong, sturdy and dependable, she had a reputation for being big on family, despite the old bastard she'd married.

Lots of young girls visited Iris while pregnant for her to do the needle test on them. She dangled a large darning needle from a piece of thread near their bump. If the needle went from side to side it was a boy, and in a circular motion it was a girl. Iris Parks was never wrong! She was often called in to help out when a local woman went into labour, too.

Good cooks like their mother, Grace and Gillian spent Sunday afternoon in the kitchen at Grace's, doing batch cookery with the back door standing wide open to let out some of the steam. It was like a Chinese laundry in there. Together they had worked out that with a few pounds of mince and lots of veg they could feed the Williamses for the next week. Both of them needed to do something to occupy their racing minds in any case.

Gillian chopped onions, complaining about her eyes watering.

'I told you to put a teaspoon between your teeth when you cut them, it stops the tears,' said Grace as she stirred a meat mixture, looking all the while at the lasagne recipe she had torn from the back pages of a magazine in the hairdresser's last month.

Gillian scooped up all the vegetable peelings and put them in a bag to take down to the City Farm for the pigs. Nothing ever got thrown away. Even though Grace had plenty in her purse to feed her family, her upbringing had taught her to cover leftover bits of dinner in foil and put them in the fridge, ready to be reincarnated into the next meal.

'Mind yourself, love,' said Gillian, gently pushing her to one side of the cooker, 'that shepherd's pie's ready to come out.' Grace stepped lightly sideways, still stirring, still looking at the recipe but not seeing it. She was in a world of her own, lost in thought and determined to find answers.

As soon as news of the discovery of Wayne's body had done the rounds the women worked out the best way of helping Sue, Terry and the kids. They themselves had been shocked and traumatised by the news, but the best way forward was to get stuck in and help Nanny Parks, who had been on the doorstep first thing Sunday morning. She had scooped up two bags of laundry and brought it back from the launderette a couple of hours later clean and folded. Back in the house she had tiptoed around, opening drawers and putting away clothes, while Sue cried steadily in the bedroom, comforted by the young WPC. By lunchtime Gillian had arrived to collect TJ and take him over to Grace's where he played happily with Benny Jr, Adam and baby Luke in the paddling pool, not understanding what was happening or even that Wayne had gone. Gillian looked at the boys and envied them the innocence of youth.

But her eldest son Jamie understood all too well. He just lay on his bed, staring at his poster of Peter Osgood, feeling frightened and guilty, even though his mum had told him it was not his fault. Gillian herself felt wracked with remorse, knowing very well that if Jamie had not gone off in the first place, Wayne would not have gone looking for him and met his own grisly fate. She was relieved that it wasn't her son, but racked with guilt for her own selfishness. Jamie's father, Benny Sr, had supported his son in the usual way – by having a lock-in at the Royal Oak.

Lucy Potts, by now exulting in her starring role in this ongoing drama, had acted immediately and picked up the Williamses' girls, Penny and Ashley. She took them over to Nanny Parks's where they ate a roast meal and watched Bjorn Borg beat Ilie Nastase in the men's final at Wimbledon. Throughout the match tears streamed down their little faces as they were held in turn by Nanny Parks and Lucy, who fetched them beakers of juice and Club biscuits and stroked their hair and told them it would be all right. Lucy had been playing mother to her own little sisters for as long as she could remember so it came naturally to her.

Grace's husband John spent the day sitting with

Terry Williams in his tiny front room while the police came and went, putting the kettle on and fielding enquiries from all the callers who came to express their shock and grief.

Grace pushed her long, black hair out of her eyes with the back of her hand and sighed with the heat. However dark their lives had become, the glaring sun continued to beat down remorselessly, almost defiantly. It was so hot she couldn't think. Nobody could. They had never known a summer like it. She took a packet of peas out of the large chest freezer and placed them on the back of her neck.

'I can't stand this, Gill.' Her sister knew she didn't just mean the heat. Despite their differences while growing up, Gillian knew Grace, and knew her well.

'None of us can, Grace, but we've just got to get on with it, haven't we?'

'Yeah, but who the fuck is doing this? Chantal, Adam, Lucy, now Wayne. Our kids, right here.' She gazed out of the window above the sink as if the answer lay in the garden.

Gillian filled a bowl with soapy water and started loading saucepans into it, shaking her head.

'It's someone we know or who knows us, gotta be. Something in my head keeps telling me that.'

'But we don't know anybody that sick. Whoever is doing this has the Devil in him. I mean, he has no heart and no soul.'

Outside baby Luke began to cry because TJ had

splashed him. Grace went out, gently told TJ, 'Be careful, eh?' and brought Luke back in where she squeezed him and held him close to her, putting her nose into the side of his little neck and drinking in his milky, baby smell. Like Gillian, she felt grateful and then guilty to feel that way. Both she and Gillian knew that Jamie and Adam were lucky to be alive.

'It'll get worse once they break up next week. There'll be kids roaming around all day long. At least you know they're safe when they're at school,' Gillian sighed.

'Well, we'll just have to make sure one of us is always with them, that's all we can do.' Grace took the dishcloth out of the bowl and wiped the baby's face and hands.

'It's not all we can do. We can get out there and find this bloke – stop him ourselves!' Gillian put out her cigarette end under the tap; it made a short hissing sound before going out. Her face flushed with anger, she looked straight at Grace. 'For God's sake, are you always going to take the back seat, or will you stand up and face this with us?'

It had always been the same; Grace was more resigned to setbacks while Gillian had always been the fiery one, the little sister with plenty of fighting spirit. Gillian was the one who used to challenge their father, tell him to stop hitting their mum. She was the bolshie little girl who always said when something was wrong. Gobby Gillian Parks! Grace, her own fighting spirit quashed by Uncle Gary, just wanted to keep her head down, avoid trouble, become invisible. And so their roles were set for life. Grace was responsible, cautious and lovely. Yet Gillian, for all her 'I won't stand for this' attitude, had gone and married an alcoholic, so who was she to talk?

'Do you always have to mouth off, Gill? Can't you just be a little easier on people? You don't always win by being mouthy and aggressive, you know.' Grace stared at her as Gillian reached for yet another cigarette. Gazing at the end of it and watching the smoke filter into the air as she took a drag, Gillian made her move. 'I've no secrets from no one, Gracie. I married a no-good shit, I was bad at school, I ran roughshod over Mum, smoked and drank, had the odd spliff . . . but no one ever took advantage of me.' She dragged again on her fag, not shifting her gaze from her sister's shocked face.

Grace flushed bright red. That knowing tone in Gillian's voice. Did she realise about Uncle Gary? Had she known all this time, and if she did, why hadn't she said something? 'I don't know what you mean,' replied Grace in a hushed tone. 'The mince is burning, Gill, you'd better stir it and turn the heat down.'

Potty had dispatched Lucy as soon as the news had reached her, early Saturday evening. Grace had agreed to take the girl home with her for an overnight stay. She would come in handy, watching the other kids. Lucy's ordeal had faded into insignificance compared to what had just happened to Wayne. Potty's baby, her girl, was alive. As usual, Michael had bolted for the door, taking himself to the local pub to seek out Benny Sr and get slowly pissed while trying to put right the wrongs of the world.

After a restless night in the terrible heat, and with her sleep constantly interrupted by a drunken Michael and visions of a stricken Sue, Potty got herself up at the crack of dawn. Something had clicked inside her. She gazed at herself in the mirror. She was a mess, and so was this flat.

Without further thought, and with the girls and Michael still sound asleep, Potty started to clean. When she was finished, the kitchen and front room looked as shiny as a new pin. It could have been a different house. Potty roused the twins, got them breakfast and proceeded to tidy their bedroom squalor. She finally sat down at lunchtime and switched the TV on and the radio off. As the final of the tennis at Wimbledon was building up, Potty made a fresh cuppa and grabbed herself a pen and paper. She was going to write a list of everything she knew about the recent events and attacks.

After four pages of scribbles, including times, locations and victims, Potty knew beyond reasonable doubt – in her own mind, anyway – that it could only be one person. She had to tell the others. Once she

160

had washed her hair and put fresh clothes on, she entered the bedroom to wake Michael.

'I've got to go out. Look after the girls. I'll be as quick as I can.' Stunned, he could only nod in sleepy agreement.

It was just the interruption Grace needed, the doorbell ringing. An uneasy silence had developed between her and Gillian and she was beginning to feel uncomfortable in her own kitchen. Grace wasn't sure what her sister knew, but she had aroused some thought-provoking questions. She must know something.

Potty stood on Grace's doorstep, looking hot and flushed but very nicely turned out. In truth, Grace was taken aback to see her so clean and tidy, something she hadn't been for years. With a smile on her face, Grace beckoned her friend inside.

Chapter Ten

With the girls over at Nanny Parks's and TJ round at Grace's, Sue finally got up and went downstairs around four in the afternoon. She hadn't wanted to come out of the bedroom while the kids were still about because she didn't want them to see her so upset. Her footsteps were heavy and laboured. Terry was in the front room with PC Watson and John Ballantyne, their voices lowered to a whisper.

Watson had been assigned to babysitting duty here after DCI Woodhouse had broken the news and taken Sue and Terry with him to the station to identify Wayne's body. Officially he was there to record details of Wayne's whereabouts on the day of the murder, but it was hard to get any sense out of the grieving parents.

Sue didn't want to hear any more talk, she was sick of it all. She tiptoed past the front room and went into the kitchen where she flicked the kettle on. Her knuckles were white from the strength of her grip on the counter top and she stared blindly at the toaster, lost in her thoughts. She didn't hear Terry come up behind her and gave a start when she felt his arms slide around her, his face nuzzling into the back of her head while he wept silently.

Terry needed her now more than ever before, but Sue was distant and cold towards him. She hadn't been able to touch him since they'd heard the news from Woodhouse the previous evening, which they'd both received in numb silence. Unable to really take it in, Sue hadn't been able to cry yet. She just knew she couldn't turn to her husband for support, and his arms gave her no comfort.

She pulled herself free from his embrace to go to the fridge and get out the milk. 'Do you want tea?' she asked.

'No, you go back to bed, I'll bring that up.'

'I don't want to go back to bed. I can't just lay there with all this shit in my 'ead.' Sue banged the kettle down after pouring the hot water into the pot. She stared at the tangerine-coloured splashback tiles, almost mesmerised.

'You should eat something' said Terry. 'There's a loaf in the breadbin. I can make you a Spam and pickle sandwich, if you like.'

'I don't want to eat, Terry,' she said, not lifting her gaze. 'What time are the kids coming back?'

'TJ is staying at Grace's tonight and I thought the girls could stay with Nanny Parks. It's not as if they'll be going to school tomorrow.' Terry shoved his hands deep into his pockets, head bowed. He was talking, but the words seemed meaningless. Why hadn't he acted sooner? Why had he let Wayne act the big man and tear off looking for Jamie? His boy was dead, his pride and joy, his Jack the lad, his first-born.

'Who says they're not going to school tomorrow? It's the last week of term.' Sue turned angrily on her husband.

Terry stood up to her this time. 'Exactly, it's the last week of term, I thought it wouldn't matter.'

'Well, it does matter, Terry. We've got to make life as normal as possible for those girls.'

'Their brother was killed yesterday. I don't think life is going to be normal for any of us ever again.' Terry's voice was getting louder. His raised voice helped him disguise the sobs that were threatening again.

'Don't you think I know that?' Sue shouted.

At that moment John came into the kitchen and looked at them both before lowering his gaze and putting his empty mug into the washing-up bowl.

'Can you get me those bits for TJ then, Tel, and I'll shoot off? Just a couple of days' clothes and a few of his toys. I can take some stuff for the girls too, if you like, drop it off on my way home.' John felt useless here and had a terrible urge to get out of the grief-stricken atmosphere and head home, back to Grace and the kids.

Terry looked at his wife, waiting for a response. Finally Sue sighed and said, 'I'll pack a bag for TJ but I want the girls back tonight.'

The two men looked at each other but said nothing as Sue made her way upstairs. Then Terry started to cry again and John enveloped him in a clumsy embrace.

'You'll be all right, mate. We're all here for you.'

Upstairs Sue sat on Wayne's unmade bed in the room he'd shared with TJ. She picked up his pyjamas and held them to her face, breathing in the smell of him. Her boy couldn't be dead. She could still feel him with her, smell him, and if she closed her eyes she could hear his voice, calling her. On the wall were his West Ham posters, and at the side of his bed stood a cereal bowl with the remains of yesterday's breakfast inside it. Messy little sod, she thought. Typical Wayne, always forgetting to bring anything back into the kitchen!

She opened the bottom drawer of the chest between their beds and took out some T-shirts and shorts for TJ. She picked up his teddy and shoved it in the Tesco bag with his clothes and went back downstairs. She wasn't ready to spend any more time in that room yet; wasn't ready to face reality.

Watson stood in the hallway, shifting uncomfortably from foot to foot. In the kitchen Terry and John were still locked in an awkward embrace and he didn't like to interrupt. He felt like an intruder. No matter what people said about the blokes round here, they were all right guys who stuck together. The PC smiled weakly at Sue as she quietly said, "Scuse me' and went round him to the kitchen.

Seeing her return, John released Terry and took the bag from Sue. Usually a larger-than-life character, today she appeared strangely shrunken to John. He wrapped his arms around her.

'You gotta stay strong, you two, don't let this bastard tear you apart.'

Sue nodded as she began to cry into his shoulder. Suddenly, she started to gasp and choke and sob so loudly that it almost deafened him. Everything suddenly gushed out and Sue was drowning in grief. Gently he released her and she turned to her husband and let out a low animal groan of agony.

This time he held her and she gripped him tightly as sobs wracked her body. Terry could contain himself no longer then, and the two of them howled and cried together. Reluctant to interrupt, Watson nonetheless couldn't leave without saying anything. He caught John's eye and pointed towards the front door. John told them that he was leaving and that the policeman was too, but they didn't hear him. They were locked together in their pain, a pain only they could understand. As the two men let themselves out, Sue and Terry Williams cried long and hard together.

It had taken its time coming, but finally Woodhouse

had the break he had been waiting for. A muddy bootprint taken from the scene of the death was a positive match for one found in the park after the attack on Lucy Potts. There was also a roll-up fag end. Lucy had mentioned the odour on the breath of her attacker and her description had included tobacco smells.

There had never been any doubt in Woodhouse's mind that these attacks were the work of one man and now he had the matching prints and could feel his investigation taking off.

The print indicated a Doctor Marten-style boot, a working man's footwear, well-worn but with the tread clearly visible. He had little doubt that such boots were common enough but the owner of these was very heavy on his shoes and the outside edges of the heels were worn down in a distinctive pattern. Big feet too, size eleven or twelve, so probably quite a big bloke. Bit by bit a description of the murderer was slowly emerging. He was tall, large, and had big feet. He was a smoker, and probably worked with chemicals of some description. He fitted in with the locals and held down a job hereabouts, either in the paint factory, one of the reproduction furniture outlets, or somewhere similar where there would be plenty of chemicals and solvents. He was known in the community and the children were not afraid of him. The victims were never carried off to another place; they always seemed either to be there already or to go off with him happily, as if they knew and trusted him.

Woodhouse also thought about those lollies. What was that all about?

Chapter Eleven

Lizzie Foster sat at her kitchen table smoking furiously. Her piercing green eyes were fixed on her daughter Mary, her mouth set in a tight furious line. This was terrible news, and made even worse by the soppy excuses her daughter had given her for not relaying it earlier. What the hell had she been thinking? Mary was fat and a total wimp. Looking at her, Lizzie just grew more and more annoyed. She was so different from Lizzie's other kids. Her Paul was so tall and handsome, and Monica, although plain, was kind and sweet. If Lizzie was honest, Mary had proved a big disappointment to her. All mothers have such high hopes for their daughters, but even as a little girl Mary had absolutely no interest in anything feminine, despite Lizzie's efforts to tempt her with pretty dresses and mob caps, pierced ears and jewellery. Mary had always preferred her own company, too, her idea of playing being a solitary game of marbles on the drain covers.

At least Monica had allowed Lizzie to do all the proper mum and daughter things. Such a shame that she and Pete couldn't have kids, but at least she had her nieces to spend time with and a high-flying job at the Education Department.

Wayne's body was found on Saturday. It was Monday now. Lizzie felt cross and disappointed that she was probably the last to hear. Why had no one thought to tell her? Her newspapers were delivered on Sunday, there'd been nothing in the nationals, and because her rheumatism had been playing up she hadn't left the house. She could understand that Sue and Terry might not be up to spreading the news, but what about Iris Parks? She was supposed to be Lizzie's mate. And what about Grace, Gillian and Potty? They had all as good as ignored her.

She ran through the events of Saturday in her mind: the hysteria surrounding the disappearance of Jamie, then the way he'd just walked back in, the cheeky little fucker. Nobody had seemed worried about Wayne then – why should they be? She'd left Sue's with Iris around two to go and visit Steven in hospital – and, Christ, hadn't that been a shock, seeing the state he was in? – but she might have got word from someone!

Truth be told, she was still haunted by memories of Steven's face, grotesquely swollen from the bruising. He just sat propped up in bed, the *Spiderman* comics they had brought him left untouched as he stared out of the window into the hot, clear blue sky, as if in some sort of trance. But it was the sight of Eileen, praying softly at the side of his bed, that had really done Lizzie in. She'd aged significantly overnight, all the colour and life drained out of her face, and there was a terrible emptiness in her eyes, which constantly brimmed over with tears. Her thin little body seemed stretched to breaking point. She barely seemed to have the strength to look up as they entered the room. When she did, Lizzie detected the despair in her eyes as she looked at her boy and then at his visitors. She knew that the two of them had been involved somehow.

Lizzie wanted to break the silence and beg her old friend's forgiveness, but out of loyalty to the others she kept her mouth as firmly shut as if it had been sealed. No words came out, just a deep sigh from the two visitors. They had colluded in the savage beating of an innocent boy, and this was the result. It was Iris who nudged Lizzie in the ribs, to indicate that they should leave. All the way back from the hospital the two women remained silent and tense, lost in their own thoughts.

Wayne had been the last thing on Lizzie's mind then. Even with everything that had been going on recently, he just wasn't the sort of kid you ever worried about. She often saw him on the streets, hanging around with a group of older boys as late as 10.30 when she came out of Bingo, even on a school night. One night she'd told him to get his arse home then immediately regretted it when the other boys began jeering and laughing at him. Worst thing you could do to a kid was humiliate them in front of their mates. She had often scolded her Paul and then realised she'd made a mistake. After all, boys would be boys, and round here, you needed to stay in with the crowd.

'How did you find out then?' Lizzie quizzed her daughter, still unable to quell the temper rising inside her.

'That Kelly Gobber mouthing off to Maria, telling her all sorts of horror stories about blood and shit everywhere. Seems like Lucy's been knocked off her perch as most popular kid at school. It's a right old carry-on.

'Mind you, you have to take what Kelly says with a pinch of salt, she's a proper little liar. She's always making up stories to impress the other kids. Can't stand her really, never works hard or does her home-work . . . not like my Maria . . . but you've got to feel sorry for her. Can you imagine, finding a dead body in that sort of a state, and actually knowing who it was?

'Apparently she was taken to the hospital for shock after she found Wayne, and that bloody useless mother of hers took so long to go and get her that in the end the police had to go and collect her. No doubt busy with yet another man!'

Mary tugged at the sleeveless blouse that was riding up around her ample waist, exposing rolls of flesh. Lizzie just looked but didn't say anything. Her daughter was a mess. If she could ever bring herself to make an effort with her looks she might just find a man . . . but then, pigs might fly! As it was, Mary looked prematurely aged and matronly even though she was only thirty-six. She had no dress sense at all, and those acrylic loon pants she insisted on wearing made her look like a pile of blubber with polythene stretched over it. Her tops were always too small, and if she had any sense of style whatsoever she would stay away from floral patterns.

She'd never had another boyfriend after Maria's father had done a bunk, and she'd put everything into that girl. She was a devoted mother, though, you couldn't knock her for that, Maria always came first with her. There was always grub in the cupboard and presents for birthdays and Christmas. All the same, Lizzie secretly wished that she had daughters like Gillian and Grace, spirited and beautiful.

'It's terrible, it really is,' Mary burbled on. 'I feel so sorry for Sue and Terry. How do you ever get over anything like this?'

'You fucking don't, Mary, for Christ's sake!' Lizzie answered in a raised voice.

'OK, Mum, keep your hair on and let me finish! You see, last night Potty turned up at mine with Lucy. Lucy had been looking after Sue's girls round at Nanny Parks's flat – she's a good girl, isn't she?' Mary didn't wait for her mother to answer before going on. 'Anyway, Potty wants me to get an application form for her for some cleaning shifts at the hospital. I told her that the money's not very good, but she seems determined.

'Sounds awful to say it, but in some ways I think that attack on Lucy has done them all a favour. Lucy's walking ten feet tall, getting her picture in the paper, gonna be the talk of the estate. Well, it's incredible to think that she fought the bloke off and escaped. And Potty seems to be getting her act together at last too. You should have seen her last night – she had make-up on and everything. Haven't seen her like it in years. Not that I think it'll make any difference to that slob of a husband of hers. "Honestly," I told her, "you're better off on your own than with a drunk."'

Lizzie just looked at her daughter and felt even more pissed off. Her own husband had been a drunk and a bit free with his fists but she'd stayed with him, thinking it was best for the kids to keep the family together.

'Anyway, Mum, I've got to go. I'm working twelve till eight today, which means I'm going to miss Maria's end-of-term concert. She's singing a solo.' Mary beamed with pride. 'I don't suppose there's any chance you can go and watch her, is there? It'd be nice if someone from the family was there. I know it don't seem right, what with Wayne being killed and all, and of course little Chantal, but life goes on and Maria's worked so hard for tonight . . .'

174

'I'll see,' Lizzie answered curtly, still smarting from Mary's comments about being married to a drunk. In truth, Lizzie had never felt very close to Maria, and out of all her grandchildren liked her the least. Funny kid. Always had her nose in a book, and when she did look up it was only to give you a disapproving glance.

She'd said nothing when told of Chantal's death, even though she was practically her cousin. She seemed happiest in the company of her mum and her books. She didn't watch a lot of TV – and what normal kid didn't like the telly? There were fantastic programmes on for kids, but Maria showed absolutely no interest unless it was a play or something really boring on BBC 2. She didn't fit in and Lizzie had no doubt that as soon as the opportunity arose, her grand-daughter would get the hell out of East London. She was only eleven and already talking about university! Of course that could just be kid's talk, but with Maria you couldn't be sure; she had an old head on young shoulders. Lizzie knew that she should be proud of her really, but there was something about that kid she just couldn't stick.

Of course, her appearance didn't help. Plump like her mum, Maria had short hair, parted on the side, which she kept off her face with a large slide. She never wore a skirt, was always in jeans, and had looked baffled when Lizzie had given her some make-up last Christmas. Lizzie prized looks in a woman above all else. She had been very careful what she ate all her life so as to keep her figure trim, and wished with all her heart that her daughter and grand-daughter would do the same. She consoled herself with thoughts of Aisha and little Trinity, though. At least they were beauties.

'Well, not to worry if you can't, Mum. She's going with a group of mates, I just thought it would be nice, that's all.' Mary understood only too well her mother's ambivalence towards Maria. She even suspected her preference for the half-caste grandkids, but never said a word about it. She stood up to go, straightened her top once more and gathered together her cotton cardigan and handbag. Mary kissed her mother's downy cheek and let herself out of the flat, closing the door softly behind her.

When she'd gone Lizzie placed the cups in a bowl of soapy water and went into the bathroom to tidy herself up before going over to Sue's. They might not be in the mood for company, but she needed to find out exactly what had happened.

Maria ran home after school, let herself in with the key hanging on a chain around her neck and made herself a couple of boiled eggs. Nothing too heavy for tea, her music teacher had told her, it affects the voice. She kept her toast unbuttered because dairy was definitely not good for the throat. It caused phlegm, and she didn't want any to build up before her big number. Her friends from the school orchestra had all been given money from their parents to eat in the café opposite the school, but Maria knew how tight money was for them and didn't like to ask her mum. She was secretly relieved that Mum had to work; it made her nervous if Mary was in the audience. Her mum always seemed to put pressure on her, even though she never meant to, and besides, she always looked so untidy and sort of squashed into her clothes. Maria wasn't ashamed of her mum exactly, but she always felt better when left to get on with things by herself.

She was feeling a bit spooked after hearing the news about Wayne from Kelly, though. Despite what everyone thought, she had not remained impervious to Chantal's death, and in her mind preferred to believe she was still around. Maria hadn't got on with her step-cousin, who was far too into boys and make-up, but her terrible death had still been a shock. She loved her Uncle Paul and Auntie Monica, but her nose had been pushed firmly out of joint when Uncle Paul met Michelle. She hated that black bitch! He had no time for his niece now, and as she got older seemed more and more distant. She still loved Monica, though. Her aunt was so clever and had always impressed Maria with her senior post in local government. One day she would hold a special job, too. She wasn't going to bother with drunken men like her dad and grandfather. Oh, no. She was going to be someone important, perhaps even famous!

Maria looked out of the windows at the bright sunshine and told herself that nothing bad could happen if she stuck to the main roads where there were crowds of people. She brushed her teeth carefully then read a few pages of her book to take her mind off the evening ahead. The rehearsal at lunchtime had gone well, she had only missed one of her top notes. She was singing a lovely song from *Oliver!* by Lionel Bart, 'As Long As He Needs Me'.

'Breathe, Maria! Breathe. Don't forget to breathe,' Mrs Davy, the music teacher, had told her. Maria had a strong voice but still stumbled over the right places to stop and draw breath.

Everybody had to be in school uniform for the concert, which came as a relief to her as she didn't have much in the way of suitable clothing. It began at 6.30. By 5.30 she was getting nervous and decided to make her way back to school. She checked her bag several times to make sure she had her music sheets, and tucked her rabbit's foot on its key ring – a present from Uncle Paul – into the pocket of her school shirt for luck. She went round the flat making sure everything was switched off and double-locked the door before she left.

It was another steaming afternoon. Despite the recent tragedies, people were milling around on the streets. It made her feel safe to know there were so any people about. She decided to pop into Ali's the newsagent's and get some boiled sweets to keep her mouth moistened. As usual, the bookmaker's next-door was exuding its usual mixture of smoke and smells. It was always so noisy in there, and some of the blokes had come out on to the street for a bit of air. The flies were bad today, buzzing all around the rubbish outside the chippy further down the road. The blokes chatted loudly and swore like troopers, and Maria thought how common they all were.

As usual, Michael Potts was there with a few others, boasting about Lucy. Maria thoroughly disliked him. He was tall and heavy and his shirt always had stains down the front. His horrible shoes were all worn and scuffed, and he lounged about looking at her with a horrid expression on his face. God, she hated drunks like that! Quickly Maria continued her journey.

She was the first of the performers to arrive at school and found Mrs Davy snapping at the caretaker over the positioning of the lights: 'We're supposed to be illuminating the performers, Mr Rush, not the audience. Ah, Maria, pop up on the stage, would you? Get in your position so that Mr Rush can train his lights on you, there's a good girl.'

Maria climbed the stairs at the side of the stage and took up her position, staring out at the sea of chairs that would soon be filled. Her heart was beating hard now and a faint nausea was swimming in her chest, which was not helped by the choking smell from the newly polished floor of the school hall. As the beam from the stage lights met her eyes Maria was momentarily blinded and realised that she would not be able to see the audience as she sang, which was probably a good thing.

'No, not that bright, Mr Rush! Just the spotlight there, and the others aimed at the backing curtains where I have clearly marked them.'

The caretaker shook his head in annoyance and Maria suppressed a giggle. She liked Mrs Davy. A lot of the kids thought she was a snob just because she spoke nicely, but Maria thought she was a real lady. There was always a copy of *The Times* in her basket, and she called everybody by their proper name. Mrs Davy tutted and mounted the stage, moving Maria over to the left and muttering, 'Stupid man.' Then, louder, 'Try now, Mr Rush, the yellow and red just here.' When the caretaker had finally positioned the lights correctly Mrs Davy whispered, 'At last!'

The other performers began to drift in sometime after six and a burble of excited chatter and laughter filled the hall. Mrs Davy went through Maria's song with her one last time: 'You take the breath there, Maria, just after the C sharp. If you can remember to do that, you'll be fine.'

'I'm nervous, Miss,' Maria confessed.

'I'm sure you are, my dear. If it's any consolation, so am I.'

'What, you get scared?' Maria's eyes widened with disbelief.

'Oh, all the time,' said Mrs Davy, sorting her sheet music into the correct order. 'You never stop feeling scared, Maria, you just learn to hide it better as you get older. Is your mother coming to see you this evening?'

'No, Miss, she's working.'

'I see.' Mrs Davy could hardly keep the disappointment out of her voice. She felt very sorry for a lot of these children, especially the clever ones who worked hard like Maria. She understood that money was tight, but still. She had grown inordinately fond of this plump little girl with the voice of an angel, and smiled at her warmly. She knew in her heart that Maria had a real gift. With her voice, she could go on to university and study music.

'I shall be right here, keeping time on the piano, rooting for you. Break a leg, as they say.'

A group of boys had grown very noisy and Mrs Davy went over to remonstrate with them. 'If you cannot control yourselves, you will not take part in the concert! Is that clear?'

At that point the first members of the audience began to drift in and take their seats, waving excitedly at their children and giving them the thumbs up. Mary had said that Nan might come and watch so Maria scanned the audience but couldn't see her. She wasn't bothered really. There wasn't much love lost between them.

By 6.30 the room was full and people were standing at the back of the hall because all of the seats were taken. Maria took her place at the side of the stage and counted down through the songs and instrumental pieces until it came to her turn. She was seventh, the penultimate act of the evening, just before the finale. The top spot, Mrs Davy had called it.

When it was her turn she walked slowly up the stage steps, trying to breathe steadily, in through her nostrils and slowly out through her mouth, just like Mrs Davy had taught her. The opening bars of her song began and Maria's mind went a complete blank. Any memory of the lyric had left her head completely. All she was aware of were the hundreds of people watching her, even though the stage lights meant that she couldn't see their faces. She looked towards Mrs Davy at the piano, who smiled, nodded, and mouthed the opening words: 'As long as he needs me . . .'

They came out of Maria's mouth automatically, without her having to think about it, and as the first verse progressed she could feel her voice expanding and becoming more confident until she was belting it out. She kept her eyes trained on Mrs Davy, who was mouthing along with her and nodding vigorously to indicate that Maria was doing well. The three minutes of the song flew by. She pulled off the tricky breath after the C sharp and followed it with a top A – an amazing sound that echoed through the hall. The next thing she knew people were on their feet, clapping and cheering.

Maria stood stunned before the appreciative audience. Even Mrs Davy jumped to her feet and clapped. Maria looked to the side of the stage where her friends and fellow performers stood, to find them cheering and smiling at her too. She stayed on stage for the finale and only afterwards, when Mrs Davy lost all composure and kissed her, did she realise just what she had achieved.

Children and parents hung around the school hall chatting until the caretaker began noisily stacking the chairs, to indicate that he wanted to close up and go home. Although he was obviously annoyed, Maria wanted to stay just a little bit longer, to soak up all the praise and accolades. She had been a resounding success!

In a daze and high on triumph, Maria went out of the school gates with three of her friends and they wandered through the light summer evening towards their homes. The sound of music drifted out of open pub doors and passing cars, and the girls giggled feverishly when a group of boys walked past and gave them the eye. The excited chatter focused mostly on how brilliant Maria had been, and how funny it was when Alan Green dropped his recorder halfway through his piece and Mrs Davy looked like she was going to have a fit.

Maria was halfway home and in the high street before she remembered she had left her precious sheet music in the girls' toilets. As she chatted with her mates, she could see a drunken Michael Potts leering at her, drinking a can of Special Brew and smoking a rotten old roll-up. Ignoring him and the others standing in a small group outside the bookie's, she told her friends she had to go back. Despite them telling her not to worry, that the music would still be there in the morning, Maria got into a panic, scared that the caretaker or cleaners would chuck it out.

'I can't lose it, Mrs Davy bought it for me specially. I'll see you tomorrow at school.'

She ran back and was relieved to find that the lights in the hall were still on and the main doors stood open. There wasn't a soul about, not that she could see anyway, but Maria felt that she was being closely watched. A strange sensation ran through her.

She looked around quickly and saw no one, but it was odd, she could feel a presence. She sprinted up the corridor to the girls' loo, pushed open the door and felt relief wash over her as she spied her sheet music on the windowsill above the row of sinks. She stuffed her music back into her bag, gave a silent prayer of thanks and squeezed her rabbit's foot in her top pocket. It was old and worn now and the claws were sharp where the fur had rubbed away. It had certainly brought her luck tonight.

As she made her way back down the corridor she heard a door slam and made her way quickly to the main school porch where a disembodied voice made her jump by saying, 'Quite the little star, aren't we, dearie?'

As he dragged her back into the hallway, he whispered into her ear, 'Keep looking straight ahead and don't try to turn round, sweetie.'

His voice was rasping and croaky, and his breath stank of tobacco. Maria could hardly breathe. An arm was wrapped tightly around her throat, and she felt something sharp piercing through her blouse and hurting her ribs. He had a knife or another sharp object.

Frozen with fear, but forced to put one foot in front of the other, Maria found herself back in the girls' toilet where she was pushed face first against the wall. Her arms had been raised, outstretched above her head, and she held on to the windowsill, her fingers turning blood red under the pressure. His hand was on the back of her head, squashing her face against the cream-painted wall. Her mouth was open. Paint was peeling off the wall and bits of it were swirling round with the boiled sweet she was still sucking from earlier.

She felt his other hand reaching up inside her school kilt, grabbing her bottom and pinching and squeezing it so hard that it really hurt. He wrenched at her knickers and she felt them tear at the side seams and start to slip down her legs. In an instant, she was naked beneath her skirt and he was forcing her legs apart. She felt her fanny being explored and squeezed, and then the sudden thrust of thick sausage-like fingers entering her vagina. After what seemed like an eternity and with the man moaning and speaking low-pitched disgusting words in her ear, he took his fingers out.

He grabbed her by the hair, warning her once more not to turn round or look at him. She flailed her arms in panic and in an instant reached into her blouse pocket for her lucky rabbit's foot. She grasped it and threw her hand back, knowing she had scratched it on something soft. She heard a sharp intake of breath. She had angered her attacker.

He pulled her roughly away from the sill and forced her down on her stomach on the stone floor. She spat out the sweet. Her arms smashed to the ground and her hand released the rabbit's foot. She watched from the corner of her eye as it flew across the floor and spun round like a spinning top until it finally stopped. She felt her knees being grazed as he roughly put her into position. Within seconds, he was raping her from behind, pushing deeper and harder, and all she could do was clench her teeth and close her eyes tight. She felt powerful blows on her bottom in time with his thrusts but he never spoke, he just got faster and harder. She felt blood flow from her mouth where she had bitten her tongue, but all she could think to do was pray and hope he would finish soon.

He withdrew himself, but her ordeal was not yet over. She felt him open her bottom and clenched the cheeks together in a vain attempt to stop him. She felt her head being lifted from the stone floor by her hair, and as she let out a scream, he smashed it to the floor and Maria blacked out.

Mrs Davy was cross with herself. She'd left her precious *Times* in the staff room and she recalled that there were a few clues left unsolved on the crossword. After all the euphoria of the evening she'd rushed out to get away from the few parents still grumbling that their children had not had bigger parts in the concert, explaining that she'd see them at the next open evening, and headed for the school car park. She had got a mile down the road in her Triumph when she remembered the paper. It was her favourite way of winding down in the evening. She loved the challenge of the crossword. It tired her out as she sipped her gin and tonic and put her feet up while Bach played softly in the background on her new music system. Mrs Davy sighed heavily, knowing she would have to go back.

As she entered the main porch, she could have sworn she heard footsteps inside the school. She ignored them and made her way to the staff room. As

187

she passed the girls' toilets, she noticed the door stood slightly ajar, and with her nose wrinkled, went over to pull it closed. She wished they'd never moved the loos inside when they'd added the new extension to the old rundown building. The smell of urine always wafted out, but the authorities had insisted on an inside lavatory for the girls.

As she started to pull the door towards her, Mrs Davy heard a faint voice say, 'Help me . . . please help me.'

Chapter Twelve

He was startled by the sound of a car pulling into the new parking spaces behind the girls' toilets. Bollocks! he thought as he looked at the back of the unconscious girl's head, his throbbing penis still tightly locked up her arse. He was in heaven, lost in satisfaction, and now he had been rudely interrupted. How dare they interfere with his special time, his precious moments of pleasure? He hesitated momentarily, wondering if he had time to finish the girl off. This wasn't the way it was supposed to be, he was nowhere near to climax, but some instinct for self-preservation made him heave himself up from the floor, hastily fasten his trousers and head for the door. He faltered again, bitterly regretting what he was going to miss, what he'd had planned for her, but he heard another noise and knew he had to get away, leaving his prize behind.

He cut through the school hall and out through the fire door at the rear; he quickly lost himself in the school shrubbery and then slowly sauntered on to the street. His heartbeat quickened. It was all he could do not to break into a run. Calm, he told himself, nice and easy, don't arouse suspicion. He made his way past the main gates at the front and did his best to look casual as he walked the hundred and fifty yards along Columbia Road to the Royal Oak. Inside he nodded at some familiar faces as he made his way to the gents' where he locked himself in a cubicle and sniffed his fingers. He could smell her but he knew that the smell alone would not be enough to bring him off. He needed more. He needed to go back and finish what he'd started, but he knew he couldn't. It was too risky, even for him.

He felt furious and frustrated and not a little afraid. He'd always taken every precaution, made sure he was somewhere he would not be interrupted and have plenty of time to finish his work. He grabbed a handful of hard toilet paper and wiped the blood and shit from around his groin, scratching at it furiously with the hard nasty sheets of paper before flushing it away. Then he ran his hands under the tap for several minutes, cursing the lack of soap, and splashed his face until his breathing had slowed and most of the muck had been rinsed away. He took out his old linen handkerchief then, not noticing the lollipop inside it fall to the floor, and wiped the excess water from his face.

Sniffing loudly, he composed himself and went out in the main bar area. He made his way up to the bar and fished in his trouser pocket for change. 'Usual, love?' asked the barmaid. His hands shook as he counted out the money. Beads of sweat still hung on his brow; his breath came in shallow bursts. The barmaid eyed him strangely as she set down the pint mug on the bar towel.

'Don't usually see you in here on a week night.' She handed him back his change.

'No, I've been working late, thought I'd just stop for a quick one before I went home.' His voice was higher than usual and had a faint tremor in it.

'You all right? You look a bit flushed,' the woman persisted.

'Yeah, bit of back trouble. Bloody pills from the quack make me hot, but nothing serious,' he replied, unable to meet her eye.

'Oh, right you are.' From the other end of the bar a group of men were calling noisily for refills. 'Yeah, all right, keep your hair on, I'm coming.'

He knew the place would be crawling with coppers soon but decided to take a minute to think. He sat himself down at a small table to one side of the open door. A plan was already hatching. He would swill this drink back, head home, scrub up, then return to the scene where he'd left his beautiful plump-arsed girlie, mingling with the others, offering help where he could, being the perfect friendly neighbour and local.

In the girls' toilets Mrs Davy knelt down next to Maria and took in the scene: the knickers ripped off and lying by the basins, her skirt hitched up around her waist, body twisted so that her bottom stuck up while her face lay flat against the floor tiles. The smell was overwhelming and Mrs Davy opened her mouth wider to try and combat the odour of shit and blood.

'What on earth . . .? Maria, can you hear me?'

The girl was drifting in and out of consciousness. Her face, already swollen and disfigured, was covered in blood from her nose, which had been smashed against the floor. She could manage only a low moan in response.

'Maria, can you sit up?' The girl tried to move herself but slumped back to the floor. 'I'm going to the school office to call an ambulance, I'll be two minutes!' Mrs Davy exclaimed. 'Christ, who did this to you?'

Maria, a tortured look on her face, turned slightly and said, 'Don't leave me, Miss,' in a tiny frightened voice.

'I promise you, I'm coming back, but you must go to hospital. Do you understand, Maria?'

The girl began to sob and reached out her bloodied hand to Mrs Davy who bit back her own tears and stroked her hair. 'Two minutes, darling. Two minutes, I promise.' Her little star pupil, such a lovely girl . . . she could hardly take it in.

She ran like the wind down the corridor to the school office only to find it locked. She rattled the handle furiously and shouted out for the caretaker: 'Mr Rush!' When no reply came she ran to the staff room where there was another phone and with a trembling hand dialled 999. 'Come on, come on!' she muttered. When an answer finally came she told the operator that she needed both the police and an ambulance. The operator didn't seem to grasp her sense of urgency until Mrs Davy bellowed down the phone, 'A little girl has been raped!'

As soon as she had finished instructing the operator that the emergency services were to come to the back entrance of Columbia Row Primary, she ran back to the toilets where Maria lay curled up on the floor, sobbing. Somehow she had got herself into a foetal position. Her bare bottom half was exposed and Mrs Davy could see that the child had not only been raped but buggered as well. That smell again . . . it was sickening. Blood oozed from the wound around Maria's anus, and together with shit flowed freely on to the concrete floor.

Mrs Davy removed her expensive lime green cashmere cardigan and placed it against the tear, in an attempt to stem the flow of blood and lend Maria some kind of decency. 'They're on their way, Maria, just a few minutes.' She looked down at the hand that held the cloth against the girl's body and saw it change colour as the blood soaked right through. She remained calm, smoothing the child's hair and trying to soothe her by repeating, 'It's OK, it's OK.'

Within five minutes, the wailing of sirens was audible and Mrs Davy hugged Maria reassuringly before leaving her briefly to go to the back entrance and show the emergency services the way. An ambulance and two police cars screeched to a halt. Within moments officers and ambulance crew were swarming all over the school.

PC Watson was among the on-duty officers and took a brief statement from Mrs Davy who was clearly in shock. A female PC was kneeling down next to Maria, her face white at the sight of the little girl's injuries. As the paramedics carried out their preliminary examination she was asking her softly, 'What's your address, love? Are your mum and dad at home?'

The WPC was new to the job and glanced up at Watson with tears in her eyes. 'Who could do this, Ian?' He could hardly believe it had happened again. It was only two days since the discovery of Wayne Williams's body. The attacker was getting cocky now, taunting them.

A crowd of onlookers had gathered to see what all the commotion was about. They saw Maria Foster being carried out on a stretcher and loaded into the back of an ambulance after about twenty minutes. The usual suspects all stood watching the scene. A few men from the local pub had gathered at the school gate. Michael Potts was vocal in leading a chorus of disapproving boos as the police emerged, and a gang of local lads from the nearby secondary school, still in uniform, were hovering, smoking fags and shouting out, 'Useless plods! Stupid coppers!'

Mrs Davy climbed in after the stretcher, but as she looked into the crowd she noticed the caretaker. 'Mr Rush!' she called. 'Mr Rush, I need to speak with you when I get in tomorrow.' And then she clambered inside and held on to Maria's hand for the duration of the short journey to the Queen Elizabeth Children's Hospital. PC Watson followed on behind in a patrol car.

The group of angry men held their ground. Michael Potts couldn't resist the temptation to corner the young WPC as she emerged from the school and went towards her patrol car, parked on the main road.

'What's a nice little girl like you doing in a place like this in uniform, eh? Out for a bit of fun?' He leaned casually on the car's bonnet and she stared at him in sheer disgust.

'If you don't mind, sir?'

''Ere, lads! George . . . Harry . . . look what I've got 'ere.'

The others merely waved him off. George looked at Harry and smirked. 'He's a right twat, that Michael. Suppose he's been boozing all day again. What's 'appened here then? I can't get in to lock up.'

Harry stared straight ahead. 'Not sure, mate. I was having a swift half when I heard all the commotion and made me way over. Think it's another murder.'

*

Upon arrival at the hospital, Maria was whisked off for examination and Mrs Davy and PC Watson stood by the coffee machine, going over the exact timings, trying to jog her memory about anything she might have seen before discovering Maria. There had been so many comings and goings with the concert, and so many people who didn't usually go near the school hanging around tonight, that it was hard to get a clear picture of events leading up to the attack.

'It had been such a wonderful evening, Officer,' said the teacher sadly, when suddenly another thought occurred to her.

'Christ, the mother! Someone needs to tell Maria's mother.' Mrs Davy's hands flew to her face.

'It's OK. Two of our officers are already on their way.'

She looked up into Watson's kind face and fought the urge to throw herself into his arms. Despite her own strong character and common sense, she felt shocked to the core.

'I can't believe it's happened in our school. I mean, aren't you supposed to be safe at school? Maria did so well tonight, such a little star. We had our end-of-term concert and she completely stole the show. Such a promising little girl . . . and now this. It's not often a child shows so much promise, not in this community anyway, but Maria is different.'

'We've got some fairly strong leads now. Hopefully it won't be long before we make an arrest.'

Watson tried to offer what consolation he could, knowing deep inside that although they had gained some ground, they were still a long way from making an arrest. This man was pure evil, but also incredibly clever. He stalked his prey, struck when he was safe, and continued to play cat and mouse with them. Woodhouse, however, had asked to see Watson just before this last attack had been reported. He knew his guv had something, but there had been no time for their informal chat. He would speak to the DCI about it when he made his full report.

'You know who it is?' the teacher queried.

'My DCI thinks he's getting close. It's got to be a local, someone who won't arouse suspicion. People would have noticed a stranger hanging around, especially in a neighbourhood like this.'

'God, that's even worse, somebody the children know and trust. How awful.' Mrs Davy gazed into the distance. Watson eyed her thoughtfully. She was young, smart and attractive. Her clothes had an air of class, and she held herself well.

'You're not from round here, are you?' he asked.

'Does it show?' She allowed herself a little smile. 'I grew up on a farm in Hampshire.' Anticipating his next question she said, 'I came here because I was bored with country life and thought I could make a difference . . . but actually I don't think I've made any at all. Inner-city kids are tough nuts to crack.

'At my last school I taught a brilliant boy, a music

scholar who won a place at a cathedral school, but his parents had to turn it down because they couldn't afford the uniform. Now he goes to a comp where they don't even study music. Heartbreaking, really.'

'Don't give up. These kids need people like you, to show them another way.' Watson coloured slightly at his own words.

'You're very kind . . .' But before she could continue a commotion broke out at the reception desk and they turned to see Maria's mother and grandmother demanding to see her.

'My little girl, my baby . . . please, where is she? I want to see her now,' Mary was saying.

Watson walked over to the desk and took the women to one side, gently explaining that they would be able to see Maria as soon as the doctors had finished their examination.

'But I want to see her now! I'm her mother, she needs me!' Mary, having only finished her shift an hour and a half before, was back in the same hospital, this time in her slippers.

'You can't stop us! We're family, we've got a right to see our own flesh and blood,' Lizzie was threatening the receptionist, who was trying to calm her without much success. The two women were a study in contrasts: Mary all tears and vulnerability, her mother dry-eyed and determined.

Lizzie had vowed before she left the house tonight that this was one battle she was going to win, and no baby-faced police officer nor high and mighty receptionist was going to tell her what she could or couldn't do.

Watson managed to quiet them with the promise that he'd see if he could hurry things along, and in the meantime he introduced Mrs Davy as the lady who had found Maria. Mary thanked her tearfully and begged for information.

'Was she badly hurt? Did he interfere with her? She'll be all right, won't she?'

Mrs Davy did her best to calm the mother, knowing it wasn't wise to say too much. 'Well, obviously she was in a state of shock when I found her, but by the time we arrived at the hospital she had come round a bit. Maria was really magnificent in the concert earlier this evening. You would have been so proud,' she said, trying to comfort Mary.

Lizzie harrumphed loudly and shot her an evil look. 'Fucking concert!'

Mrs Davy shot her an evil look right back. She wasn't afraid of the likes of Lizzie Foster; she knew that type only too well. The teacher stood her ground and turned back to Mary. 'Maria's a wonderfully talented little girl, and a pleasure to teach. She has a rare musical gift and I'm proud to be her teacher.'

Lizzie opened her mouth to say something scathing then but Mary implored, 'Mum, leave it!'

'Well, what sort of a teacher are you, leaving kids on their own at school anyway?' Lizzie got in.

'I can assure you that every single child had left the premises before I went home. I don't know why Maria went back. I definitely saw her leave with two other girls before I left the building.' Mrs Davy could feel herself growing rigid with outrage.

'Yeah, right.' Lizzie's mouth tightened in disgust and Mrs Davy was bracing herself for a sharp reply when PC Watson came back and informed Mary that Maria had now been placed in a side ward off the main children's ward, if they wanted to follow the nurse waiting for them by the desk.

Mary made to follow the nurse then turned back, quickly hugging Mrs Davy and saying tearfully, 'I'm sorry, I know you did your best, and I know you like my Maria.'

Mrs Davy just nodded, afraid to speak in case she cried herself. Mary had to break into a little run to catch up with the nurse and Lizzie, already marching purposefully along the corridor. Mrs Davy watched them go and stood in silence with Watson for a few moments before gathering together her things.

'If you wait a minute, I can get one of our officers to take you back to the school to get your car,' he offered.

'It's OK. I'll take a taxi, thank you.'

'If you're sure. It must have been quite a shock for you too?'

Mrs Davy just nodded. He was right, she was

trembling inside. That gin and tonic would be a very large one tonight.

'Quite sure, thanks.' She hesitated before asking him, 'You will catch this man, won't you?'

'We're doing our very best.' Silently they shook hands and then Mrs Davy made her way out of the hospital towards the taxi rank.

Lizzie went into the room ahead of Mary and immediately took the big chair by the side of her bed. The sight of Maria's swollen and bruised face made Mary give a little cry.

'Oh, my baby, what has he done to you?' She placed her arms gently around her daughter, afraid of hurting her.

Maria began to cry. 'Oh, Mum! I'm sorry, Mummy, I just went back to get my music. I know I shouldn't have . . . I'm so sorry.'

Mary cuddled her daughter gently and the pair of them cried and comforted each other. As she hugged her daughter, Mary was filled with guilt. She should have been there, she should have gone. Lizzie's face was impassive, betraying nothing.

The nurse looked on awkwardly before gently saying to Mary, 'Miss Foster, when you're ready, the doctor would like a word.'

Mary nodded and followed her out of the room and into an office where a middle-aged black doctor was waiting to speak with her. A handsome man, his tight, wiry hair flecked with grey, she recognised him as one of the paediatric consultants, apparently one of the hospital's best. That was something, at least.

He took her arm gently and led her to a chair where he motioned for her to sit before he took her through the list of injuries that Maria had sustained.

'Miss Foster, your daughter has suffered a terrible ordeal. We have managed to clean her up, but she will need surgery in the next couple of hours. She's on a drip at the moment, and will shortly need some blood. Do you know your own blood group? We try to encourage relatives to donate when necessary. She's weak at the moment, but with surgery we hope to put her back together. Her rectum has been split in several places, and her hymen is broken.' He paused to look at Mary. 'Do you understand, Miss Foster?'

She nodded, gulping with the shock.

'We haven't been able to ascertain the full extent of Maria's injuries as she is obviously in great pain and we want to wait until she is under sedation. I need your signature to proceed, Miss Foster.'

He placed a form in front of Mary which she signed without even reading it. She was still lost in the realisation that her child had been brutally violated, that she was no longer a virgin. The doctor interrupted her thoughts.

'I want to get her into theatre as soon as possible. If you'd like to wait, I will talk to you again as soon as I know more. The nurse will take you off to check your blood type and to take some if it's a match. Don't worry, Miss Foster, Maria will be OK.'

Mary felt herself lifted from the chair. She steadied herself and managed a bleak smile at the doctor. The nurse, who had been standing quietly by, took her by the arm. 'This way, Miss Foster.' And she gently led Mary out of the office and down the corridor to the pathology lab. As Mary walked slowly, her arm held tight by the nurse, she stopped and looked over her shoulder.

'My baby! I want to see my baby before they operate.'

'Its OK, Miss Foster, there's plenty of time. Her gran is with her, and I promise to take you back as soon as we're finished.' The nurse led her back down the corridor and the pair of them disappeared around a corner.

Back in Maria's room, Lizzie picked up her granddaughter's hand and studied the grazes on her knuckles. She'd never felt close to this child, always thought she was different, but she was a Foster nonetheless, and tonight Lizzie felt strangely proud of her.

Maria had shown she was a survivor. 'Right then, young lady, stop crying for a minute,' said Lizzie briskly, 'I want you to tell me everything you can remember.'

'Oh, Nan, please! I'm tired and I want to go to

sleep. Everything 'urts, can't it wait? I've just done all this with that police lady.'

'Never mind them, this is me. Now, talk.'

As Maria whispered quietly into Lizzie's ear, the nurse came in and gave her a sedative shot. A new drip was being placed in her hand and the nurse told Lizzie, 'She's got to be prepared for surgery now. She's going to get drowsy in a few minutes.'

'I know,' Lizzie replied harshly. 'I'll stay with 'er till her mum gets here and then I'll leave.'

Mary walked back into the side ward, looking ashen-faced. She laughed grimly. 'My blood don't match hers. I can't even get that right.'

Lizzie kissed her grand-daughter's head. 'You're a brave girl, Maria. Mummy's here now. I'll see you later.' She made her way over to the door and in a no-nonsense fashion whispered to her daughter, 'I've got things to do, Mary. I'll call Monica and 'ave her come and sit with ya.'

With that she was off down the corridor and heading towards the hospital exit.

Chapter Thirteen

Grace had taken to grinding her teeth at night and woke every morning with aching jaws. The murders and assaults were always uppermost in her mind and as she slowly tortured herself, trying to find answers, she got little or no sleep. Now she fished around in the medicine drawer for soluble Disprin with baby Luke on one hip and Adam tugging at her dressing gown, saying he was hungry. It was a good sign. He had been off his food since the attack but was finally beginning to get his appetite back.

Usually John brought her a cup of tea before he left for work, but he must have gone at the crack of dawn to try and get as much done as he could in the morning, so that he could leave for home early. There had been no tea in the caddy and Adam had tried to help himself to cereal, only to knock the box of Rice Krispies all over the floor. Grace was treading on them, grinding them into the floor under her tired feet.

Her thoughts returned to her troubling dreams which had been filled with horrendous visions where she couldn't prevent what was happening to the children, and all she could hear were the echoes of their screams. Tiredness making her snappy, she shouted at Adam to wait in the front room while she tidied up the kitchen floor and sorted out a tin of stewed apple for the baby. This was very out of character for her. She was usually calm and considered in her dealings with her children, but the endless sleepless nights had robbed her of her patience.

Adam slunk away, looking tearful, and Grace's irritation was replaced by a wave of guilt. With her head spinning, she prayed silently for God to give her strength as the two Disprin dissolved in a glass. She knocked back the cloudy mixture then put the baby in his highchair while she opened the tin for his breakfast.

'Mummy, the telly's broke!' Adam called from the living room, and Grace bit back a scream. It was obviously going to be one of those mornings.

She went in to see what was up. With a watery smile, she said softly, 'It's all right, babe, it's just not plugged in. Hang on a sec.'

Grace bent over the telly, knocking the aerial off the top. Christ, she wished John was here! The others were all going to arrive in a few minutes and she was still in her dressing gown, feeling like she couldn't cope and looking like something the cat had dragged in.

'Half-nine at your place,' Lizzie had stated, without asking if it suited her. If the circumstances had been different she might have told Lizzie to shove it, but in the wake of the news of the attack on Maria she had just nodded in agreement, too down and miserable to argue.

The doorbell rang as Grace found something on the telly for Adam to watch. Through the window she could see her sister standing on the doorstep. She opened the door to find Gillian looking bright as a button, in full make-up and wearing a sundress and a pair of cork wedges, brand new by the looks of it.

'Christ, look at the state of you!' Gillian said, walking into the hallway and dropping her bags on the floor.

'I overslept.'

'Right, I'll get the kettle on,' said Gillian, as she went into the kitchen. 'Oh, my God! What's happened in here then? It looks like World War III.'

'Adam tried to help himself to breakfast and had an accident.' Grace pushed the hair out of her face, feeling clammy.

'Go upstairs and sort yourself out, I'll clear this lot up.'

'But the kids haven't had their breakfast yet, Gill.'

'I'll do that, you go and get some clothes on.'

Grace didn't need telling twice and gratefully went into the bathroom where she ran a cool shower for herself and stepped under it.

As the water poured over her, her mind returned once again to recent events. Over and over she traced the web of her suspicions and fears. Darkness filled her waking moments as well as her nightmares. Downstairs she could hear the doorbell ring again and the sound of Potty's voice drifting upward.

Grace could do without this. She was sorry for what had happened to Maria, desperately sorry, and as for poor Wayne . . . well, Sue's agony didn't bear thinking about. But she wouldn't stand for another vigilante attack, not after the one they'd got so horribly wrong. She knew what was coming, knew from the commanding tone of Lizzie's voice that she wanted action once more, and Grace realised she was expected to go along with things, no matter what her scruples.

She closed her eyes and allowed the water to run over her face, lost in that moment. Noise filtered up the stairs and she knew she would not be able to indulge herself much longer. She covered herself with an expensive white bath sheet, sat on the towel box and gazed out of the open frosted window.

Grace had popped round to Sue's the previous day, to drop TJ off, and found Lizzie there with murder in her eyes. Sue sat silently at her kitchen table while Lizzie assured her, 'We're gonna sort this, Sue, we really are.'

Another ring of the doorbell and more voices; she'd have to get dressed and go downstairs, she couldn't hide up here all day. Grace slipped into a simple sundress and combed her wet hair. She looked into the mirror then at her make-up bag but thought, Sod it, I'm not in the mood. She underestimated her own natural beauty. With fresh skin and dark hair drying in the heat, the others were still no match for her.

In the kitchen Gillian, Nanny Parks and Potty were drinking tea and smoking. Gillian had a fag in one hand and a spoon for feeding the baby in the other. Grace didn't bother with the niceties but angrily opened the back door. 'Can you at least let some air in if you're going to smoke around the baby?' The other three looked at each other and raised their eyebrows.

'She didn't sleep well last night, did you, Sis?' Gillian offered by way of explanation, and glanced at her sister.

'Who can in this bloody heat?' asked Grace. 'Morning, Mum. Morning, Potty.' She scooped the baby out of the highchair and stood with him by the back door to get some fresh air. 'God, those fucking cancer sticks will put you all in an early grave!'

'I got a job, Grace, at the hospital. Head of Housekeeping said I could cover Mary's shifts while she is off, and do general holiday and sickness cover until a permanent job comes up. I gotta alternate between Queen's and Bonner Road Chest Hospital, but they're minutes away from other each so it's great.'

Potty looked pleased with herself, like a child

asking a parent to admire their painting. She was wearing a clean cheesecloth shirt and denim shorts, her hair tied up in a bushy ponytail.

'You lot will all be in Bonner Road if you keep lighting up, one after the other,' said Grace sarcastically, then added, 'Anyway, I'm pleased for you, love, I really am. How's Lucy?'

Potty shifted uneasily in her chair and twisted a lock of curly hair around her finger. 'Not bad. She was as high as a kite last week, despite that bloody Kelly and all her shenanigans, but when we heard about Maria it knocked the wind out of her sails. Even getting her picture in the paper didn't lift her spirits. She was quite low yesterday, took herself off to bed early – unheard of – you know what a cow she is about bed-time usually.

'Anyway, I did my first shift yesterday and they're a nice bunch of girls to work with. The money will come in handy and you get to see all sorts of comings and goings in a hospital, you really do. Some of those doctors are really dishy!'

Grace smiled to herself. Good for you, Potty, she thought. Find yourself a nice boyfriend and get shot of that useless lump you're married to.

'Did you see Mary?' Nanny Parks asked.

'Maria's on a different ward to the one I've been cleaning, I've been up in the baby unit on the top floor. Got a baby in there with mumps . . . fuck me, his little balls are huge, and he's very sickly.

210

Everyone's talking about Maria, though, you can imagine. Old Bill in and out all day.

'I did see Mary briefly, to get her keys so I could go round to the flat and collect some of her clothes and toiletries she'll need while she's staying with Maria. I put a few bits in the fridge and opened the windows to let some air in.'

A loud clunking sound approached and they all turned to the door to see Adam dragging his Fisher Price garage along the floor until he came to rest by Nanny Parks. 'See my garage, Nanny? It's got a lift.'

'Ooohh, isn't that lovely?' cooed Iris. 'How many cars have you got, darlin'?'

'A red one, a blue one and a fire engine.' Adam demonstrated the wind-up lift which took cars to the top floor then ejected them to slide down the ramp. For a few moments the women looked on smiling, lost in his touching innocence, marvelling at his recovery. Every time he successfully got a car to slide down the ramp, the women all gave a big clap and called him a clever boy. He was smiling broadly, revelling in all the love and attention, when the doorbell rang again. Grace moved to put baby Luke on the living-room floor and gave him a large plastic Tupperware shape ball to play with. With a furrowed brow he tried to put the square piece in the round hole and she moved over to the kitchen counter to top up her cup of coffee.

'That'll be Lizzie,' said Nanny Parks, jumping up to answer the door.

'Oh, goody, can't wait,' said Grace as she took another glug of coffee.

'Try and keep a civil tongue in your head, young lady,' Nanny Parks warned her daughter. 'She's shattered after what happened to Maria.'

From the kitchen Grace could hear them talking in whispers by the front door. She knew her mum was right and she knew she was being ratty, but she felt so irritable and tired, and the Disprin hadn't worked. Her head was still thumping. A minute later they came into the kitchen where Gillian jumped up and offered Lizzie her seat.

She doesn't look shattered, thought Grace, she's loving this. For a few minutes they exchanged desultory small talk about the heat and the flies and having to pour Jeyes Fluid down the drains to keep the smell away, then Lizzie launched into her tale of woe. It was all 'my Maria this' and 'my Maria that'. Like you give a shit, thought Grace.

'And I've had a long chat with Sue,' Lizzie carried on. 'She won't be coming today as she's got a lot on, getting ready for the funeral tomorrow, but she agrees.'

Agrees with what? thought Grace. She sensed what was coming and dreaded it.

'Anyway, I've just come from the police station

and that Woodhouse bloke isn't even there. I wanted to get as much information as I could before seeing you all. He's supposed to be in charge of this case, and the desk sergeant tells me he's over near the City, somewhere around Shoreditch, dealing with an armed robbery. Fucking disgrace!' Lizzie thundered. 'No wonder people have to sort things out for themselves round here.'

Grace bit her tongue. The others were hanging on Lizzie's every word, nodding eagerly and agreeing with her.

'Well, at least we know who it is now,' said Lizzie with finality. The others all nodded. They must be privy to some information that had been kept from Grace.

'Who?' she asked.

'George,' said Gillian, looking at her sister sheepishly.

'George who?' Grace didn't have a clue.

'The caretaker. Slimy George, the kids all call him.' Lizzie looked Grace right in the eye, challenging her to disagree.

'How can you be so sure?' She tried to keep her voice level but anger was rising inside her.

'It all adds up, doesn't it? Gotta be a local, gotta be someone the kids know, gotta be someone who knows the area.' Lizzie paused. 'Any chance of a cup of tea, Grace?'

She filled the kettle and flicked the switch before

saying, 'But that could be anyone really, how do you know it's him?'

'It's not just that, Grace,' said Potty. 'That Kelly who found Wayne told my Lucy that George was hanging around outside Sue's the morning Wayne went missing.'

'So?' Grace spooned three spoons of loose tea into the pot and reached for the glass bottle of Camp coffee for herself.

'Well, he told Terry Williams that he'd been in the betting office all day, but obviously he couldn't have been if that Kelly and her mates saw him. And another thing,' Lizzie added triumphantly, 'he didn't turn up for crib at the Birdcage on Monday night, and according to Harry he never misses it.'

'And that's your evidence! Kelly and the other girls told me they'd seen Harry the Horse too. Are you gonna sort him out as well? For God's sake, you can't just decide someone's guilty. You have to have proof.'

'Grace!' Nanny Parks shot her daughter a murderous look.

Gillian intervened then, trying to play peacemaker. 'There's more. It's all sorts of things . . . like the smell, for a start. Both Lucy and Maria mentioned the smell of this bloke. Fags and drink and sweat and a kind of chemical smell, like the stuff they use on the floors at school. And he's a big bloke, a heavy bloke. They both said he weighed a ton. George is a big bloke, you can't deny that.'

Grace quickly replied, 'So is Harry, and if we're talking big men, so is your bloody Michael, Potty!'

She just stared at Grace with her mouth open, shocked at the very idea that someone might accuse Michael of trying to harm his step-daughter. Grace reacted to that look. 'I'm sorry, Potty, but can't you see how hysterical all this is getting?'

Gillian tried some logical persuasion then. 'Look, you've got to remember that George is a bit of a weirdo, a real loner. I mean, nobody I know has ever been in his house and he must have lived around here for, well, nigh on thirty years. Has anyone ever seen that wife he had? Rumour has it she just disappeared, and her elderly mum too.'

'It's bloody strange, whatever way you look at it,' Nanny Parks chipped in, but Grace stayed silent. She couldn't be bothered to argue, they'd obviously made their minds up.

She poured the water into the teapot, stirred it and placed it on the kitchen table. She cupped her steaming mug of black coffee and sipped at it slowly, turning her head away and concentrating on the strong liquid. She needed it! Finally, after a long pause, she spoke to them all.

'Well, you can do what you like, but I don't want my John involved.' The other women just looked at each other and an uncomfortable silence descended once again on the kitchen until Grace continued speaking. 'Five minutes away down that road, in a hospital bed, lies an innocent retarded boy who was beaten to a pulp because you thought *you* could take the law into your own hands. Well, I say enough. You've got to let the police catch this man.' She surveyed the others in the faint hope that they might relent. 'What does Sue think?'

'She wants fucking blood, obviously.' Lizzie stared back at her, hard-faced.

'That wasn't the impression I got yesterday,' Grace retorted, standing her ground.

'Well, you were only there for five minutes. I was with her most of the day, and I'm telling you she wants revenge. Old Bill keep saying they're making progress with their enquiries, but it's obvious they haven't a clue. That detective chief inspector isn't even down at the nick! That young bloke Watson is all right, but he's just a constable and doesn't know anything. No, I'm sorry, Grace, but if we wait for the police we'll be waiting for ever. If we don't do anything, he'll be at it again. We've already got two dead and three badly injured – one of them your own son, I might add,' Lizzie said with a flourish of her hand.

Grace turned on her furiously. 'Don't you think I'm aware of that! My boy's in there now, afraid of men, and still can't take a piss without crying.' A crash came from the front room then and a wail broke the tension between the quarrelling women. Luke had tried to touch Adam's garage and knocked all the cars down.

216

'OK, that's enough, the pair of you!' Nanny Parks pulled herself up to her full five foot one and made a gesture with her hands to indicate that they should stop. Both Grace and Lizzie fell silent.

Gillian cleared her throat nervously before saying, 'Look, there's no point tearing each other apart over this, we've got to pull together. We can't let him set us at each other's throat.'

Potty nodded vigorously and added, 'You're right, Gill. Divide and rule, that's what he wants.'

The rest of the women looked at her, wondering where she'd learned a phrase like that. Her recent transformation was making her unrecognisable.

Grace wandered out of the back door and into the garden. She went round pulling up a few weeds that were appearing in the dry earth between her bedding plants. Inside she could hear the conversation returning to more normal matters. Gillian was telling Potty that she'd picked her wedges up in the sale at Dolcis. Grace's head was still spinning. She really didn't know what to think. What if they were right? What if it really was George and they didn't do anything? What if it was Harry or, even worse, what if it was Michael? The killer could strike again. Every single woman in that kitchen had been personally affected by him. Even Gillian had had that false alarm over Jamie the day that Wayne was killed.

Grace wished again that John was there. She felt powerless in the face of such strong feeling. Finally she wandered back into the kitchen where they all looked up at her expectantly.

'I honestly don't know what to think, but I'll talk to John. I'm not promising anything, though, so don't include us in your plans. Let's just get Wayne's funeral out of the way first.'

'Oh, that reminds me,' said Potty, jumping to her feet, 'I'm supposed to be picking the flowers up. I'm sending a wreath from Mary, 'cos obviously she won't be going.'

'Good girl, Potty,' said Nanny Parks.

'Do you think Maria is up to visitors yet?' asked Gillian.

'I don't see why not,' said Potty. 'Besides, I expect Mary would appreciate a bit of support.'

'Wanna come with me, Grace?' offered Gillian.

Grace shook her head. She wanted to be on her own.

Chapter Fourteen

Grace had another bad night. After only an hour or two of sleep she woke up to a grey sky and a fine drizzle. She had been haunted by those terrifying dreams again and the sheets clung wetly to her. There were beads of sweat on her face and a cold damp shiver running over her body. At least God wasn't mocking them with another beautiful sunny day for the funeral. She closed her eyes and breathed in the cool air that filtered through the open window. Was all this real? How she wished it was only part of her nightmare, but she knew only too well that today they were burying a child.

Downstairs she could hear John already up with the kids and the faint background noise of the telly. She turned to look at the clock and saw that it was already nine; panic shot through her and she leaped out of bed, fastening her dressing gown around her as she went down the stairs.

She had arranged to collect TJ from Sue's at half-nine so that Nanny Parks could look after the younger children at Grace's while the rest of them went to the funeral. It had been a joint decision not to take the younger kids. Sue was still mindless with grief; anger was next on her list of emotions, followed close behind by devastation and pain. The kids didn't need to be around that. Nanny Parks loved a funeral, saying they had more soul than weddings, but had agreed to baby-sit on this occasion as Grace and John had not been able to go to Chantal's while Adam was still so ill.

'Why didn't you wake me up?' Grace asked John, lifting the kettle to check how much water it had in it then flicking the switch. She felt angry with him already and she'd only just got up.

'Because you've been tossing and turning all night, I thought I'd let you lie in for a bit,' he said, trying to spoon some breakfast mush into Luke, who was refusing to eat in his high chair.

John glanced at Grace appealingly. Ignoring his puppy dog eyes, she answered curtly, 'I'm supposed to be picking TJ up from Sue's in half an hour, I'll never make it on time.' She dropped a teabag into a mug and reached for the sugar bowl, tutting when she saw two ants scurry out from beneath it.

'Don't worry about it, Grace, I'll go. The kids have been fed. All you've got to do is have a bath and get dressed. Anyway, the funeral isn't till twelve, there's no rush. Come on, son, just another couple of spoonfuls and you can get down.' John held the teaspoon against Luke's firmly pursed lips.

Grace rubbed her eyes and wondered how she was going to get through the day ahead. This was one of those moments when she wished Gillian was here to nag and tease her into getting on with it.

From the front room she could suddenly hear Adam laughing at *Wacky Races* and stopped to listen to the unfamiliar sound. 'He's laughing, John,' she said, amazement in her voice.

'I know. Bloody brilliant, isn't it?' he said, winking at his wife. For the first few days after the attack on Adam they'd wondered if he would ever speak again and now here he was, chortling away. Grace wondered if in time he might be able to forget the attack on him completely, then quickly banished the idea as wishful thinking. Adam still had a long way to go. Hopefully further surgery would correct the physical damage he'd endured, but the mental scars would take a lot more healing.

Anger surged through her body then as it always did when she allowed herself to think of the attack on her baby. Luke continued to protest noisily from his highchair.

'I've had enough of this,' said John jokingly, putting down the bowl and spoon. 'Right then, son, you're a free man,' he said, hoisting the baby out of the chair and placing him on the floor where he quickly crawled away into the front room to see what his brother was up to.

Grace turned away to stare out of the kitchen window, just in time to catch next-door's cat crapping on her bedding plants. She rapped noisily on the window and the startled cat leaped over the fence. 'Bloody cat! I wish he'd crap in his own garden.'

John came up behind her and wrapped his arms around her, enfolding her in a strong embrace and kissing the side of her neck. A flicker of desire ran through Grace and she turned to kiss him deeply. It had been a while. He responded hungrily and within moments they were necking like a pair of teenagers by the kitchen sink, John's hands reaching under her dressing gown and pulling her tight towards him.

'I've missed you, babe,' he whispered.

Grace felt herself go limp with the strength of his embrace and her mind flashed back to their love-making in the past. John was the most wonderful, gentle man. His height and muscular build always made her feel every inch a woman, but he was soft, considerate and tender with Grace. She was his queen.

'I've missed you too. It's just that I . . .'

He silenced her with another kiss. 'It's all right, Gracie, I know. Now come on, get yourself ready, I'll go and get TJ and your mum.'

Reluctantly she let him go, wrapping her arms around herself, trying to hold on to the feeling, watching as he gathered up his keys and wallet. A wave of love for her husband washed over her. John was everything to Grace. He'd shown her how love could be, how it should be, had made her feel safe again and able to trust a man – something she'd thought she'd never be able to do after Uncle Gary.

As he reached the front door Grace called his name and he turned to see what she wanted. She smiled and said, 'I love you, John.'

He smiled back and said, 'See you in about half an hour,' winking as he closed the door softly behind him.

Grace sniffed the air and caught the smell of her husband lingering close to her. It was warm and familiar, protective and reassuring.

The drizzle kept up all morning and by quarter to twelve the streets were slick with a fine veil of moisture. Cloud protected them from the scorching sun but it was still desperately humid. People stood around talking on the pavements, waiting for the funeral procession to pass. It felt like the end of the world. The sky hung low with blackened clouds as the morning dragged towards noon. Faint rumbling could be heard in the distance and drizzle fell then stopped as abruptly as it had started. People huddled together and hung their heads low.

Finally, as the two black horses turned the corner on to Columbia Road a hush descended and shopkeepers came out and stood in their doorways in reverential silence, waiting for another small coffin to pass by. All activity ceased. Everything seemed to move in slow motion. So large in life, such a force of nature, Wayne was now just another young life snuffed out before its time, his body consigned to a short white coffin covered with lilies. Sobs broke the silence. In the distance a fire engine could be heard, but right now, in this East End street, time stood still.

Behind the horses and the coffin, two large black cars carried the mourners, the first bearing Sue, Terry and their two girls, at Sue's insistence. The second car carried both sets of grandparents. Sue kept her head bowed, her handkerchief covering her face, as Terry gazed solemnly out of the window of the car, occasionally nodding his thanks to the people lining the streets, some of them familiar to him, some he'd never seen before. Outside the betting shop Harry the Horse wept openly, punters occasionally resting a hand on his shoulder for consolation. The men shuffled about, too angry and irritated to stand still, and an air of anger hung over them.

Having discovered little Adam's body all those weeks ago, Harry felt more personally involved than many. He couldn't quite quash the thought that had he gone out to the bins earlier he might have caught the attacker dumping Adam there. The thought still haunted him. He felt he bore some responsibility in the matter. Though logically it made no sense at all, as a community elder, watching these children being picked off one by one, his sense of personal failure ran deep. He knew in his bones that the person responsible for all this was someone familiar to him.

He didn't know why he felt this, but a strong conviction that it was true washed over him as he saw Wayne's coffin go past. Someone close by was doing this, some stalking creature who forced a smile and only pretended to belong.

Mourners arrived at Christ Church to find a sea of flowers and wreaths laid out in the churchyard, their bright colours at odds with the drab, rain-streaked brick and concrete surroundings. As it grew warmer, steam lifted off the pavement and swirled over Wayne's wreaths and flowers. A white satin pillow on which to rest his head, a silver key to the gates of heaven, and a flower-patterned book to chart his journey lay amongst the many floral tributes, and kids' drawings and messages were pinned up on the gates before the church. Children huddled next to their mothers, some in school uniform, holding the claret and blue scarves and flags of Wayne's beloved West Ham.

The church was packed to the rafters. Grace and John squeezed into a pew halfway down the aisle behind Gillian, Jamie and Benny and took their seats as the organ softly played 'God Be in My Head'. As she quickly scanned the crowd, Grace's heart went out to Robbo and Michelle as they cried, not just for Wayne, but for little Chantal too. Potty sat with Lucy and Lucy's aunt, who Grace only saw rarely. Just in front of them were the empty seats that Sue and Terry would shortly occupy, along with the pall-bearers and the girls.

Grace gazed towards the altar and felt a flicker of annoyance to see Lizzie Foster sitting right at the front in the first pew on the other side, usually reserved for immediate family only. That bloody woman! She was decked out in full black regalia, including a mantilla like some Mafia widow, turning occasionally to greet people behind her and thank them for coming.

Candles flickered softly and mourners spoke in hushed whispers, waiting for the funeral procession. A collective throat-clearing signified its arrival and people shifted uncomfortably in their seats, turning to see the pall-bearers, Paul Foster, Terry's brother Aaron Williams, and two other men Grace didn't know, make their way down the aisle, holding Wayne's coffin aloft, its canopy of lilies leaving a strong scent in its wake. Sue and Terry followed behind, holding their daughters' hands, with the grandparents bringing up the rear.

When they had all taken their seats in the two front pews, the Vicar shuffled some papers for a moment or two to get his composure before beginning: ' "*The Grace and Mercy of our Lord Jesus Christ be with you.*" ' The congregation responded, ' "*And also with you.*" ' Sue let out one small sharp cry and Grace craned her neck to see Terry slide his arm around her. ' "*Our faith in God consoles us in*

226

our sorrow and he is with us now. Let us draw near to him with confidence, and in a few moments of silence confess to him our human weakness and our failings." ' Grace asked God to forgive her for her resentful feelings towards Lizzie and prayed that he would help her be of whatever service she could to those around her. She thanked him for sparing Adam's life and asked that he keep Wayne safe in heaven, in the hope that he would meet up with Chantal there and tell her that they all loved and missed her. Grace's faith allowed her to believe that the two children were together now, out of harm and free from pain.

The congregation stood then for the hymn 'Abide With Me'. Grace was grateful when it ended and she could sit down again. After a summer spent in flip-flops her feet felt crammed into her high heels, swollen and puffy, and she was grateful to take the weight off them. Her black tailored suit was now a little too big, due to the weight she had lost, but she still looked elegant and sophisticated even in mourning.

Looking around her, she spied many familiar faces, some she hadn't seen for years. It was extraordinary how a funeral brought everybody out of the woodwork, she thought, unable to decide if this was a mark of genuine respect or just plain nosiness. Looking again at the two unknown pall-bearers and trying to think who they were, she decided they must be from Sue's Hoxton family.

The Vicar then announced that Wayne's best friend would give a reading, and Grace's heart beat faster as she watched her nephew Jamie make his way down the aisle and mount the steps to the lectern. She crossed her fingers and made a wish that he wouldn't stumble over his words. He stood there silently for a few moments, suddenly such a tiny figure in a black suit that looked two sizes too big, and Grace held her breath, willing him to hold it together.

Finally he took a gulp of air and began to recite, '"*All things bright and beautiful, all creatures great and small, all things wise and wonderful, the Lord God gave them all.*"' He faltered then and cleared his throat. Grace's heart went out to him and she turned her head to see John wipe a tear from his cheek. She squeezed his hand and they both watched Jamie who breathed deeply again and finished the spoken hymn. It had been familiar to both boys. They sang it often in school and it was the boys' favourite.

Then Jamie pulled a scrap of paper from his over-sized pocket and started to read aloud from it. 'Wayne was my mate, and he looked after me. He taught me how to ride my bike and how to play better football. He was like a big brother, and I'm sorry . . .'

A huge sob filled his throat then and he couldn't force it down. Sorrow had him in its grip again and he looked out into the sea of faces for guidance from his mum.

Gillian left her pew and went up to him. He wiped

his face with the back of his hand and flushed with relief to see her approach. She held out her hand and he descended the steps from the lectern. His head bowed, he held his mum's hand tightly all the way back down the aisle.

Grace felt a swelling of pride for her nephew and reached her hand forward to squeeze her sister's arm as she sat back down with a distraught Jamie by her side. Gillian turned and gave her a tearful smile and for a moment they held each other's gaze as if to say, Didn't he do well?

They all stood for the next hymn, which passed in a blur for Grace as she gazed at Wayne's coffin before the altar, feeling so sad for Sue and Terry but so grateful that it wasn't her Adam lying there when it so easily could have been. As they sat back down an audible sobbing from the front pew competed with the Vicar's voice as he led the congregation in their prayers. Everyone joined in and a murmur of prayer filled the church.

The swelling voices said 'Amen' again before the Vicar finished the service by looking towards Wayne's heartbroken parents. His gaze on Sue and Terry, he spoke directly to them when he said, ' "*Almighty God, Father of all mercies and giver of all comfort: Deal graciously, we pray thee, with those who mourn, that casting every care on thee, they may know the consolation of thy love; through Jesus Christ our Lord.*" '

The vicar signalled to the pall-bearers to take up the coffin once more and bear it to the burial ground. As the service ended, people began to speak quietly while they waited for Sue and Terry to walk out after the coffin. The pews slowly emptied behind them, Grace and John moving slowly in the awkward procession, jammed in with the other mourners trying to get out through the narrow church doors.

Grace looked around her at all the people, smiling at some she recognised, thinking it incredible that so many had turned out to say goodbye to a boy who had not been entirely popular in the neighbourhood. Most of them had had a window broken or a car stripped by Wayne and might have thought he needed to be taught a lesson or two, but no one had wanted this.

As they filed past the final pews at the back of the church, a stocky figure dressed in scruffy work clothes caught her eye. He stood out a bit with his casual dress and dirty unkempt look. His head was bent, revealing greasy dishevelled hair. She couldn't work out who it was. Finally he looked up, catching her eye, and she recognised him. It was George. A cold shiver ran through her then and she looked quickly away. But she couldn't stop herself from looking again and he was still staring at her – and in that moment she *knew*. She had seen that same look before, that predatory gaze and the steeliness beneath the faint smile.

230

Suddenly unsteady and with her tummy turning over, Grace gulped back a wave of sickness. She thought she might faint. She grabbed John's arm roughly, to steady herself, and as he turned to her and mouthed softly, 'You all right?' she replied, 'No.'

And still George held her gaze, sensing her discomfort, mocking her. In a flash, she saw Adam, frightened and in pain, struggling with the nasty, smelly man. She felt her face grow hot, her knuckles clench into fists. As soon as they got outside she motioned John to one side.

'What's up, babe?' he asked, full of concern.

'It's him, that George! He did it, John, I know he did.' Grace's voice was trembling with barely suppressed rage. 'Don't ask me how, just trust me, I know it.'

'How come?'

'From the way he looked at me in there . . . something about him . . . God, I don't know how, John, but I just know it's him! He hurt our boy, and he murdered Wayne and Chantal. You've got to believe me!' Desperation filled her voice. 'What are we going to do?' She looked nervously around, hoping that nobody had overheard.

John looked at his wife intently, trying to decide. Her instincts were usually bang on, but this was hardly the time or the place.

Grace scanned the crowd and tried to calm down, hoping no one would notice her manic air. She squeezed her legs together. Fear always made her want to pee. Her whole body was trembling. Her mind raced. There were other things too that made her certain . . . Her heart was suddenly thumping so loudly she thought everyone would hear it.

'We're not going to do anything yet, just hold your horses.' John pulled her to him, held her tight and stroked her hair. 'Easy, baby, easy.'

'I can't go to the wake, John. I'm shaking like a leaf.' Grace held out her hand and watched it tremble. The drizzle was building into a fine rain and umbrellas were going up all around them. John fished in his pocket for some cash and pressed some notes into his wife's hand. 'Grab a cab and wait for me at home. I'll go for one drink then join you back at the house in about an hour. Try not to get yourself in too much of a state.' He held her face in his hands and kissed her, keeping eye contact all the time. 'All right?'

She nodded but still looked anxiously at the door of the church, waiting for *him* to come out.

'He's in a church, a house of God . . . the bastard! I want to kill him, John, really I do. I just want to kill him.' Grace's eyes were brimming with tears now.

'Just go. I'll see you in a bit, all right?'

She nodded and made her way down the stone steps and out on to Brick Lane. Gillian came up to John and said, 'What was all that about? Where's she gone?'

'Not now, Gill, later.'

Surprisingly, Grace got a cab easily. A few had lined the street, sensing the opportunity for a fare, and while other mourners milled about, talking and looking at the flowers, Grace made a quick exit. She sat back in her seat, trying to breathe deeply and regain her composure. The taxi driver made small talk and Grace nodded here and there, pretending she was listening, but all she wanted now was the comfort of her home and her babies in her arms. Something pure that would take away that image of George Rush now fixed for ever in her mind: his slight smirk and those dark yellow teeth.

Chapter Fifteen

Grace and John sat up half the night, going over it all. It wasn't that he didn't believe her, he knew only too well what she had suffered in the past, but he needed to understand what made her so sure. He was worried that she was too emotionally involved because of Adam and the others.

'Look, babe, everyone's upset about this, especially as our kids have been affected, but maybe we'd be better off speaking to Old Bill first?'

'And tell them what, John? He's got this funny look in his eyes? That I can feel it in my bones? Oh, yeah, I'm sure they'll arrest him for that. Look, I can't put it into words. I just *know*.'

Grace drained her glass of Bacardi and Coke and stood up to get another. She wasn't much of a drinker but tonight her nerves were feeling shot through and she needed something to steady them. Looking deep into the bottom of her glass, through the tears in her eyes, she continued speaking, dry-mouthed as she relived her worst childhood memories.

'For years all my senses were tuned in to Gary. The way he looked at me, his behaviour, the way he strutted about because he controlled not only me, but everyone. That atmosphere he created when he walked into a room. Always the big I am, with his money and his jokes. Tickling me, and Gill . . . making my mum roar with laughter. I was the only one who knew what was really going on, and that's too much for a kid to handle.'

She poured the Coke slowly into her glass, and a slight smile crossed her face as she remembered Gary was dead.

'Besides, if we tell the police we think it's George and then he gets a pasting, it's a bit of a giveaway, isn't it? I'm surprised they haven't come knocking already about Steven Archer.' John was stung by her comment; she could see him flinch. Feeling remorseful, she sat back down next to him on the sofa and said, 'I'm sorry, love, that was uncalled for. But this time it's different, John, I know it.'

'No, you're right in a way . . . about young Steven. It's why I'm feeling dodgy about this. We got it wrong last time, and you were so upset, Grace. I don't want anything else coming between us, we've been through enough.'

'I know, love, I know.'

'Look, if you can be as sure as is humanly possible that it was him who hurt our boy then I personally will rip the fucker limb from limb. But my first duty is to protect you and our kids, and I can't do that from a cell in Pentonville.'

Grace could see that she wasn't getting far and

decided to change tack. She needed John to take the lead.

'Did you speak to Terry at the wake?' she asked.

He nodded.

'What did he say?'

'Not much. Pretty dignified really. You could see he was fit to murder, but he was holding it together for Sue. She just sat in a corner, not speaking to anybody. There were crowds of people standing around her but you could see she wasn't really there. She ain't half lost a lot of weight. Terry says he can't get her to eat a crumb. It's all a terrible strain on them, Gracie. They seemed to be together, but apart too. I can't imagine what this is going to do to the pair of them.'

'Mmm,' murmured Grace, remembering how she had felt in the immediate aftermath of the attack on Adam. She knew in her heart how easy it was for a grieving couple to blame each other, to look in vain to the other to take away the pain and guilt, and knew that a lot of marriages failed for far less. 'I'll see her tomorrow when I take TJ back. Michelle spent an afternoon with her the other day, couldn't get a word out of her apparently.'

'Yeah, but I'm sure it helps, just being with someone who knows what you're going through. Michelle has been incredible. I don't know where she gets her strength. Maybe it'll help Sue through.'

John looked terribly sad and Grace gazed at him,

236

wondering if he spoke to his mates about what had happened to them, and if any of them really understood. It must be lonely being a bloke, she thought. Women were always talking, but men, well, they just held it all inside, didn't they? She stroked the dark hair back off his forehead and gazed into his handsome face, gently massaging the back of his neck.

His eyes closed with pleasure and his dark eyelashes looked even darker against his pale skin. He sighed and reached across for her, pulling her towards him. They stayed like that for a while, saying nothing, Grace massaging his neck and shoulders as John's breathing became slow and regular, his eyes still closed.

'You tired?' she asked.

He opened one eye and, smiling slightly, said, 'A bit. Not that tired, though.'

With her other hand Grace stroked his thigh, squeezing it.

'Shall we go up?' he asked, excited at the prospect after so long.

'No, let's stay down here. TJ's a light sleeper, don't want to wake him.'

Grace moved across the sofa and straddled her husband's lap, taking his face in her hands and slowly kissing its familiar contours. She heard him draw in his breath sharply and thought he was going to sneeze, but when she pulled back she could see the tears begin to roll down his face, her tenderness pushing him to the brink. A surge of love shot through her then for this big, beautiful man who now appeared so vulnerable, almost lost. She pulled him down on the sofa and lay on top of him, gently moving against his body.

That night they made love like they hadn't for years; not since the kids had come along anyway. It was a role reversal of kinds as Grace took the lead and tenderly made love to her husband, taking her time. A new, stronger bond of passion was forged. Afterwards they lay in each other's arms on the sofa, a gentle breeze caressing their naked bodies, their legs entwined.

'We'll be all right, John, really we will.'

'I don't know, Gracie . . . I don't know if I can handle this any more. I'm scared. I look at Adam and realise how close we came to losing him and the fear just rips through me. I feel out of control, helpless.'

Not in all the ten years she'd known him had he ever made an admission of this kind. Her John never showed fear.

'We can handle anything together, John, because we've got each other. We just have to stay strong.'

He buried his face in her breasts and fell asleep like that. The next thing Grace knew, sunshine was streaming through the window and Adam was standing by the sofa saying, 'Mummy, why hasn't Daddy got his pyjamas on?'

*

DCI Woodhouse tiptoed round the broken glass and rubble from where the explosives had ripped their way through the vault beneath the Old Street branch of the Royal Bank of Scotland. The whole place was a bloody mess, and this was the last thing he needed right now. Initial estimates placed the bank's losses at somewhere around two and a half million pounds in cash and valuables. Empty safety deposit boxes littered the floor along with discarded pieces of silver and jewellery deemed not worthy of such a grand theft.

The gang, five men in balaclavas bearing sawn-off shotguns, had entered the building through the back entrance around 6 p.m. the previous evening, while the last of the cashiers were totalling the amounts in their tills and placing them in the vault before going home. It was an audacious robbery, carried out in the middle of rush hour, but who was to know? Everything had seemed just as normal from the outside.

The bank had closed for business at 4.30 p.m., its plate-glass doors locked and blinds drawn. Only those staff remaining inside the building, who had been gagged and tied up and made to lie on the floor, had any notion what was taking place. One of the cashiers, a woman in her forties, a single mother of three, had gone for the emergency button beside her till early on in the raid, before they had all been made to lie on the floor, and had paid for her bravery with her life as two shotgun cartridges were released into her chest.

Now there were ambulances on the scene, and shocked members of staff were being wrapped in blankets despite the heat. An innocent employee had been killed and someone needed to tell the family. The DCI was short-staffed enough, what with the attacks on his own patch. Now he was well and truly bogged down. As if he didn't have enough going on back in Bethnal Green and Dalston, his superiors had insisted that he supervise the preliminary enquiries into the robbery and the murder of the cashier as well.

In truth, he was on much surer ground with this sort of crime. His years in the force had given him an unparalleled knowledge of the criminal gangs who might undertake such a professional operation and he was able to issue a list of possible suspects to the investigating officers within half an hour of arriving on the scene. This had been a carefully organised raid, not the work of chancers or amateurs, and he guessed the shooting had been carried out in error. These gangs usually liked to keep their work clean; it was money they were after, not blood.

He had dragged Watson along with him, for company as much as anything else but also to delegate a list of tasks that needed to be tackled back at Bethnal Green while he was held up at Old Street.

'Make sure all the evidence sheets are back in the

right files, won't you? Those two rookie investigators from West End Central will have papers strewn everywhere. You could see they didn't have a clue when they arrived yesterday. I need more experienced detectives, preferably trained men from Homicide, not these Work Experience teenagers they keep sending me.' Woodhouse was busy making notes as he issued his instructions to Watson. 'Any joy at the funeral yesterday?'

'Didn't make the service, sir, got held up by a burglary at the paint factory. Little thugs, I imagine, didn't really get away with much, just a few sprayers and that. I did manage to poke my head in at the wake later.'

'And?'

'Well, there's a definite undercurrent of hostility and impatience. People want to know why we haven't made an arrest yet.' Watson shuffled his feet uncomfortably, hoping his words didn't sound like a criticism.

'Can't blame them really, but without going round and taking bootprints from every man within a two-square-mile radius there's not much else to go on.' Woodhouse broke away to shout at a young officer, 'Can you not touch those boxes until they've been dusted?'

'I did overhear an interesting snippet though, sir. It might be nothing, but I thought anything was worth paying attention to at the moment. You never know, even in idle gossip there may be some truth.'

'Oh, yes, lad, everything's worth considering.'

'That Foster woman, grandmother of Chantal and Maria . . . I overheard her talking to Lucy Potts's mother about George Rush, the caretaker at Columbia Row Primary School.'

'Yes, Mrs Foster. Quite a leading light that one. You've got to watch her, though, a right sharp piece of work. I knew her old man. The Fosters aren't exactly squeaky clean. I went through Rush's statement about the night Maria was attacked but he has a rock-solid alibi from the barmaid at the Royal Oak. It seems he may have just popped out for a pint straight after the concert and before locking up, leaving the way clear for the attacker to get into the school. Certainly that teacher said he was nowhere to be found when she arrived. What were they saying about him anyway?'

'That he's a weirdo and a pervert, the usual stuff.'

'You mean, the usual stuff people say about all single men? You have to be careful with hearsay, Watson.'

'Yes, sir.'

'But when you get back there this afternoon, you might want to go walkabout . . . see what the word on the street is. And get down to that betting office again; see what the word is there too. I don't trust that Jew Harry either.'

Watson took his leave after this and Woodhouse stared after him, wondering.

After her first decent night's sleep in weeks, Grace felt clear-headed and resolute. Their lovemaking had restored her to her usual level-headedness and the morning found her brisk and businesslike. She felt glowing, contented and loved. John had taken the van to work, so she loaded the Jag with the three kids and some food she had bought to take over to Sue's. TJ had been an angel but he wanted his mummy after twenty-four hours away from her. 'Not long now, sweetheart, we're on our way home.'

'Can we get an ice lolly, Mummy?' asked Adam.

'After lunch, babe,' said Grace, checking in her rear-view mirror as she pulled away from the curb.

'Oh, that's ages!'

'Adam, make sure TJ doesn't play with the windows, will you?' she said, fishing in her bag for a few barley sugars that she knew were knocking around. 'Here you go, you can have two each.' She reached back and handed the crumpled bag to him.

'But I want an ice lolly, it's hot!' Adam threw the paper bag of barley sugars on to the floor.

'You keep that up and you won't get anything. I mean it, Adam.'

She and John had spoken about this the night before, the way they had to start laying down a few rules with their eldest again. Their talk had resolved a lot of issues, and deep inside Grace knew that despite everything she and John were more solid now than ever before. Since the attack they had taken a softly, softly approach with Adam, letting him watch telly all day. Like any kid, he was beginning to push his luck now and they had decided it was time to start getting him back to normal.

The traffic inched along painfully and Grace lowered her window to poke her head out and see if she could spot what was going on up ahead. A bus had broken down on the corner of Hackney Road and the cars trying to get past it were blocked by traffic coming the other way. Oh, great, she thought to herself.

She was stuck in traffic for fifteen minutes, and all the time she sat in the car she was thinking furiously. The attack on Chantal had been less than four weeks ago. Since then there had been attacks on Adam, Lucy, Wayne and now Maria. Five kids in four weeks, two of them dead. It beggared belief.

When the car finally pulled up outside Sue's house after the painful journey there was relief all round. It would have been quicker to walk.

'Can we play in the paddling pool, Mummy?' asked Adam.

'We'll see,' said Grace, struggling with the baby, TJ and bags of shopping. 'Adam, wait a minute! Don't get out that side, get out on to the pavement, love.'

As she tried to organise herself, Potty came bounding down the street looking like a pools winner. She was dressed in a pretty yellow sundress and her hair was pinned up. She looked the best she had in years.

'You're looking lovely, girl, what's his name?' Grace said with a wink.

'Oh, you're such a tease, Grace. Here, give me those bags, you look like you're going to topple over with that lot.'

'You coming in to see Sue?'

'Yeah. What happened to you yesterday? Didn't see you in the pub after the church.'

'I'll tell you in a minute, when old flappy ears isn't about.' Grace nodded in Adam's direction.

'Got ya.' The front door was open and they pushed it back to let TJ, who was struggling to get inside, be the first through. Grace could see Sue stand up from the kitchen table and walk towards her son. She scooped him into her arms and squeezed him to her. 'Hello, my little soldier. You been a good boy for Auntie Grace?'

'Good as gold,' she said. 'How you feeling, love?'

'Oh, you know.' Sue smiled weakly. 'I don't really know what I feel at the moment. I'm still numb from it all. Come in, come in, I'll put the kettle on.'

'Terry not about?' Potty asked.

'No, he took the girls to school and then went on to work. I think it's doing his head in sitting around

245

all day so I told him to go in. The sooner we try and get back to normal, the better. Besides, the girls have got the dress rehearsal for their end-of-term play tomorrow. I didn't want them to miss it. Mind you don't slip on the floor, it's still a bit wet.'

Sue seemed a bit erratic, moving rapidly from one topic to another. The mop and bucket were propped up against the kitchen door and there was a strong smell of bleach in the air, as if she'd been trying to clean all the bad feeling away from the grieving household. Potty and Grace followed her into the kitchen, with Adam behind her. Lizzie Foster was sitting at the table with a cup and saucer in front of her. She always refused to drink out of a mug, she was of that generation who always had to have bone china.

'Morning, where's my mum?' said Grace without any visible warmth.

'Grace, Potty.' Lizzie nodded a greeting. 'Your mum's took some bits to the cleaners.' Lizzie was speaking to Grace but couldn't help noticing Potty. 'Blimey, girl, you're looking good.'

'I'm feeling good, Lizzie. This job's the best thing that ever happened to me. Gets me out of that bloody flat, instead of looking at him drinking all day. Head of Housekeeping has put me in Bonner Road Chest Hospital for the next week, and I prefer it over there. Breaks my heart looking at all those sick kiddies at Queen's. You know half of them are never coming out of there, poor little sods.

'Anyway, I decided to spend a bit of money on myself, for a change. Now I know I've got some money coming in each week, it don't half make a difference. First time I've bought something in years that hasn't come off the sale rail,' said Potty, lifting up the skirts of her sundress with pride.

'You look gorgeous, love, you really do,' said Grace before Lizzie had the chance to make any sarcastic remark.

'Right then, tea,' said Sue. Grace noticed that her clothes were hanging loose on her. She must have lost half a stone in a week. She went and put her arms around Sue and said, 'I'm sorry I didn't come to the wake.'

Sue could feel herself go limp and tearful, as she did at the slightest display of emotion or kindness, and moved Grace gently away from her.

'Didn't you? I didn't even notice.'

'I did,' said Lizzie pointedly. She and Grace held each other's gaze for a moment.

'I won't bother with an answer to that just yet, Lizzie, there's something we need to discuss urgently.' Grace took a deep breath then and admitted, 'You were right, it is him. It's George.'

Potty and Sue turned to look at her in surprise. Lizzie just smiled thinly.

'You've changed your tune,' she said quietly.

'When I'm wrong, I say it. Put my hand up and admit it. Don't fit me up, Lizzie. You were wrong about Steven, but I didn't speak up strongly enough. This time, I know. Did you see him there yesterday, sitting at the back?'

The other women shook their heads.

'Well, I did. And I'm telling you, he did it.'

'This is all a bit of a turnaround, if you don't mind me saying so?' Potty coloured slightly as she spoke. The last person she wanted to offend was Grace, but she had been shaken by the violence of the attack on Steven and was scared at the thought of yet another mistaken reprisal.

'I was walking out of the church with John and I saw George sitting in the last pew at the back of the church. He had this awful leer on his face . . . a look I've seen before, believe me. I don't know, I can't really explain, but I felt it in my body then . . . it shot right through me. I felt sick and shaky, and I just *knew*.'

Grace lowered herself into a chair with a sigh. The other women all nodded at her. They didn't need convincing about the power of intuition, as women they relied on it, but what exactly made Grace so sure? She still had no real evidence, nothing concrete.

'I think you might be letting your imagination run away with you, Grace.' Potty looked away from her as she said it, nervous of Grace's reaction.

'What do ya mean, you've seen it before? Seen what?' said Lizzie astutely.

248

Grace looked down at the floor, wringing the folds of her skirt between her hands.

'Looking at the facts,' said Lizzie, as if to distance herself from Grace's display of emotion, 'we know that whoever done this is a heavy bloke. Both Lucy and Maria say he was a big fucker, nearly crushed them. He's a drinker and a smoker and has that smell of industrial cleaner about him. Both girls said he whiffed of that polish they use on the floors at school.' She held a finger up to itemise each fact as she reeled them off. 'Plus George is a single bloke, and for the thirty odd years I've known him he's never had a woman. And . . .' she paused for emphasis '. . . he never turned up for crib on Monday night, the night he got hold of our Maria. I only found that out by chance when I was chatting to Harry. He was moaning that he didn't have enough players to make up a team, and I said, why not? And he said, because bloody George didn't turn up. Never misses a game usually.'

'Doesn't mean he did it, though,' said Potty, 'I mean, it could have just been because he had to lock up after the concert.' For the first time she looked visibly afraid, like it was all becoming a bit too real. Talking about someone's possible guilt and giving them a beating was exciting, but close to the actual event her nerves were beginning to fail her.

'What do you think, Sue?' Grace asked softly.

Sue put her head in her hands and rubbed her eyes.

She looked shattered. 'I don't know what to think any more, to be honest, but my Terry did say that George had told him he'd been in the betting office when Kelly Gobber reckons he was out here. Mind you, she also said she'd seen Harry, but he was in the betting office all day so I don't know who to believe.'

'It's not Harry,' said Grace quietly, 'it's George. You must listen, I know I'm right. Please let me finish what I have to say.'

She raised her head from staring at the floor and looked past all of them, travelling far away in her mind, back into the past – and describing it all for them.

'I was dressed in my school uniform, I'd just got back from the last day of the spring term. Uncle Gary's car was there so I was pleased someone was in, otherwise I'd have had to go and find my dad down one of the pubs. I hated the thought of that. All the smoke and beer and men shouting. Mum was out shopping with Gill for her new stuff for school. You know Gill, she always hated hand-me-downs!' Grace forced a smile, but her eyes were dark with memories. 'I trusted him, but he was different that day. He grabbed me and kissed me. My books fell to the floor, and my school pencil box broke and all the pens and pencils spilled out over the floor as it dropped from my bag. I tried to push him away, to make him stop, but he was too strong, too big . . . and he was Uncle Gary.

'He raped me that day, and he continued to rape me on a regular basis for the next three years. It only stopped when he was killed, when he crashed his car, pissed out of his head, and I was so *glad*. I never told anyone, not even Gill, although she seems to have known something was going on. But it would have killed Mum to hear it.'

A silence fell over the kitchen then. Lizzie looked at the floor, deep in thought, while Sue and Potty sat speechless.

Grace continued, 'Don't you see what I'm trying to say? Ever since that happened to me, I've felt I can tell when someone's dodgy. I sense a difference in a man when he looks at me that way . . . the way George looked at me from the pew in that church yesterday. These men have a way of getting inside your head. Just one look and they can cause a sickness deep inside that makes you feel faint, ill, frightened . . . and the worst part is that no one will believe you, that much I do know.

'We've got to act, and act fast. Men like that don't just go away. I don't know what would have happened if Gary had lived, maybe I'd have killed him myself, but that's over with. Now George is here taunting me instead. Worse still, he's getting away with it! No one thinks it could possibly be someone like him. But we do, and I think it's time we did something. Before it's too late. Before he gets his filthy hands on someone else's kid.'

251

'Hear, hear!' agreed Lizzie. The two women caught each other's eye briefly and in that moment all their previous disagreements and hostility were forgotten. They were united. 'You're a brave and special girl, Gracie. I'm only sorry I didn't understand that before. No one else needs to know your secret, do they, girls?'

Sue and Potty mumbled their agreement, still in shock that someone so beautiful had experienced something so ugly.

Grace looked at Lizzie with new respect. She had as good as ordered the other two not to talk about this to Gill or Iris, respecting the decision Grace had made all those years ago. Besides, they had more urgent things to consider.

'My John is a bit all over the place at the moment but I know he'd be willing to pay George a visit, and I know Paul Foster wants to help,' Grace said, looking at the other women and waiting for their reaction.

'My Terry will be in there like a shot if I give him the green light, but I'm frightened he'll go too far and kill the nonce, the state he's in at the moment. But after what you've said, who gives a flying fuck? Last night when I went up I found him sitting on Wayne's bed, crying like a baby. He thinks it's all his fault, like he's let his family down by not protecting them. I keep telling him not to be stupid, that nobody could have prevented what happened to Wayne, but he wouldn't have it. Funny, isn't it? You see a bloke crying and it kind of makes you step back and pull yourself together.'

Sue lit a cigarette and inhaled deeply. Grace's mind went back to the night before and her thoughts about John. Women had their kids and each other, but blokes, well, they had nothing to fall back on really.

'I'm not sure Michael would be much help,' said Potty in an apologetic tone. She was right. He'd be a hindrance. Too drunk, too gobby, too sloppy by half. Grace felt a sudden wave of pity for her friend, being married to a useless lump like that. How lucky she was to have John.

Sue pulled TJ on to her lap and cuddled him hard, holding on as if he were a life preserver. Thank God she's got those other kids to keep her going, thought Grace.

'What we need is a bit more proof to convince the men,' said Lizzie. 'I suggest we keep our noses to the ground, sniff around, get some more hard facts. We need to be sure about his movements, check them all out with Harry and the barmaid at the Royal Oak. Then, if we can convince the men, we'll get it done properly this time.'

At that moment Gillian arrived, walking down the passageway into the kitchen carrying a loaf and a couple of pints of milk she'd picked up for Sue. The other women all nodded hello.

'Well, I'm ready if you are?' said Grace, looking round at all their faces.

'Ready for what?' asked her sister.

'Never mind that for a minute. Grab a cup of tea,' said Lizzie.

As they all sat at the table, Grace held her cup high. 'To Justice!' she said, and then everyone said in unison, 'To Justice!'

Chapter Sixteen

Everybody lay low for the next week. It had been decided that nothing was going to happen in a great hurry, not until they'd had a chance to watch George closely and make detailed plans, but happen it would. This wasn't going to be a quick wallop to some loud-mouth for saying something nasty, this was going to be a well-executed punishment which befitted his depraved crimes. Justice would then be served, the East End way.

Everyone was sick of the lack of progress by the police, who still had no one in the frame, and the tight-knit community was tired of having to function as best they could, knowing that a killer was still at large in their midst. Women took to keeping the children indoors, even though the long summer days were baking hot. No child was even allowed down to the sweet shop on their own, they had to be with an adult at all times. The streets and parks in the neighbourhood, usually thronged with children, were eerily quiet. People were angry at being forced to live this way, but powerless to do anything about it.

*

Grace's admission about her own suffering at the hands of Uncle Gary had united the women as never before, lit the touchpaper of their determination. Having confessed her secret shame to the others, she knew that she would have to come clean to her sister, and found this the most difficult disclosure of all.

Afterwards she knew she would never forget the look on her sister's face when she heard the truth. Gillian rushed to hold Grace, to say how sorry she was, and Grace felt the years of silence between them fall away. Gillian had a clearer view of her sister now, and almost hated herself for what she had previously believed about Gary and Grace's relationship. As a young girl she'd sensed something going on between her favourite uncle and her big sister – sensed that Grace was special to him in some way. The jealousy and spite she had harboured towards her sister then made her cringe with shame now. What a fool she had been to ever think that way! Gillian, feisty as ever, immediately wanted vengeance for Grace. She wanted Gary named and shamed, and the love she had hidden from her sister all these years poured out in her craving for retribution.

Grace, now more calm and contented in herself, was determined that Iris should never know the truth, despite Gillian's urging her to come clean. For days she went on at Grace to tell their mother, and wouldn't let it drop. She grew more furious and upset, and as the days went by more guilty that it had happened to Grace and not to her. 'Mum's gotta know, Gracie!' she thundered.

'But what good would that do? She idolises the memory of the bloody man, there's no point,' Grace reasoned.

'Why should she idolise a fucking animal who raped her own daughter? It's all wrong, Grace.'

'Maybe, but telling her the truth won't achieve anything. Mum is getting older now, Gill, she clings to her memories of the past. She's had enough to contend with lately, she would feel a complete failure as a mother if we told her about Gary. I love her too much to let that happen. No, let sleeping dogs lie, Gill. Besides, it's the here and now we gotta deal with. And we have to do it before that George gets his filthy hands on another kid.'

Gillian didn't disagree with that. The day after Grace had dropped her bombshell she had literally bumped into George as she walked round the corner to go to the newsagent's. She had been squabbling with her boys about how much money they could each have.

'I mean it, tenpence each and not a penny more. I'll be broke at this rate and all your bloody teeth will drop out of your head . . . I can't keep this up for the whole summer holidays!'

The boys had surged into the shop with Gillian close behind them just as the caretaker was coming out with a newspaper tucked under his arm and a small white paper bag held in the other. Gillian nearly jumped out of her skin. Fear shot through her like ten thousand volts as she collided with the man and his stale smell reached her nostrils, an odour of grease and fags and something curiously sweet and sickly . . . She didn't know George really, only well enough to say good morning to, but seeing him that day, terror caught her by the throat and all her fighting talk counted for nothing.

Gillian didn't scare easily but she felt sick at the sight of George Rush, knowing what he'd done to those children. He smiled and said hello, just like normal, and for a moment she wondered if they had the wrong man again. He didn't *look* guilty . . . but then who ever did? Uncle Gary had managed to hoodwink the whole family!

Later, when she recounted the incident to Potty down at the launderette, her friend nodded her head vigorously in agreement.

'I know, he's bloody terrifying. I saw him walking down Bonner Road the other day when I was coming out of work, and I had to cross the street to avoid him. Lucy had come to meet me from work and I had to pretend I hadn't seen him 'cause I didn't want her to think anything was up, but I'm telling you, I was shitting it!

'Lucy obviously didn't realise it was George who had attacked her because she went sauntering past him without a care in the world. I was hoping in a way that she might be reminded of her attacker but she wasn't and he made no eye contact with her, it was as if she wasn't even there. He just kept walking by with that carrier bag full of tins weighing his arm down. He must live on Spam and tinned soup.'

The beginning of the summer holidays brought with it a new wave of fear. To them the summer holidays were a pervert's paradise. The children, however, especially the older ones, didn't need to be told twice to be careful and always stayed in groups, fiercely protective of their younger brothers and sisters. Parents complained vociferously that their children's childhood was being stolen from them as a culture of fear and suspicion held the neighbourhood in its grip.

The air remained thick, the sky cloudless and the sun tortured all those who stayed out too long. Hospitals were kept busy treating cases of dehydration in young and old alike, and the local papers suggested that the most vulnerable should stay in with their curtains drawn and windows and doors open, and should keep drinking water. Not one electric fan could be found for sale in the whole community, and every DIY store had sold out of watering cans, hosepipes and even buckets.

Mothers watched like hawks as children played on swings, and complained that they couldn't get on with their housework because they were having to play minder all day and night. It was the summer of the clacker and the sound of those two hard plastic balls banging against each other was driving the women to distraction: 'Take those bloody things outside!' was their constant cry, only to realise then that that meant they'd have to go too. There was also a Space Hopper frenzy and lots of kids ended up in Casualty with cut knees and bangs on heads.

It was as hot as hell. Each day the newspapers had more pictures of scorched and cracked earth as crops failed and the country struggled in the grip of drought. People were pictured queuing for water with any receptacle they could find, and the papers didn't miss a chance to report another heat-related death.

Scaremonger tactics were used to frighten the public into keeping their rubbish tied up and bagged properly. A report in the paper had told the story of a baby bitten by a rat. They had said it was an outbreak of bubonic plague, but it turned out to be a boy who'd been bitten by his pet gerbil! Many kids had taken to playing on the streets, no further than a few steps from their front door, squirting each other with water from old washing-up liquid containers to try and stay cool. Tempers were frayed as children were constantly told off for being out of their mother's sight for more than a minute or two. Many of them were wishing the holidays away so that they could get their kids back safely inside the school gates, the strain of having to stay on top of them all day proving too much.

And then there were the latch-key kids to keep an eye on too. As if the stay-at-home mums didn't have enough on their plates, they had the added responsibility of looking out for the kids of parents who had to work. It went without saying that they would be watched by friends and neighbours, but everyone was all too aware that the attacker lived in their community and some parents were left not knowing who to trust any more. Jobs were put on the line as mums asked to take time off to be with their families and protect them, which didn't please local employers. With uncertainty over jobs, families were struggling to put food on the table each night. Single parents suffered the most, and the whole area was in turmoil.

To help keep the children closest to him off the streets, in the first week of August John had bought an extra-large paddling pool and installed it in their garden where it took up most of the lawn. Despite the hosepipe ban, they filled it up under cover of darkness, an operation that due to the size of the thing took several hours. Grace and John's home, being bigger than everybody else's, proved an ideal place to while away a few hours with the kids. Grace filled the freezer up with ice pops and choc ices, now in great demand at the local supermarket, and got ready for a long summer.

Lucy Potts had taken to coming over with her little

sisters while Potty was working, and would spend her evenings with Maria Foster, who had recently come out of hospital. Even though Maria was doing well and getting her strength back, Mary was refusing to let her leave the house, despite Lizzie's urging her to get things back to normal as soon as possible. Aside from Grace's, Maria wasn't allowed to go anywhere.

Lucy and Maria had formed an unshakable bond that summer because of their shared experience at the hands of the attacker. 'I don't know what those girls talk about but they're in that bedroom for hours,' Mary complained, though she was secretly glad that Maria had made such a good friend. A mother's love would get you so far, but Mary knew that it could only be the companionship of a great mate that would do the rest.

In the privacy of the bedroom Lucy and Maria spoke little of their respective ordeals, but Maria taught Lucy about music and Lucy concentrated on teaching Maria basic judo moves.

Sue Williams was also grateful to have somewhere to take her children during the long hot days that summer. In previous years she had helped to run summer play schemes, working as a supervisor. It was a handy way to amuse the kids and earn a few bob at the same time. But this year she didn't feel up to it, understandably, and had drawn closer to Grace in the wake of what she'd learned about her past. She had always thought Grace a bit snotty and aloof, but now she saw her in a different light. It was funny how people's attitudes could change. The jealousy she had harboured against Grace for so long was diminishing. She had been spending time with Sue, encouraging her weight loss and helping her with her hair and appearance. In fact, Grace loved having a house full of people and didn't mind the mess and chaos one little bit. A quick whizz round with the Hoover each night was a small price to pay for the companionship of the other women and children. They talked about fashion, make-up and hair and Grace was in her element.

These idle chats helped to get them through the more difficult conversations about their kids and George Rush. Adam blossomed under the attention of all those bossy little girls – Sue's two and Potty's two – and loved having his cousins Jamie and Benny over every day. A month after the attack, his physical wounds had nearly healed and he was becoming much more adventurous again. He had taken to climbing the garden fence, getting a foothold in the panelling and jumping from it into the paddling pool, to make a huge splash.

Lizzie Foster and Nanny Parks would come over to give the younger women a break so that they could go off and get some shopping done or accomplish all those other chores that become such hard work with the kids under your feet all day. The women were coping, and coping well. Following the tragic circumstances that had changed their lives for ever, they were tougher, smarter, bonded.

Lizzie had become their chief investigator, hanging around the local shops and market stalls in the hope of catching sight of George, and when she did she would follow him. Now that school was finished for the summer his movements had changed and the only place she knew for sure she'd find him was in the betting office where he went most days. She followed him a couple of times from there to his maisonette, but there was nothing very suspicious to report there apart from the fact that he never used his front door, only the side gate from the alley and then in through the back. He was always weighed down with two stripy blue and white carrier bags full of tins.

Following him back from the shops a few days earlier she had nearly been caught. Lizzie was walking briskly to catch up with his long strides, when suddenly George stopped. She just managed to get behind a huge delivery van in time before he saw her. She stood shielded from view by one of its open doors and her heart quickened; she would have to be more careful in future.

Sue Williams's place was only half a street away from George's. While she was there Lizzie would crane her neck over the fence to get a peek into his back garden, but the view was interrupted by lines of washing and panelled fences so that she could see only the shed in the bottom corner. She wondered if George could see into Sue's garden from his upstairs windows, and if he had spied Wayne from there.

Lizzie was more reckless than the others, figuring that, as an old woman, her life was nearly over so what did it matter if she went to prison? She was not naturally a fearful person, and unlike the others did not jump out of her skin whenever she clapped eyes on George Rush. He was a paedophile, a murderer, a monster, but she wasn't going to be frightened off by a look or a glance from him. She had survived a brutal marriage. It would take a bit more than the likes of George Rush to force her to retreat.

Seeing him just made her angry; it was her temper she was having trouble controlling, not her fear. It was all she could do not to go up and drive a knife through the bastard, to laugh and enjoy the feeling as she did it, but she had promised the others that she wouldn't do anything hasty; they were going to plan this one properly. No going off half-cock like they had with Steven Archer.

Lizzie felt sure that once the beating was administered it would alert the police into investigating George Rush more closely. Everyone knew he was a bit odd; that he had been living on his own for years after his wife and mother-in-law suddenly left. Most people felt sorry for him, but once the police investigated him properly he would get everything he deserved. Lizzie saw this revenge as twofold. The angry and grieving parents and relatives would have their day, and then the police could step in and make sure Rush spent the rest of his sorry life behind bars with the other pieces of human scum who preyed on innocent kids.

Reporting back to Grace and the others, Lizzie was a study in frustration. 'There's no pattern, from what I can work out. Now he doesn't have to go to work, he spends all day in that bloody maisonette. He only leaves the house to put a bet on or to go to the local shop for tinned crap! He still wears a jacket every day, even in this heat. He must be sweating like a pig, the dirty bastard.' Lizzie fanned herself with a folded copy of the newspaper and blew the smoke from her cigarette upwards; she knew how fussy Grace was about smoking near the kids. 'I mean, what does he *do* all day? He does go to crib, though, and he likes a drink . . .'

'Well, we can't do anything in the daytime anyway, there's too many people around,' said Grace.

'Not at his place there aren't.' Lizzie had been arguing for a while that the best way to deal with George was to pay him a visit at home, but the others thought this would be too risky. Those maisonettes had walls like tissue paper; the neighbours would see and hear everything. In any case, if they did get caught they would be breaking and entering too, and after one narrow escape already – thanks to Eileen Archer not wanting to press charges – it was definitely too risky.

'Well, your only other chance is crib night on a Monday. He always goes to crib.'

'John reckons that's our best bet too. Wait till George leaves the pub. It'll be dark by then and he has to go down Gossett Road to get to his place. It's pretty deserted along there at night, with only the garages. No one hangs around those garages at night.'

'My Wayne and his mates used to,' Sue put in quietly.

'Oh, Sue, I'm so sorry, I didn't mean . . .' Grace's face flooded with colour. It was so hard not to say the wrong thing round Sue. Even an innocent remark could come out wrong.

'No, you're all right, love. I'm just saying, it's usually only kids up to no good round there, but I'd be surprised if any of them were allowed out at the moment.' Sue spoke calmly but had a haunted look about her. She had continued to lose weight and, strangely, looked better and more youthful with her new figure, but the old fire in her belly and her habitual cockiness had evaporated. 'TJ, come here and let me wipe your nose.' She pulled on his arm, drew him towards her and tidied up his face with a tissue. He struggled free to run back into the garden and Sue's gaze followed him. 'He's always got a runny nose, that kid, even in the summer. It's his lack of immunity. Kids like him can't fight off the bugs like normal ones.'

'How often does he see the specialist, Sue?' asked Nanny Parks, moving the subject on.

'Every six months. He's got his three-year check-up the week after next, actually.'

'He's a happy little soul,' said Nanny Parks, smiling.

'Well, he's in a world of his own, isn't he?' said Sue. 'And I'm glad he is. Sometimes being special gives you protection against the world and the evil in it. I know how Eileen must feel now.' She bowed her head in deep shame as she said that. She knew she had been the main instigator of Steven's beating, and bitterly regretted it now.

'Has TJ said anything about Wayne?' Grace didn't really like to ask, but she was curious.

'No, love, not much. He only asked if he could sleep in his bed. Terry tried to explain it to him, that Wayne was with the angels, but course he doesn't understand. Not like the girls. They're all right in the day, but they still cry at night.' Sue paused then added, 'We all do.' The kitchen fell quiet for a moment as the others pondered the irreversible sadness of her life. Finally Lizzie steered the conversation back to matters in hand.

'So when does your John plan on doing this then, Grace?'

268

'Anytime now really. Paul Foster's ready to go.'

'And my Terry's ready to kill,' added Sue. 'What about Robbo?'

'I'm not sure what's planned. John is handling that side of things. I think it's best if we keep it small, don't you? The more people who know about it, the more likely it is that something's gonna get out.' Despite her determination to act, Grace was fearful of John being caught. She couldn't stand it if he had to go away.

'I don't think anyone round here would grass them up. More likely give them a pat on the back and buy them a pint,' said Nanny Parks, washing up the cups at the sink.

'Yeah, probably, Mum. But all the same, let's keep it tight, shall we?'

'Don't panic, Grace. We've got their alibis sorted. If anyone asks, John was at my place plumbing in the washing machine,' said Gillian.

'What – at eleven o'clock at night?' Potty, having listened closely, piped up for the first time. 'Don't be daft, Gill. Who's gonna fix a machine at that time of night? Let's get this right.'

'Well, something like that. We'll think of something,' she said, dismissing Potty's concerns.

'Potty's right, Gill,' said Nanny Parks in a warning tone. 'You need to come up with something watertight.'

'It's sorted, I've already spoken to Harry,' said

Lizzie. The other women turned to look at her and waited for an explanation; this was a new development.

'Harry's said he'll leave crib early – say he went for pie and mash with all of them. Oh, and Robbo *is* in. Terry spoke to him yesterday and he's up for it.' Lizzie's eyes held a glint of triumph as she spoke.

'Do you think it was a good idea to bring Harry in on this?' asked Potty. 'I can understand Robbo wanting in . . . after all, Chantal was George's first victim and he's been a different man since she died . . . but Harry?'

'Harry's as sickened as the rest of us by what's been happening. He's had his own suspicions. Don't forget, it was him who told us George never showed up for crib the night that Maria was attacked. As far as Harry's concerned, you can count him in.'

'You're right,' Grace conceded. 'Poor Harry feels so guilty about my Adam, he keeps going over it every time John sees him in the pub. How he should have found him earlier, how bad he feels. Christ, these shorts are tight,' she said suddenly, pulling at her waistband.

'You putting weight on?' asked her mother.

'No, just a bit bloated, I think. It's this heat.'

Lizzie, impatient with all their chatter and wanting an agreement, spoke over their voices. 'So – Monday then?'

The women all looked at each other and nodded

before saying in unison, 'Monday!'

*

John, Terry and Paul had a quick pint in the Birdcage, just to check that George had showed up for crib, before moving on to the Royal Oak and meeting up with Robbo. They occupied a corner table there and didn't say much to each other beyond, 'Another pint?' for the next two hours. Each man knew what he had to do. John, as the tallest, was to approach George from behind and hold him while the other three went in and did the damage. John and Terry were the most nervous while Paul and Robbo remained calm. Paul had boxed for a few years, and although he was not a big bloke, he was fast and accurate. He'd felt helpless and emasculated in the weeks after Chantal's death, unable to help Michelle in any way. Now he had his chance to put things right, and to support Robbo in his grief and misery too. There wasn't a lot of love lost between the two men normally but tonight they were united.

John, more cautious by nature, was good ballast for Terry who was fit to be tied. He'd always been a bit of a hen-pecked husband who'd do anything for a quiet life, but since Wayne's murder his character had changed completely. 'Don't go mad, Terry. We wanna give him a good beating, not find ourselves up on a murder charge,' John warned him. Terry nodded vigorously in agreement but John could see his leg bouncing up and down under the table. He was straining at the leash. Getting him away was going to be the real problem. Terry would want to finish the job. But the whole idea behind all of this was to bring the police in, to get George officially investigated and then charged and convicted. 'And whatever you do, remember, we're not to call each other by name at any point.'

'He'll see our faces, though, even if it is dark,' Paul said reasonably.

'Yeah, but I don't think that's gonna matter. He's not going to go crying to Old Bill, not after what he's done.' John looked at the clock behind the bar: 10.20 p.m. 'Harry should be here in a minute.' He had agreed with the others that he would leave crib before the final game, claiming a headache, and tip them the wink that George was finishing up before he walked home.

Slightly later than anticipated, Harry came into the Royal Oak and ordered a half. He didn't speak to the other men, but nodded in their direction to indicate that they should be making tracks along Columbia Road. They had worked out that George would come out of the pub and turn left into Gossett Road to reach his maisonette, a five-minute walk away. Halfway down, they would be waiting for him in the shadows by the garages, in the gap between the two blocks of flats where the streetlights had been out of order for months. Thank God for the council taking months to fix anything!

Terry was so worked up that he muttered, 'Christ, I've got to have another piss,' even though he'd already been before they left the pub. He was standing in the corner of the garages by a stairwell leading to the flats, unzipping himself, when a faint whistling reached their ears. The men held their breath. Footsteps followed and within seconds George's large frame came lumbering down the street. They watched as he passed and when he was a few yards in front fell in behind him.

'Now,' said John quietly.

He ran up behind George and grabbed him round the neck, winding him and making him go momentarily limp. Robbo swept his legs from under him and he fell backwards. By the time George had worked out what was going on and started to try and struggle free, Paul and Terry had gone in, fists flying, while Robbo put in heavy sickening blows with his boots. George was probably unconscious within a minute, such was the ferocity and speed of their attack.

When he curled up on the ground all four of them finished him off with a good kicking. John, sensing when enough was enough, was the one to call the others off, but Robbo turned out to be more enraged than the rest of them.

'This is for my baby, you sick cunt! I'll finish you now, here in the street, you bastard!'

For a moment, all three of them watched as the

father of the first victim continued to kick the unconscious man. Finally John stepped in. 'Help me get him off, you two!' He and the others pulled at Robbo to stop the onslaught of kicks and punches.

John held him pinned against one of the garage doors. 'He's had enough, mate. Calm down! This ain't gonna help no one. Now let's get out of here.'

With calm restored they separated and made their way home in different directions. It had taken less than two minutes to fell a man of about sixteen or seventeen stone and leave him lying in a crumpled bleeding heap on the pavement.

Potty was in her element. As a result of his injuries, George had suffered a massive heart attack and been admitted to the Chest Hospital somewhere around midnight. When she came on duty at eight o'clock the next morning, there were policemen hanging around the main reception desk. After making a few surreptitious enquiries she was told that a man in his fifties had been admitted with heart failure after a brutal beating. A quick glance in the admissions book confirmed that it was George Rush. It was all she could do not to punch the air in triumph.

He had been discovered minutes after the attack by a group of men who had been drinking in the Birdcage. They confirmed to the police that he had left the pub somewhere around quarter to eleven after playing crib there, and ten minutes later they'd found him bleeding profusely from a head wound and unconscious.

Potty had wanted to go rushing over to Grace's then and there, but they had agreed that no one was to do anything out of the ordinary. It was to be business as usual. They had to act as surprised as the next person when the news became public knowledge.

It took a lot to shock the nurses at the hospital but at tea break Potty overheard a couple of them having a conversation. She strained her ears to catch one of them saying, 'I've never seen anything like it. There's no way that was just a fight with another bloke, there had to be a gang of them to do that kind of damage. He's black and blue from head to toe and his face has swollen up like a pumpkin. No wonder the police are getting involved.'

Potty was elated. They had done what they had set out to do. The police were involved now and soon they would be swarming all over George's house, delving into every aspect of his life. No one took a beating like that without good cause.

Meanwhile George was in intensive care and there were several police officers stationed outside in the corridor, waiting for him to come round. Potty felt fearful at the sight of them and kept her head down so that they couldn't see her guilty expression as she walked past with her mop and bucket. It was a bit of a scare when she spotted PC Watson coming up the stairs, but she managed to avoid being seen by slipping through the janitorial supplies department door and waiting there until the coast was clear. It was irrational, but her heart was banging hard for the whole shift and she had never felt more relieved than when it finished at two o'clock.

She went straight to Grace's. She could have gone home and waited for Lucy to bring the girls back, but she had to share the news. She knew she had done well. She was proud of herself and her part in the whole scenario. Grace was as eager to hear it as Potty was to tell it. All John had said when he came back the previous night was, 'It's done, and I'm going to bed.' She knew not to push or press for any further information and in the morning he had got up for work and left early. He obviously wasn't going to talk about it.

Paul Foster had been similarly tight-lipped with Michelle. It was only Terry who relived the entire incident with his wife, all two minutes of it, second by second, deriving some small satisfaction from knowing that the man who had killed their son had himself been badly hurt. Robbo had gone off to lie low. His knuckles had been badly bruised and he didn't want to arouse any suspicion. Nobody knew how much damage had been done to George until Potty arrived with the news that he'd suffered a heart attack.

Grace and Sue looked panicked when they heard

about that. Christ, he wasn't supposed to die, that would be murder! Assault and battery or GBH might put their husbands away for a few months, even a year, if they were caught, but if they were found guilty of murder they'd be inside for years.

'What did the nurses say?' Grace asked, shushing Adam who was after another choc ice.

'Well, they don't really talk to us cleaners, but I overheard a couple of them say he was black and blue all over. I could hardly go up to a doctor and ask for any details, though, could I?' Potty lit a cigarette and drew on it deeply, her hands trembling. 'I'm sorry,' she added. 'But I did see Constable Watson. I avoided him and he didn't see me. I'll find out more on my next shift.'

'It's not your fault, you dope,' said Grace, then turning to Adam irritably, 'I mean it, this is your last one,' as she reached into the freezer for another choc ice. She was feeling tetchy, the certainty of the last few days giving way to an uncomfortable weight of anxiety in her chest.

'Well, I'll just bloody well go up there and ask,' said Nanny Parks emphatically.

'No, Mum, leave it!' Grace turned the full force of her jitteriness on her mother.

'Why, where's the harm? They're not going to suspect anything of me, are they? I'm just a nosy old biddy.'

'I think Grace is right, Nanny, there's police

everywhere at the moment and they'll only want to know why you're asking,' said Potty.

'What do you think, Sue?' Nanny Parks asked her, looking for an ally.

'Let's leave it for a day or two, shall we? The news is a bit fresh at the moment. If we wait until everybody has wind of it, it won't look so strange. When are you at work again, Potty?'

'Not till Thursday, tomorrow is my day off,' she said, looking guilty, as if the rota were her personal responsibility.

'Well, we'll just have to sit tight,' said Grace, eyeing her mother. Nanny had a face like thunder and didn't like being undermined by her own daughter in front of Sue and Potty. She gathered up her old shopping bag and cardigan and said, 'I'll be off then. I said I'd go round Lizzie's this afternoon and give her an update. She's arranged for Michelle to pop in too.'

Grace rolled her eyes heavenwards. God only knew what her mother was capable of with Lizzie Foster egging her on. She made her promise that she wouldn't do or say anything, and they all agreed to meet at Grace's again in the morning, to see if there had been any developments.

Nanny Parks was as good as her word. Although, frustratingly, nobody had been able to ascertain anything conclusive, they all kept their nerve. The rumour mill, of course, was in full swing:

George was brain-damaged . . . he'd never walk again . . . he'd lost an eye. All kinds of snippets of information reached them, none of which proved to be true.

It wasn't until Potty came off duty on Thursday afternoon that the full picture emerged. She had managed to ask one of the nurses casually why the police had been there the other day and had been told that a patient had been attacked and suffered a heart attack but that fortunately there was no long-term or permanent damage.

'Do they know who did it to him?' asked Potty, hoping her voice didn't wobble as she asked what she really needed to know. The nurse shook her head and said that he had been unable to identify his attackers as it was dark and they had come up behind him, but that there had definitely been a couple of them, maybe as many as three or four. Potty shook her head in mock concern and said, 'Terrible, isn't it?' The nurse agreed.

She went on to tell Potty that the victim was out of intensive care and down on the ward, where they would probably keep him for a week or two until his head wound had healed and so they could make sure there had been no internal bleeding. The police visited him there regularly, but as yet they didn't have a statement from him.

George Rush had been moved down to Howarth

Ward, and although that wasn't one of Potty's she pretended she was looking for one of the other cleaners and crept along its length, hoping to get a peek at him. It was a huge ward, mostly full of old men who looked as if they didn't have much time left in this world. She had to scan it carefully before she found him. He was asleep. Although badly disfigured by bruising and swelling it was undoubtedly George Rush, the same greasy hair and big stomach sticking up from under the covers. A shiver ran through Potty and she realised that he still had the power to terrify her even from his hospital bed. But the immediate danger had passed. She was able to report back to the others later that he had been badly hurt but would survive.

A mood of jubilation swept through the women and that hot Thursday afternoon cups of tea were jettisoned in favour of Bacardi and Cokes for the younger girls, and for Nanny Parks and Lizzie Foster Mackeson milk stout.

But in the days that followed their jubilation was replaced by a feeling of intense weariness. They all complained of feeling drained and strung out by the events of the last month. They had been living in a perpetual state of high alert. Now that the menace had been contained, they could finally relax.

John and Grace planned a holiday abroad, the first time either of them had ever left the country. They asked Nanny if she wanted to go with them, but she was adamant that she would rather die than set foot on a plane. They couldn't decide between mainland Spain or Majorca, but both wanted to get away and forget about it all for a fortnight. Sue and Terry planned on taking their kids to a holiday camp on the Isle of Wight if they could scrape the money together.

For a week or two it began to look as if life might be returning to normal. Questions were asked around the neighbourhood for a few days about who might have beaten George up, but they soon died down and people lost interest as they invariably do. Harry said the police had been in only the once to make enquiries in his betting office. Clearly, finding George's assailants was not a priority for them.

This bothered the women. They had been so sure the police would investigate George, but it seemed they'd decided he was just another victim of random street violence.

Lizzie Foster kept the pressure up. She'd made several visits before this to DCI Woodhouse down at the police station, nagging him about his progress on the case and asking if he was close to catching the man who had attacked and murdered all these children. To stop now would only arouse suspicion and she was too smart for that. PC Watson sensed a change of mood in the neighbourhood but couldn't quite put his finger on it. Most of the women still hovered over their kids nervously, and his job was to soothe and placate them. There had been no further progress towards finding the attacker and Woodhouse had been kept busy by the bank robbery at Shoreditch. Watson could only repeat over and over that they were using all the resources they had, a phrase he had been taught at the police training centre in Hendon.

Grace was idly flicking through the clothes in her wardrobe one afternoon, alone in the house for once. Nanny Parks had taken Adam and Luke down to the swings then over to her flat for their tea so that Grace could clean the house. Afterwards she had taken a long bath followed by a nap and was now going through her wardrobe, looking for something that wasn't too tight. She had obviously piled a few pounds on in the last couple of weeks and would have to get a few new bits if they did go on holiday as nothing seemed to fit. She'd found a button-through sleeveless denim dress and was relieved that she could still get the buttons done up when there was an urgent banging on the door, shattering her peace. What is it now? she thought. The banging started up again, this time more insistent.

'All right! I'm coming . . . I'm coming,' she shouted as she made her way down the stairs. Through the glass panel in the front door she could clearly see the outline of her mother with the two boys. Grace immediately assumed that something must be wrong with either Luke or Adam and took the last few steps two at a time, opening the door to find her mother ashen-faced and the boys looking sullen.

'What on earth is going on? What's happened, Mum?'

'Oh, Grace!' said Nanny Parks, her eyes filling with tears.

'Quick, get inside, what is it?' Grace took the baby out of his pushchair and closed the door behind them.

'Nasty man, Mummy,' said Adam.

Grace's mind whirled. 'What do you mean? What's happened?'

'It's TJ, Grace,' sobbed Nanny.

'What about him?' Grace's heart began to beat faster, as if she already knew what was coming next.

'He's gone.'

Chapter Seventeen

When they found him he looked as if he had just lain down and decided to take a nap. His soft downy hair lay flat against his head, and his lips were pursed together, forming a perfect cupid's bow. He was curled up on his side, one thumb in his mouth, his other hand clutching the half-chewed drumstick lolly that was stuck to the side of his face. Small cuts blemished the near-perfect skin of his face where his eyelashes had been cut off, and his body, naked except for a red T-shirt, had gone a strange shade of blue.

He had been dumped by the old railway arches in a side street off Hackney Road, just down from the bridge. It was a dark area where the sun never managed to shine. The cobbled narrow street was home to a variety of black cabs and cars as most of the arches were used by shifty mechanics.

Four boys had been standing around, arguing about who was going to retrieve the ball that had fallen in front of Nobby's archway garage. Nobby had a fierce reputation in the neighbourhood, but today his garage was closed. He was with a few of the guys that worked for him, on a beano in Clacton. He was always shouting at the kids for riding their bikes past the black cabs he took in for repair as they often managed to scrape the paintwork or hit a ball at the newly washed bodywork. As one of the boys made his way in the general direction of where the ball had landed, he saw what he thought was a coat or some other item of red clothing that had been dropped. It was only as he drew closer that he realised it was a little child, in nothing but a red T-shirt, perfectly still and lifeless. His mates thought he was mucking about when he screamed at them to get the police, they were always pulling those kinds of stunts on each other, but then he kept on screaming for much longer than he would have done if it were a joke. In fact, young Albie, as he was called, couldn't stop screaming, and when the lad was found he was kneeling with his back against the fence, face buried in his arms, still yelling. He refused to look up.

Woodhouse was first on the scene shortly after 5 p.m. and knew before he even arrived that their man had done it again. This child was barely three, and Woodhouse's guts turned to ice as he lifted the blanket and saw the shock of fine blond baby hair lying in a pool of blood. The body was still warm and soft and seemed to glow with the sheen of death. The scene was all too familiar, although there seemed to be no instruments around to suggest the assailant's usual sexual preference. However, a thin tube was

285

found to be protruding from the child's bottom, and a strange-coloured liquid was congealing at one side of the body. There were obvious traces of semen present, so Woodhouse could see that this attack was sexually motivated, like the others. He thought he recognised the child but couldn't quite place him. It was only when Watson arrived with the Missing Persons report filed earlier that afternoon that he was able to make a positive identification.

Woodhouse sucked in the warm air, closing his eyes in disbelief as he realised who this child was. It would be his second trip to the Williamses' home in three weeks to inform them of the death of one of their children, and even with Watson at his side he wasn't sure he could do it.

But do it he must, just as he'd have to answer some furious questions about their slow progress on the case. If he didn't make an arrest soon he would be out of a job. If nothing else, this latest development would help him press his case to his senior officers for more manpower, but thoughts of the job seemed suddenly insignificant compared to the loss of another life on his beat. Looking at the forlorn little figure of TJ, he doubted he even wanted to stay in this line of work any more. His stomach churned and his hands went clammy.

Watson stood nearby, and Woodhouse was conscious that the young PC was watching his every move. He was not a religious man himself but found that in the light of this terrible series of events he could no longer dismiss the concept of evil as the product of a primitive imagination. He couldn't understand how one person could do this to another; how fleeting sexual gratification could ever be worth the life of an innocent baby.

He couldn't figure out how the attacker had gone unnoticed either. The arches were not a busy place, but people were living on the other side of that fence, for Christ's sake, and a group of passengers were usually gathered at the bus stop, some twenty yards around the corner. There were always lots of comings and goings from the hospital about a three-minute walk away, yet this baby had been murdered under their noses. Had no one seen anything?

This crime, like the others, had been carried out with a certain methodology; it was not the work of a man in a hurry or liable to panic when he saw blood on his hands. Watson followed Woodhouse around the garages in silence as medical crews and crime scene officers went into a swarm of subdued activity around them. His notebook was poised and at the ready, awaiting instructions. He studied his boss's face for signs of his intent but found none. Woodhouse wore the look of a defeated man, sickened and beaten by the events of the last months.

Finally, he turned to Watson and said, 'In the morning we're going to bring in every man on our list of suspects.'

'All sixteen of them, sir?'

'All sixteen.'

Watson cleared his throat and suggested nervously, 'We don't have much to check them for, beyond that bootprint. There isn't much in the way of definite evidence, sir.' Their list focused chiefly on men with form for mild sexual assault, peeping toms, flashers, but no murderers, nothing in this league.

'I know, Watson. I've read those files a hundred times, but he's right under our noses. I know it, I can smell it. Time to apply a bit of pressure and see who squeaks first.'

'Yes, sir.' But Watson couldn't imagine the DCI applying pressure, it wasn't his style. He was a by-the-rules man, thorough and straight as a die. The PC watched Woodhouse carefully as he briefed the other officers on the scene in his calm, concise way. Woodhouse never flapped. Even when three of the top brass arrived on the scene, demanding an explanation, he didn't look flustered under hostile questioning; in fact, his face betrayed little emotion beyond a quiet weariness. Watson watched him nodding but saying little as his superiors spoke to him. Once he glanced over and gave Watson a look that said, I'll be with you in a minute.

When his bosses had finished with him, Woodhouse called Watson over. They walked to his car in silence and climbed in, each dreading the task ahead.

'Ready then?' asked the DCI.

'I think so, sir. I can't believe we've got to tell them that they've lost another son. How do you do that?'

'I don't know, Watson, but unfortunately it's our job. Did you radio ahead for the WPC to join us?'

'Yes, sir, she's waiting at the station for us to collect her. It's the same one who looked after young Maria at the school. She's a good girl.'

'OK, let's go.' Woodhouse pulled away from the kerb and headed east along Hackney Road. 'Watson?'

'Sir?'

'I'm pleased to have you with me. You're a good officer.'

Woodhouse seemed embarrassed by his own words and Watson wasn't sure how to receive them so just mumbled his thanks.

Sue and Terry already knew before the blue flashing light appeared on the street outside their house. TJ just wasn't the sort of kid to wander off. He could stay happily absorbed in a single task for hours, but never go far from Sue's side. TJ couldn't cope with the unfamiliar. He needed routine and order. Other kids might grow adventurous or curious or forget for a moment that they weren't to leave their parents' side, but not TJ.

They couldn't fault the police really. TJ had gone missing around three, and it was just before six when Woodhouse and Watson arrived with the news. Sue and Terry took it with a kind of numb acceptance. Shock, Woodhouse supposed. It was Lizzie Foster, waiting with them in the kitchen, who went for him.

'Who else, eh? Who else is gonna get killed before you do something? You're fucking useless, the lot of ya!'

She coloured to the roots of her wispy grey hair and let fly at him then with every insult at her disposal. Woodhouse had seen some angry people in his line of work but she seemed to be in the grip of some especially powerful emotion and he wondered briefly if there was more to it than simple grief.

Woodhouse, Watson and the WPC stood and took it calmly, as they had been trained to do in these circumstances. It was Terry who finally told her to shut up and go home. Woodhouse was able to offer the grieving parents very little in the way of comfort beyond the assertion that TJ would have lost consciousness very quickly, a fact of which he was not at all certain.

Gillian, who had been out with Grace scouring the streets and asking in all the shops for sightings of TJ, arrived exhausted and clueless at Sue's house to find the police car outside and a group of neighbours standing around on the street, trying to work out what was going on.

'Have they found him?' she asked one of the women hopefully.

The woman shook her head and shrugged her shoulders. 'I dunno, love. Three of them turned up here about quarter of an hour ago but they didn't have the little 'un with them.'

Gillian stood rooted to the spot. It couldn't be, it just couldn't. TJ had to be all right. Someone would find him somewhere. They'd found their guilty man and dealt with him. He was tucked up in hospital and now their kids were safe again, weren't they? Gillian's mind whirled and she hesitated on the doorstep before knocking, not knowing what she would find inside or even if she wanted to go in. People continued to gather outside the house.

It took a while for anybody to come to the door but when Terry answered his face told Gillian everything. In his blue eyes she saw the despair and disbelief of a broken man. She stepped inside the hallway and he crumpled against her shoulder, sobbing like a baby and asking, 'Why us? Why us?' over and over.

She cradled his head, softly stroking his hair, and held him as she would her own child for as long as he cried. She noticed how light and insubstantial he felt, as if a stiff breeze would blow him away. There were no words for what was happening to him and Sue, no clichés of consolation she could offer, nothing that came close. Gillian was struck by a sudden fear that

Terry would do himself in, that the strength required to carry on in these circumstances was simply beyond any normal human being. Certainly, she would have given up by now.

When they walked through to the kitchen Sue looked up at Gillian and said simply, 'He's killed my baby, Gill.'

Gillian held her hand out and Sue gripped it tight, beyond tears now, filled with mute incomprehension.

Woodhouse didn't like to bring it up but someone had to identify the child's body. He knew that the crowd outside wanted answers too, and he had to move quickly. Terry said he wanted to do it on his own and that Sue was to stay at home but she wouldn't have it, insisting that she be the one to go with the police and that Terry should stay with the girls.

In their anguish they screamed at each other, and Woodhouse and Watson looked on helplessly while Gillian and the WPC attempted to bring some order to the situation. As if tipped off, the crowd could be heard outside, shouting and taunting the police. If Woodhouse wasn't careful, he'd have a lynch mob on his hands.

In the end Gillian stayed with the girls and the WPC while Sue, Terry, Watson and Woodhouse made their exit from the house and on to the street. The jeers from the crowd quietened to a hush as they waited for news. Terry and Sue remained in a daze. Woodhouse stayed tight-lipped. It was Watson who took the initiative. In a bold, strong voice, he urged the crowd to disperse and go home. They were doing no good to a grieving family.

At the force of his words, the onlookers mumbled to each other and started to leave. Watson climbed into the car and they made their silent journey to the morgue.

Sue remained quiet and composed as they descended the cold stone steps into a bright, white-tiled room where a small figure was laid out beneath a plastic sheet on the hard metal table. Terry walked into the room and straight out again, not willing to confront the moment of truth. Sue stayed and silently nodded at the mortician, signalling her readiness to see what lay beneath the sheet.

He looked so peaceful, her baby, with his milky skin, that she drew a strange sense of comfort from the sight. But then she looked more closely and saw that something was not right. TJ didn't look the same. She studied his face hard before realising what it was then drew in her breath sharply: the long silky lashes that drew so much attention, so many compliments, were gone, leaving just a short stubbly line.

It was then that something inside her hardened. It was as if a switch had been flicked that would change her for ever. For the first time in her life, Sue Williams felt pure hatred and it made her strong.

DCI Woodhouse sat at his desk the next day, looking at the folder on top of his pile of paperwork. He needed a cup of coffee before he read the grisly notes on the cause of death of the Williamses' baby.

Just like the others, TJ had been sexually assaulted before death. This time a thin plastic tube had been inserted into his bottom and a dark green liquid poured inside him, almost like an enema. The child's bottom had been extensively slapped and bruised. Handprints etched into the flesh and the extent of the bruising suggested the hands had belonged to someone quite big. Death had been fairly instantaneous after the child's skull had been smashed against the ground. There had been some interference to the boy's genital area, but it was his anus that had borne the brunt of the attack. The MO couldn't determine how long the baby had suffered before he died.

Woodhouse closed the file. Sipping his coffee, he could taste his own tears mingle with it as they rolled down his face.

The next day was the hottest of the summer so far. Grace heard on the radio that they expected the mercury to hit 96 degrees by midday. The Minister for Drought went on air to say in a public broadcast that unless water consumption was halved, it would be standpipes only until Christmas. He urged Britons to place bricks in their cisterns and said that dirty cars were patriotic. The water in the paddling pool had turned lukewarm; dead flies lay marooned on its surface. Grace fished them out with a little net that John had bought Adam in Devon last year when they'd gone rock-pooling. It had been such a lovely innocent time. She was pregnant with Luke then, feeling as sick as a dog and able to do little more than paddle in the surf with Adam or lie propped up on pillows under a parasol. That was before all this had come into their lives and turned everything upside down.

She closed her eyes as if doing so could take her back there and she could change the course of events. She used to do the same with Uncle Gary, close her eyes, and as he raped her brutally would lose all sense of reality, as if that meant she wasn't really there and he wasn't doing those things to her. Gently Grace traced the surface of the water with her net, scooping out bodies and laying them on the parched earth. She did so in a meditative trance, stupefied by the news of TJ's abduction and murder. She'd had to get out of her kitchen where Nanny Parks, Gillian and Lizzie Foster were gathered, all smoking furiously and drinking endless cups of tea.

To Grace's surprise, Michelle had arrived too and was joining the others for a cup of tea and a fag. Michelle was clearly nervous and perhaps wished she'd stayed out of the whole thing, but she was committed now and part of their group. She was the only one brave enough to mention the attack on George.

'I don't see how he can be responsible for TJ's death when he was stretched out in a hospital bed.'

Lizzie shrugged her shoulders.

'Who knows? But I wouldn't feel too bad about it. He's a horrible bugger and deserved a hiding anyway!'

Grace felt as if she had spent her whole summer with the same people, talking about the same things, and now her head was ready to explode. Their triumphant mood had evaporated into one of stunned panic as they tried to come to terms with the thought that they had got the wrong man once again. Nanny reported that police cars had been pulling up around the area all morning and dragging men off to the police station. 'They're pulling everyone in – they're bound to get him now.'

In the background the TV was playing the opening ceremony of the Montreal Olympics, though nobody cared. The children had lost interest and wandered off, even though Lizzie had told them, 'Look, it's the Queen.' Every few minutes one of the women would sigh and say, 'I don't understand it,' so sure had they been that George Rush was the attacker and that they had put an end to his reign of murder and mayhem once and for all.

In between expressions of disbelief, Gillian fed back snippets from the previous night: like the difference in Sue before and after her trip to the morgue to identify TJ's body.

'I tell you, she was weird when she got back from that police station. When she left she looked proper upset, like you'd expect, but by the time she came home something about her had changed . . . she had, I dunno, a kind of hardness. I didn't see Terry, he came in and went straight up to bed, but she came into the kitchen, put the kettle on, then asked me and the WPC to leave. She wasn't rude or anything but she wanted us out of there. Not a tear in her eye. I tell ya, it was strange.'

'Well, it's shock, isn't it?' offered her mother.

'I don't know, Mum. I can't explain it, but I got this really funny feeling off her.' Gillian tasted her tea and stirred another sugar in. Lizzie Foster just shook her head, quite unable to comprehend the sequence of events.

'It all happened so quick, that's what gets me, Lizzie,' said Nanny Parks. 'I remember the ice cream van came along and stopped on the kerb outside the park and then all the kids mobbed us at once for money, rushing outside the gates to be first in the queue. Sue was looking for her purse and I was trying to hang on to Luke and keep an eye on Adam. Anyway, we get all the ice lollies and cones and hand them out, and Sue's taking the wrapper off TJ's Fab and she turns round to give it to him . . . and he's not there. Just like that. There was a big queue of people at the ice cream van so we think he must still be standing with them somewhere, but he's nowhere to be seen. So we look around the swings and slide, thinking he can't have gone far, but he's gone, just gone. It all happened in two minutes flat, didn't it, Gill?'

'Definitely. I remember him playing on the slide with Benny when we heard the van, then they all jumped off and started yelling for ice creams and he was definitely there in the middle of it all. It must have happened in a matter of seconds. Nobody saw or heard a bloody thing, that's what's so scary about it all.'

'So if it's not George Rush, who the bloody hell is it, that's what I'd like to know?' Lizzie's cigarette end made a hissing sound as she extinguished it in the bottom of her cup. For somebody so fussy about what she drank out of, she didn't mind where she dogged out her fags.

'It's got to be somebody we know, it's got to be,' said Gill. 'If there was some strange bloke hanging around, one of us would have noticed.'

Michelle nodded her head in agreement.

'When's George out of hospital anyway, any idea?' asked Lizzie.

'Can't be long now, Liz, he's been in there going on three weeks,' said Nanny, draining her cup.

'What a fucking disaster this all is, I can't think straight. And what's your Grace doing out in the garden with that bloody fishing pole all this time?'

Lizzie stood up to get a better look out of the window and saw Grace staring dreamily into space, the fishing pole hanging limp in her hand while the children ran screaming around her. She was oblivious to the noise they made.

'That Black Panther – Neilson I think he's called – got sent down, didn't he? Five life sentences he got,' said Nanny. 'I saw it on the news.'

'They can catch them sometimes then,' said Gillian bitterly. 'But what do they do then? Give 'em a warm cell, a TV and a university degree, that's fucking what!'

'You're right there, my girl. Bring back the noose, that's what I say!' said Lizzie. 'I don't know whether to go round to Sue's or just leave it for a while. You know, give them a bit of room to breathe. I don't know what to do for the best.'

'From what I could tell last night, she just wanted to be left alone, but it couldn't hurt just to turn up and see if they need anything. I'll come with you if you like, Lizzie, see if she wants me to take the girls off her hands for a bit,' Gill offered.

'I might come too,' said Michelle. 'It takes my mind off things and maybe I can help a bit more . . . you know.'

'Those poor kids have been pushed from pillar to post in the last few weeks, God knows what they're going through, that's both their brothers they've lost now.' Nanny pulled her cardigan closer around her as if to ward off a chill even though the air was thick with heat. Grace wandered back into the kitchen then, not looking at the others, just wishing they would leave.

'All right, love?' asked her mother.

'No, Mum, not really,' Grace replied. 'I feel a bit sick actually.'

'Well, you're bound to be feeling out of sorts, we all are, it's such a shock.' Grace wished her mother would shut up and was relieved when the doorbell rang.

'Not expecting anyone, are you?' asked Lizzie.

No bloody business of yours if I am, thought Grace irritably, but she said nothing and went heavily to the door.

Potty was on the doorstep, jiggling from foot to foot as if she desperately needed the loo. 'Quick, quick, let me in!' She was visibly out of breath and looked up and down the street before pushing her way past Grace and hovering in the hall. 'Are the others here?'

'What's up?' asked Grace.

'You won't believe this! I tell you, you won't believe it . . .' Potty walked into the kitchen and said excitedly, 'I can't stop, I've got to be back at work in half an hour. I told them I was off to the doctor's, I lied . . . I had to get here somehow.' She acknowledged the others. 'All right, Mich, Gill, Nanny?'

'You heard about TJ then?' said Lizzie.

'Course I've heard about TJ, that's why I'm here.' The other women looked at her, waiting for her announcement. She seemed manic.

'So you know it couldn't have been George,' said Lizzie.

'But that's just it. It's what I've got to tell ya – it could have been George!'

'What do you mean?' they all chorused.

'Yesterday . . . he got up yesterday, said he was going for a walk in the grounds to get some air apparently. I only found out by chance when I got to work this morning and overheard the nurses talking. One of them was saying that she didn't think he was ready to go home, and the other said, "Well, he was OK enough to go out for two hours yesterday." I asked them what time that was, and they both looked at me as if to say, what's it to you? So I said, "Oh, just wondering, I thought I saw him when I came off duty, that's all." Trying to sound all casual and concerned for a patient like. And they said that he went out after lunch about two and didn't get back till half-past four, and if he was that well he could free up the bed for somebody who needed it.'

The women all looked at each other in disbelief. It was Gillian who was the first to speak.

'Fucking hell.'

Chapter Eighteen

Grace couldn't remember the last time she had been to Mass. It was one of those things she had outgrown along with homework and knee-length white socks. She had a deep personal faith upon which she called in good times and bad, to guide and protect her, but aside from weddings and, latterly, funerals, she had ceased to be a worshipper in the House of God. Deep down, Grace still believed but she saw no reason to go to church to prove her faith. Sometimes, late at night, when she had been tossing and turning with nightmares about Uncle Gary or, more recently, the assaults and murders of the children, she had closed her eyes and given herself up to her God, praying for help. Her faith had taught her never to ask for more than knowledge of God's will for her and the power to carry it out.

This morning, however, she had surprised John by getting up before him and was dressed and ready to go when he finally stirred. John blinked at his watch. 'Where you going, Grace? It's only quarter to eight.'

'I'm off to church. See to the boys, will ya?' She bent down and kissed her husband's forehead, which was still clammy with sleep. 'I'll be back by half-nine. We can go to the market then if you fancy it.'

Sundays were usually family days when they had a cooked breakfast and then wandered down the market so that Grace could get her barrowload of flowers and say hello to friends and neighbours. There was always a roast lunch – whatever the weather – and this was followed by John falling asleep on the sofa in front of the telly while the kids played on the floor and Grace got on with some ironing or just read the paper.

He studied her sleepily for a moment, searching for the right words, then thought better of it, turned over and said, 'All right, babe, I'll see you later.'

Grace tiptoed down the stairs, so as to escape without waking the boys. She grabbed her bag and keys and closed the front door quietly behind her. She placed the key in the door of the car then thought better of it and began the fifteen-minute walk to St Anne's on Underwood Road, the Catholic church she had attended regularly as a child.

She felt a cool breeze lifting her white cotton dress as she marched along. In her mind she knew what she had to do, and was beginning to feel a steely determination run through her as she walked the familiar streets of her childhood. Iris used to be a stickler for church when her husband was alive, dragging Gillian and Grace out of their beds and making them accompany her there. Grace, as the more biddable of the two, was happy to go along with it, always believing and never questioning the word of God, but Gillian was defiantly anti-religion and would loudly argue with her mother, using the mess in Northern Ireland as just one example to justify her position that religion was the cause of all the trouble in the world. 'It's not God who starts the wars, Gill, it's us,' Grace would say. It seemed obvious to her.

Since her husband's death, Nanny Parks's need for formal prayer had lessened to the point where she now only attended at Christmas and Easter, but she'd still never forgiven Gillian for marrying in a register office.

Grace tied a small white scarf under her chin and entered the cool of the church, inhaling its familiar scent of incense and beeswax. She walked to an empty pew halfway down, remembering to genuflect and cross herself before she took her seat. Instantly she felt calmness descend and a deep sense of belonging. It was as if she had never been away.

She was surprised by the number of people there, a quick head count totalled more than seventy, and wondered why she had stopped coming herself. She loved the way that church made her feel and in that moment realised why so many people still came here to worship.

Gazing up at the altar she vividly remembered taking her first Communion here and the enormous fuss that had gone into making her dress, an elaborate garment of ivory silk with puffed sleeves that Nanny had scrimped and saved to buy the material for. Grace smiled at the memory of the missing hair ribbon bordered with antique lace, bought specially to match the dress, that they simply could not find on the morning of the ceremony. It later turned up in one of Gill's drawers though Grace never told their mother that. She remembered the Communion photo too, all curls, lace and teeth, and how it still sat proudly on Mum's sideboard with a rosary wrapped round it.

The priest, a bent old man with wispy white hair, walked past her down the aisle then and Grace squinted at him in disbelief. How incredible that Father Tom was still alive. He'd seemed ancient when she was a child, and he was still going. But when he started the service, the same strong Irish accent boomed around the church, helped now by a microphone that had been installed so that people in the pews at the back could hear. Grace wasn't paying much attention to the words of the service, lost as she was in her own thoughts and prayers to God. She had come here with a specific request in mind and wanted to get clearance from the Almighty before she committed an act in defiance of one of the Ten Commandments.

She knew the Commandments by heart, though she also remembered '"Vengeance is mine," saith the

Lord.' But didn't he gain His vengeance through the actions of mortal beings? God had given her free will for a purpose. Grace was determined to use it to extinguish the evil around her. Evil was dwelling amongst her people, her family, her community, and she had to trust to her strength and God's guidance to save them all from it. She had rarely felt so sure of anything in her life, and was strangely free from anxiety about what she faced. It was simply the right thing to do.

Grace knelt up at the altar rail to take Communion, and as he placed the paper wafer on her tongue Father Tom smiled at her and gave her a wink, pleased to see her back in his congregation after all these years. Grace was flattered that he remembered her and smiled back. She took a bigger gulp of Communion wine than was strictly necessary and the flavour exploded in her mouth, leaving her with a warm feeling of wellbeing.

When she returned to the pew, she knelt down and prayed hard. She prayed for John and her boys, for her mother and sister and all their friends and family, but mostly she prayed for the souls of the little children that had been taken from them and promised God that she would avenge their memory.

Silently, she spoke to Him of her plan and asked him for a sign, just something that would tell her He understood. As she knelt deep in concentration a shaft of light shone through the stained glass window. Grace opened her eyes and looked towards it, seeing the Madonna and child brilliantly illuminated. That would do.

After the service the congregation filed out, pausing to exchange a few words with Father Tom who stood outside bidding his farewells. When it was Grace's turn he shook her hand and smiled broadly, exposing several missing teeth. 'What an honour to have you back with us, Grace,' he said.

'I'm amazed you remember me,' she said, smiling back. 'It must be twelve or thirteen years since I've been to Mass.'

'Ah, you're not to worry about that, Gracie girl. There's always a welcome for you here, and God never leaves us, wherever we are,' said the priest, squeezing her hand before moving on to the next person.

Grace felt buoyed up and curiously elated as she made the fifteen-minute walk home, recalling the feeling from all those years ago. A good Mass really did sort you out. Time to think, time to be still and gather your strength before you went back out there and got on with life again. She promised herself she would start going back to Mass, John could cope with the kids for an hour or so on a Sunday morning.

She put the key in the lock and pushed open the front door – to be met by the smell of frying bacon, which made her empty stomach roll and boil until she realised she'd have to run upstairs and be sick. It must be that Communion wine, she thought. Drinking on an empty stomach was no good for you. Next week she would have some toast before she went.

Grace wanted to speak privately with Sue before she let the others in on the plan; everybody would be needed to see this idea through to its successful conclusion but Sue was the key. If she could get Sue on her side, the others would fall into line more easily.

Once the necessary police enquiries and funeral arrangements for TJ had been made, Terry took the girls off to his sister's in Broadstairs for a few days as they all needed a break. There was nothing to be achieved by staying at home; he and Sue rowed over every little thing, they were pulling each other apart. If Wayne's death had drawn them closer, TJ's abduction and murder had stuck a bomb under them and blown their lives to smithereens. He couldn't understand why she didn't cry and she didn't understand why he couldn't pull himself together. The two girls were completely distraught and seeing Mum and Dad fight was too much on top of everything else. So Terry had taken the initiative to get them away, have a short separation to give them all more space and time.

Grace made a point of getting to Sue's first thing

on Monday before anyone else had the chance to turn up. She knew Sue was a morning person and liked to wake early and get on with her housework. Sure enough, when Grace arrived with her boys at 8.30 a.m. Sue was steadily working her way through a pile of ironing that threatened to topple off the kitchen table. Noel Edmonds was doing his morning show on Radio 1, and Sue seemed to draw reassurance from listening to him as usual and getting on with stuff. Grace could tell from the way she was standing, almost hiding, behind her ironing board that she wasn't in the mood for hugs or comfort of any kind, so she made do with a quick peck on the cheek before shooing the boys into the garden and putting the kettle on. 'Hope you don't mind me turning up at the crack of dawn like this, Sue, but I wanted a word while nobody else was around.'

'Fire away,' said Sue, the steam from her iron hissing upwards as she straightened the creases in a West Ham duvet cover. Wayne's, Grace supposed.

'You've heard the news from Potty then?'

'What, about George going on the missing list from the hospital?' She looked Grace in the eye. 'What about it?' Sue's tone was steely. 'If you've come here to suggest another beating, you can forget it. It's too good for him. It didn't work. Nothing works!'

'Well, that's what I've come about, Sue.' Grace hesitated then continued, 'I think it's time we took care of him ourselves, left the men out of it.' She coughed nervously, suddenly dry-mouthed, and Sue put her iron down and said, 'Go on.'

'Well, it seems to me that the police aren't going to do anything. You'd have thought they might have looked into it after he got that beating, but according to Potty he's got meals on wheels and everybody going "Poor George". Makes you sick, really.'

'Makes *you* sick? Lizzie saw him yesterday, limping round to the betting office like nothing had happened. Bloody do-gooders, always getting it wrong. What 'elp have I had, I ask ya? Nothing, that's what.'

'Well, that's what I mean. I think we should take matters into our own hands. We can do better than the police or our men.'

'Well, if you're looking for someone to go round and stick a knife through him, I'm your girl.' Sue lifted up a pair of little jeans and laid them on the ironing board. Grace wondered why she was ironing TJ's clothes but said nothing.

'I don't think it should be any one of us.' Grace drew breath and added, 'I think it should be *all* of us. You know, all for one and one for all?'

'What. Like the Three Musketeers? Got it all worked out, have ya?' Sue smiled bitterly and proceeded to clamp the steamy iron down on the little jeans, and for a moment Grace wondered if she was mad even to think of it, let alone mention it. Sue looked drained. Maybe Grace's timing was all wrong, but she was here now and she had to get the message across to Sue, make her understand that she was serious.

'Kind of,' Grace said softly. 'But we need to get him out of that maisonette first.'

'What? And take him round your place? So we can murder him? What with . . . your Hoover?' Sue laughed hollowly.

'No, but he's got that garage round the back, hasn't he? You see him there sometimes, tinkering with that old Cortina he never drives.'

'What, the place with the red door?'

'Yeah, that's the one, number forty-nine. I checked it out this morning. It's pretty quiet there. You've only got the back of the flats overlooking those garages.'

'You're serious, aren't you?' Sue put her iron down and looked directly at Grace.

'Totally. It's the right thing to do, I feel it in my bones.'

'You and your feelings!' Sue shook her head and smiled. 'So quite apart from how you get him there in the first place, what you gonna do with him when you do? He's a big bastard.'

'I think we do everything to him that he's done to our kids.'

Grace didn't look up; she didn't want to see Sue's reaction. A charged silence hung in the air for a few seconds before Sue came out from behind her ironing board and joined her at the kitchen table. Grace could tell from her expression that her mind was racing. A killing? Justice? God, what she wanted to do to him was no one's business.

Arms folded and now giving Grace her complete attention, Sue stared at her. 'And then what?'

'Then we finish him off.' Grace looked up for the first time and Sue held her gaze. 'We finish him for ever.'

'Fuck me,' said Sue, staring into space. 'Well, you're full of surprises, Grace, I'll say that for you. Never thought you had it in you, but then again I never thought you'd been raped either.' Grace visibly flinched. 'I'm sorry, mate, it's just that you look like butter wouldn't melt in ya mouth, and yet you're tough, Grace, tougher than I'd ever imagined.'

'Oh, I've got it in me all right.'

The air between them crackled with excitement and tension and Grace could see Sue's brain doing some quick calculations as she straightened in her chair. 'So, just me and you then?'

'No, this is going to take all of us; it needs to be all of us. Me and you wouldn't be strong enough to kill a big bloke like him, but together, as a team, we can do it.'

Grace sounded very sure about this. Sue looked a little disappointed and shook her head, nonplussed. 'So, talk me through it then. How's it gonna happen?'

'I've gone through it time and time again in my head. I thought if I could get him to the garage, you and the others could be waiting there for me.'

'No, that won't work, he'll know something's up and do a bunk. Anyway, how are you going to get him there?'

'He won't suspect anything. Why would he? I've always been nice to him. I'll get him on a promise,' said Grace meaningfully. 'You know, give him the come on, let him think he's in for a good time.'

Sue put her head in her hands, and tried to think.

'I don't mean to offend you, love, but I don't think you're his type. He likes kids, remember.' She lit a cigarette. 'And even if you do get him there, and even supposing that the rest of us can join you, don't you think other people will hear?'

'We'll gag him. And as for me not being his type, I remember the way he looked at me at the funeral. I'm his type all right.' Grace remembered that sick, longing look of sexual desire.

'What?'

'Gag him. Stick a load of rags in his mouth and tie him up. And if I can't get him there on a promise, I could always tell him someone has broken into his garage, get him there that way, but I know he wants me, Sue. I could tell. It was the same look my Uncle Gary had, the same horrible leer.'

'And how are we going to break into his garage?'

'Potty. She's brilliant – she can break into anything

with a pair of tweezers and a pen knife. She used to do all the lockers at school and get people's sweets out.'

'God, yeah, I remember. She was such a girl, wasn't she? Shame marriage to that twat has knocked it all out of her.' Sue laughed.

'Oh, I think Potty's having a comeback. She's really getting her act together. This cleaning job is the best thing that's happened to her for years.' Grace looked at Sue eagerly, waiting for her reaction. 'So, what d'ya think?'

'We gotta get this right, Grace, there's no room for fuck-ups this time. If we do it, we gotta do it properly,' said Sue. 'And how do I know you won't lose your nerve when it comes down to it? We are talking murder here, plus kidnap and torture. We could all go away for life!'

'I know, but I won't bottle out.' Grace sounded absolutely certain.

'What about the others?' Sue asked.

'Well, we need them. We can't do it on our own, and they deserve the chance to be in on it. I just wanted to talk to you first, that's all.' Grace looked at Sue and reached her hand across the table. Sue took it and squeezed her fingers.

'Thanks, Gracie, you're a good girl, and a brave one.'

'So, are you up for it?' Grace asked gently.

Sue started to bite her nails. Revenge for her boys?

A chance to feel justice had been done? A chance for her to move on? 'Definitely.'

'Shall I tell the others to meet up at my place later, after tea, when I've got the kids to bed?'

'What about your John?'

'I'll send him down the pub, tell him we're having a girls' night in. About half-seven then?' Grace picked up her bag and called the boys in from the garden. Sue stepped towards her hesitantly then opened her arms wide. They stayed locked in an embrace for several seconds. 'Thank you, Grace,' whispered Sue. 'I need this. I can't let it go this time.'

'I know, Sue, and I understand. None of us can.'

The air crackled with a sense of apprehension at Grace's house that evening. The children were bathed and bedded early, Grace having made sure she tired them out during the day with a trip to the playground and a go in the paddling pool at the park. She had been going over everything in her mind and an urgent need to act had taken her over, body and soul.

She had gazed at Adam, splashing in the pool, and held baby Luke over the edge, his tiny feet dangling in the cool water, and she had thought about their future. She wanted nothing more than to see her life pieced back together, to see her boys grow and develop into happy, confident children. And there was no chance of that happening unless she acted to rid the area of the canker poisoning its heart.

Lizzie Foster and Nanny Parks had taken up residence in the comfiest chairs, with ashtrays balanced carefully on the arms. Grace had told them in no uncertain terms that they had to be there this evening, but had refused to explain why. 'I'll tell you everything later, Mum,' she had promised.

Gillian and Potty arrived together, having stopped at the off-licence to get a bottle of Bacardi which Potty insisted on paying for. She was looking fantastic in a pair of midnight blue velvet flares and a chiffon bell-sleeved blouse. Her hair was straightened and hung down to her shoulders, and the new navy blue mascara she'd bought suited her freckled complexion.

Sue was the last to arrive at quarter to eight, having stopped to pick up Michelle on the way. Grace looked at Michelle, trying to work out if Sue had told her anything, but if she had Michelle wasn't letting on.

The seven women sat in the front room, some on the sofa, some perched on the edge of chairs and the others on the floor. The whole place seemed suddenly small and crowded but Grace pulled the curtains, adding to the sense of confinement even though it was still light outside. She didn't want to arouse suspicion unnecessarily. It was hard to do anything in this neighbourhood without somebody noticing.

316

If anybody did say they'd noticed she had visitors she'd say it had been just a few friends gathered to help comfort Sue in her hour of need. When they were all settled with their drinks, Grace was the first to speak.

'First off, I need everybody here tonight to promise that what is discussed here won't go beyond these four walls. You might not agree with what we're suggesting, and you might not want to play a part, but we do need you to swear to secrecy. What I'm proposing probably won't sit comfortably with everyone here, but we are all good friends so I feel I can ask for your trust and secrecy, no matter what. Am I right?' The women all looked at each other and nodded vigorously in agreement. Potty let out a nervous laugh. 'I mean it, Potty, we've got to be able to trust each other or this won't work.'

Grace went on to give a summary of what they already knew about George and his movements on the day of TJ's murder. Everybody present agreed that it had to be him. Michelle then angrily told the group how she had seen him coming out of the supermarket shortly after his hospital discharge and he'd said hello to her: 'Bold as fucking brass, like nothing had happened.'

'That's what he was like the day I saw him with Lucy. He just blanked her, like he didn't see her. I don't think he even knows her name! He must have recognised her, though. He's a proper psycho. He doesn't see others as people like him, they're just sexual playthings. That's what I find so scary,' Potty declared.

Gillian agreed that she found him terrifying. 'Men like him are capable of anything, they don't have any kind of conscience at all. You'd think he'd feel some kind of shame, but nothing. He's not part of us or our community, and I want him gone.'

'He looks more disgusting than ever now that his lips are all swollen and he dribbles where the stitches were,' chipped in Nanny. 'They always used to say that a wet bottom lip was a sign of madness.'

Gillian and Grace looked at each other moment-arily and rolled their eyes as if to say, What's that got to do with it?

They talked around George's guilt for a few minutes more, Grace and Sue eyeing each other, waiting for the right moment to drop their bomb-shell. It came when Michelle stated that Robbo was willing to finish him off this time. She took a long gulp of her drink and it made her shudder. She wasn't a drinker, but tonight she knew she had to face the others and share her nightmares. Drink was a good way to relax and get fired up!

After talking non-stop about Chantal in the days following her death, she had gone silent about her baby in the weeks that followed. It was as if she couldn't bear to think about her, to be reminded that she was no longer around. It had all been a bit of a blur at first, but reality was beginning to bite and she found her life desperately lonely without her beautiful girl in it. Michelle needed friends around her, the company of others who understood. Her anger was deep-rooted and she needed to offload.

'No, we don't want the men involved,' said Sue emphatically.

'What, you gonna wait for the police to do something then?' harrumphed Lizzie. 'You'll be waiting for ever, girl, let me tell ya. That creep George is covered in well-wishers like a rash, and the police are out in sympathy with him! Bloody bastards.'

'No, Liz, no police, we're going to take care of this ourselves.'

The other women looked puzzled for a minute, not sure what Grace was suggesting. It was Gillian who asked the obvious: 'So when you say "take care" of it, you mean we attack him?'

'To start with, yes,' confirmed Grace.

Sue added, 'Then we kill him,' and her face glowed at the prospect.

There was an audible intake of breath around the room. Michelle almost dropped her glass. Silence fell momentarily, to be followed by a chorus of voices all speaking at once. Some were crying out in agreement, others calling for caution.

'I really don't think I could kill anyone!' protested Potty.

'You won't have to,' promised Grace, 'but can you still pick locks?'

'Is this some sort of joke?' asked Potty, looking flustered. 'I mean, you really do intend to kill someone?'

'No, not someone, something. You can't call him human, can you? I'm serious about this, Potty – do you reckon you could get into his garage?'

'What, the one round the back of the flats?' asked Potty. Grace nodded.

'Easily. But why?'

'Because that's where we're going to do it,' said Sue. 'If we can get him to his garage we can do it. It's quiet there.'

'Does anyone mind if I ask how this miracle is going to occur?' asked Lizzie sarcastically. Sue then outlined the plan in brief and as she did Lizzie's eyes widened with the realisation that the pair of them were absolutely serious. Grace was nodding as Sue spoke, while the others exchanged nervous glances.

'Well, I think it sounds absolutely mad. You'll never get away with it!' Nanny looked terrified. 'You'll end up going to prison, Grace, and then what's going to happen to your kids? Have you thought about that? And what if something goes wrong? What if he takes you up on your so-called offer? What if he hurts you?'

'I'm not going to prison, Mum, because we're not going to get caught. And with you lot there, I won't

320

get hurt.' Grace stayed calm and unflustered. Gillian looked at her sister as if seeing her anew. First the revelation about Uncle Gary, now this. She was certainly full of surprises. It was always the quiet ones.

'Well, I'm in,' said Michelle, draining her glass. She spoke without hesitation. Memories of Chantal's funeral came flooding back and then a sense of resolve filled her. There was no doubt in her mind. George had murdered her child, and he would die for it.

'Me too. I'm in, Gracie,' said Gillian.

'Oh, Gill, please,' implored her mother. 'Grace, stop it, you're encouraging her to commit murder.'

'Mum, it's the only way, believe me. The police are never going to pick him up, or if they do it'll be too late. He's done enough. Time we stopped him.'

'Well, I'm not sure . . . what do you think, Lizzie?' Nanny looked at her friend, desperately seeking some kind of back-up. Lizzie pursed her lips and stared at them all for a few moments before speaking.

'Fuck it, why not?' she said. 'It's high time we got some justice for those kids.'

'Lizzie! You can't be serious? Old women like us, we're no use . . .'

'You can be very useful actually,' contradicted Sue. 'We want one of you to look after the kids, and the other parked up in a car outside the garages – on the lookout.'

'We can do that,' Lizzie answered for them both.

'Right then, let's plan this properly. Got a piece of paper and a pen, Grace?' Sue asked.

For the next hour and a half they went over timings and movements. Potty would break the lock on the garage, then she, Sue, Michelle and Gillian would be waiting in the parked car when Grace arrived with George.

Grace would go to his place and tell him that she'd seen some kids breaking in and he'd better come with her. On the way she would say how sorry she was about what had happened to him, and meaningfully suggest that she might perhaps make it up to him. She would wear a provocative outfit, something like a schoolgirl's. If George wanted young, she could do that.

'We want him confused, like he doesn't know what the fuck's going on,' said Sue.

The next bit of the plan was unclear, but somehow Grace would get him into the garage, pretend she wanted him and that they needed to be alone, act suggestively, maybe let him touch her a bit until the others joined her.

'Do you think you can do it, Grace?' asked Gillian.

'I can do anything now,' she replied, steely and determined.

'You need to be able to give us some kind of signal once you have him in there. It won't be easy,' Michelle warned.

'I'll bang once on the garage door, you'll be able to hear that from the car.'

'Potty, can you get the enema gear from work?' asked Sue.

'Are we really going to do everything to him that he did to the kids?' Gillian felt sick at the thought.

'I am going to grease a baseball bat and rip that fucker's arse right open – and that's just for starters.' Sue's eyes gleamed as she imagined it. There was some disagreement over the best way to kill him when they'd finished torturing him, with Michelle bent on suffocation by strangling, just as he'd done to Chantal, and Sue favouring a knife through the heart.

It was Nanny Parks who came up with the best solution. Having listened in stunned silence to most of the talk she suddenly suggested that perhaps the best way would be carbon-monoxide poisoning. Attach a hose to the exhaust pipe of his car inside the garage, start the engine and leave it running. He'd die alone and no one would know for days.

'We need to be able to get his body in the car first and he's a real lump,' warned Gillian.

'We can do it with five of us,' said Grace. 'It will be a struggle, but we'll manage.'

'I'm not sure I can, sorry,' Potty apologised.

'Don't worry about it, Potty. Just break that fucking lock and get us in there,' said Sue, and Potty nodded vigorously.

'I can't be part of it, girls, I hope you understand,

but I could create a diversion with the police. Call them up and say that I've had kids trying to break into the flat or something?' Nanny Parks was offering to do what she could.

'Well, I want to see it, and I don't wanna miss a second.' Lizzie was adamant about that.

'But we need you to wait in the car, Liz,' said Sue.

'I'll wait in the car,' said Potty, relieved to be able to offer something that did not involve taking a life. Her Lucy had survived; she didn't need an eye for an eye like the others. Least, that's what she told herself.

Grace stood up to open a window; it was getting close in there with all of them smoking and it was making her feel a bit nauseous. As she passed Potty she gripped her shoulder in a reassuring gesture, as if to say, It's OK, I understand. Potty looked up at her with tears of gratitude in her eyes. They twittered nervously amongst themselves until Sue called for order again and went through her list, point by point, making sure they all understood.

'The only question now is, when?' said Grace.

'Well, it's got to be before Terry gets back with the girls on Saturday, so it's either tomorrow or the day after.'

'The day after,' they all chorused in unison. They all needed time to get their nerve up, but not too much in case they lost it altogether.

'Are we going to tell the men?' asked Michelle.

'Not till it's over,' said Sue. 'They'll try and talk us out of it. Besides, this is between us.'

'I'll mind the kids then,' said Nanny Parks.

'Do you mind, Mum?' asked Gillian.

'No, I'll have them all round here then call the police, say I've seen somebody trying to get over the garden fence. They'll come quick if I tell them it's just an old lady and a load of kids.'

Without becoming directly involved she was giving her tacit approval to the whole scheme. Grace smiled gratefully at her mother. 'I still think you're mad, the lot of you, but that's all I'm going to say on the subject.'

Nanny Parks stood up awkwardly, the effort of getting out of the chair playing hell with her arthritic knees.

'Right, I'm gasping, anyone for a cuppa?'

The last boy had proved tender, young and easy pickings. For all that he had done, they were still so stupid. He was glad of the beating. In a way, he'd almost enjoyed it. It had covered his tracks so well that now no one suspected a thing. The future looked bright for him and he felt safe and secure as he stroked the fur on Twinkle's back. It would be time soon for a visit upstairs, after he'd eaten the dinner the local authority provided for him. What a lot of prats they were, fussing round him, bringing him meals and showing concern! He gently put the cat on the floor, stretched his long muscular arms above his head, and felt excitement stir at the prospect of reliving his latest conquest. He discarded his dessert, tinned peaches and cream, in favour of something more satisfying.

His muscles still hurt, he had trouble climbing the stairs, but once he was back in his favourite room he felt a surge of pleasure rippling through his body. The last one had been nice and easy. He preferred a struggle, but the kid had been placid and trusting. He was damaged anyway, so what good was he to society? Just another burden on over-stretched resources. Far better to let the kid satisfy him and then be done with it. The real kick had lain in snatching him from right under the mother's nose. Two in a bed, the big boy and then the brother . . . heavenly!

As he pulled open the drawer and gazed at the eyelashes, he felt an erection stir almost immediately. It had been difficult to wank in the hospital. A little black nurse had had a nice firm arse and caused him to fumble with his penis under the blankets, but seeing that mad fucking Potty woman walking round the ward had put him right off. He had pretended to be asleep, but he had seen her. They were all so stupid! Getting out, getting the brat and fucking him had proved too easy. By suppertime he was back in bed, tucked up with the perfect alibi.

He carefully removed the eyelashes and laid them

out on paper tissues. They were so distinctive against the white background. The curly dark ones belonged to the black kid – she'd been a fighter; then the soft brown downy ones . . . now he was nice . . . and the dark lashes of the big boy who'd really loved having his arse spanked. Now he had added another set to his collection from the idiot baby. It was all too much for him. He climaxed over and over, and finally fell in a heap on the nearby bed.

Chapter Nineteen

The following day the funfair came to Victoria Park and Lucy begged Potty to take her: 'Please, Mum, please! All my mates are going!' She hovered over her mother as she was unpacking the shopping in the cramped kitchen. Posters announcing the fair had been pinned up for weeks, but no one had seemed that interested until now.

'Oh, love, I'm shattered. I've been on my feet all day at work. Can't you see if your dad wants to take you and the little 'uns?' But Potty knew before she asked that there was no way Michael would give up his evening in the pub to do anything with the children. She listened in as Lucy went into the lounge where Michael lay flat out on the sofa, a can of beer by his side. She could hear the pleading tone in the girl's voice and his mumbled reply. When Lucy came back into the kitchen looking deflated, Potty knew what his answer had been. Michael had little or no interest in any of the kids these days. It seemed his life was just one long piss-up.

'He says he's got to go out. Oh, Mum, come on, it'll be better with you anyway. It's been ages since we've done anything as a family and I really would like to go.'

Lucy hung around expectantly while Potty noisily put tins and packets away in the cupboard, feeling her anger rise. At the bottom of her shopping bag she came across the tobacco which she'd bought for Michael, always thinking of him first in everything she did. Rather than give it to Lucy to hand over, she took it into the front room where she flung it at his prone form. It hit him on the side of the face and caught him unaware as he watched the news.

'What was that for, you stupid lump?'

'Me, a lump? You lazy good-for-nothing! What are you doing tonight that's so important you can't take the girls to the fair then?' Potty's voice betrayed her increasing impatience with her husband.

'I'm meeting John tonight. He said he might have a few weeks' work for me on a job he's doing in Spitalfields.' She knew that was a lie.

'When was the last time you did anything with the kids?'

'Oh, don't start, I've been looking after them all day!'

'You call lying in bed all day looking after them? They've been round Michelle's since I dropped them there on the way to work – you could at least have picked them up. There's a fucking maniac out there on the streets, but you don't seem to give a shit.

329

You're happy to let them wander around by themselves or let other people look after them. What sort of a fucking father are you? Your own daughter was nearly raped and murdered and you act like nothing even 'appened.'

Potty's face had coloured with rage to the roots of her newly styled hair. What had been taken for granted for years was finally becoming intolerable to her. He hadn't even flinched when she mentioned Lucy. He just didn't care. Michael Potts was dead weight and she was sick of carrying him.

She looked around the lounge at the dirty plates and cups he hadn't bothered to pick up, the socks and other random items of clothing which had been dropped where they'd been taken off, and felt a surge of pure fury.

'I don't need another kid, Michael, I've already got three. You want to buck your ideas up or else!' she cried, furiously banging plates and cups together as she swept through the room.

'What's the matter with you?' He was baffled. She never used to be like this. Silly cow, must be taking the wrong tablets.

'Well, I'm having trouble working out what exactly it is you contribute around here. There's got to be more to life than this, you know. I don't want to live like this any more. I want to set our girls a good example, let them see that decent people work for a living. Move your feet!' She snatched up one of the girl's dresses which was scrunched up in a ball beneath his crossed ankles.

'Oh, what, now you've got some poxy cleaning job, suddenly we're the Brady Bunch?' Michael licked the gummed edge of his cigarette paper and rolled it between the fingers of one hand. He looked at her and smirked.

Stung by his comment, Potty finally saw red.

'Actually, there's a supervisor's job coming up and I'm going to put myself forward for it. It might just be a shitty cleaning job to you, but I love my work and I love the dignity it gives me. Shame you don't have any pride, you useless piece of shit! I like what I can do with the extra money, and I want my kids to have the same things that other kids have, instead of hand-me-downs all the time.'

'Piss off!' Michael lit his roll-up and pulled at a strand of tobacco which had become stuck to his lip. Potty looked down at him and knew then that he wasn't worth the effort of a reply. Deep in her heart something had changed, but it had taken a long time for her to understand its significance. Was this really the man she had laughed with and loved so much? His face was unshaven and his eyes puffy from non-stop drinking. She knew then it was just a matter of time before she gave him his marching orders.

She dropped the dirty items of clothing in the washing basket in the bathroom and dumped the plates and cups noisily in the sink while Lucy waited at the kitchen table, where she had been listening with a sinking heart.

'Well, Mum, can we go? Please!'

Potty turned and looked at her girl and felt a surge of love for her. They'd be all right together, they didn't need him. She knew she and the kids would survive.

'Yeah, go on then, get yourself ready. We'll pick Sara and Jessica up on the way.' Potty laughed as Lucy jumped up and down in delight and rushed her mum at the sink with a huge hug and a kiss on top of her head. Lucy was already taller than Potty and was going to be a big, bold girl. She'd grown up a lot this summer, surviving that attack and growing stronger from it. Lucy was growing up fast and Potty could see traces of the woman she would become. She felt hope rising in her chest at the prospect. She was proud of her girl, and proud of the way she had come through her ordeal. She was proud too of the help she had given Maria. All in all, Potty knew Lucy would be OK. She looked at her daughter with tears in her eyes.

Lucy looked back at her, bewildered. 'You all right, Mum? And are we gonna have some tea before we go? I'm starving.'

Potty smiled back. 'No, I'm not cooking after a day at the hospital, I'll get you a hot dog or something at the fair.'

Lucy whooped with delight. They never ate out

332

because they couldn't afford it so this was a real treat.

'Give me ten minutes to get this shopping put away and change into some clean clothes. I'll call Michelle and let her know we're coming.'

Potty approached her new red phone with deep pleasure. It had only been put in the week before, their first phone; no more rattling around in her handbag looking for two-pence pieces to go down the phone box. She carefully opened the red address book she had bought herself and looked up Michelle's number. She loved her shiny red phone and the way it smelt so new, not like that horrible greasy thing in the phone box outside the flats.

She dialled the number and was thrilled at the sound of the double ring at Michelle's place, half a mile away. Michelle was definitely up for a trip to the fair. She'd been stuck in with the four girls all day and was desperate for a change of scene.

'It'll be good to see you, Potty. I've been freaking out all day about this other business, and I think Paul knows something's up. I just gotta get out the flat for an hour or two. I ain't never been good at fooling that man, ya know, and he knows I'm bothered over something.'

'Yeah, me too. See you in about quarter of an hour then, Mich.' Potty carefully placed the receiver back on its cradle. She didn't bother saying goodbye to Michael, what was the point? She brushed her hair and painted on some pink-tinted lip shine, smiling at herself in the mirror, pleased with what she saw. Sod Michael.

It was a sultry evening as the two women and their five girls made their way towards the park. From a distance they could hear the thump of loud music. 'Harlem Shuffle', a tune familiar to Potty, got her quickening her step, and the four younger girls pulled eagerly on their mothers' arms, asking for goes on every ride.

Lucy kept quiet, knowing not to push her luck. They were going out and she might see some of her mates, that was enough for her. She hoped she might see Maria, but was sure Mary wouldn't let her out of her sight. As the lights of the fair came into view, growing bright in the dusk, Potty found excitement rising in her own chest; she was as bad as the kids.

'Can you remember the last time you went to a funfair, Mich?'

'I was just thinking that, it must be years. Great, innit?' The two women smiled excitedly at each other. God, it felt good to be out and having fun.

The music filled their heads and they swayed as they walked. Soon, without thinking, they were both singing the familiar words out loud.

'We're definitely going on the waltzers!' Michelle skipped along, holding Aisha and Trinity by the hand. The two girls looked gorgeous in their little summer dresses and with their hair braided. Compared to

Michelle's girls, Potty's Sara and Jessica looked like a pair of scruffy orphans and Potty resolved to sort them out with some nice clothes from her next pay packet.

'No way, I'll be as sick as a dog!' she protested, laughing.

'Oh, you always say that! You're just chicken, Potty!'

As they drew closer the words of another familiar song rang through the night. *'Sugar! Ah, honey, honey, you are my candy girl, and you've got me wanting you . . .'*

Michelle exclaimed, 'Oh, I love this song!' and punched Potty on the arm. Lucy felt happy just to see her mum smile. She was looking better and younger than Lucy could ever remember seeing her, as if she'd been sleeping for years and had suddenly been kissed by a handsome prince and brought back to life. Potty twirled girlishly in her new jeans and Lucy noticed how tight her T-shirt was. Mum had stopped wearing baggy gear and looked lovely for the first time in years.

'Now, nobody wander off. I mean it. We stick together or there'll be no candy floss, do you lot hear me?' said Potty.

The girls all nodded eagerly and drew closer into a huddle, moving en masse through the gathering crowds as they advanced towards the heart of the fair.

'Right, we'd better sort these little 'uns out first, Potty,' said Michelle, leading them to the stall where they could fish for ducks. Sara and Jessica fished out the first numbered duck they could grab and were happy with the little furry spiders they won, but Trinity took her time, studying the toy ducks as they whirled around in the water. She was determined to win a goldfish and the stallholder became engaged in her game, gently encouraging her to keep her hook low. Occasionally he would look up and catch Potty's eye and wink.

Michelle saw the way he looked at her and nudged her in the ribs, sniggering. 'Oh, sod off,' Potty whispered, trying to suppress a laugh. The man was in his late twenties with startling blue eyes and a shock of dark hair which hung over his forehead. He was handsome and cheeky, and his flirting reminded her of how things had been for her in days gone by.

She watched the stallholder as he took his time with little Trinity and remembered how it had been when she'd first met Michael. He had been handsome and cheeky once, too, and she had been swept off her feet by him. It was the attention he gave Lucy, too. The fuss he made of her, the way he didn't seem to mind that she was someone else's child. All this had made her love him more, and she realised now she'd probably felt grateful too, because she was being given a second chance at love. He'd never asked her questions about Lucy's father, didn't seem to want to know about the past, just seemed to care about her and the baby.

Lucy would have been about four at the time and he used to spend hours with her, playing silly little games, making up stories, tickling her so that she laughed so hard she couldn't breathe. Lucy adored him and for a while all had been golden. But then something went awry, Potty didn't know what, life got in the way, the two younger girls came along, and then they didn't have the time for each other that they used to. They had fallen out of love, she supposed, but it still hurt her. How horrible Michael had become to her and to the kids.

Potty wanted to cry then for what she had lost. She wasn't really afraid of the future, but she was definitely wistful for past happiness with Michael, and the realisation that it was too late to get it back.

When Trinity had finally chosen a duck – her little tongue poking out of her mouth with concentration as she painstakingly raised it out of the water – it didn't have the right letter underneath for her to win a goldfish. Her face crumpled and her huge brown eyes filled with tears. The stallholder told her to choose a fish anyway and smiled broadly at Potty as they all gushed their thanks at him. She noticed that he had the most incredibly white teeth. 'Come back later,' he said, looking straight at her. He had the direct gaze of a man who knew his way around women.

Potty could feel herself blush and Michelle cackled loudly, 'God, it's good to laugh, innit, Potty?' She placed her arm through Michelle's and kicked her heels in the dust of the dry earth. Too right it was good to laugh! They had been living under so much pressure, crushed by the fear that had held them in its grips for months, that they had nearly stopped breathing. How good it was to remember that there was nothing better than a man's eye on you for making you feel special. The stallholder looked at Potty like he wanted every bit of her, and she was warm and receptive to the idea of a man's arms wrapped around her.

Potty smiled a seductive smile at the young man before turning on her heel to leave. She felt light as air as they drifted past the shooting range and the haunted house where the girls squealed in protest, adamant they would not go in. Potty nearly jumped out of her skin as a siren suddenly went off and announced the beginning of another ride, voices shouted at them to ''Ave a go, lovie' and the pungent air was filled with the sweet smells of fried apple fritters and sarsaparilla drinks. Potty was heady with happiness and squealed with delight as another stallholder pulled gently at her arm and whispered in her ear that he'd like to go round the back with her for a kiss and a cuddle.

Lucy hung back, smiling, and kept an eye on the four little girls as Michelle and Potty wandered arm-in-arm about the fairground. She thought the two women looked like schoolgirls together, and had a sense for the first time in her young life that her mum had once been a girl too and must have had her dreams, just like Lucy did.

Her dream was stronger than ever now. Back in June, before the attack, she'd been for trials for the London Youth Judo Squad. She hadn't told anybody except Maria. If she got through, she wanted it to be a surprise for her mum. It had been nearly six weeks since the trials and she still hadn't heard so she doubted it would come to anything. But if not this time, then next, and she would keep going until she got where she wanted to be. 'It's all about stamina, this game,' Lucy's coach had told her, 'it's the people who keep at it who get the prizes.' She had secret high hopes for herself and was sure that one day she would get her chance.

He lurked in the shadows, dizzy with all the wonderful sights around him: the nubile young things in their shorts and little skirts. It all made his mouth water and his head feel so light that he had to grip the side of a caravan for support. He was comfortable here in the shadows where he could gaze uninterrupted at the wonderful sights that walked past him. No one noticed him, no one knew he was watching. Now that darkness had fallen he could really get down to business. He desperately wanted to pluck one of them, to feel their soft skin under his hands, to embrace them . . . and then watch the life slowly leave them as he fucked their brains out.

But tonight it seemed everyone was holding on tight to little hands. He already knew that pickings would not be easy here, and it could prove a little dangerous. No, tonight he would just content himself with watching, and as he did he rubbed himself and climaxed over the thought of what might have been.

Twilight slowly gave way to the first stars of the evening and Lucy breathed in a deep lungful of fairground air. The scent of candy floss and diesel oil and hot dogs filled her nostrils and lifted her spirits. There was excitement blowing on the breeze. Their group came to a shuddering halt when Michelle and Potty stopped by the ghost train and insisted they all get on. Squeezing into a couple of carts, the girls all squabbled amongst themselves. 'Stop squashing me, Jessica!' her sister shouted.

The bell rang and the wheels moved jerkily down the track, meeting the metal swing doors with a loud crash. They all screamed in joyful unison. A few seconds into the ride, however, as the simulated sounds of horror blared in the darkness, the little ones became afraid and hid their faces against their mothers' breasts. Michelle and Potty told them not to worry, reassured them that it would soon be over, but the ride was longer than expected, the little cart jerking on its track in a stop-start fashion, and even Lucy was beginning to feel anxious. By the finish Sara and Jessica were nearly in tears and Potty had to bring them round with the promise of a hot dog.

'Think I might have gone a bit over the top with them there, mate, I was starting to freak out a bit myself,' Potty said quietly to Michelle.

'Nah, they'll be all right in a minute. Get a bit of grub down 'em,' Michelle said reassuringly. Her large gold hoop earrings were twinkling in the darkness and her teeth looked whiter than white against her dark brown skin.

The little party stood around, munching on their hot dogs and chips and debating which rides to go on next. The girls wanted the carousel while Michelle demanded that Potty should come on the waltzers with her. 'Over my dead body,' said Potty flatly, turning to find a bin for her greasy tissue. As she did, a white caravan lit from within by a soft light through warm orange curtains caught her eye. A blackboard hung outside reading: Madame Marla, Fortune Teller. 'Oh, look, Mich, they've got a clairvoyant!'

'You won't get me going in there. I don't want to know what the future holds, thank you very much. Come on, Potty, let's go on the waltzers. Lucy'll mind the girls.'

'No, wait up,' begged Potty, 'let me have a look.' Michelle rolled her eyes and tapped her foot impatiently while Potty walked over to study the board outside the caravan. It was a bit steep at £1, but for that she could choose between crystal ball, palm reading or tarot. She looked in her purse, which was bulging with change, and had a quick count up.

A woman of about sixty in a flowered dress and vivid eye make-up opened the door to let a customer out. She looked at Potty without smiling and said, 'You coming in?'

She turned back to look at Michelle who just shrugged as if to say, It's up to you. 'Five minutes,' Potty shouted over to them. 'Lucy, keep an eye on the girls.'

Still not smiling or offering much of a welcome, the clairvoyant looked Potty up and down as she settled herself on a bench behind a table covered with a white lace cloth.

'Close that curtain behind you unless you want everyone looking in,' she instructed. She sounded surly and Potty wondered for a minute if this was a mistake. 'OK, let me get settled here,' said the woman, closing her eyes and breathing deeply, 'now give me your hand.'

Potty reached across the table. As she placed her hand in the clairvoyant's, she noticed that in contrast to her own it was tanned and warm and covered in gold rings. The nails were beautifully manicured and painted red. They sat like that for a minute and Potty began to wonder if the woman was ever going to speak when she raised her head and opened her eyes to look straight into Potty's. She had that same direct stare as the guy on the fish-for-a-duck stall. Potty wondered for a moment if the clairvoyant could be his mother. Then she felt like the woman could see right inside her, and shifted uncomfortably on the bench.

'Cards for you,' said the woman, reaching behind her to an occasional table and picking up a velvet scarf wrapped around a set of well-worn tarot cards. Unwrapping the deck from the velvet, the woman handed the cards to Potty. 'Shuffle them, then split the pack into three.' Potty did as she was told. 'Right, now I want you to put them back into one pile, in any order you like.' Potty studied the cards for a moment then shuffled them back together, left first, then right, then middle. 'OK, let's have a look,' said the woman, turning the cards over, three in the middle and the rest around the edge.'

Potty scanned the illustrations on the cards, some beautiful, some bleak.

'Right then, this is you, the High Priestess. What this card says is that you're coming into your own, you're growing and becoming a wise and loving woman. It tells me your judgement is good, that you can be a leader of others.'

Potty nodded. She liked the sound of that.

'But you see this one here?' continued the woman, pointing to a skeleton on a black background. 'That's

343

the death card.' Potty drew in her breath sharply. 'It doesn't always mean somebody is going to die, but it does mean that some part of your life has ended and needs to go. Does that make sense?'

She swallowed hard and nodded, not looking at the woman, still staring at the card.

'And this one here, the Tower. You see it's crumbling and falling down? That's the same thing. Something has to fall apart before it can be built up again. Does that feel right?'

Potty looked up at the other woman and for the first time saw a glint of warmth in her eye. 'Don't worry, love.' She allowed herself a small smile. 'It normally just means you gotta get the dead wood outta your life. It's for you to decide what the dead wood is.' Then she ran one long red nail along the cards down the side. 'You got three kids, right?'

'Yeah' said Potty, impressed.

'Girls?'

'How'd you know that?' she asked. The woman just tilted her head to one side as if to say, Well, it's my job, love.

'One of them is going to have a lot of success. I can't see which one it is, or how old she'll be, but that's the Star there, one of your girls.'

'Bloody hell!' said Potty.

'Hold up, there's more.' The woman's face clouded into an expression that Potty couldn't read. 'It's not clear,' she said, shaking her head, 'but it's a kind of shadow . . . I don't know, something dark . . . you have to fight it. I just know you have to see it off, even if it scares you. And, remember, you are not alone in this. You think it's bigger than you, but it isn't. Just like David and Goliath, you can do it against the odds, that's what this card tells me.'

The woman abruptly swept all the cards together in her hands. Potty waited for something else but she just said, 'One pound, please.'

'Is that it?' Potty asked.

'Yes, that's it,' said the woman, looking straight at her with a look that Potty didn't want to challenge.

'Oh, right then. Cheers.'

'Be lucky, sweetheart,' the woman called after her as she descended the caravan steps.

Potty didn't look back but went straight over to the hot-dog stand where Michelle and the girls were waiting.

'Well, are you going to meet a tall, dark, hand-some stranger?' said Michelle, smirking.

'No, nothing like that.'

'Well, what then? Come on, don't be shy, tell me what she said?' Michelle shushed her girls as they nagged her to go to the carousel.

'Not now, Michelle, later. Come on, let's take them on that carousel before they explode.'

Impatiently the girls waited for the ride to come to a halt and before it had even stopped moving were clambering up and rushing for their horses. 'Be careful!' Potty shouted after them, her voice lost in the noise of the engine and the music. Lucy rode the carousel with the four younger ones, telling them to make sure they hung on to the pole with both hands or they'd fall off. Michelle and Potty smiled as they watched their girls fly past, huge grins plastered all over their faces, hair flying out behind them.

Both women firmly refused when they whined for another go after their ride had finished. 'No, you'll be sick after those hot dogs, let them go down for a bit. We'll take you on the dodgems later.'

'Come on, Potty, come on the waltzers with me, please!' Michelle tugged at her arm like a child.

'No, Mich, they're too fast for me.'

'Oh, come on, Mum, please. Just once, just for me,' pleaded Lucy.

'Yeah, come on, Potty, you gotta live a bit,' Michelle teased her. And so they got her into the seat, squashed between them on the red leatherette with the bar firmly clamped across their laps. The music was so loud Potty couldn't hear herself think. As they began to move butterflies rose in her chest. She watched the man who collected the money walk past with his apron full of change, heavy black boots and hands dark with grease. As he passed he flicked the back of their seat and sent them into an early spin as they rose up the ramp and descended into a fast turn. Michelle threw her head back and screamed with delight, as did Lucy, but Potty began to regret her decision to try the ride. She could feel the bile rise in her stomach and cursed herself for having let them talk her into it.

She endured the next four minutes by breathing deeply and keeping her eyes closed, concentrating on Suzi Quatro singing, 'Come alive, come alive, down in Devilgate Drive!' The noise was ear-splitting and she fought down her panic when she opened her eyes briefly and caught Sara and Jessica looking up at her with concern as she flew past them. She wanted to get down, get off the bloody thing and be with her girls, not feel so sick.

The force of the ride had her head pinned against the back of the seat and she felt powerless to move. Lights flew past in a blur of colour and, seeing her in a state, the guy manning the ride spun their chair extra fast for the last minute of their time. 'You fucker!' she managed to scream, and by now tears of real distress were gathering in the corners of her eyes.

Michelle and Lucy apologetically helped her out of the seat when it finally came to a stop and Potty staggered off, nearly tripping down the steep step, and made it to the ground looking green.

'Mum, are you all right?' Lucy was worried now, sensing the joke had gone too far.

'I feel sick.' Potty leaned over and put her hand to her mouth.

'Come on, over here.' Michelle took her hand and

led her through the maze of caravans and generators and leads that bordered the edge of the fairground.

'Stay with the girls, I'll go on my own,' said Potty, lurching forwards and coming to a stop about twenty yards from the bandstand where her stomach finally gave up the fight and released its contents. 'Oh, shit,' she mumbled between lurches of nausea. She threw up several times and when it finally came to a stop knelt on the grass, dribble rolling out of her mouth on to the ground. She spat several times to clear the taste then sat back on her heels to steady her breathing. It was quiet here and she could get herself back to normal.

She crouched in the grass like that for several minutes, looking up to watch a plane descend over London, its lights flashing in the night sky. Closing her eyes, she took a final breath before climbing to her feet. As she straightened and brushed the dirt off her trousers, a voice said silkily from the darkness, 'Hello, sweetie.'

Chapter Twenty

Potty nearly lost her balance as she shot away and headed for the bandstand, tripping on her own bell bottoms and toppling sideways on her platforms as her foot slipped over the edge of her shoe. She felt a sharp pain in her ankle which nearly stalled her, but she managed to lurch towards the lights and the rumble of the generators without stopping to look back. She was panic-stricken, almost forgetting to breathe in her frantic effort to keep running.

She clambered over cables and tow-bars on trucks and cars, trying to glimpse the rifle range where she had left the others behind before she had been thrown off course by the whispering voice of the man hiding in the shadows.

The band had already packed up and headed off home and the audience had gone by the time she reached the open space, leaving only litter in their wake and a few empty deckchairs not yet collected by the park officials. As she heard their voices trailing off into the distance Potty leaned breathlessly against the podium of the bandstand and gulped for air. That smell . . . that terrible smell of tobacco, stale beer and cleaning fluid.

She wiped her hands over her face in an effort to clear her mind and regain her composure. She needed to find Michelle and the kids, and find them fast. She had been inches from *him*, she was sure of it. She'd recognised that hoarse whisper, she knew the voice, and she had to get back and warn the others, take them home.

She could see the light bulbs twirling round on the rocket ride in the distance. She must have gone full circle round the caravans. It took her a moment to get her bearings. She scanned the darkness, looking to see if anyone had followed her. Her heart was in her mouth, pounding heavily. There was no one close by but she slipped off her platforms, hitched up her trousers and ran in the direction of the rocket ride.

Potty swerved and sprinted through the crowds, eventually reaching the rifle range where she saw Michelle and the kids. Struggling for breath, she said, 'Let's go! Let's get out of here . . . *he's* here!'

Michelle held out her arms to her frightened friend and soothed her. 'Easy, easy, just slow down a minute. What's going on?'

'He's over there, Mich, amongst the caravans, about twenty yards from the bandstand. He spoke to me, must have been right beside me while I was throwing up, but I didn't see anything . . . just this voice, this horrible voice, and that smell!' Potty panted.

'How do you know it's him?' asked Michelle, and instantly regretted it.

'It's him, I know it! It's all clear to me now. It sounds like madness, but Grace is right! I just *knew*.' Potty screamed.

Sara and Jessica started crying then and little Trinity clung to Michelle while Lucy tried to bring order. Aisha stood frozen-faced, staring beyond the caravans into the darkness. A group of teenage boys with long hair and tanned faces swaggered past, laughing at the state of Potty, thinking she had just come off a ride.

'All right, love? Look like you've seen a ghost,' they jeered.

Michelle didn't miss a beat. 'You can fuck off an' all!' she shouted, then gently started smoothing Potty's sweaty hair off her forehead. She felt cold and clammy and looked a sickly grey colour. Michelle looked angrily over her friend's shoulder towards the bandstand. 'I've half a mind to go over there and wring the bastard's neck. He thinks he's got us on the run, does he?'

'I'll come!' offered Lucy eagerly.

'No, you will not, nobody is going anywhere,' insisted Potty, getting her breath back. She pulled Sara and Jessica close to her. 'It's all right, we've got each other, let's stick together! This is not the time or the place to do anything. Let's just get out of here.'

'But we should tell somebody or get the police,' Lucy insisted. Michelle and Potty rolled their eyes at each other, knowing he'd be long gone by the time a squad car arrived.

'There's no point, love, honestly. I'll go to the station in the morning and tell them what happened, but they're not gonna find him tonight. We're better off getting out of here.' Potty desperately wanted to cry but knew that she had to take charge and keep it together. Her three girls were looking to her for protection and reassurance. She couldn't let them down. She'd already come so far, she couldn't allow this monster to rob her of all she had achieved. Sandra Potts was going to stand her ground!

'Come on, let's get everybody home, we'll grab a cab,' said Michelle, leading them back through the maze of bodies. The fair was teeming with noisy crowds, surging and swelling, and the girls became afraid of being separated from Potty and Michelle, clinging ever tighter to their legs and arms, making it difficult to get anywhere. Potty felt as if she was moving through a film in slow-motion, her head swimming with images and sounds, but trying desperately to stay focused in the here and now and get her girls home safely. The sound of a bell ringing pierced her ears, and the thunderous rumble of the rides went right through her.

Where was Michael? she asked herself. The fucking useless pisshead! He should be here, minding them all, instead of down the pub with his mates. He was no good to anyone, no help to her or the kids.

Even when the other guys had beaten up Steven Archer, he'd been deliberately left out because he was a complete liability, a useless drunk! Potty felt a stab of loneliness as she realised that she was the only one holding her family together. The man she had seen as her saviour and protector was in fact nothing of the kind. Women laughed at him; other men avoided him. He was the local joke. He spent every minute he was out of the house getting falling down drunk, ending up pissed and sick in some gutter. He was nothing but an embarrassment to her.

She would have screamed at her girls to stop crying but knew it would only make matters worse. Desperately she tried to hold it all inside and not let her own tears of panic escape. They spilled out of the park gates and on to the road where she finally seemed able to breathe normally, but there were no cabs to be found.

She hid her mounting agitation and said to the children, 'Come on, we'll walk. It's fine out here on the street.'

Michelle looked unsure, still peering into the sea of traffic for the orange light of a cab. They walked in fearful silence for a minute or two until Michelle said, 'Here's one,' and stood out in the road to signal to the approaching cab, its orange light like a promise of rescue. She rushed up to the open window and Potty heard the cabbie say, 'Sorry, love, I can't take seven of you, it's against the law.' Michelle said something

353

else to him which Potty didn't catch, then the back door swung open and Potty piled the girls inside. Michelle was last to get in, saying, 'Cheers, mate,' as the taxi quickly pulled away from the kerb.

'Just drop me off, Mich, I'll be all right,' said a still sweating Potty.

'Not on your bloody nelly, mate. You're staying with me tonight.'

'Honestly, I just want to get back to the flat.' Potty felt overwhelmed with tiredness, and tearful as she felt Lucy's hand grip hers and squeeze it. They shared something more than a mother-daughter bond now. They had both survived.

'No way. You're staying with us. We've got plenty of bedding. You can go on the couch in the front room, and the girls can all squash down together in their bedroom.' Michelle's two girls gave a little cheer at this.

'Oh, please, Mum, can we?' whined Jessica.

'I think it's a good idea, Mum.' Lucy was sounding more and more like an adult every time she spoke. Who was taking care of who here? wondered Potty.

'I've got work in the morning,' she protested feebly.

'So? We'll be awake at the crack of dawn with this lot anyway, you'll have plenty of time,' Michelle declared.

Potty surrendered then, too exhausted to argue and secretly grateful not to be alone with her girls in the flat tonight. Michael rarely made it back before the middle of the night anyway. God knows where he got to after the pubs chucked him out, but she was too drained to care.

The cab came to a halt beside Michelle's block of flats. The two women went to scrabble in their purses but the driver said, 'You're all right, girls, this one's on me. Be safe.'

'What did you tell him?' Potty asked.

'That you'd had a fright, that's all. Nice bloke, eh?'

'Yeah, really nice,' said Potty, gazing after the cab as it moved off down the road.

'There are some nice blokes out there, Potty, some really good men, you gotta believe that.' Michelle fished her keys out of her bag and let them into the flat.

Potty loved this place. It had big rooms and high ceilings and was freshly painted throughout. Most of the furniture was second hand but Michelle kept it spotlessly tidy and clean. Potty immediately felt a sense of calm and order in here. Michelle was the only person she knew who had floor-to-ceiling curtains in the front room which she hung without nets. She was a bit different, Michelle; had a bit of style that was all her own.

Everybody drank hot, sweet tea before bed. In front of the girls Potty said that she would go to the police station in the morning and report what she had heard and they were not to worry – the police would soon find the man and lock him up. Only Lucy sensed this wasn't true.

When all the girls had settled down in their bedroom and the giggling had stopped, Potty and Michelle spoke openly. 'How you feeling then?' Michelle lit a cigarette and inhaled deeply.

'Terrified, kind of, but more angry than anything else. It makes me really fucking *angry* to think of the hold this animal has over us. We can't go anywhere or do anything without him being there the whole time. I feel as if he's stolen our lives. It didn't seem real at Grace's the other night, talking about killing him, but now I can imagine myself doing it. I don't think it would be wrong any more. As a matter of fact, I want the bastard dead!'

'I agree it doesn't seem real, but I don't reckon we've got any other option left. Besides, it's not like just one of us feels this way, we all do. How wrong can it be?' Michelle slipped off her shoe and rubbed a blister on the back of her heel.

'I can't believe we're really going to kill someone. Actually take a life. What if we go to hell?' Potty whispered.

'Potty, we're already there,' said her friend as she lit another cigarette.

Victoria Park was a desolate scene now that only litter and trackmarks from the rides' machinery remained. The fair had already left. A lazy wind blew round the bandstand and flicked the candy-striped cloth of the deckchairs around it, lifting them slightly off the grass. An eerie mist swirled round the band-stand's circular wall and the solitary figure sitting on the steps leading up to the platform. Smoke billowed from the end of a cigarette and then the powerful figure stood up, hitched the belt on his trousers and began to walk away in the direction of Cambridge Heath Road.

The caravans followed each other in a neat little convoy, over the canal bridge, round a back road and then down towards the roundabout that would take them on to the motorway junction.

A mother cradled the limp body of her baby as others looked on. She kissed his head and whispered softly into his fine hair, telling him all would be well. The man from the fish-for-a--duck stall stood beside his common-law wife, unable to speak from rage but chewing the skin inside his cheek as he looked down at his boy, battered, buggered and bruised.

His grandmother held court as the others in the caravan raised angry voices, demanding revenge. But she knew only too well that there was no justice for travellers like them. Their sorrow and grief would go unheard; the authorities listened to householders, not people passing through. Madame Marla held their gaze with her own and spoke calmly. They had to believe her, she told them. This crime would be avenged and the person responsible would meet a grisly end.

She had seen it tonight in the cards.

Potty didn't sleep much. She watched the sun come up through the gap in the curtains, feeling curiously calm and still, and smiled to herself when she heard little voices in the girls' bedroom. Her love for her children was her greatest strength. She could feel it lifting her up. Without them, there really would be no point to any of it. She got up and quickly jumped in half a bath of not quite warm water, sliding beneath its surface to wet her hair. She emerged ten minutes later feeling refreshed and ready. She squirted some of Michelle's Opium behind her ears, its deep, sharp tones making her feel powerful.

'Oh, my God, Mum, how much perfume have you got on?' asked Lucy, coughing, as she came into the kitchen.

'It'll settle down in a minute, it's just a bit strong to start with. Do you want some cereal?' Potty opened cupboards, looking for bowls and spoons.

'No, I'm not hungry.' Lucy was still half asleep.

'I want you to take the girls over to Grace's today, Lucy. Nanny Parks will mind them. But we need to stop off at home first to get some clean clothes.' Potty whistled as she filled the kettle with cold water from the tap.

'Are you going to work then, Mum?'

'Yeah, I'm doing ten till four,' Potty lied.

'Are you gonna go to the police station?'

'Yeah, I'll do that on my way,' she lied again, hoping Lucy would leave it alone. Michelle came into the kitchen then wearing just a T-shirt and a pair of knickers, exposing her long beautiful legs and pert bottom. Her hair was fanned out around her face in a large halo and through the light from the kitchen window Potty thought she looked like some kind of avenging angel.

'You seen my fags anywhere?' she asked sleepily.

'Yeah, on the coffee table in the front room where you left them last night. Tea, Mich?' asked Potty.

'Please, Potty. What time you off then? It's only half-seven.' Michelle squinted up at the clock.

'I'm going to get cracking and pick up some clothes for the girls at the flat before I go to work,' said Potty, stressing the last word and winking at Michelle.

'Right, got ya,' she said, winking back. 'You'll call me from work, though, let me know how you got on at the police station?' They continued this pantomime for several minutes, for Lucy's benefit. They'd already made their plans the night before.

Grace would meet them round at Sue's with Lizzie and Gillian at about ten; give them time to get the kids up, washed and fed before dropping them with Nanny Parks. Terry had decided to stay on with the girls at his sister's in Broadstairs for a few more days, so that was him out of the way.

Michelle's Paul had come home the night before to find Potty and her kids staying and hadn't questioned it once Michelle explained what had happened at the fair. He had just shaken his head wearily, beginning to despair that this monster would ever be caught. All the fight had gone out of him. They'd done everything they could; it was down to the police now.

John thought Grace was a bit jumpy and off-colour but had no reason to suspect she was up to anything. She was bound to be in a state. They were all fried with tiredness, and he just wanted to take his family away to the sunshine for a few weeks, give them a chance to get their breath back and relax.

As he watched her apply make-up in the bathroom mirror that morning, and took in her provocative outfit of tiny denim shorts and red vest, he let out a wolf-whistle. 'What's all this for then, you off to meet your fancy man?' he chided her.

She just smiled and said nothing, her stomach doing somersaults all the time. She couldn't eat a thing but that wasn't unusual. She struggled to get anything down her most mornings except for a cup of tea, and even that was tricky.

'I'll see you later then, love,' John said. 'I might be a bit late, I'm gonna try and get that Spitalfields job finished today.'

Grace had to stop herself from rushing him as he let himself out of the front door; had to fight back the part of her that wanted him to know and to put a stop to it. But she didn't. She let him go, not knowing what would have changed by the time she next saw him.

After running through everything with Nanny Parks concerning the kids and what food there was in the cupboards, Grace was the last to arrive at Sue's just after ten. Nobody said much. They huddled around the kitchen table, talking in whispers, waiting for Potty to come back from the garage where she had gone to break the lock. In the quiet a sudden loud knocking at the door made them nearly jump out of their skins. Sue leaped up to open the door, expecting Potty, but found only an empty doorstep. She looked to left and right and saw a group of five children running for cover into the stairwell of the block opposite. 'It's just bloody kids playing knock-down ginger,' she said, sighing as she came back into the kitchen.

'Christ, I nearly had a bloody heart attack,' said Gillian.

'I wish Potty would hurry up, she's been gone ages. I hope she hasn't been caught,' said Lizzie. 'Be just like her to fuck things up.'

'Come on, Lizzie, she had the fright of her life last night, I think she's bloody brave. You wouldn't get me breaking into a garage in broad daylight,' said Michelle, defending her friend.

'Yeah, I heard all about that carry-on last night,' said Lizzie. Michelle filled in the details for the rest of them, who had only been given the short version by Potty. 'He was just waiting there in the darkness, fuck knows if he got hold of anyone.' Gillian and Grace listened attentively, not speaking but giving each other meaningful looks – looks that said, We're gonna kill him.

'It's the fucking audacity of the bloke that gets me.' Gillian twisted a lock of hair tightly around her finger, one knee bouncing up and down nervously under the table.

'Jesus, I feel sick.' Grace dry-heaved a couple of times and lurched towards the sink. Sue went and rubbed her back.

'You sure you're up to this, Grace?'

'Not, it's not that. I always feel sick at the moment.'

'Morning sickness,' Lizzie pronounced.

'No, I can't be.' Grace wasn't having any of Lizzie's diagnosis.

Have you eaten this morning?' Sue asked. Grace shook her head. 'Has anybody eaten this morning?' All the women shook their heads. Nobody had been able to manage food. 'Right, more tea and fags then,' said Sue, emptying the ashtray into the bin.

'Go on then, Sue, I'll have a bit of toast,' said

Gillian, changing her mind. 'Don't want to get light-headed.'

Sue slipped four slices of Mother's Pride under the eye-level grill on her Canon gas cooker, and as the smell of the toasting bread filled the kitchen they all decided to have a slice. Tea plates and knives came out of cupboards along with a jar of Marmite. Even Grace managed half a slice of dry toast, and they all felt better for having a bit of food inside them.

Potty arrived back just as Sue was filling a bowl with soapy water for the breakfast plates. She looked purposeful and calm, though a slight breathlessness in her voice gave a hint of her true feelings.

'OK, it's done. I knocked over a couple of tins of paint and hid a few tools so he'll think kids have been in there nicking stuff. Oh, and I keyed that Cortina of his, wrote "Sex Case" in capital letters right across the bonnet!'

'You didn't?' asked Gillian, horrified.

'Yeah, I did, I couldn't help it. Once I got inside that garage I was buzzing, couldn't stop myself.' Potty wore a slightly manic smile. Having previously insisted on confining her role to picking the lock and then waiting in the car, her experience at the fair had made her want to get stuck in and do some real damage.

'Not one of your best ideas, Potty,' said Gillian, sounding irritated. 'Bit of a fucking giveaway.'

'Well, it's too late now. We just gotta get on with

it. No use rowing,' said Lizzie to shut Gillian up.

Grace took a deep breath and pulled her long hair back behind her shoulders. 'We fit then?' She looked at her friends, checking to see if anyone had second thoughts. They all nodded resolutely and stood up. They clustered in the passageway and ran through their plan one last time, making sure everybody knew exactly what was expected of them.

Sue was adamant. 'I mean it, we got to stick together. Anyone bottles out and the whole fucking thing collapses, one of us could get hurt and he'll get away scot-free.'

'That's not going to happen,' said Michelle. The others chorused their agreement.

'Ready, Grace?' asked Lizzie.

'Ready as I'll ever be,' she replied. The others kissed her warmly and wished her luck.

'We'll be right outside, Grace. You just gotta bang on that door and we'll be in there, we won't leave you on your own, I promise.' Gillian was afraid for her sister but also in awe of her bravery. Grace handed Gillian the keys to John's Jag so she could drive with Lizzie in the front, Sue, Potty and Michelle in the back. They would be parked up fifty yards from the garages along Gossett Road where they would be able to see Grace go by with George. Once the two of them were inside, they would cruise quietly down the road and park opposite number forty-nine itself. The garages were often deserted even in broad daylight, but it was a risky strategy nonetheless and one they would not be able to account for should they be caught.

They had argued endlessly amongst themselves about the best thing to say if somebody came along and asked what five women were doing parked up in a Jag outside a garage, and it was a circular discussion that never found a resolution. The one thing they all agreed on was the speed with which they needed to act.

'No fucking around, no hesitation, we get stuck in and finish the job quick,' Lizzie had instructed them. 'Get in there, finish the cunt off and get out again.'

'Lizzie, please, you know I hate that word.' Gillian wriggled uncomfortably.

'We're about to do a bloke in and you're worried about bad language? Get a fucking grip, Gill,' Lizzie harrumphed and then lit a cigarette as the car pulled away.

Grace watched the Jag move slowly up the road and lifted a hand in final salute. She took slow, measured strides over the seventy yards of pavement to George's maisonette. She arrived outside his corner unit, looking up briefly to see one window open, and knocked on the door steadily, four times. The letterbox was jammed stiff and could not be used.

Grace detected some movement from within and braced herself, but no answer came. She knocked again and this time through the frosted door panel saw a shadowy presence make its way down the passageway from the kitchen at the back. The figure stopped behind the door but made no move to open it.

'It's stuck. You'll have to come round the side, through the gate in the alleyway.' He sounded irritated at the disturbance and for a moment Grace was caught on the hop. She hadn't planned on going round the back, wanted to stay out on the street in the open, not go into his house; if she went round the back she would be in his garden and she didn't know that she wanted that.

She lifted the latch on his back gate and pushed open the six-foot door panel to find him standing behind it, closer than expected, shielding her view of his back door. 'What do you want?' he barked.

'George, I'm sorry, but it's your garage. I think some kids have broken into it . . . the red one, number forty-nine . . . that is your garage, isn't it?'

Her words came out in such a rush that she could feel herself tripping over them. Her heart began to bang now; he was really close. A look of confusion drifted across George Rush's sweaty unshaven face and he said defensively, 'Yeah, that's mine, number forty-nine.'

Grace steadied herself and tried not to look flustered as the sweat started to bead on her forehead and trickle down the sides of her face.

'Well, I think you'd better come and have a look. I was on my way back from the shops when I saw a group of kids running out of there with a load of tools – they'd left the door wide open. Do you think we should call the police?'

George didn't seem unduly worried until she said the word 'police', and then for a moment Grace wondered if he'd tell her to mind her own business, but he said, 'No, don't bother with the police, there's no point. I'd better go and get a shirt on. You wait 'ere, sweetie.'

He looked at her in the same way he had stared when she was leaving the church after Wayne's funeral. It made Grace's stomach tighten, but she held her ground. She waited by the gate, casting nervous glances up and down the alleyway for the minute or so it took George to get his shirt and jacket, exhaling slowly through her mouth so as to stay calm.

They walked together towards the garage, a good three minutes away, and she struggled to find something to say, finally managing, 'Are you feeling better now, George? I mean, have you fully recovered?'

'Like anyone around here gives a fuck about me,' he snorted bitterly.

'People do care, of course we do,' said Grace, thinking how bizarre this all was.

He looked at her sideways, trying to weigh her up, taking in the pert breasts straining through her vest and the slim waist above her denim shorts. His big dirty cock began to stir in his trousers and he fell behind her slightly to take a better look at her arse as she walked. Not ideal, but he'd fuck it anyway, given a chance.

Grace turned and gave him a smile which said she liked him looking at her, and it threw him. Women never gave him a second look so why was this beauty giving him the eye? He'd fucking show her what happened to a cock-tease like her!

'What's a pretty girl like you worrying about an old man like me for?'

'Just looking out for you, George, same as I'd do for anybody else. Look, there it is.'

Grace pointed to the garage door, up on its hinges, one corner bent back, as they rounded the corner and reached the garage block. Just before she turned she spied the shiny blue of her Jag parked up Gossett Road and walked wide to make sure they saw her. She wanted to wave but knew she had to stay cool.

George let out a sigh of dismay and Grace followed him into the darkened garage where tins of paint and varnish had been strewn around, with boxes of nails and screws and spirit levels and spanners scattered over the floor. They picked their way carefully through the debris.

'Take me bloody ages to clear this lot up,' he grumbled.

Grace stroked his arm. 'I'll help you,' she offered,

and bent down provocatively in front of him, picking up six-inch nails and putting them back in their box. She heard him breathe deeply behind her and kept going.

'They've taken my Black and Decker drill, cost me a bloody arm and a leg that did,' he said, surveying the shelving for missing items. He straightened a couple of paste boards and buckets, tutting and cursing under his breath. Then he saw it. Potty's childish hand had scratched 'SEX CASE' across the bonnet of his blue Cortina and his face went puce as the graffiti came into focus.

Grace pretended she hadn't seen it and found a broom in the corner with which she began to sweep up some broken glass. The garage door was still open so she pulled it lower, saying, 'You don't want everybody looking in, I'll just close this a bit. Have you got a light in here?'

George pulled the cord on the overhead bulb and dispelled the gathering darkness.

'Just the two of us then,' he smirked.

Grace knew that this was her moment. She hadn't been able to plan for it, but now it was here she had to act. She sidled around the edge of the car and stood in front of him. 'That's all right with me,' she said, gazing straight into his eyes.

She looked for a sign of something, but found nothing. There was nothing at all behind his eyes, nothing she recognised as human. He took her hand

and steered it down to the growing bulge in his filthy trousers.

'Rub my cock! Go on, rub my big fat cock.'

She felt giddy at the thought of actually touching him. His filthy talk and dirty trousers made her want to gag. She was twelve years old again and in her pink and white child's bedroom, rubbing Uncle Gary in the same way George wanted her to touch him, and it was all real and happening again. Grace forced herself not to give way to panic. This time it was her in control, and she knew what was going to happen next.

She grasped him and gently moved him back and forth in her hands, feeling him stiffen beneath the greasy fabric. 'Oh, yeah,' he sighed, his eyes closing, 'go on, rub it harder.' She did so until he was quite rigid, planning her next move as he panted for her to speed up.

Then, lowering his head, he swiped his tongue against the corner of her breast by her bra strap and licked her, hard and wet, across the entire width of her cleavage. She felt completely sickened and hurriedly straightened up; she had to break free for a moment, regain the upper hand.

'Let me close the door properly, someone might be able to see.'

He just leered at her and unzipped his trousers, letting them drop around his ankles, settling on the top of his scuffed boots. He made no move to take them off but stood proud with his large cock swinging beneath his bulging gut, its tip glazed, bulbous red and angry.

Grace pulled the door to with a loud bang and hoped to God the others had heard because there would be no going back now. Dead or alive, she wouldn't be coming out of this garage unfucked if they didn't move soon.

'Come here then, give me some loving. What's the matter, doesn't your old man know how to love you properly?'

Grace knew she couldn't stay leaning against the garage door for ever but was reluctant to move forward. But the harder she looked at George, the more she saw her Uncle Gary and all the other sick fucks who got their kicks from spoiling the innocent, and then she felt strength burn through her like a flame. This time she was in charge. 'Lay down,' she said simply.

'What?'

'Lay down. You're gonna work for it today, George.'

'What do you mean? Come here and bend over. You know that's why we're here. Come on, darling, suck it.'

'No, *you* suck it.' Grace's voice was firm, not loud but assertive. George stood before her, trousers round his ankles, rubbing himself to try and maintain his erection.

'I want you to get down on that floor, George, and

then I'm gonna sit on your face, and you're gonna eat till you're all full up and then some.' Grace's eyes challenged him: Defy me if you dare.

George's lecherous expression changed to one of confusion. All the time Grace was thinking, Come on, come on, come on, hurry the fuck up! But she was holding it together, she was doing it, it was happening. They'd talked about it and imagined it and planned for it and called for it – but now it was here, and she was driving the engine, it felt fucking wonderful.

George lowered himself slowly to the ground, encumbered by the hastily dropped trousers above his boots, but still holding on to his cock like a talisman and snorting with effort.

'I'll eat you then, you little slag, but I'm going to poke my fingers up your arse until you scream!'

This man was not human at all. She thought instantly of her baby, Adam, and the destruction and damage caused to his little mind and body. She was now delirious with the taste of sweet revenge.

'Not till you make me come you're not.' Grace slowly moved forward until she was standing over him. She stood above his face, one heel to either side of his head, and popped the button on her denim shorts before slowly lowering the zip. George breathed harder. One leg at a time she removed the shorts and exposed the crutch of her black skimpy knickers at him. She swivelled her hips and sucked her fingers while she stared down into his sickening face, faltering briefly.

He spotted her moment of hesitation and seized his chance to regain power here. He reached up and grabbed at her thighs. His grip was vice-like, and momentarily panic shot through Grace then. She smiled at him, licked her lips and pushed his hands down but was at a loss for what to do next. Then, finally, she heard the metal door of the garage begin to move. There was a whisper of 'Quick – get in!' and then the sounds of four women falling over each other in their rush to get in the garage and close the door behind them as quickly and quietly as possible. Potty had come instead of Lizzie, she saw.

George started muttering beneath her, 'Who the fuck's that?'

Grace stepped to one side, looked down at him and said, 'You filthy, dirty scum!' And then from behind her they all rushed in at once, each going for an arm or leg, exactly as planned, except for Michelle who had a screwed-up tea towel in her fist, soaked in paraffin. The others were clumsy and fumbled to bring down their full weight on his meaty limbs as he thrashed about beneath them, but Michelle simply dropped on him like a stone and lay full-length on top of his body. She had the tea towel in his spluttering gob in a matter of moments.

'Get the fucking rope!' Sue hissed then.

'I haven't got the rope!' Potty hissed back.

'I've got it, here,' said Gillian, dropping the two cut pieces of sisal rope they had bought that morning from the ironmonger's.

George kicked out and caught Sue in the hip, making her yelp as she struggled to get the rope around both his feet while Gillian sat on his legs to keep them down. He was strong and put up a fight, but it was his size that let him down. He was too fat. He had power but lacked speed. The women were all over him like a rash.

Once Sue had managed to loop the rope around both his ankles and yank it into a tight knot, she straightened up and got her breath back before pulling herself into a standing position and surveying his prone form. Then she landed an almighty kick across his backside, making him groan audibly through the stinking gag.

Michelle pushed the paraffin-soaked rag into his mouth, harder and harder, pulling back the flaps of his cheeks and his lips to really cram it in until the corners of his mouth began to bleed and the paraffin turned the red parts of his mouth white.

While she was down there she lifted him by his hair and cracked his head against the concrete until Sue said, 'Stop it! We don't want to knock him out, we want him to feel it.'

Crouching down next to his head, she stared into his face. 'You hear that, you dirty fucking animal?

We want you to feel it, every bit of it. Every fucking nook and cranny you think is your own we're gonna take from you . . . just like you took it from our kids! I hope you like pain, you cunt, 'cos you're gonna be getting a lot of it today.' She spat into his face then stood back to let Grace through. She was trying to retrieve her clothes.

'Don't worry about your sodding shorts!' Gillian bellowed. 'Come and help me hold him!'

Busy at the top end, Potty and Michelle had tied his hands together behind his back so that his body lay in a twisted position, chest down and his bum sticking out to one side in what was obviously an excruciating manner for a man of that size. With trembling hands Potty assembled the enema kit. She reached into her jacket pocket and pulled out five pairs of rubber gloves, courtesy of Carnegie Ward, which they stretched over their hands.

Grace hushed the other women into silence and they formed a circle around his twisted body. 'George Rush, it's the unanimous verdict of this group that you are guilty of the rape, buggery, assault and murder of our children. We know you don't care about their souls, or their mutilated bodies, or the memories that will haunt the survivors all their lives, but you will feel their pain and our pain, and suffer as they did.

'Sue, the broom handle. You don't need gel, do ya, George? Ram it up his fucking arse, Sue, like he did to your Wayne! Michelle, ram that cloth further down his throat, and then grab his cock and rub it off till he comes.'

George was not in pain. In fact, he was loving it. He'd always wanted to be buggered and was happy to let the women continue. He felt himself come and his eyes rolled back in his head with the sheer ecstasy of it.

Sue removed the broom handle and shit and blood oozed from George's anus, but he still seemed quite unmoved. Potty prepared the tube for the enema. 'This is for little TJ.' In seconds, she was pouring a jugful of soapy liquid into the tube that had been inserted as far as possible into George's arse. To deny him any release, Michelle grabbed another tea towel and slowly began to push the material up into his anus. His back passage was now blocked completely and the enema was building up inside his body.

George started to colour and his face turned red and blotchy. Sue had started the wanking process again, but she used more force than the others. Semen started to spurt, but this time it was mixed with blood. Relentlessly she continued. Slowly, water burns seemed to erupt the length of his penis. George tried to raise a scream, but no sound came out. His eyes rolled again in sheer pain.

With total abandonment Michelle raised her foot and kicked him in the stomach. Potty followed with a judo punch to the back of his head, and before long all five women were scratching, punching and kicking him. The garage was silent apart from the deep thuds raining down on George's body. Blood squirted from his nose and ears, and his battered penis lay shrivelled and inert on his left thigh, covered in blood and semen.

Suddenly, in unison, the women ceased the beating. Potty wiped her mouth with the back of her jacket sleeve, and Sue began to laugh, silently at first and then hysterically.

Michelle dashed to her side and placed a hand over her mouth. 'Shut it, you stupid bitch, or the whole estate will be in here.'

Gillian drew back, anguish on her face, but Grace slid one arm around her shoulders and pulled her sister close. 'It's OK, Gill, it's nearly done.' Grace looked up as if to heaven and said a silent prayer, closing her eyes for a few seconds and sucking in some much-needed air. Then, taking control again, she gathered them into a circle. 'Right, girls, brace yourselves, we need to get 'im in the car.'

Sue, Potty and Gillian took his top half while Grace and Michelle scooped up his tree-trunk legs and hauled him towards his car. Somehow they managed to cram him in. Potty took control of the hose that she'd attached to the exhaust and slowly uncoiled it, feeding it through the open car window before winding the glass back up to leave only the smallest of gaps.

'Fucking hell, the poxy car key!' screamed Sue then.

'Shit! God Almighty, I forgot all about that,' replied Grace, biting her bottom lip and trying to think fast. 'Check his trouser pockets, I'm sure he went back in his flat and got the keys for something.'

Sue wrestled with his legs and forced her hand deep into his pockets. 'Panic over, ladies,' she said, raising one hand with a bunch of keys clasped in it.

Grace hushed the giggling triumph of the other women. 'Before we start the engine, Potty, check outside and get Lizzie to start my car. Mich, you got the lollies, babe?'

Michelle produced a white bag holding six drumstick lollies, peeled the paper off each one and licked them thoroughly.

Then she reached across the limp body in the driver's seat and squashed them heavily into George's face. Quietly she whispered in his ear, 'This one's for my beautiful girl. Rot in hell for ever!' as she pressed one lolly deeper and harder than the rest.

Gill, quieter and more sedate than the others, moved towards the garage door. She cleared up the mess as she went, placing everything in a stripy plastic carrier bag that they would get rid of later. The whole place stank of blood, shit and paraffin. 'We need to move it, ladies, time's ticking by,' she said.

Potty peeped out of a gap in the doorframe.

378

'Fucking Ada! It's only that poxy kid Kelly Gobber and two of her mates.'

'Quick, shut the door, Potty. Gill, stay still. Sue, Mich, don't move a fucking muscle!' Grace held them all to silence as they heard the clip-clop of three pairs of feet and the giggling laughter of the girls passing by. If those kids noticed anything strange, they'd be fucked.

For what seemed like an eternity, the five women held their breath and an eerie silence stretched. Eventually the clip-clopping sounds faded, along with the giggling, and Grace exhaled.

'That was too fucking close! Let's start the engine and get the fuck outta here.'

Potty secured the garage door after them as well as she could. Grace arrived at the Jag to find Lizzie crouched down across the passenger seat, still hiding from Kelly and her mates. The girls had vanished, though, and once again the back street was quiet and empty. The low purring of an engine could faintly be heard, but no one would notice for a while. The women all scrambled into the car, each with her own thoughts and each deathly quiet. They knew George would die, and each of them believed that an all-seeing, all-wise, compassionate God would forgive them their actions.

Chapter Twenty-One

The women went to ground the next day, keeping away from each other's houses. It had been decided that they would carry on with their daily lives as normal and they had made a solemn oath not to tell their menfolk just yet.

Terry came back from Broadstairs with the girls, calmer and more resigned to his double loss, and he and Sue set about finalising arrangements for a quiet funeral for TJ. Terry felt more able to cope now. Spending time alone with his girls had shown him that although he would never stop missing Wayne and TJ, there was comfort to be drawn from his daughters' love and need for him. For a long time, Terry had lost his grip on family matters and put too much responsibility for them on to Sue. He had decided while he was away that he needed to become head of this family again.

The funeral was to be attended only by family and close friends, the people who had known and loved TJ the best. He and Sue agreed that they wanted to keep it simple, too tired and drained for another parade of grief on the scale of Wayne's funeral. Besides, TJ had been a quiet little soul who didn't like crowds. Sue was aware that the area expected more, but she had been a sideshow for them once already and felt she was doing right by her baby this time.

It was excruciating for all the women to try and carry on as normal, not knowing if George had been found or even if he was really dead. Every moment seemed to last an eternity, but they just went about their daily rounds, waiting for the story to break. There hadn't been much life left in his body when they'd finished with him in the garage, and the exhaust fumes would have done the rest, but they still didn't know for sure . . .

News was hard to come by, despite Lizzie's frequent trips to the shops for snippets of gossip and Potty's radar on high alert at the hospital.

DCI Woodhouse had originally ignored the call-out to the garage, thinking little of it. He sent a junior detective and PC Watson along instead. He had so far made little progress with the Shoreditch robbery, and after TJ's abduction and murder knew he had to concentrate all his efforts on finding the sex attacker. Locals were disgusted by the police's lack of progress on the case and had begun to taunt them, jeering at patrol cars as they moved through the streets and throwing stones after them. Relations between the police and the community had never been good hereabouts, but now they had sunk to an all-time low and Woodhouse was getting censure from above as well. It had been the worst summer of his career. He felt it was only a matter of time before they pulled him off this case and replaced him with one of the flash young upstarts from West End Central.

Upon arriving at the garage and switching off the car engine, officers had to stand back for ten minutes to allow the carbon monoxide fumes to dissipate before they could get to the body. It was during this respite that Watson radioed back to the station for Woodhouse. Getting him on the line he said, 'I think you'd better get down here and see this, sir. George Rush has been killed.'

'Nobody move him or touch anything until I get there,' Woodhouse instructed. 'I'm on my way.'

He definitely wasn't prepared for what he found in that garage. George Rush's corpse had been subjected to a frenzied and vicious attack of a plainly sexual nature. It was immediately obvious to the DCI that Rush had suffered the same sexual violations that all the child victims had suffered. There was dried blood around his genitals, and his anus was still leaking a sticky mixture of blood and what looked like soap. The same sticky mixture also trailed across the concrete floor of the garage, and matched the liquid used in the attack on the last child victim.

The dead man's trousers were still down around his ankles and there were several wounds to his head which had dried into a congealed mass of blood and

382

hair. His body was covered in large raised bruises, probably from being kicked, and this had clearly been the work of several men as there was no way just one could have done all this.

But it was the six drumstick lollies stuck to the side of the corpse's swollen bruised face that told Woodhouse everything he needed to know about the attack. This was the work of vigilantes through and through, the kind of thing that was anathema to anyone paid to uphold the law. But now, staring at the bruised and battered remains, Woodhouse privately decided that, provided they had got the right man, he felt nothing but relief. It seemed jungle justice had achieved what he couldn't. Please God, just let it be the right man!

Of course, his superiors would want an investigation, and as was the victim's right he would have to instigate a full enquiry, but as he gazed at the disgusting remains of what had once been a human being, for once he felt absolutely nothing.

'Watson, I want you to come with me when they've taken him away and sealed this place off. We're going to go through George Rush's house from top to bottom,' the DCI instructed.

The body was zipped into a bag and taken away in an ambulance in front of a crowd of onlookers who had gathered to see what all the fuss was about. There were a few muttered comments and some booing as the police came out of the garage, but Watson quickly took control and dispersed the crowd. DCI Woodhouse instructed his entire team of officers to remain tight-lipped about exactly what they had found in the garage, which was padlocked before the scene was vacated.

Woodhouse and Watson then walked in silence – ignoring the low-voiced criticism of the few remaining onlookers – to George Rush's maisonette where a patrol car full of crime-scene officers were waiting to receive Woodhouse's permission to break down the door.

Having gained access, and told the SOCO crew to wait, he walked through the ground floor, taking in the bare furnishings and lino in the front room, then on into the kitchen where he gagged on the stench from the cat's litter tray. Watson accompanied him. He opened doors and windows to get some air through, in the hope of clearing the stench, while Woodhouse checked the food cupboard. It was something he always did. If he wanted to build a profile of a person then he needed to check their larder, and in George Rush's he found Fray Bentos meat pies, tins of Whiskas, a couple of packets of tobacco and a white paper sweet bag from the newsagent's containing four drumstick lollies.

He opened the fridge and reeled back as the smell of decay hit him full in the face. Inside it was half a pint of milk, virtually congealed, a block of lard and a bag of off-cuts from the fishmonger which had evidently gone off.

Upstairs was just as miserable, with a few threadbare pieces of furniture and a bed with a big hollow in the middle where the mattress had given way, all covered by a grubby, stained candlewick bedspread.

'In here, sir,' called Watson from the second bedroom. Woodhouse stood in the doorway and could only stare at the wall in front of him which was covered by images of children, pasted into a collage that took up its entire length and breadth. He was speechless. They were not especially provocative images, but they betrayed a clear obsession. The whole room held the sour odour of stale semen and damp, long-forgotten laundry.

Watson was gingerly lifting stacks of magazines, muttering, 'Oh, Jesus,' and replacing them when a black card index box caught his eye. Thinking it must have been where Rush kept his addresses, he flicked back the top to find a series of envelopes carefully filed inside, with dates and times written on them.

'Have a look at this, sir,' he called to Woodhouse, still standing transfixed by the images on the wall, sick with the realisation that their man had been under their noses all this time, even briefly on their suspect list. Why hadn't they caught him? They'd had some evidence – why hadn't it led them to this sordid, threatening room? Woodhouse flicked through numerous envelopes, all inscribed with different dates and times, going back years, and placed in date order. He took one out and looked inside. Bearing the date 22 June 1976, 4.15 p.m., was a blue Basildon Bond envelope containing what looked like tiny snippets of black hair; upon closer inspection he realised they were eyelashes.

He closed his eyes and images of the murdered black girl, Chantal Robinson, filled his mind. He opened his eyes again after a few seconds, gazed around him and knew that this enquiry would be a long one and that evidence-gathering would prove difficult and distasteful.

Woodhouse looked directly at the PC. 'We need to get the ball rolling here, son. I'll get back to the nick. Don't let any big-footed plod roam around the place until I have all I need officially.'

At that moment, he heard a purring sound at his feet. A cat had silently approached him, and was wrapping itself around his legs. He bent down and picked the animal up. 'I bet if you could talk, you'd tell us a few things.' He stroked the cat gently before placing it in the arms of a surprised Watson. 'Get it to the animal rescue place. We can't leave the poor little fucker here, can we?'

Later, when he was back at the police station doing his paperwork, Woodhouse's phone rang and the duty sergeant informed him that it was a reporter from the *Hackney Gazette* on the line. In cases like this there was usually a media blackout until a statement had been drawn up by the officer in charge, so the receptionist was surprised when Woodhouse said, 'Put him through.'

If John had noticed anything different about Grace he wasn't letting on. Life for them seemed back to normal. She moved about in the days after the attack in a trance-like state, going through the motions while endlessly debating with herself about coming clean and telling John everything. The women had sworn secrecy to one another, but still it seemed unnatural to Grace to have done such a momentous thing and not to share it with her husband. What would he think of her if he knew the truth? John had set her up high on a pedestal, bolstered by his love and respect. Did she really want him to think differently of her?

She was girding herself up to making a confession when he got back from work on Thursday night, but just as she got the children to bed and all went quiet the moment disappeared. John announced that he'd had a pig of a day and needed a pint. He was standing jiggling his keys in the hallway as she came down the stairs and she took this as a sign that now wasn't the time. She fell into a fitful sleep, to be awoken by an excitable John at 1.30 a.m., smelling strongly of beer and shaking her shoulder.

'Babe, wake up! Guess what?'

Grace stirred and reached for the bedside light.

'What, John? What time is it?' She glanced at the clock. 'Oh, Christ! It's gone one in the morning, can't this wait?'

'No, babe, listen – this is great, you're gonna love it. George Rush has topped himself! Everyone in the pub was talking about it. Old Bill found the body this morning. He's gone, babe.'

Grace sat up in bed, rubbed her eyes and asked him to say it again. John repeated the news, his voice getting louder and louder, and she had to shush him so he didn't wake the boys. 'I'm not surprised he couldn't fucking live with himself after what he'd done,' said John. 'Good bloody riddance!'

'How?' Grace asked then.

'What d'ya mean, how?'

'How did he kill himself?' If another chance had presented itself for Grace to tell the truth, she wasn't taking it. It was almost as if she really knew nothing. Over the past few days, her mind had slowly started to rewrite events. She had virtually convinced herself by now that she had played no part in George's death and neither had any of them. Better by far to accept that it was suicide.

'Stuck a hosepipe on the back of his exhaust and gassed himself in his car in the garages,' said John, smiling broadly.

Grace threw her warm, sleepy arms around his neck and over his shoulder whispered, 'Thank God,' meaning it more than he would ever realise.

TJ's quiet funeral was held in the smaller St Anne's Church, rather than Christ Church where they'd had Wayne's. Sue and Terry didn't want people witnessing their grief any more, no matter how well-intentioned they were. These events always seemed to turn into a circus, and people gossiped about how many cars were there and who wore what. Only those who had known TJ and had a close relationship with him were invited.

When Terry had returned from Broadstairs with the girls he'd suggested that they should move down there and start again. 'Otherwise we'll always be the family people point at and say, "Two of their kids were murdered."' But Sue had no intention of going anywhere, though she didn't have the heart to tell Terry that yet. There was no way she was leaving her two boys behind.

She didn't want any black at the funeral, everything – from the girls' dresses, to the restrained flowers and the coffin – had to be white. The coffin wouldn't be paraded through the streets this time. There wouldn't be a funeral procession, and the undertakers had arranged for everything to be in place when the mourners arrived. Sue insisted there were to be no flowers from anyone except family. If other people wanted, they could make a donation to the cerebral palsy charity instead. There were no hearses. John drove Terry and Sue with their girls to

389

the church in his Jag. Grace and the boys followed behind in a mini-cab. There were no more than twenty people gathered together to say goodbye to little TJ, but each and every one of them was a person he had known and cuddled and played with.

His tiny coffin was raised up on a trestle, adorned with a simple bouquet of lily-of-the-valley, and this symbol of a brief life moved everybody to tears except for Sue, who found solace, peace and simple satisfaction in knowing that she had avenged her babies' deaths.

There was no wake after the service, the women merely exchanged brief goodbyes and meaningful glances, waiting until their pre-planned meeting the following day.

Grace was awake with the lark on Saturday morning and for the first time in weeks felt able to eat something. As she whisked eggs together and sliced bread for toast, she felt an unfamiliar sense of peace. After John had told her the news about George, she had gone back to sleep immediately and slept the whole night through without any dreams, nightmares or sweats. She'd now had several nights of uninterrupted sleep and was feeling as if all her old energy was back. She had a smile on her face and, as a favourite song of hers came on the radio, cheerily joined in and began to dance around the kitchen like a teenager. She was looking forward to seeing the others and sharing her euphoria with them.

It had been days since George's body had been found, and there had been no visits from the police and no enquiries. Grace felt safe. John breezed into the kitchen, smelling of Old Spice aftershave, and wrapped his arms around her waist, swaying Grace across the room to the song she was singing.

'I gotta go out for a bit and check on a job. I thought I'd take the boys with me. The drive will do them good and Adam loves to see the diggers at work. That OK with you, hun?'

Grace turned and kissed him. 'Course, babe. Me mates are coming over soon. I think Terry's taking his girls to the swimming pool, Lucy and Maria are off to Roman Road Market, and Paul is taking his two up to the farm. Seems like a day for fathers and kids.

Potty arrived first at 9.30, with a beaming smile on her face and a letter crumpled in her hand. 'Lucy, bless 'er, has taken the girls with her and Maria. Michael's fucked off to see his bruv in Bournemouth, so I'm childless, promoted and completely made up!' She shoved past Grace and went straight into the kitchen, almost skipping. 'Who'd 'ave thought it, me a bloody supervisor?' Potty could contain herself no more and let out a scream of sheer delight. Grace found it impossible not to be swept up in her excitement. As they skipped around joyfully the doorbell went again.

This time Sue and Michelle stood on the doorstep,

grinning like two Cheshire cats. Grace drew in her breath in pleasurable surprise. Sue looked so radiant and slim, and Michelle had on a lovely pink and white trouser suit with her hair in a perfect Afro. The kettle was soon boiling, the women chatted and smoked, and once again the bell rang.

Gillian looked like the cat that'd had the cream, and Nanny Parks and Lizzie harrumphed a few times as they bustled in behind her, almost jamming each other into the doorway. It was too much for Grace who started to giggle again, and this time her mum and Lizzie joined in.

From beneath her arm, Nanny Parks pulled a rolled-up copy of the *Hackney Gazette* and leafed through its pages until she reached a small item on page sixteen.

'Listen to this,' she said. 'The body of a man identified as George Rush, 59, was discovered in a garage on the Columbia Row Estate at 10.40 a.m. on 26 August. It is believed that the man died by suicide as a result of carbon-monoxide poisoning. The police say that there are no suspicious circumstances surrounding the death but that there will be a standard Coroner's enquiry.'

Nanny Parks looked up at their expectant faces. They were braced for more. 'That's it, five bloody lines is all. The police must know it wasn't suicide, God knows what they're playing at. Still, if we're in the clear, who gives a bugger?'

A chorus of laughter rang out. United together in joy and relief, the women laughed and laughed!

Considering how long it had hung around, everyone was amazed by the quick exit of the hot sultry summer. They went from shorts and T-shirts to coats in a matter of weeks, and autumn rushed into early winter with a flash flurry of snow as Christmas rapidly approached.

Grace's house looked stunning with a large tree taking centre-stage, all decked out in red and gold.

Lights twinkled brightly as the evenings drew in, and the whole area seemed to have returned to normal. The air held a fresh, clean crispness, the flies had long gone, rubbish had been cleared, and the pubs overflowed with crowds bent on seasonal merriment.

The girls all arrived at Grace's on Christmas Eve to exchange their gifts and sat around with full glasses. It had been a strange few months, each of them silently acknowledged.

Potty looked amazing tonight in a beautiful new suit. Michael had decided to give Bournemouth a permanent go, and Lucy had been chosen for the London Youth Judo Squad. The twins were thriving in their beautiful new clothes and clean and orderly home. Michael's decision to leave had turned the dynamic of their home life on its head, and now the Pottses were no longer the family other people looked down their noses at. Potty thought of their presents waiting under the tree. Her new job had provided a lot for them, most of all freedom for herself in her new life without Michael.

The fair had come back to the area in the autumn. She thought of how she and the girls had revisited the park as a happy family and had thoroughly enjoyed the rides in the autumn sunshine. The children laughed and ate their fill of hot dogs and candy floss.

She was glad she had seen Madame Marla again, and the young man with the beautiful blue eyes. They didn't seem to hold the same sparkle any more, but she'd seen the satisfaction in the eyes of the tarot reader when she saw Potty's cards for a second time. Something there seemed to please her, but she had taken Potty's money once again and said no more. A young lad sat in her caravan, playing with a toy train, and Madame Marla glanced at him several times, saying nothing.

Something Potty couldn't see, hear or feel happened that afternoon and put any last traces of guilt or unease right out of her mind.

Nanny Parks was in her element. All the babysitting last summer had paid off and she had got herself registered as a child minder. She had turned a favour into a job and was rushing her drink tonight so as to get ready to go to the community church hall for the kids' Christmas party.

Gillian snuggled up next to Grace on the large cream sofa, and thought how close the two of them had become. Not telling their mother the secret about Uncle Gary had been the right thing to do, she could see that clearly now. Grace had been right. As usual.

Sue and Michelle gazed at the large star on top of the Christmas tree and Grace knew where their thoughts lay. For a few minutes, she joined them in their silent prayers for Chantal, Wayne and little TJ. Life would never be the same without them, but it would go on. A tear formed in the corner of her eye. They had all come so far. Their actions had finally instigated a full investigation of George Rush, albeit after his death.

In the months that followed George's maisonette had been searched and the garden dug up. It would never be ascertained just how many people George Rush had hurt or murdered in his reign of terror. The remains of his wife and mother-in-law were found and reburied at St Anne's. The turnout had been small but respectful. Envelopes containing eye-lashes had been found dating back to the early sixties. The police remained unsure how many exactly had been taken from dead victims, but it was generally believed that Rush had claimed many more lives in the past.

Woodhouse and Watson sat opposite each other at the DCI's desk in the smoky back office of the police station. The ashtrays were piled high, and on the corner of the desk stood a bottle of whisky and two paper cups.

Woodhouse wasn't a big drinker, but he liked to know it was there if he needed it, and during the last few months he had needed it more often than not. He knew George Rush had been murdered but had no hard evidence to lead him to the killers, and the only witnesses near the crime scene, Kelly Gobber and her two giggling mates, swore they had neither heard nor seen anything. No one was giving up any information on George Rush, and local enquiries had resulted in a big fat zero. The fathers of the victims all had solid alibis, and there were no other likely suspects.

The big robbery case had proved more successful for the DCI. A local gang had been arrested and placed on remand until the court case next year. They still hadn't retrieved all the money, but he was satisfied he had the right men locked up.

Now file upon file was stacked to either side of Woodhouse and Watson. With heads leaning on hands, they waded their way through the paperwork, ballpoints working furiously.

Suddenly the door burst open and the young WPC blew her Christmas paper horn. 'C'mon, sir, it's the Christmas party! Everyone's waiting for you.'

Woodhouse smiled at his young constable. 'Let's go then, Watson, can't keep the whole station waiting. And besides, this lot will still be here in the morning.'

The beautiful, melodic voice of an angel filled the school hall. 'O Holy Night' had never sounded so wonderful. Maria felt strong and confident as she reached every note effortlessly. Mrs Davy stood with tinsel round the neck of her black polo jumper, hands clasped to her face and tears of joy in her eyes. Maria had come so far, and with Mrs Davy's help was now assured of a place at a local grammar school for the following year.

Mary sat on a narrow plastic chair in the front row and clung to Lizzie's arm, watching her daughter and beaming with pride. Lizzie also felt remarkably humble before the bravery and sheer determination of her grand-daughter. Maria was a Foster after all, she thought.

As the crowd from the school dispersed, Lizzie chose to walk to Grace's rather than get the bus. She kissed Mary and Maria goodbye and made her way down the high street. As she walked through the familiar catacombs of alleyways and paths, she gazed up at the cloudless dark sky. 'We're in for snow,' she mumbled to herself. She decided to get some sweets for the kids and made small talk with Ali at the newsagent's for a while. When she came out Harry the Horse was standing outside the quiet closed betting shop, dragging on a cigarette and making circles with his mouth to form smoke rings.

'It's bleeding freezing, ain't it, Harry?' she laughed.

'Yeah, it's 'taters, love, you don't want to be hanging around outside too long,' he replied. 'Ere, fancy a nifty Lizzie?'

'Thanks Harry, that's real nice of ya, but I'm off round me girls, see the grandkids, ya know.' Lizzie thought for a while as she walked away.

'I'll take a rain check though if that's alright?' Lizzie smiled back at him.

Harry looked made up, 'Righto Liz, I'll hold you to that. Lizzie was flattered.

Lizzie rounded the corner, and glanced at the flats. George Rush's maisonette was boarded up and covered in graffiti. 'Pervert', 'Nonce' and 'Cunt' were all scrawled across the chipboard that had been put up after the windows had been smashed in. A few bunches of dead flowers were still pinned up on the back garden gate, a token to mark the deaths of the two women who had disappeared from their midst unnoticed. Lizzie felt someone step on her grave then and she shivered. Not for the first time since the murder, she gained comfort from the memory of the lost children. She felt no remorse and no guilt for what had happened to George. Justice had been done. It was the cold night air that sent shivers through her body, not the memory of George Rush for she was sure he was burning in hell.

The lights from Grace's house could be seen in the distance and Lizzie quickened her step. The door opened to the smell of cinnamon and candles, and Grace hugged her. Michelle rushed over to her mother-in-law and threw her arms around her. Lizzie was home, she had her family around her, for she knew that she had found real friendship and love with these remarkable women.

Gillian, Potty, Michelle, Nanny, Sue and Lizzie all filled their glasses in a toast to Grace. Drinking orange juice and patting her swollen pregnant tummy, she raised her glass too.

'To us, for ever and always, and Happy Christmas!'
'Happy Christmas!' they all cheered.

THE POWER OF READING

Visit the Random House website and get connected with information on all our books and authors

EXTRACTS from our recently published books and selected backlist titles

COMPETITIONS AND PRIZE DRAWS Win signed books, audiobooks and more

AUTHOR EVENTS Find out which of our authors are on tour and where you can meet them

LATEST NEWS on bestsellers, awards and new publications

MINISITES with exclusive special features dedicated to our authors and their titles

READING GROUPS Reading guides, special features and all the information you need for your reading group

LISTEN to extracts from the latest audiobook publications

WATCH video clips of interviews and readings with our authors

RANDOM HOUSE INFORMATION including advice for writers, job vacancies and all your general queries answered

Come home to Random House
www.rbooks.co.uk